MARIONETTE

MARIONETTE

ANNIKA SINGH

AUSTIN, TX   2023

©2023, Annika Pandya Singh

All rights reserved. No part of this book may be reproduced or translated in any form or by any means, digital, electronic, or mechanical, including photocopying, recording, or by any information storage and retrieval system, without permission in writing from the publisher, except for the use of brief quotations in a book review or related article.

www.annika-singh.com

YOUNG ADULT FICTION
Magical Realism
Romance / LGBTQ+
Coming of Age

Print: 979-8-218-26057-6
Ebook: 979-8-218-26979-1

Book Design by Jennifer Payne (Words by Jen, Branford, CT)

Printed in the U.S.A.

FOR MY BIG SISTER, ALI

CHAPTER 1

Hj igh school football games are the most pathetic excuses for school spirit. Especially the ones in Florida.

The crack of an opposing side's jeer, a screech from the field's other end, a revolting number of freshmen in one humid place chanting *"Torquet Paup High,"* and not nearly enough seniors for me to chat with. Not to mention football games are an American school sport.

I halt my thoughts, sick of my own pessimism. It's difficult, however, to stay positive when the only record repeating in my head is the constant drone of strangers' and acquaintances' voices. I can handle parties, out-ings, festivals, but this hodgepodge of sweating teens my age who are way too close to adulthood to be enjoying this? I'll pass.

A palm invades my back, jolting me forward. "C'mon, Connor. Why do you look like you wanna kill yourself? We're here to support Brandon — it's his first game on the varsity team." Fritz, the back-slapping culprit, grins.

Before I can protest, he drags me to the front row, avoiding plastic cola bottles and spilled popcorn. I squint at the players lit by football-season moonshine, scan past the cheer squad, then stop and scan again.

I blink. "What the — is that…Quinton in there?" I tug Fritz's shirt, helping him find Quinton in the crowd with a, hopefully, subtle finger point.

Fritz narrows his eyes. "Uh, yeah, I'm pretty sure." His smile then deepens, and he lifts an eyebrow.

I scrunch my nose; years of friendship shared with the boy have taught me that his coy grins only mean bad news.

But my attention returns to Quinton, spectating as he snickers and converses with the other cheer members. My lips tug upward, slightly endeared by the glee on his face. I'd spoken with Quinton prior to this horrific football event — only a few sentences here and there. Unfortunately, we've never had a chat solid enough to call a *conversation*. We've never gotten past acquaintance, never felt the need to.

But I'd always noticed how stupidly strong his allure is — how his cheer skirt seems to fortify his masculinity, the manner in which he dances his routines, his infamous gaze.

Quinton is the American Dream. Wealthy — *wealthy* — blond, white, male, green-eyed, and freckled. Honestly, give the world a ration of all you've been handed.

So, sure, he's a bit of a hallway crush, so what?

I snap out of my thoughts when Fritz taps my shoulder. He glances at me expectantly.

I purse my lips, and pry my eyes from where Quinton's body is stretched in the grass. He's stationed by the staircase leading just behind the fence that separates us. Finally, I turn to Fritz. "Oh, what? Sorry, did you say something?"

Fritz grins wide with a knowing tease. "Well, I asked you a question, but I guess you're too busy staring at Quinton over there so…another time, Connor." He chuckles at my flush before focusing back to his phone screen.

Attempting to drain the red from my cheeks, I curse the, admittedly, lovely Quinton. I'd have little luck pursuing him seeing as he's desired by many — girls and boys alike. But respectfully watching him from afar does no harm.

Though, even if I tell myself that, rationality wins, and I permanently turn away from him. Unfortunately, my head moves just slowly enough for my eyes to catch the most prized fish of the sea.

Quinton.

His eyes link with mine. I remain caught in his eye contact, mind ricocheting in panic. And as seconds pass, I grow curious, wondering when he'll look away. I surely don't have the nerve to do so.

With gentle horror, I recall how easily he could walk up the steps and confront me for staring. Yikes.

Much to my shock, my brown eyes never avert, playing the waiting game with his green ones. His head tilts, interest seeming to get the better of him. He grins. He waves off his fellow cheer members, promising to return quickly. He then heads up the few stairs with a gaze that never abandons mine.

Oh, my God.

I turn to Fritz for assistance, scared of the situation I've caused.

But my brown-haired best friend is far off — I spot him bantering above with another student. A finger taps my shoulder, and I snap my head from the crowd. I blink, eyes floating up to find Quinton standing before me.

He expects me to speak first, but after a long — and awkward — pause, he eventually caves. "Well, you seem awfully quiet for someone who has been staring at me for the past ten minutes."

I *blush* at the accusation, eyes locked on his self-assured smile. I consider myself brave, daring — but it's different with Quinton. He's popular, attractive, and currently looking down on me.

But maybe he's not. I shouldn't assume he's here for a mean laugh to share with friends the moment half-time ends.

"Fine then, Connor, I guess you don't want to talk."

I shake my head, rising to my feet. "Wait, wait, sorry, I just — " I inhale, chest burning with adrenaline. Fuck it. " — I just, um, get nervous around generally attractive guys is all." I muster a toothless grin and silently cheer myself for not stuttering.

Quinton raises his eyebrows and chuckles, clearly aware that I'd love to slap a hand over my mouth and dart off.

"Consider me won over. Your staring was quite an ego boost, anyway." Quinton's eyes search the ground, and after a few beats, he clicks his tongue in triumph. He swiftly crouches down and plucks up a slightly dirty gum wrapper. Fishing in nearly invisible pockets, he grips a mini-pen and scribbles quietly on the gum wrapper.

My jaw hangs lax as I replay the events that just occurred with disbelief. No chance that eyeballing the shit out of Quinton somehow worked in my favor.

"Just for you." His voice draws me back to reality, and his hand takes one of mine. In a swift movement, he presses the paper into my palm. My heart pounds. "Catch you later! The game's about to start." He encloses the wrapper-holding hand with my other, positioning me as he pleases. And he leaves.

Holy shit.

I swallow, my open mouth morphing into a grin for the century. Either I have award-winning game, or Quinton is crazy. I chuckle to myself, carefully slipping my new possession, which as expected has Quinton's phone number, into my pocket.

Maybe high school football games aren't so bad after all.

QUINTON

I blow a kiss, earning one right back from the members of my cheer team. The weight of the game begins to mellow out as I slam my car door shut. Shifting the gears, I stretch my neck, tired after a night of dance and less-than-pleasant weather. But even with my post-game soreness, Connor is at the front of my mind. How his hair falls on his face, his outfit, his traits. *How did I not pick up on it before?*

My white house sticks out like a sore thumb against the night sky. After a ride of skeptically pondering Connor, I pull into my driveway. I don't greet Mom, I only wave with an arm that says I'm not in the mood for chit-chat. Seconds from my goal, and room, a notification beeps from my phone. Submitting to curiosity, I flick my screen on.

Unknown Number

407-***-****: *Hii*

Huh?

407-***-****: *It's Connor lol :)*

Oh. Let's go.

Quinton*: hello. what's up, Connor?*

As I wait for his response, I plug a contact name in.

When no response comes, I shrug it off, remembering the coincidence that piqued my interest in him in the first place. Finally, my eyes find the doll, neatly perched on my marble nightstand.

The doll's clothes, too similar to Connor's.

Its face with a resemblance too strong for comfort.

Fuck, even its glasses mirror Connor's exactly, white-rimmed and round.

Coincidences exist, of course. But for a human being to be wearing identical clothing, have the same eye color, the same hair, and the same general form as my childhood doll?

What the fuck?

I stare, bewildered, my arms unsure of what to do. I eventually decide to pick the doll up and inspect it. I compare it to my memory of Connor, swallowing at the similarities. Carrying the doll to my closet, I quickly close the door, handling it like it's an antique waiting to break. A haunted, scary antique.

Keeping the doll out of sight frees some of the panic from my chest. My mind clears enough for me to begin asking myself coherent questions. Do I confront Connor? Research humanoid dolls? I should probably research tomorrow, it's late. Maybe see if he has anything to do with this? He's cute — so I'm not complaining if I have to spend time with him. But….

I stop overthinking and fiddle with my lamp switch.

Worry is Future Quinton's problem.

CONNOR

My own yawn awakens me, and the sun pulls me further from slumber. My limbs whine at the movement, irritated and oddly chafed. I blink, confused at the ache, seeing as I've put in the physical effort of a goldfish this past week. Assuming I slept awkwardly, I blindly gravitate toward my phone, mind still tipsy with fatigue.

I squint at the message from Quinton I'd ignored for the sake of getting a good night's sleep, whispering a curse to myself. Fuck, he's gonna think I'm a careless text and dipper. Sniffing once, I read his message.

407-***-****: *hey Connor, what's up?*

I grin, wider than expected, and shove the phone into the covers.

My giddiness subsides, nose baited by a waft of Mum's cooking from across the hall. Stretching with a foreign delight, I buzz up and out of my bedroom. But even with this joy, a weight still forms in my stomach. Another day of considering my medical career despite not planning on going to college — I could never leave Mum behind like that — and watching my few friends with money excitedly babble about their futures.

But I'll be fine. "G'morning Mum." I squeeze Mum from behind, pressing a kiss to her shoulder before peeking out from behind her. "Whatcha cookin'?" I throw a treat into my Labrador's crate, smiling as she eats it up with no remorse.

"Morning sweetie." She extends her arms in a stretch. "I prepared some toaster waffles for your enjoyment."

I grin, too familiar with her never-ending strength. Managing to provide delicious breakfast minutes before work and arrive on time? The power of single mothers.

My phone vibrates, interrupting my absentminded bite of her home-made waffles.

--****: *left on read for 8 hours? that hurts.*

I lift an eyebrow at his shameless call for my attention and chuckle. I suppose when you're popular, you can get away with double-texting.

Me: *Sorry, I accidentally fell asleep :p*

I notice his blank contact, adding his name before my phone vibrates once again.

Quinton: *i'm truly heartbroken*

   but i guess i can forgive you. on one condition

Me: *Haha*

   That is?

Quinton: *meet me after school by your locker. let me take you somewhere in school?*

I reread the text several times, my stomach warm once again. Did Quinton fucking Hansley just offer to hang out *at* school? Suppressing nerves, my tingling fingers manage to type out —

Me: *Pff sure. Sounds like a plan :)*

I breathe.

Quinton: *see you then, Connor*

Stuffing my pockets full of a phone and a skittish hand, I swallow the remains of my food. But in an instant, the recollection of school stampedes on my parade.

Wait, fuck, I have school today.

Clambering toward the family-shared car, or I suppose the shared car between Mum and me, I start the engine. Once the old car is humming with life, I twist the volume button clockwise, smiling ear to ear. However, a sort of shame follows the grin, guilty for feeling so motivated after only talking to one simple man.

But the shame dissipates as quickly as it comes. Self-sabotage is a fatal flaw, but I can't let it be mine. Quinton talked to me. *Me.* I'm pretty wonderful, so it makes sense, but does it make me wonder how he picked up on that? Why me, and why wait until that very game to make a move? I sigh until I adjust to the idea of serendipity. Let fortune favor me for once, just until the end of today.

My foot abuses the vinyl floor with relentless taps. Groaning at my skirt's crumples, I curse myself for dressing intricately — the risk of an outfit malfunction has increased.

Though the thought only hangs for a second, my eyes are soon preoccupied entirely with the longer hand of the clock. Next class is my second to last class.

Next class is my class with Quinton and Fritz, and it's coming up quickly.

I spend the last minutes of the class period wondering about dinner. Lunch was light today, but I'm sure I can make *something* appetizing with Mum. Despite her long work hours thanks to the "American Dream," she comes through in a way that puts the wealthy to shame. She's surviving in a system designed to work people like us to death. Still, hard as she works, here I am, stressing over if I'll find dinner tonight.

The bell chimes, providing an escape from this hell of a class. I inhale, prepare, and speed walk from the classroom.

"God, fuck." In my rush, my backpack snags on an object, halting me. I twist my neck, seeing that my backpack has caught on a locker knob. As I struggle to detach it, a stranger unhinges the hold, chuckling from above. I look up as the gracious figure moves in front of me.

My lips part.

Quinton.

"You're welcome."

I clear my throat, and my heart hammering quicker than before. "Thank you. I could've undone the catch myself, though."

Quinton only snorts, teeth shining behind his smile. "Sure you could've. But to avoid any "catches" like that again, mind if I walk you to class?" It's not the smoothest segue, but it'll do for me. He emphasizes his offer by gently brushing his fingers over my hair for just a moment. I freeze at the touch, my heart buzzing. Reaching his arm out, Quinton adds with a smile, "C'mon."

I take the offer, looking down to hide the undoubtedly pink flush on my face. Stupid Edward from fucking *Twilight* skin. *God, Connor, why are you referencing a decade-old franchise?* "Okay. But hurry up and walk faster, class starts soon." Pestering him in order to fill the silence, Quinton hums in agreement.

"So nagging, Connor, we have…oh fuck, like, thirty seconds. Let's go." He jolts us forward, and we both chuckle with wide smiles.

"Let's."

CHAPTER 2

Quinton enjoys following my lead. As I wanted him to, he hurries, feet pounding on the linoleum hallway tiles by the time we reach the class's entrance. We laugh in synchrony, eyes lingering on one another for a sweet couple of seconds. But I don't let myself swoon quite yet. After all, I don't know Quinton, and it's only been one day since we've felt comfortable speaking casually to each other. He's just a very attractive, talented man with manners who has taken a mutual liking to me.

However, does it get better than that?

Suppressing any more giggles, I look to Quinton to pick our seats.

But catching my expectant gaze, he simply smiles. "Where would *you* like to sit, Doll?"

My brow furrows at his posh, mocking British accent. "Oh shut up, don't call me that. You choose." I cross my arms to divert focus away from my smile. *Doll.*

Quinton, angled slightly behind me, clutches one of my wrists and lowers his head to my ear. "No."

My breath quickens at the movement, allowing the man to paint my cheeks red yet again. I note his bravery with the gesture as well — Quinton has a large sum of confidence. I'm excited to one day learn if it's earned or not.

Exhaling softly, I lift a feeble arm to point to a pair of plain desks in the back row.

Quinton immediately leans away and tips his head, leaving me yearning for the proximity again. "Thanks for your compliance." It's hard to say whether he purposely worded his thank you like…that or not, but I move on, sitting in the chair Quinton has pulled out for me.

Any quippy response I had prepared is soon interrupted by Fritz barging in beside us.

He blinks at the two of us at our joint desks. "Huh, this your new 'best friend,' Connor?"

My eyes soften. "No, Fritz, you, unfortunately, already fill that role."

Quinton butts in, offering a short wave to Fritz. "Perhaps I could fill a different role in your life, Connor?" He swings an arm over my shoulder, and my hands beat it off.

"You're bad at flirting," I say, despite my internal reaction. Cowering from his suggestive expression, I clear my throat.

Quinton only blinks. "I was kidding," he murmurs, but he makes sure I hear him say, "Sort of."

⁓

I loop my bag over my shoulders, the old straps hanging lower than meant. Quinton leads the way to the cafeteria — as he's told me, it's his typical lunch spot. I'd already alerted Fritz, Tina, and Theo that I couldn't join them for lunch today — our usual "spot" is the third-floor balcony or Fritz's car.

I blank out for the majority of Quinton's and my walk — nothing on my mind but unrealistic scenarios with him. Reality soon returns sharply.

This is definitely not the path to the cafeteria. "Hey, where are we going?" I tilt my head toward Quinton's face.

He smiles, but he doesn't respond, prickling my skin. Where are we going?

It doesn't take long for me to form an educated guess, and upon arrival, my suspicions are pleasantly confirmed. Right by our school's environmental course hall, a mini-forest sprouts. Part is planted deliberately, but the other half grows naturally. A small picnic table, old and periodically tended to, rests on the natural side.

And fuck, it's stunning. My eyes travel around the grassy land, pausing on a small turtle pond. Sunlight flits across it, illuminating the few animals rummaging the waters. I haven't been here since freshman year, and, God, it's changed since. Like, where did all of these vines come from? "Whoa."

⁓

QUINTON

Whoa." Connor's voice is quiet — almost like he's intimidated by the scenery.

I refrain from puffing my chest — kudos to me for picking the spot. "I know, I know, I found the one not really ugly place on campus. C'mon through, let's eat."

Connor scurries to the bench and heaves his bag onto the right side of the seat. "What are you waiting for? Sit down, Quinton." Connor's unreadable smile teases me once more.

"Jeez, you're so bossy, Connor." I plop beside him. "Tone it down." Zipping my bag open to retrieve food, I recall a dangerous object squashed behind the nylon.

The doll *identical to the man beside me.*

Honestly, I'm not a hundred percent sure why I brought it. My original plan, obviously thought of by an idiot, was to possibly show him the doll. But at school? With no warning? That idea now seems fairly dumb. He'd probably run away and think I'm a creep, or something.

Frantic, I seal the bag with a speed that only a legally blind person wouldn't notice.

He cocks his head. "Are you having an aneurysm? Trying to win the Olympics of bag-zipping or something?" With a riled smile, he inquires, "What're you hiding in there?"

I chuckle, trying to distract him. "Oh, c'mon, Connor, I'd never hide anything from you. Even if you're British."

But despite my flirty tactics, Connor stares, unsatisfied.

"Oh, really? Then what's the harm in showing me, weirdo?" Connor responds to my energy by meeting it with equally playful behavior.

Before I can respond with "none ya' business," Connor snags my bag and holds it above his head.

"Hahaha! Got it!" His thumb slides toward the zipper.

My instincts split on whether to jokingly grab for it or freeze in terror. "Connor — Connor, give it back. Let's not play this game. I don't want to accidentally scratch you — "

Connor's head snaps upward, his smile *smiling.* "Oh, yeah you're just so big and strong and don't wanna scratch me, whatever." His curious eyes trail back to the incriminating backpack. "I mean what could possibly be *in* here?"

A doll that I've had since age two which happens to look exactly like you.

"Nothing. Just — What the hell is wrong with you? Come on, give it back." I try to sound serious, but I can't help but giggle.

Connor simply laughs and flips me off.

The audacity.

Unlike my attempts to gently reach for the bag, Connor rebels with all his might, set on keeping the backpack as his. After minutes of my politely trying to retrieve the backpack, he holds it high above his head, grinning.

Fine then. "Connor." I try to wear a serious tone.

However, despite my intent to come off strong as a rock, Connor perceives me as a pebble.

As expected, he responds with a teasing tone. "Yes, Quinton?"

"Give it."

"Make me."

Oh, he did not. My mouth slightly opens before morphing into a smile, and I allow for rougher banter on my end. My arms fly upward, prying his hands apart by his wrists 'till his fingers finally unclasp.

The bag falls into his lap.

His yelp of surprise is *tuneful* but brief — soon, his gaze hardens and stills, as though he's mapping out some plan in his head.

As usual, I was right. Connor suddenly tugs hard against my grip — and his own head lurches forward — right in front of mine.

I tighten my grasp on his wrists. His closeness is *gorgeous*. Although the sun is hidden behind various trees, Connor's face shines brighter than diamonds. I, stupidly, continue to stare at his almond-shaped eyes and perfectly oval-ish face.

Connor, perfectly aware of what he's doing, takes advantage of this. He pulls with great force once again, breaking one hand free from my own. We both decorate the air with a high-pitched, competitive laugh, and random strings of "oh my, God"s and "ugh"s.

I react before he does, shoving his body on the grass and off the short bench. I roll with him and eventually splay out on dry grass. Connor snickers and snakes his arm toward the bag that's just a few feet away.

I grunt under my breath. "Oh no, you don't." I spring to my feet, channel my strength, and seize his wrists just before they reach the bag. I fasten his hands together and pin them to the ground. Hair hanging, I do a once over on the boy *literally pinned beneath me*.

This definitely escalated.

CONNOR

"Must — must have some secret in there, huh?" I swallow, red, nervous, and staring dead into Quinton's eyes. I'm met with intensity — the much larger boy seeming merciless. As my breath grows heavier, I speak again. "Come on. Let me see the backpack." My words shrivel, and I cower before Quinton. It's difficult to keep my voice from growing small in this position.

Quinton scoffs, tightening his grip. "Oh, come on now, why would I think about doing that when you've been a little rascal for the past five minutes." I'd bet he is equally nervous — pretending to be cool and confident as most do in this sort of situation.

"Oh, fuck off." I roll my eyes and attempt to rise from beneath him.

But Quinton is unrelenting, and he pins his knee to my lower thigh. "Connor — " his volume plummets, " — quit being a little shit, and promise me right now you won't go for my backpack."

Fuck, color me swayed.

I swallow. "I, um, promise." Equally annoyed by and attracted to what just played out, I begrudgingly surrender.

The change on his face is quick. It seems like a mischievous mask has slipped off to reveal a look of nonchalance. Quinton stands and ruffles my hair as though he wasn't on top of me a few seconds ago, eliciting an odd cloud of disappointment. Though what was I expecting, a kiss? It's been one day. *Pull yourself together.*

The taller man reaches an arm out. "C'mon, let's eat, we have, like, twenty minutes left of lunch." Quinton hauls me up onto the seat beside him, the backpack stored safely between his feet. Not even father penguins exhibit such solicitous protection. With a defeated sigh, I back off and allow Quinton to keep his privacy.

I inhale sharply as Quinton's hands suddenly rush toward my face. Bracing, I feel him adjust the lopsided clout goggles hanging across my eyes.

I smile. "Thanks, weirdo."

He grins. "No problem, idiot."

Rushing from English class to find Quinton has transformed into routine. I'm a fan of said routine.

Gathering my items in a hurry, I set out to find him, waving my teacher off with a smile. I quickly trek past the lockers and giggle. I'm sure the textbook romantic that has waited for me this past week will remain there once more — Quinton himself. Perhaps at some point, we can relocate our lunch meetings to somewhere off campus. However, him being the far more popular one, he's entirely responsible to invite me.

"Hey, Connor." A figure much taller than me breathes on my head.

"Hi, Quinton." I grin.

He links our arms. He has grown familiar faster than I could've predicted.

We continue onward, chatting about Quinton's favorite philosophies and my favorite foods…while insulting Quinton for his philosophies. Passersby watch us which furrowed eyebrows and pursed lips, wishing it were them rather than me. Knowing we're both envied in one way or another, we speed up our pace to his car, but it's still impossible not to suffocate under the stares. Especially when their eyes are so devoid of altruism.

It's expected, of course. Quinton, again, is popular. Setting foot in popular's territory, otherwise known as Quinton's car, risks safety. Everyone adores him, save for the homophobes — however, they'd hop in the drool-over-Quinton boat if his parents hadn't *allegedly* outed him. Pretty cruel of them — if the rumors are true.

"Sorry about everyone staring," Quinton's voice pulls me from my head after we've piled into the car. He fires up the engine. "I guess I'm just a bit of a hotshot around here."

Quinton attempts to clear my mood with sarcasm.

His attempts work.

"It's fine, I suppose." I act reluctant, humoring his joke and kicking back in my seat.

After minutes of small talk about whatever we drive past, a lovely neighborhood inches into view. Its entrance seems to be built with money itself. Homes laced with luxury always ignited envy in me. I'd normally look away to spare myself the anger.

Quinton, however, turns the wheel toward the neighborhood.

Wait, what? "You live here?" My voice vibrates with accusation, more so than I intended.

Quinton blinks like a lectured schoolchild. "Yes? It's nice, right?" He chuckles nervously, bringing a hand to the back of his neck.

Swallowing, I remind myself that he didn't choose to be born here at the expense of people like me. It's nothing to dwell over. "It's beautiful," I reassure him, staring at the flower beds and verdant grass.

Quinton pulls into a house reeking of modernity, but I can't help but marvel at its beauty. Once led inside, my nostrils are assaulted by swathes of lavender. I ignore a nag in my throat, and now nose too, by keeping my vision steady on Quinton.

He escorts me to a double-door room and swings it open. There's a round bed with sheets that'd have you slip and slide from the silk. The nightstand is spotless and Bocote. The throw pillows and chandelier match. The *throw pillows* and *chandelier* match. Beggary is no fun compared to this.

Quinton's nonchalance increases, almost as though he's desperate to distract me from his wealth. "Okay, whatcha wanna do, Connor?" He hops on his bed, tossing his open backpack toward a corner.

I waddle to the bed, plopping beside him. "I dunno, it's your house, you decide."

Quinton shifts along the bed, inching toward me with an unreadable expression. When I think it's high time for him to back up, he moves in even closer.

My breath picks up, soon struggling to stay afloat in the drowning proximity. But, he quickly retreats and takes an LED light switch in his hand. Ah. "So…where are your parents right now?" I choose parental conversation to soften the air, fairly well-versed in what to say during tension-thick situations.

Quinton's expression goes through a *metamorphosis* at the unremarkable question. "Ah.. they aren't home right now. They're, um, sweet!" He flashes a quick smile and leans against his bedframe.

I raise an eyebrow. What a random, vague description. If there was any innuendo in his phrase, it wasn't pretty.

Before I can decide whether to pry or not, Quinton pats the spot on the bed directly beside him. "C'mere, let's watch something." Quinton plucks his remote off his second nightstand and activates the flatscreen before us.

I conceal my exasperation.

Throughout the viewing of *Catch Me If You Can*, we begin to inch toward each other, giggling over the script every now and again. Halfway through the film, I readjust and note how squished our bodies are beneath the covers.

"This movie is so stupid." Quinton pauses it, slowly turning his head to stare me down.

I twitch under the blanket, meeting his eyes with a buzz in my chest. "Not as stupid as you. Do not insult *Catch Me If You Can*." I lower my tone as he did.

"Oh yeah? What are you gonna do about it?" Quinton's face rises and moves forward, lips curling into a subtle grin. The simple movement causes my head to reel.

I let out a meek, "I don't know, what do you want me to do about it?"

Quinton doesn't respond. I silently remain millimeters from him and examine his expression for millennia.

His hands raise to cup my face, his eyes flutter shut, and —

"Wait, what the fuck?" I shoot backward. My finger stabs toward a... whatever the hell that is, hanging out of Quinton's backpack. Is that a doll?

Quinton springs upward, confused and embarrassed. "I'm so sorry — I should've asked if I could. I'm — "

I silence him with a finger and glare at his backpack. "No, Quinton, it's not that, but what the fuck is that?" I roll from the cushion and strike the area with another stab of my finger.

Quinton's expression morphs from a tame mortification to extreme and utter terror, furthering my suspicions.

Instinctively, I dart toward the doll before Quinton can. I grasp the doll from his backpack, inspecting it.

And with the inspection, fear swells.

This doll really *does* look exactly like me. My eyes didn't deceive me.

With its delicately stitched features, the doll possesses a sinister lookalike-ness. Eerily, its hair, eye color, and glasses are identical to mine. It wears the clothes I had on the day of the football game. I glance at the doll, and then at Quinton, feeling the air dry and freeze between us. What I'd thought to be a small, embarrassing object he was careful to hide turned out to be a...*something* stuffed with cotton and...creepiness!

My hair stands on end, and I clutch the doll, scooting closer to the door. When I look at Quinton again, my throat dries.

Quinton rises slowly while I study him. Despite this freakish doll, Quinton's behavior never pointed to psychopathy or ill intent. Unless I'm blind.

"Okay, okay, Connor, listen. I swear — I know this looks weird as hell but please, let me explain. Is that okay?"

His friendly exterior persuades me, and I agree with a reluctant sigh. "...okay. Go ahead." I keep my distance. He appears hurt, but before he can experience a lick of pity, I need an explanation.

"Listen. I have had this doll for, like, years. Honest. I got it from some random sketchy toy shop Mom took me to. Look, look — " Quinton spins to his closet, fishing around frantically for a moment.

And all of a sudden, the handsome man a few feet away from me is a stranger again. I'm in a stranger's house — someone I have only recently met. I consider bolting to prevent the conversation's inevitable continuation.

But I stay, unable to follow through and leave.

Quinton finally turns around and holds up an old Polaroid victoriously. "See? Look, I have baby pictures with it. How could baby me possibly be a creepy stalker?" His eyes beg me to say what's on my mind as he taps the photo over and over and over. "I don't know how or why this looks like you, but I noticed the uncanniness at the game." He pauses, stuttering in a flurry. "Okay, now — that's not in any way *why* I like you, of course, because yes, I like you. But this doll," Quinton sighs, a bit defeated. "I guess it piqued my curiosity and — I mean, I have no idea why it resembles you, honestly. Sure it's why I went up to you at first but, you gotta believe me, I genuinely like you." With that, his speech ends.

My chest warms at his nervous confession, but I stay silent. My hand stretches outward, a wordless demand for the toddler photos. He gives them.

I scan the Polaroids several times over and draw one conclusion: It's clearly the same doll. It even has the same ketchup stain as the one in our present day. "Okay, Quinton. I believe that you didn't maliciously get this doll of me, but it's still, um, weird."

Quinton nods, a little too fast. "Yeah, no, no — I get that, of course. I mean, imagine how weirded out I was when I saw one of my childhood dolls at a football game. Or — yeah." His eyes are wide and nervous.

"It's okay." I skip toward the bed, reclaiming my spot on the mattress. "I trust you're not some crazy murderous person." For the most part. This could be the most idiotic decision I've ever made.

Quinton laughs, the sound freeing the air of its tension.

With a cluttered head, I add, "And, forgive me if I'm wrong but — " my eyes taunt, " — did I hear you say you like me?"

Quinton pauses. "Well, um, let's talk about this first th — "

"Son, who is this?" Quinton is interrupted by an older man's voice, surprising us both.

Quinton rises to his feet, and I follow the action, hurling the doll across the room. It hits the wall with a thump. Ignoring — but not forgetting — a jolt of pain in my shoulder, I turn to the adult man I presume to be the mighty Mr. Hansley. Quinton's father.

Quinton croons. "Oh, he's my new friend. He was *just* telling me what girls like to hear — am I right?"

I wince at the undercover misogyny Quinton spews to forge a bond with someone, apparently, like Quinton's dad.

Quinton remains composed. It's frightening how honestly he can lie. "He'll be gone in about ten minutes or so. Tell Mom I'm helping her with dinner tonight!"

Mr. Hansley appears pleased with himself. "Ah, my boy's a heart-breaker. I'm glad this boy is breaking you out of your, uh, bad habits."

Immediately, my eyebrows raise to the tip-top of my forehead. There it is. Confirmed. Quinton's parents, or dad at least, hate women *and* are homophobic. Cute.

I glower as his father exits.

The blond cheer captain beside me releases a strung-out sigh, ditching the player act. "God."

I swipe my hand over the sore spot on my back. "So, your dad is…"

Quinton snorts bitterly. "Yes, homophobic." He averts his eyes from my own sympathetic ones. "It's not fun, but he and Mom love me a lot. I'll live. They truly believe my being gay will get me into Hell or whatever. They…know I'm gay? But they believe I can change — and they think I'm on the right track." He hunches his back with a small sigh. "They think they're saving me, you know?"

I slip a hand over Quinton's shoulder. "Hey, it's okay. I'm so sorry you have to live with that. That's really fucking dumb of them."

Quinton graces my hand with his own, squeezing once. "I'm fine, it's fine. But thank you. Let's focus on this weird doll lookalike of you, yeah?"

I'm too lost in thought to respond immediately. My eyes pin to the floor, feeling endlessly thankful for Mum's unconditional love, even if that shouldn't come at a price. Dad never had the chance to offer such love. But, I'm sure he would've too.

While I'm staring at the floor, my eyes catch the doll again. Right.

Quinton lifts himself to his feet. "Connor. What d'ya think we should do with it?" He picks it up from the ground, juggling it lazily.

I'm about to chuckle at his antics, but Quinton throws it particularly high, and the doll plummets into his palm.

And, fuck, I react. An impact brought by God-knows-what punches at me, sending tingles throughout my stomach.

What the *hell* was that?

I fail to hide my pain, and Quinton notices my shocked expression. "Whoa, hey, are you okay?" He chucks the doll on the bed, and a second impact hits my bones.

It can't be.

Quinton rushes over after hearing my new groan. "Connor, answer me, are you okay?"

I think hard, horrified.

It couldn't possibly be. "Ow, I'm fine, I just…" Because that'd be crazy. "I'm sorry, no way, this is too weird."

When I look at the doll again, it appears far more sinister than before.

"What is 'too weird'?" Quinton presses on, urging me to look at him.

I slowly tear my eyes away from the doll. "Quinton, when the doll hit the wall, I felt a random, I don't know, shot of pain. And when the doll hit your hand after you threw it, I felt a hit too. Plus when you threw it on the bed just now." I pray he'll call me insane. Pray for a perfectly reasonable explanation.

Quinton doesn't reply, though his jaw unhinges. He backs away, glances at the doll, and *carefully* picks it up. "Okay, I promise I will not hurt you. I'm gonna test something pain-freely, okay?" Quinton turns around, spiking my nerves. His thin promise is too weak to completely calm me down.

Still, I decide to trust him. "Okay." I screw my eyes shut, and a progressive dizziness begins overpowering my senses. "Dude, what are you doing?"

Quinton turns to face me once more, dangling the doll. "Okay, did you feel anything?" He guides me to the bed, handling me like a confused grandpa.

I nod and bat the guiding hand away. "Yeah, I felt super dizzy. Like I was spinning or something."

Quinton goes pale. "Shit. I was twirling it."

Fuck, I've never hated a hypothesis for being correct so much before.

With a dry mouth, I manage to croak, "Okay, um, okay. This is weird and scary. What do we fucking do?" The unfamiliar walls around me grow menacing, reminding me that I've been friends with him for only a short week and a half. I do not know this man.

Quinton takes a comforting approach. "It's okay, Connor. I promise, I swear, I won't do anything to it." He plants it far away from me on the bed for emphasis and pulls me in for a consoling embrace. It's a strange gesture. It helps, a little. "I have no idea what the hell is going on either," Quinton continues. "Come by my house tomorrow, okay? We can test more and brainstorm ideas on what to do with it. For now, we can just relax or test more if you'd like." Quinton places a surprise kiss on my forehead.

I offer a smile but lower my head. "Okay, thanks for the kiss or whatever, but dude, why the fuck are you acting so calm about this?" I march to the bed, snagging the doll from the sheets. "This," I jab a finger at the doll, "fucking *inanimate object* is literally connected to my real, human body…I think. A doll — a *doll* is directly transferring, or something, to me." My breath quickens, progressive worry and wonder clouding my mind. I step toward him, finding his eyes. "Get your laptop out or something! Also, I'll take the doll home, thank you. *'We can just relax or test more'*," I quote him aggressively, my fear coming off as anger as I take a step closer. "Obviously I want to test more. What, do you just expect us to relax and chill out after discovering, like, whatever the hell this is? I mean, what the f — "

"Quinton?" A middle-aged voice interrupts us, not sweet-sounding enough to hide a tinge of horror. I back up from Quinton. I didn't notice how close we'd become during my speech.

Quinton freezes. "Mom?"

Oh, fuck.

CHAPTER 3

Parents are made to protect. They earn, foster, and co-parent; prioritizing their children applies to parenthood as a role. Quinton's mother's expression and father's behavior suggest that neither has carried out parental responsibilities properly. Or at least the critical ones, e.g. accepting your child.

Ms. Hansley wears a cold, firm smile. "Quinton." Her eyes beckon him to stand with a quick squint, and Quinton takes the hint. He follows his mother out of the room, sending a reassuring look my way.

I do not feel reassured. Maybe I would've if he didn't also look downright mortified.

After debating with myself for a few seconds — okay, less than a few seconds — I decide to eavesdrop and tilt my head toward the cracked open door.

"We've had this conversation so many times, Quinton," a scolding voice echoes across their long hallways, reaching my ears. "I know high school is the time when kids get all curious, but you're setting yourself up, sweetie. What did we say about you and your male friends?"

Quinton sounds spent. "Mom, it's not — you're really jumping to conclusions right now." It sounds like he's had this conversation a number of times, and he's tired of getting a lecture every time he smiles a man's way in front of his parents.

She replies with little mercy. "Jumping to conclusions is part of parenting, Quinton. Kindly tell your friend to go — I just can't trust you anymore after Marco. Perhaps it is innocent, but you broke our trust with him, and we're *still* trying to save you from damnation. I know you think it's a bunch of crap, but we just want to ensure your safety." She treats caring

for your child like charity work. "The least you could do is understand —
just think of the testaments, okay sweetie?" She breathes before masking
her poison with a prettier tone. "Now go, I made brownies downstairs for
you to enjoy when he leaves."

Quinton clears his throat. "Okay, Mom. I'm sorry, I know." How does
he hold his tongue? I never could've guessed Quinton's home life would
involve this. Mega-rich? Very believable. However, homophobic parents
he's had to remain patient with his whole life? Yikes.

A slow thump of footsteps sends me flying back to my original spot on
the bed. Once settled, I can only frown, picturing whatever nightmare of a
childhood Quinton had to live, and understanding how little I deserved to
hear such a personal chat.

Once he's back in sight, our eyes find each other's before I quickly
turn my head.

When Quinton speaks, his voice is shrill. "Yeah, so, you heard her, I
don't think you can come by tomorrow."

I can tell he cares little about my eavesdropping when his eyes darken
a few shades. "Maybe if my mom didn't treat me like a walking fucking
sin." He trudges over with my backpack, lifting it toward me politely.

I accept the bag. "Oh — thanks, yeah, no, that's fine." A beat of silence.
"I'm really sorry you have to deal with that." I would've been able to think
up a more sympathetic condolence, but the doll still heavily distracts me.

He grins. "It's cool. We can meet at yours — to discuss the doll the day
after tomorrow. If that's all right?"

My lip twitches, and I remember the luxury stained marble lining
every inch of this household. But I'm not letting insecurity over money
keep us from figuring this doll out. "Oh, um, sure."

With a brief smile, Quinton tugs my hand and ruffles my hair. "Great!
Come on now, we need to get you out of here before my parents actually
throw a fit."

I nod. "Bye, Quinton."

"Bye, Connor."

When his front door shuts in my face and I'm halfway down the block,
I slap my forehead with a deep sigh. I left the doll at his house.

———

"Man. That is actually so fucking crazy. You sure Quinton didn't just drug
you or something? Or — dude, if you're pulling my leg right now..." Fritz
is chewing while he talks on the other line.

I throw my black Labrador her ball, bored from repeating the story to him for the 15th time. Fritz knows I'm not crazy, but he's a logical man. I doubt he's gotten around to fully believing my tale about a human-connected doll yet. *"I'm sure.* I'm actually very curious, though. Freaked out overall, of course, and especially because I forgot to take the doll with me from his house. Like, God, I'm so stupid."

A low-quality drone comes from the other line, which I assume is meant to be a hum of agreement. "You're strong, dude. I'd have refused to leave if that happened to me, or not trusted the guy. I can't believe it's *Quinton* of all people. I mean, I won't tell anyone, but hell that is juicy. Imagine what people would say if y'all told others." He swallows his food. "That's really fucking scary still. Like, what if someone just sits on it, you know? Or like a cat gets to it. Would you, um, get hurt?"

My mouth dries. Fritz's theories are too possible. "Fuck. Um — yeah, I think? I don't know, we haven't tested that yet." Instinctively, I bring my knees to my chest, sit up in bed, and scan my skin for any bruises or cuts.

Whew. I find nothing. Maybe it's a good thing I left the doll at Quinton's house. I turn my head to Birdie, and then her long teeth. Labradors are known to chew up everything they find — and I can confirm that with plenty of torn-up stuffed animals of mine now in landfills. I speak again, breath quickening. "You know, I'm — I'm getting tired, and I have loads of homework. See you at school tomorrow, yeah? And don't, like, tell people about this. You have a lot of friends and a big mouth."

"Yeah, yeah, I promise, I already said I wouldn't. I was the one who warned you not to tell. People would just call me *absolutely ludicrous.*" He snickers. "Sleep well. But, again, that's insane. Are you sure you're gonna be okay because — "

I accidentally hang up before Fritz has finished his thought, sucking in a sharp breath. I consider texting a "good night," but I decide I'm too tired.

Sleep well. Sleep well, sleep well, sleep well. *As long as I don't get maimed by a housepet that takes its hunger out on a certain doll.* Does Quinton have a pet?

I blink, blindly submerging myself in the bed covers. Whatever.

Quinton's eyes put Achilles to shame. How could a simple mortal hold a green lovely enough to trump a Greek god? I don't express gratitude for his appearance often enough. A glance at him is equivalent to a shot of vodka — he's cocaine, in the right lighting. If he were a fox, every hen house's door would swing open with a welcoming cluck. He's just —

"Connor!" Mum taps her foot in front of me, unamused. "You've been vacuuming the same spot for a whole minute. What's all this for, baby?"

I sniff dismissively and wander toward the sink. "This guy friend is coming over tomorrow. He's hella-fucking-rich, so I'm cleaning up." He's also definitely the cutest guy I've brought over. I select my words carefully, deciding Mum can hear about him at dinner tomorrow night. I'm not keen on telling her about the doll, however. Part of me still believes I dreamt the whole ordeal.

Mum pauses, as if she's planning to pry, but she then shrugs and leans against the pale wall. "Ah, okay. Thank you, son. I gotta go now, but I left some money on the counter so you can order pizza, okay? Bye, love you."

"Love you too. Enjoy the night shift." I return to vacuuming.

QUINTON

I scrub my hand into my hair, frustrated at it for not doing what I want. I need my messy strands to be normal just this one time — I'm going to Connor Jones' house. I must show respect for that adorable, witty boy.

I splash my face with lukewarm school water a final time before turning a corner to look for Connor. I first survey the parking lot. In the midst of the student body sauntering to their cars and the buses, I spot the small brown-haired boy, dressed in a thigh-length sweater and long wool socks.

He, too, is eagerly looking around. Looking for *me.* I glide through the crowd, walking toward him from behind.

I lean down to whisper in his ear. "Hi, Connor." I can't help but smile to myself when goosebumps appear on his neck.

"Agh, why do you always do that? That little 'Connor' all in my ear." He yanks me by the arm toward what I believe is his car.

I find myself not alarmed by this roughness. Connor is still a stranger budding into a good friend — but we get along so well, it creates an illusion of familiarity. It's hard not to feel like we've been friends for years. "You know you love it."

"Whatever. Do you have the doll?" Connor halts beside a baked black car.

I nod and hop into shotgun. "Yes, now start driving, idiot."

Connor scoffs at the insult but hits the gas anyway.

Ten minutes pass before we turn into a neighborhood, and soon after, Connor's car snakes into the driveway of a small house. The exterior is painted baby blue, decorated with a tin rooster and a clay sun, and the front yard is covered in flowers and buds.

Connor exits the car, jumps onto the pavement, and curtly nods his head toward the house.

We enter the house, and I look around, enjoying the simple, but contemporary design. "Wow."

Connor frowns deeply. "You seem a bit too shocked at how nice the inside of my house looks." He clutches his chest, offended.

I immediately backtrack. "No — *no*, it's not that, you just really talked it down. I was expecting a dirt hut based on how you described it, honestly."

Connor doesn't seem to buy what I say. But, he smiles. "I was joking, doofus." Oh. "But also, don't lie, I get it. Thank you anyway."

"I'm not lying! I don't give a flying fuck about how expensive your house is or not. I came to chill with you and test the doll, not ogle furniture."

Connor stretches his arms with a smile, but the grin soon vanishes. "Thanks, but I'm not casually 'chilling with you — '" he does dramatic air quotes — "until we get to the bottom of your freaky-ass doll."

Understandable. The doll feels heavier in my bag than it should, but I can't find it in myself to care as much about the doll as he does. And I have no clue why.

Connor's mother, I presume, emerges from a small bedroom door and greets me before taking her leave for what Connor explains is her final shift of the day.

Connor waves her off with a few exchanged 'I love yous' and leads me to his room. The room is compact, and there's not too much wiggle room for testing. But, it's organized and tidy. A few pictures from his childhood are hung across the wall. I grin — I've always been a fan of documenting moments with strung-up photos as well. My parents thought it messed with our classy rep, and that we needed to "keep up appearances," even in our own home. I slow my pace to look at the photos of Connor.

Only one has a father present, and Connor couldn't be older than two in it.

His walls, frames, and sheets all happen to be the same color. I think out loud. "You seem to like the color blue."

Connor sets his backpack down, a low yawn strolling through his words. "Well, yeah, it's one of the only colors I can see." He snorts once. "Protan color blindness."

The more you know. "Cool, cool, so you like, can't see red or purple or, like — "

"Get the doll out." Connor reminds me in a firm tone.

I nod, clearing my throat. "Right, let me grab it." I reach for my bag and pull it out delicately. "I won't do anything to hurt you, promise."

CONNOR

Hours of swimming in internet nonsense must've passed by now, and I still come up short. The only video similar to our doll situation is a grown bearded man rambling about how the Earth is flat for the second half of the video. Which leaves us here. Testing the boundaries of touch.

Quinton's fingers find the fabric, caressing the doll.

I click my tongue, nodding a weary 'no', to indicate I didn't feel anything.

Quinton nods at the quiet command, massaging the doll with more strength.

I lift a hand. "All right, I feel something. But it's not very strong." I lean back against my bed frame, accidentally slapping a glass of water from my nightstand.

But the mistake is hardly severe because Quinton catches it with impressive reflexes.

"Damn," I say aloud, eyes pinned on his hand gripping the glass.

He sets it down and snaps twice. "Focus, Connor, I thought you wanted to only test." But, Quinton's proud smile mellows out when he notices the doll in his other hand has gone missing. "Where the — " he pauses, looking like a lost puppy. "Aha! Found it." He digs behind the bed and holds it in the air, wrapping his fingers around the doll's torso.

My face heats up. "Move your thumb, you massive idiot!" Stomach pooling at the new touch on my waist, I reach upward and yank the doll from him.

Quinton cocks his head, most likely not expecting me to steal the doll from him. However, with my red face and wide eyes, he catches on. "Oh! Oh, my God, I'm so sorry." He snorts, holding out a hand for the doll, which I give him, and nestling it — *carefully* this time — into his palms. "I'm sorry — won't happen again."

I smile. "Don't stress it."

Quinton nods, a grin teasing at his lips. "Maybe we could utilize that function later."

I huff several times at the insinuation and twist my head away from the weight of his beating gaze. "Quinton! What is wrong with you, oh, my God."

"Sorry, sorry," he apologizes with sincerity.

It's nearly disappointing.

I mean, what?

I open my mouth to offer a delayed reply, but before I can, a scream rips from Quinton's phone. It cries out with a number of chimes before ceasing. "Jesus, Quinton, change your ringtone. I felt like a dog listening to those…dog whistle things."

Quinton chuckles. "It's my parent's personalized ringtone." He adds with a sad smile, "Can't miss a call from them." His pointer finger must be a masochist because it presses the green *accept call* button with zero hesitance. "Hello? Yes, yes, I know…Okay! Okay — look, calm down, don't worry…I *know*. I'm coming home right — yes, I understand…Okay, bye. I'm sorry, love you too." His shoulders slump, indicating what his mouth doesn't.

Misery.

Quinton rises, a dread stronger than gravity visibly pulling him back toward my bed. "I can't believe they're so strict — and just because you're a fucking guy." He spits every word out. "I'm so sorry. I know how stressed you probably are about the doll. I'll just — we can maybe experiment more tomorrow. Test its limits more? Here."

My heart sinks; I'm entirely unsettled and completely aware that I'm getting zero sleep tonight. Knowing there's a magical doll out there linked to your body is definitely a risk factor for insomnia. But as much as I *need* to continue testing, Quinton needs to leave.

I look at his outstretched hands holding the doll before pushing them away. "It's all good, I'm sorry your parents are such assholes. But, you keep the doll. Our dog — Birdie — tears through every toy she finds. And you saw how big she is. Do you have any pets?"

Quinton nods his head no.

I swallow, understanding what I'm trusting my *very* new friend with. "Then please, keep it safe. We haven't tested injury yet but…I'm not taking any chances. I'll come over as soon as possible, and we will build some sort of case to keep the doll in — to make sure nothing can get to it. Then maybe I'll take it home. Like a glass case in a safe sorta thing?"

Quinton looks astonished, oddly amazed. "I can keep it? Really?"

It comes out nearly a whisper. "Really."

QUINTON

The air is not my friend today. Humidity and heat aren't suitable weather for cheer practice, but I'll have to deal with it. I wave goodbye to my Uber driver, still annoyed Dad took my car for the day. It's a stupid punishment for seeing Connor without asking, in my opinion. It has only resulted in me wasting money on Ubers who don't get paid enough to care about driving safely.

I squint through the mist, spotting my cheer coach several yards within the fog. I admire how mysterious my team looks hiding inside the mist before remembering Connor exists.

Soon, my thumb is above Connor's contact on my phone. It's been seven days since our first meeting at his house, and since then we've met up every single day for vigorous doll-training sessions. It's insane how the doll exists. It must have been fate, or something, for us to find each other like that. The doll often comes to my mind, but I have never been too afraid of it. Maybe my crush on Connor is just that strong, but he, separate from the doll, is on my mind way more often.

With our daily meetups, my free time is shrinking, but going to his house on the daily does get my parents off my back. I've been leaving at around seven p.m., and assuring them I'm headed to our bank to study more so I can properly "take over the family title" when they retire. Little do they know I've been putting my developer skills to work. They think my "obsession" with coding is a pesky distraction. Turns out, rerouting your phone's location when tracked by your helicopter parents is easy with the right clients and when your left hand is basically a source code editor. When they track me, it always appears that I'm at the bank.

So: in your face, Mom.

I've found my way around it.

God knows how much Connor trusts me — he can be hard to read — but, we're discovering this *magic* together. One step at a time.

After a few more steps in the damp grass, I've reached my team. Quickly, I schedule today's daily meetup with Connor.

Me: *wanna pick me up from cheer in an hour? we can go to your place*

Connor: *I guess I will. Only for you, idiot*
Me: *you're the idiot*
Connor: *A hot idiot*
Me: *true*
Connor: *Shut upp*
        See you in 60

I transfix on his texts a minute too long before my phone is sent to my pocket with a giddy shove. *See you in 60.*

Quinton!" Connor sticks his arm outside the car window, banging the metal below with his small palm.

I duck inside and chuckle. "Is that your way of kindly asking someone to join you?"

Connor turns his key. "I've been impatient my whole life. Probably longer than we've owned this rusty ass car. How was cheer?" Connor taps the pedal, and the car lurches forward. His eyes widen, startled by his own action.

I grip my seat. "Connor! It was — good, very tiring, but damn."

"Glad to hear. And, sorry — " he stretches the 'y' " — the car does that sometimes."

I smile.

He taps the pedal again, far more gently this time. The car reacts well, nudging forward correctly.

I sniff, thinking of lines to drop later today. Something to completely win him over. We've never discussed romantic or sexual histories together, and Connor's reputation isn't common knowledge, like mine. He could be a heartbreaker for all I know. "You should get this thing repaired, you know," I say mindlessly to encourage a conversation.

There's a second of silence. Connor's lower lip twitches.

"We can't." Connor's eyes remain trained on the road. He doesn't say anything else, causing me to panic.

Shit. "Oh — fuck, I'm sorry that was stupid. Where are my manners?" I slump in my seat with an awkward chuckle. *Idiot.* "I meant it as a safety joke thing, nothing more, promise." The vapor gathers in the sky above us, and more clouds begin to form. Way to encourage the mood, traitor clouds.

Connor shifts in his seat, flicking his left turn signal on. "It's not — you didn't say anything wrong. I just don't bring up my, um, working-class status often." His eyes stay pinned on the never-ending asphalt road.

I rest a hand on Connor's shoulder and screw my lips shut. Sure, I whine about my parents often, but I've still tried to be aware of the tremendous privilege that I have even outside of my socioeconomic status.

"It's — " Connor continues — "I don't take things very personally anymore. People have…I don't know, I'm sorry, I'm rambling. You didn't even say anything wrong; I'm taking shit out on the wrong person." He finally blinks.

I shake my head, horrified under my caring grin. Why the fuck would I say that? "No, no, no. Connor, you aren't oversharing. Whatever you say, I'll listen."

Connor opens his mouth and closes it twice over, looking for the right words.

I wait patiently.

"People…" He sighs. "People don't have to verbally say how they're feeling about the appearance of, like, everything I own for me to know what they're thinking. But they still often do. I don't know, I'm used to comments like that, is what I'm trying to say. Everyone says things like that."

"Well, then, I don't want to be 'everyone.' Connor, I'm so sorry — "

He raises a finger, poised and focused on the road. "I have a single immigrant mother, who I care about. She doesn't get paid for what she's worth. She's smart, funny, and so hard-working but — " Connor's tone approaches a breach, halting to avoid a voice crack. "Give me a moment."

"Of course." My hand slips into his, my chin resting on my other palm propped up by the seat divider.

Connor speaks. "Damnit, it really hurts when, you know, people point out *things* about her. Or at least her accomplishments. Like buying her first car." Connor speaks low and clear, as though he's careful to not appear too offended at what I said.

I cringe, feeling guilty.

"People bringing up my house or sly comments about, I don't know, whatever. It's like a blow to all the hard work it took my mum to live happily." He wears that look again, the one that begs me to not see him as a sensitive buzzkill. "But I mean it's fine, she doesn't deserve it, right? She was lied to — this country sucks — not to say the UK doesn't in its own ways. I mean, imagine how much more horrible it'd be if she wasn't white like — " a humorless snort — "I hate it here." Connor pulls into his driveway at last and sits, unmoving. I don't move either.

"I'm so sorry, Connor. Your mother sounds strong and incredible. I'm sure your conditions have put a lot of pressure on you as well." I swipe a thumb under his eye.

Connor smiles, his nose bright red. He leans his head on my shoulder from the other seat. The car's crowdedness does me a favor, bringing Connor closer to me than he would've been if this were my car.

He chuckles near my neck. "I'm sorry, I didn't mean for the conversation to turn into me tearing up on your shoulder."

"I don't mind in the slightest."

I drop my voice to a murmur, almost inaudible against the drizzle outside. "You don't have to worry Connor. This has been an awesome couple of weeks of getting to know you. The last thing I'd want to do is upset you — please call me out on my bullshit."

Connor lifts his head from my neck, but he doesn't move any further away than that.

He chooses to stay near me.

"Thank you." He tilts his chin up, and I notice his tears are gone. Moments pass, and soon, the red on his face is there for a different reason. Different intention.

My fingers provide a rest for his cheek, and my eyes find his. "You're so pretty."

He blushes like crazy. The sight catalyzes my heart rate. "Heh, yeah?"

"Yeah."

He breaks eye contact, disappointing me. But I soon pleasantly realize he's intensely staring somewhere else now. My lips. He stares a little longer, his head tilts to the side, and *fuck* our lips meet.

Connor kisses me.

Sweet and sinless — unless you count the whole gay thing — Connor kisses me. When he pulls back, his eyelashes are nearly touching his eyebrows. My hand quickly finds his jaw, guiding him in for a second kiss. Connor accepts eagerly, and his mouth parts within a few moments. Once the kiss deepens, we break apart, lips easing into grins.

"That was...nice," Connor says, squeezing my hand and facing the windshield to blush in private.

I shift in my seat, heart pounding underneath my cheer uniform. "Damn, only nice?" That was beautiful.

Connor only shrugs. "I guess it was all right." But his sparkling eyes and broad smile confirm he enjoyed it more than he's letting on.

I kiss his cheek. "Oh, shut up."

CONNOR

I call for Mum, singing her name out to alert her that I'm home. I shout it once more, and my heart squeals in anticipation when she doesn't respond. Normally, I'd be hoping to find her, but today, Quinton and I are eager for her absence.

I lead Quinton into my bedroom, excited snickers painting our dim, pale walls pink.

He sits on his usual spot on my bed, though with a far different intention than normal. I smooth the bed covers, pushing away any thoughts of the doll and feeling Quinton's hard stare on each of my fingers. Neither of us have addressed the other since the kiss.

Quinton decides to take the initiative and scoots closer until we're side by side. I blush, studying him with a small shiver.

"Connor," his voice dips as he eyes me. *Leers* at me even.

I shift toward him and my heart rate jumps, because how could it not? He's just so fucking *hot*. I curve my neck to properly loom over his sculpted face, and we watch each other, flustered.

Quinton frowns, displeased with me being above him, so he scoots his broad body upward. "Connor," he tries again, a question dancing across his pink lips. "Can I kiss you again…and maybe go a little further?"

My mouth parts as I once over Quinton, trying to convince myself this is in fact happening. When I meet his ardent eyes, reality feels mythical. But at this moment, he's my fantasy, and my reality.

With an eager hum, I reply. "Yes, please."

CHAPTER 4

The sun urges me to wake up with an unforgiving shine. I screw my eyes shut to defend myself against the brightness while aimlessly patting the sheets next to me. "Jesus, curtains." A delirious request meant for Quinton leaves my lips. My bones crack as I fumble around, and I smile to myself, remembering the previous night. Okay, I more than smile.

Once I adjust my eyes to the sun, I look for Quinton. My bleary, goggle-less vision scans the room for a tuft of blond hair, but I can't seem to find him.

I sit up in bed and grind my teeth as I try to avoid immediately overthinking.

Maybe he had to go? Or he's in the bathroom?

He probably texted or left a note somewhere.

I pat the covers, unearthing my phone from the clothes and bedsheets surrounding me.

Not a single text or notification from Quinton on any platform. Asshole.

I drag myself out of bed, mortified to see that his bag containing the doll and its safety case are gone.

I blink. Was I only a hookup to him? No, no, we pretty much have to be friends because of that damn doll. Wait, was the doll an elaborate plan to get me in bed? If that is the case, should I be flattered or call the cops?

No way, not even Quinton and all his dollar bills could pull that off.

Trying to understand his wordless departure, I head to the bathroom. With every step thumping down the hall, a new dreadful theory as to why he's gone comes to mind.

Was I bad at sex? The inevitable question finds me.

I scold myself, no, it couldn't be that. But despite my experience and self-confidence, Quinton manages to make me doubt myself. With a lump of coal in my chest, I brush my teeth. After a lazy self-care routine, I discover Mum standing in the kitchen.

She jumps when my arms rope around her waist, twisting her head to see me. "Good morning, sweetie. Happy Saturday." She leaves a barely-there kiss on my forehead.

"Morning, Mum. Did you see Quinton lea — " I cut myself off. She didn't know he'd spent the night.

She raises an eyebrow. "Are you having a stroke?"

I clear my throat, giggling. "Sorry, I meant to ask if you saw anything Quinton left behind. He said he left a pocket chain of some sort?"

Mum narrows her eyes. "You mean when he left this morning?"

My eyes widen. "…Ye — no?"

She makes a brusque turn toward the counter, finding envelopes eager to be sorted. "You're eighteen and soon to be nineteen, Connor. You don't have to lie about boys spending the night. What you do is none of my busin — "

"Thanks, got it, sorry!" I grow pale, knowing no matter what age, any discussion of my sex life with my mum will feel criminal.

She turns, grabs a tray of toast and bacon, and plops at the dining table, clearly amused by my embarrassment. "You're welcome, prude."

While she serves herself, I pull out my phone and twitch at the zero notifications from Quinton. If he's ditched me, he should at least have the decency to leave behind the doll bound to my body — come on. Without thinking, I cave, and begin to type.

Me: *Good morning*

Now to wait for a response.

—

I groan at the length of my homework and answer the first physics question.

And check my phone for a text from Quinton.

Moving on to question two, I scribble another thoughtless explanation about calculating acceleration with kinematics.

And check my phone for a text from Quinton.

Coming toe to toe with the final question, I find myself stumped, once *again* defaulting to Quinton's contact.

I slap my forehead, kneading the skin into my palm. I've been incessantly triple checking my notifications the past two days as if I'm expecting a surprise call from the president, unable to remove my stare from the screen *just in case*. Every passerby in this coffee shop most likely assumes I'm a chronic screenager.

And tomorrow's Monday. I might have to watch Quinton prove all my nightmare theories correct — that I was a dare, that he's a psychopath, that he's simply a player, or some other scenario where no one loses except me.

It's safe to say he's sullying my mood, because where the fuck is he?

I give in once more, rereading all my unanswered messages while my anxiety crawls into my head.

Me: *Good morning*

Me: *Hi I hope ur alive*

Me: *Quinton?*

I dissect every interaction we had. Did he console me in the car to win my consent for sex alone? And did I let that *work*? Was the doll, like, a ploy to keep me coming? I refuse to believe I'm that stupid.

But every second he doesn't respond is another second spent worrying that I was a fling. Which would've been fine if discussed prior. We didn't have the "what are we" conversation before or after we had sex — he didn't give that conversation the chance to be had.

His window of time to respond has far closed. I have reached my limit of three texts; can't come across as desperate and needy. Speaking with him soon is necessary, though. I need my doll back. And despite my recent impulses to try and curse Quinton, my anger is secondary to my sadness.

Moments after our encounter, I spammed Fritz with elated text messages. How *embarrassing*.

I slump into the hardwood of my seat. The toasty coffee shop environment has lost its appeal. I shove my pencils and laptop into my backpack and exit annoyed with myself. I shake my head when I reach outside as if the motion would dispel all my negative thoughts.

It doesn't, but for the rest of the day, I will blindly believe that Quinton got grounded. Yeah. After all, he *was* sleeping at a boy's house — something strictly forbidden under his parent's rules.

When I arrive home, I decide I'm too exhausted to eat, and I spend the rest of my energy brushing my teeth and crawling into bed. I pull the sheets over my shoulders with a small sigh. Please let tomorrow be bearable.

Today is every scientist's favorite day. Hypothesis testing. Is Quinton grounded? An asshole? Dead? Stay tuned to find out.

It's important to know if it's right for me to shit-talk him to my friends. Wouldn't want to accidentally punish him more if he really is grounded.

Perhaps I'm being dramatic. Missed a memo that it was obviously a one-time thing. If that's the case, I'll lower my weapons. Still, the pit in my stomach deepens as I step out of the car and face Paup High School. I liked him. As a friend, and as more.

Students fumble past me, waddling their way to class as an indescribable stress thickens the air. I get it — final exams are inevitable for most of them. Thankfully, my above ninety averages in each class have exempted me. The only thing I have to shiver and shake about is my medical career. Especially since I am far too unremarkable for a scholarship, and far too poor for any worthwhile college.

I sigh as I head to class, joining the throngs while my stress levels heighten.

After two long class periods, it's lunchtime. As in my opportunity to have a *chat* with Quinton.

I walk and drag my hand across the lockers. Quinton tends to sit in the cafeteria, so I check there first.

My eyes scan the room, and I'm greeted by at least a hundred talking heads.

Focusing my vision only on dirty blond hair, I finally spot him. My heart speeds; I haven't seen his face since it was wonderfully red and primitive. Since he was grinning as his breath came hard and heavy. Since we had sex.

Aware of my stalker-like glare, I look away, but inch closer.

Just before I gain the courage to go up to him, I notice him loop his toned arm around the girl beside him.

She's beautiful. Though I don't know her by name, I've witnessed her chuckle and chat with Quinton almost every year since high school began. It was pretty much common knowledge to everyone they were never more than best friends.

But still, I instantly stop in my tracks, narrowing my eyes to study them better. You can fall in love with your best friend.

The two giggle, bodies far too close for comfort. Quinton attempts to swirl her tight curls, prompting more snickers from the both of them.

What an *asshole*.

Quinton suddenly pulls his phone out. Lightly taking her chin, he… kisses her on the cheek, snapping a photo to save the moment forever.

Jealousy simmers as I involuntarily step closer. The girl's russet eyes gleam as the two slowly separate from each other.

Quinton lifts his head and, by chance, catches my expression. In an instant, his bright smile drops. I swear I can see his lips mouth the words, '*Oh no*'.

Knowing his next move will be to stand and run toward me, I speed walk in the opposite direction. I'll spend lunch with Fritz as usual, Quinton is one man, a popular one too, and it's okay. What'd I expect? He's, again, a man. Sure, I'm not used to rejection, but I'm used to this vague type of hurt, and I'll get the doll from him once I've cooled off. Yeah? Yeah.

I leave and take a deep breath.

Jesus, Connor, have some self-respect.

The manner in which Quinton hollers my name is *desperate*. It does feel good in a way I couldn't admit out loud. But still, I skid away. I pretend as though the cafeteria voices could ever be loud enough to keep me from hearing him call my name.

I reach the school's couches with a groan, positively exhausted by the scene we caused. At least once school is out, I'll never have to see a face from Paup High again. I crawl onto the cushions, and my bones meet what feels like rock.

Once extended across the couch, which could very well be a boulder in disguise, I half expect Quinton to waltz in with a godsent apology. However, the logical side of me has already accepted reality. I grab my phone from my pocket. Fritz's contact seems like heaven beneath my pointer finger as I press the call button.

And straight to voicemail. Of course, it goes straight to voicemail. I cry quietly for a moment, in utter awe and terror of the hold Quinton has on me. Once my tears begin to disappear, a sudden sleepiness leaves me snuggling into the couch. Getting played and discovering magic is real is a lot for three weeks.

I fight to stay awake. But I lose, and my eyelids shut.

Ah, what the fuck?" I blink slowly, moving my hand to lazily scratch my back. I pause. "Shit!" I jump to my feet, beet red.

My eyes fly open. People must've seen my public nap on the community couch and scrunched their noses in some form of putrid judgment.

I shake my head; no, that's dramatic.

Still, not a great way to promote my reputation.

I wipe a finger below my eye and catch a hint of liner. Bringing life back to my limbs with a quick stretch, I haul my backpack onto my shoulders. I cried for a number of reasons. Accusing Quinton solely of making me cry is too much of an honor.

I arrive to class late. My teacher's face contorts from scolding to pitiful after one look at my red eyes and runny nose.

Glad to have a few buddies in this class, I'm not scrutinized by my classmates. Ponk and Alyssa would defend me endlessly anyway. The people here will only look at my puffy cheeks with sympathy, not scorn. For the most part.

Still in nap mode, my eyes struggle to stay open. The clock's ticking begins to sound so rhythmic, my mind almost mistakes it for a lullaby.

I think of Quinton to wake myself up. *One guy, it was one guy.* Just snatch the doll from him, stick it in its safe, and be glad you have the ability to pull hot flings, right?

I chuckle. This was the sexiest blunder I've ever made.

CHAPTER 5

QUINTON

Two Days Earlier

My face wrinkles, and I enter my house with a *tangible* anxiety. My parents send text after text, a tactic to stress me out to the max.

Although he was in my arms a little less than thirty minutes ago, I miss Connor. As I twist the doorknob to meet my eternal damnation, I can't help but wonder about him, and the night's…endeavors.

"Quinton?" Mom's voice sounds melodic as it pipes from the dining room.

"Hi, Mom! Um, so, yeah, hi." I kick my shoes off and notice how calm she is compared to her flurry of texts.

Does she know where I was? If she does, what's in store? Punishment? Belittling? Hitting? I walk to the dining room slowly, breath heaving all on its own. I'm not a genius, but I'm pretty sure eighteen-year-olds aren't supposed to be this scared of their parents.

I try to calm down.

Father is in the dining room as well when I arrive.

I look away, nervous. I keep from thinking about what I've done so I can lie more easily, but it's hard when there are at least ten crosses hung on every one of our walls. Sitting down across from my parents, I return my gaze to Mom whose fingers tap the table expectantly.

She clears her throat. "So, Quinton, we know you were gone all last night. Would you like to tell me and your father where you were?"

My tongue dries. Mom can cause a drought in my mouth with a simple side-eye. "I, um, I was at a friend's house. I'm sorry for not letting you know."

Terrifyingly enough, Mom smiles.

I slouch in my seat, recoiling as she leans forward to pick a short, brown hair strand right off my shirt. Connor's brown hair strand. "Right. What was the gender of this friend?"

I remove my damp palm from hers and pretend to be casual. Or *try* to pretend to be casual. I've always been a great liar, but parents are different. Like my kryptonite. They're tricky — their punishments are crueler than anyone else could inflict on me. They raise the stakes. "Oh! He was a guy. That kid, Connor, you know, brown hair, um, glasses. Can I go upstairs now? Got a test coming up." Lying is a breeze unless it's to your procreators' faces.

Mom's grin gets a little tighter. "Connor! Thank you for your honesty, seriously." My mom tilts her head toward Dad, tugging his shirt so his head lowers to her level. They share a few whispers until her eyes find mine once more. "Quinton, what did you do at Connor's house?" Her gradually lowering voice is suspenseful, I'll give her that.

"We didn't do anything."

We did.

I limply beg myself to not cry as I try to keep my voice from wavering. It's hard. And the fact this is a seven-a.m. confrontation after I accidentally fell asleep with Connor for only five hours steals an abundance of my energy. I've been so careful in the past. Of all my encounters, I wished to not get caught for this one above all, and look what happened. Fuck you, universe.

Mom's calm demeanor breaks, and a heavy disappointment and darkness flow from the cracks. "Quinton. Lying is not welcome in our household. Why was his hair on your shirt? Why is your shirt backward? Want to keep lying, or will you be honest with us?"

She smiles.

My face reddens, and my upper lip shakes. How dare she act all cool and collected? I scrutinize the emotional impurities that she believes are *so* well masked. At least Dad is upfront with his horror at who his son is. Mom is a hurricane who believes she's a drizzle.

Mom makes another face of disappointment. Shit, my time to respond has run out. "I guess we know what happened then." Her brown eyes deepen with disgust. "Something against God."

Dad's face burns, but beneath the flames, he seems scared. "Just think of our gospel we preach studiously. If we didn't think your *habits* would send you to hell, we would be fine with them. What do you not get? Where are your principles?" God knows what my dad suffered as a kid to get him to be so…him. Maybe he was beaten too. Maybe they both were.

I look to the side to hide from their stares.

Despite dropping to their knees in prayer every Sunday, my parents don't have half the Bible interpreted correctly. They use the holy book as your standard '*How to Raise a Child: 101*' and don't even understand the text. "Look, Mom, I know, but I'm eighteen years old. I am a full adult. I can make my own decisions."

Dad scoffs, stabbing at my confidence. "You're barely an adult. Turning eighteen doesn't suddenly sharpen your brain — you're clearly still very immature. You realize if we allow you to get away with this behavior, we are punishable as well? Do you want us to go down there too?"

Punishment by association? Since when does the bible adhere to Western-style law? Thought God would be too divine to follow rules written by sinners.

Dad continues, head slowly shaking left and right. "When did my son become this selfish?"

When I was born liking men. I'm sorry, Dad.

My thoughts go to the darkest places, wondering what their plans are. What will they do to me with this new information, because what *can* they do? I'm going to the University of Texas after the gap year they forced me to take next year — they can't stand the thought of my independence — but, after that, I'll be shipped a good thousand miles away. What then, Mom?

Mom nods. "Son, I know you think you know what's best for you, but unless you want us to go to hell, you will not speak to Connor. I know you think you're *gay* or…'*bisexual*,'" she says with air quotes. "But you're simply falling victim to temptation. You can resist. And we're your parents, so we will help you. You will not text Connor, call him, or interact with him in any way in real life, school or outside. Will you do that for us?"

My father groans at my mother's kindness, clearly wanting her to take a more disciplinary approach.

But this is punishment enough, because I am horrified. "No. No, Mom, I like Connor, a lot. You can't do this. He's made me happier than anyone ever has since Marco."

"*Marco* — " her fist hits the table — "was a mistake and a horrible influence. You're just having another episode." Her voice softens. "Hormones make us do crazy things, I know." She's trying to be persuasive by using logic.

But she's not using logic, she's using manipulation. Better for her anyway. If my wonderful parents have taught me anything, it's that logic has nothing on manipulation.

I grow angrier by the second. "Mistake? Marco is a person. Someone I liked and could've loved. The same thing is not going to happen to Connor. I don't care if I go to hell or not. I like men. Make up your mind; is it 'my attraction isn't real', or is it 'we'd accept you if it weren't for the Bible?' So many inconsistencies, like, grow the fuck up, no one's gonna die because I fuck men!" It's my fist's turn to slam the table.

My mother's sugary smile finally leaves, and she gasps. "Marco was taken away and punished because of *you*. If you would control yourself — if you *can* control yourself, nothing will happen to Connor. But for now, know your place." My mother shakes her head.

"What do you mean? What would you do to Connor?" I begin to feel guilty, and it weakens my words. Marco wasn't my fault, it wasn't — it was theirs. They wouldn't touch Connor.

Mom ignores the question. "Quinton. You will not speak to Connor."

I huff, adding with venom and spite, "I will do worse than speak to him."

Dad's face drops as he barrels toward me, grabbing the collar of my shirt.

Shit.

"You will do *nothing* with this boy. Do you understand? Fucking brat, you should be grateful. Look at this beautiful house I've worked to give you. All the crosses hung to protect *you*. We are protecting *you*. Get that through your thick head before something happens to that boy you think is so precious." Dad spits everywhere. He kicks my chair, stealing my confidence and causing me to jump in my seat.

What would they do to him? I stare at the white marble floor and walls, blinking dreadfully. I think of Connor's stained walls and unswept floors, our wealth gap. They could do anything to him and his single mother and get away with it. "You wouldn't do anything to Connor," I lie through my teeth, half to them, half to myself. They would. They did to Marco.

Mom looks me in the eyes again, gritting her fake teeth behind thin lips. "We would do anything to protect our son from Hell."

I feel tears built up during the conversation unleash at last. My parents drone on about how I can never speak to him, they're monitoring all my texts and calls, and how they have a family friend's son that will ensure I do not speak to Connor at school either. You can truly do anything with old money. My lower lip curls back and shakes. I want nothing more than the comfort of Connor. I wish I was with him and far, far away from this situation. But if I tried to escape with him for a second, my parents would look for us at all costs, and do God knows what when they'd find us.

Once their rant about my new rules is over, they release me to my room.

I always hated Sundays, mostly because of being forced to go to church, but this was the nail in the coffin. With the delicious closing of a door, I hear my parents leave the house for work.

I cry. I cry, fucking loud. I stay in bed all day, and my parents do me a favor by not bothering to knock on my door. I don't have my phone either. They locked it in a fucking safe. Phoneless, I eventually drift off upright in my bed. I dread school when I wake up.

Shockingly, my parents announce at the breakfast table that they will permit me to take my phone to school. I chew morsels of scrambled eggs, uncomfortable with the atmosphere, but happy with the silence.

My happiness is short-lived. "Quinton, please don't hate us. We love you, and you'll get privacy privileges back once you prove your hetero-sexuality to us! We're saving you, darling, trust me, we don't wanna be the bad guys."

Prove my heterosexuality? *Privacy privileges?* I tense up in anger, but quickly relax. Being rude and snappy won't help me get Connor back any quicker. I've gotta use my brain this time, and maybe, I even have to be nice to them. I've always disliked the one method needed to get you what you want from your parents. It's like a paradox — obey them more so you'll have to obey them less. But it's part of the only plan I've got.

I nod stiffly and stare back down at my breakfast.

Prove to them your heterosexuality. Prove it. I glance at my poster of Deepika Padukone. It can't be too hard when I like girls as well, right?

I arrive at school, waving to friends as if I didn't just come up with a plan to push a heterosexual agenda onto myself this very morning. I block every thought of Connor's face. It's pointless for me to think about him until my plan is executed. Plus, if I went up to him my parents might actu-ally disown me, so.

I hold my head high when I sit down in class, searching for a partic-ular girl friend of mine and smiling when I see her backpack in the seat next to mine. Nia. Nia is beautiful, smart, and hilarious; however, since we met in freshmen year, her never-more-than-platonic energy destroyed any romantic feelings on my end. I could never fall for her now, even if I tried. Reciprocation of feelings is important to me and necessary for love; one of the most important things life has to offer. Or, scratch that: *life* is one of the most important things love has to offer.

I wave in Nia's direction — who's negotiating her grade with the teacher — and gesture her over. She looks confused, but walks up to me anyway.

"What's up?" She uses her teeth to hold a hair tie, pulling her dark, braided strands into a bun at the top of her head.

I greet her with a smile. "Okay, Nia, listen. I'll explain after class, but, can you like — " I hold my breath, " — fake be my kind-of-girlfriend, but kind-of-not-girlfriend?" I use my body language to convey what I'm getting at. I lower and shake my head, knowing that couldn't be worded more poorly.

She eyes me and giggles for a second, pushing her charcoal pencils away on the desk so she can rest her elbows. "Erm, what?"

"I'm, okay — it's, listen — it's hard to like, oh, my God." I lightly punch myself on the head for being unable to properly explain.

With a small smile, one of her white, glued nails traces my hand. "Take your time, Quinton. Just not too much. We gotta pay attention." She points to the teacher writing away on the whiteboard while fiddling with her curls nervously.

I nod and inch closer, lowering my voice to a whisper. "Okay, listen. So, Connor and I, that white, short skinny guy from London in your fourth period, are, like, a thing."

She retracts in surprise, her face brightening. "I knew it!" She whisper-yells with a grin. "I fucking knew something was certainly going on!"

But her joy falters as she sees my more solemn expression. "Is there no longer a 'thing' going on or…" She bites her lip, impatient for a response. "Wait, how did you know I'm in his fourth period?"

I look away, grinning. "Well, obviously I told him about my best friend."

Nia smiles. "Aww — "

"Shut up," I chuckle. "Anyway, it's complicated. My homophobic parents found out about him and restricted me from texting, calling, or talking to him. I was wondering if I could, like, I'm sorry this is weird, but if you could be my fake girlfriend — but not actually my girlfriend — maybe just a girl I'm talking to? To prove my heterosexuality to my parents so I can text Connor again? Like message me and take pics as if we're dating, you know?"

Nia's face undergoes all five stages of grief, before settling with gold; acceptance. "God, I am so sorry about that. This is a horrible situation, as well as a horrible plan, but, sure. Fuck it, I already finished all my AP classes' homework and got time on my hands." She ducks under my arm, placing it over her shoulder. "We start now?"

"We start now."

Nia clasps my arm in the hallway, seeming weary of the stares and murmurs. She simply smiles at them with grace, already a pro. "Do we want to be public? Or…"

I exhale. "Yes, if there are rumors my parents will most definitely hear them from other drama-loving trust-fund kids telling their parents, making it way more believable."

Nia nods in determination like she's on a top-secret mission. It warms my heart to see her still my friend after four years. Our overall friend group of normally either five or seven has adapted and changed throughout time, but she and I stick together like gum to the underside of a table. We haven't spoken much the past few weeks, thanks to Connor, but it's nice having time to catch up on our daily adventures — my post-UT acceptance stress, and her MIT anxieties.

We bounce down the stairs and turn into the cafeteria, laughing about our sophomore-year English teacher — the poor guy doesn't know we relentlessly bully him to this day. Shouldn't have failed all your students after *you* lost our assignments, Mr. Mullen!

I take my seat next to Nia, who asks to put her hand on my chest. I nod.

She looks around the room, giddy. "Ahh, this is crazy! Everyone's looking at us. My friends are gonna freak out." She pauses, gaze lowering. "They all probably can't stand to see a black girl hooking arms with Mr. Porcelain Popular, amiright?"

I bite my lip, and my eyes darken. "God, I'm really sorry about that. You know, if you ever, *ever* get uncomfortable with this ploy — "

Nia squeezes my hand, chuckling and highly amused. "Jeez, it's fine, Quinton, you're so funny. I'll get used to it."

I sigh deeply while our lunch table members engage in their regular conversations about how scary it is becoming an adult, cars, music, and more. But the only thing on my mind is Connor, especially since he thinks I ghosted him.

Connor's and my friendship is rare. People don't click with others as easily as we did. I believe everyone has many platonic and romantic soulmates, and I don't believe in them because of religion or faith or whatever, just logically. Scientifically speaking, there's gotta be people you get along with out there somewhere, people where your personalities simply match, no matter who you are — our population is nearly eight billion. I was already growing convinced he was one of those people — one of the many soulmates I was lucky enough to meet. When you crush on people as passionately as I do, when your parents beat you at the slightest hint you are loving the wrong gender, you have to have this belief set about love and soulmates. If I wasn't so dramatic or passionate about love, my parents might've been successful in beating the will to love out of me. Which is why this plan has to work.

I miss Connor deeply; the familiar voices of my main friend group are barely a distraction.

Nia notices my distress, resting her head on my chest and blinking up at me with blue liner. "You good?"

I offer a tender smile and bob my head "Yes." And for a second, my distraught emotions lessen.

Deciding to move the plan along more quickly, I shift Nia off my chest and cup her face. My expression hardens. Grabbing my phone, I lean into her ear and ask, "Can I kiss you? Just on the cheek and take a picture of it for evidence?"

She immediately flusters, leaning away from me for just a second before an unbreakable look appears in her eyes. "Sure, buddy. Anything to get those parents off your ass."

"Thank you," I whisper earnestly. I plaster a smile on my face and lean forward. A wad of guilt engulfs my heart as my lips approach her face. When I finally kiss her cheek, I nearly hate myself. I rest there for a moment, barely remembering to take the photo. Unconsciously, I snap the image. When I hear the camera click, I jolt away from her, feeling uneasy. The pounding in my heart subsides, and I slow my breath. I hadn't noticed it'd quickened. The things I do for the boys that steal my attention. However, Connor has barely seen the worst of the punishment that comes from being mine.

For some it's more dire.

Marco is most likely out of jail by now. I don't know the exact sentence length for a minor possessing LSD, but I blame myself partly. I brought him into my life — brought my parent's religious bullshit to him while knowing what they were like. He swore he was holding the LSD for a friend — and he *was*, but a court isn't going to believe the Hispanic minor over the rich white adults — my parents — who swore he was offering it to me.

I no longer have contact with Marco; Mom and Dad made sure of that. I don't want to either, because the sharks could strike again. I could never risk dragging another man I care about into that. And I hope I haven't already dragged Connor. But the doll complicates him — complicates everything. How was I meant to keep from catching feelings during each testing session?

Nia's hand slowly comes up to her face, touching the spot I kissed like it's an open wound before giving me a calm look. I feel her hand touch my shoulder. "It's gonna be okay. I'm sorry you gotta deal with those freaky parents."

I revel in the affection for a moment, letting my guard down for the first time today. "Yeah, thanks for letting me do this. And if you ever need a favor, you know where to find me."

After a few more 'thank-you's, I stare at my evidence. We look like a happy couple. I cringe at the sight of me kissing *Nia*, but it's over now. And maybe when my parents see this, I can hopefully have Connor back. I take a breath of fresh air, lifting my head toward the cafeteria's entrance to scan the random flow of students moving in and out. I leave my eyes there for a moment until my stomach drops to the *fucking floor*.

Connor.

Connor Jones standing right fucking there. He stares at me with furrowed eyebrows and a deep frown. A mix of ache and disdain spills out of his face.

No. No, Connor it's not what it looks like.

I promise it's not.

Please believe me, Connor.

I try to speak, but I can't. I jump to my feet, take a deep breath, and prepare to run toward him.

Finally, my vocal cords decide to work. "Connor!" Thankfully, only a few people's heads turn, so I manage to ignore my embarrassment. But public image is an afterthought right now. Nia looks wildly confused, but I'm already twenty feet away from her. I desperately scan the room for him, soon forgetting about her entirely.

But he's gone.

I sprint outside the cafeteria and into the hall, mesmerizingly blank walls passing me on both sides. I feel a sensory overload come with my panic, brought about by the sound of my squeaky shoes, the repetitive scenes in front of me, and my physical exertion. I try not to lose focus, calling his name one last time. "Connor!" My breath quickens, and I stop in my tracks as panic short-circuits my athletic ability.

Slowly, my self-awareness begins to bleed into my forehead again. If I'm caught speaking to him, that'd compromise the plan completely. Mom sent out students to watch me like a hawk. No matter how horror movie-ish it sounds to have a bunch of kids watching my every move, it's my reality. It could be anyone — even my friends. My parents paid them to do this, and money is more tempting than friendship. It could sway an angel.

Besides, what good would talking to him do? What if he doesn't listen to me or believe me? What will I even *say*? Finding time to figure out a proper game plan is vital.

I turn my head, guiltily hoping to catch a glimpse of his pretty face looking back at me from across the hall. But of course, he's gone.

I trudge back to lunch.

CONNOR

I shoot upward in bed and squint at the vast, warm sunlight peeking through my blinds.

After brushing my teeth for two whole minutes, I hop downstairs and wrap my arms around Mum from behind for a tight hug.

"Goodness, Connor!" She pauses, turning around. "You seem…much happier than you've been. Gonna take the day off school again?" Mum asks, obviously hoping I won't.

I shake my head 'no' vigorously before splashing lukewarm water into my glass. "That's 'cause I am much happier. I'm not skipping a second day." I roll my shoulders before sitting down. "I am much happier. Realized my worth, is all." I stare down at my phone charging beside me, and a familiar stress clenches in my stomach. Five missed calls from Fritz.

I skipped school yesterday. I'll admit, I was a little shaken after seeing Quinton the previous day, but I've learned in these last 24 hours that he's inconsequential. And I'm better than that. I'll get the doll from him today, and we never have to speak again. Fritz can be my new doll-testing partner, I guess.

I skip to my car, gleefully pressing play on my 'Happy Playlist'. Through the car ride, I suppress any Quinton-related stress, and I arrive at school with a smile on my face. I'm ready. I'm okay.

Lunchtime is when my stress begins to grow, so I quickly distract myself with my friends. Criss-cross applesauce on the second floor rooftop, I laugh — harder than I have in a few days — at one of Fritz's stupid jokes. As I give a quick apology for not answering my calls, I notice how much I missed him. In response, Fritz steals my goggles off my face with a quick snatch, mightily amused.

I giggle hysterically as I blindly reach for my goggles. "Fritz! What is wrong with you?" When I finally retrieve them, I launch for Fritz's white headband as Bennet tries to separate us.

Fritz dodges and throws his hands up in surrender. "Bennet, fuck off, this isn't your fight. Connor, you win anyways."

I holler in victory, grabbing my turkey sandwich for a bite.

Fritz smiles. "I'm glad you're talking to me again." He takes a generous bite out of his pizza slice. "You have no idea how much I'm trying to not find Quinton and beat the shit out of him right now."

I chuckle and punch his arm, ignoring how much I didn't want Quinton's name to be brought up. "I'm glad too." I swallow the raging moths in my stomach as my class period with Quinton inches closer.

While I stare at the clock like a predator does to prey, Fritz rests his hand on my knee. "Look, don't think about that right now. Besides, I'm in that class, dumbass. I'll protect you if you need it."

Leave it to Fritz to read my mind. Even though I don't credit him enough for it, and tease him relentlessly, he's truly the best-best-friend. "Thank you, Fritz, seriously. As much as I never tell you, you're an awesome friend."

Fritz leans back in his bench table seat, crossing his legs. "Yeah, I know. It's only since you helped me with my boy problems so much last year. Does this mean you'll stop killing me on the SMP?" He smile-yawns through his words, flicking my cheek.

I flinch, hitting him back and rubbing my cheek. "Psh, no way, idiot." I grin at him until a loud beep signaling it's time for class startles all five of us. Fritz reaches his hand out and pulls me out of my seat. He takes my arm, and we walk to our next class in silence. Our next class with Quinton.

Once we push through the front door, I face the front of my class, smoothing down my sweatshirt. I see Quinton's hand out of the corner of my eye. I feel light as air while Fritz tugs me to a double-seated table. Momentarily, I witness the sharp stab of Quinton's eyes piercing mine.

Eye contact.

He averts his gaze and pretends he didn't notice it happened.

Noticing how on edge I am, I calm myself down.

Okay, fine.

Maybe I'm not as okay as I thought. Or happy. Or entirely immune to being sad over this. In my defense, he's very attractive, and again, I basically just discovered magic is real. So.

I tap my pencil on my desk. The longer we remain in the same room, the more my bones turn to jelly. *Just get the doll back.*

I can feel Quinton's stare bore into my back, and I grow annoyed. Make up your mind, do you want my attention or do you want to ghost me for two days?

The blood pumping through my veins speeds up when he stands and moves one desk closer to Fritz and me.

He's a sadist.

He gives me inklings of his voice by yawning, stretching, sniffling, just being himself. If these are tactics for my attention, it's working a little too well.

I can't focus for the life of me. Even though he kissed Nia, my heart swells when he looks in my direction.

Fuck this. I swallow every time he does, yawn every time he does, unintentionally mirroring his actions just to be closer to him.

I hate him for not coming after me in the bathroom. But I like him so, so much for every other moment we shared. It was only a little bad that came with so much good.

Fritz notices my discomfort but can't console me without getting in trouble, so he sends me empathetic eyes instead.

I bury my face in my arms, easily keeping awake with Quinton a few feet away. How does he have this much power over me?

I hate it.

I hate this.

I bite my lip, continually locking eyes on the clock. I could grab the doll and ignore Quinton, forever, for the rest of high school. I could forget about him and never be blessed, or cursed, with an explanation.

But I *need* an explanation.

Letting out a slow breath, I decide I'm too nervous to simply strut up to him and demand the doll. Especially with students surrounding us. So I settle for ripping out a piece of paper from my journal to write a non-threatening, threatening note.

"ill give you two sentences. TWO SENTENCES to explain what happened. After class. Return the doll to me. I will literally drive to your house and take it if you refuse."

I let out a slow breath, fold the paper, and turn to face Quinton. He perks up immediately like a puppy offered treats. His questioning eyes flick down to the note and then back up to me.

I respond by launching the paper directly at him, smiling when he flinches in pain. I've been wanting to hurl an object at his marvelous face for a while now. The satisfaction comes from Quinton's reaction to the note. His hope, his fear, his need to know what's written as he unfolds the page and inhales a choppy breath — it's priceless.

Until class ends, I quietly sit and eagerly wait.

The bell rings. I rise out of my seat steadily, turning to see Quinton all prepared with his backpack hanging over his shoulders, and my note in hand. He looks at every corner of the room before reaching for my hand.

The air seems to freeze.

I outstretch my arm.

He pulls me along, not speaking a single word until we're safely rushed into the boys' bathroom.

Again, his eyes wander around the room — I only allowed him two sentences. Huffing, he finally speaks. "I — Connor, hey, I know you're mad which is completely understandable, but it involved my homophobic parents and I can't explain it all yet, but I'll give you the doll tomorrow when I have it." He pauses to take a breath and hold an index finger in my face. "Give me a chance and meet me outside of school tomorrow and, please Connor, please trust me." He finishes by holding up a second finger, and then drops them both after an awkward moment.

I bring my hand to my chin, ridding myself of any impulsive response I wanted to spit. I blink hard, processing a nasty mix of shock, relief, and pity. I take a breath to respond, but realize he has left the room. *What?*

The hole in my chest expands.

And then the guilt arrives.

I've internally accused him of things that may have been far out of his control. Staring at the floor, I shuffle around in my jacket pocket and uncover my phone. With a few shaky taps, open my tacky calendar app to meet up with Quinton a few days from today. Hours later when school is over, I stare out of the bus window, and I don't bother to text Fritz about what happened.

I slam my keys into my front door, grateful the bus decided to shortcut today. By the time I get the door open, I toss myself into Mum's arms and inhale her familiar honey scent. Boy, is she about to get the longest TLDR about my current life.

QUINTON

If there is one word that least describes me, it'd be religious. But little me would have strongly disagreed with that statement. Despite religion being the reason for my overspilled tears, I've prayed in a Christian manner, whether it be to the stars, Jesus, God, the Bible. I've yet to receive my cosmic transmission of the promised hope, understanding, and love I supposedly earned the day I was born into this "quintessential holy family." It's tough being left on read by *God*. Now that I'm older and know I'm bisexual, I no longer expect anything from Him. I've heard the terminology for what's happened to me — "religious trauma," "abuse," or any other similar words. But the word "traumatic" feels all too small and short to render my childhood.

My parents tried to abuse love out of me. Their methods were physical, verbal, or manipulative. They'd go to any length to make me stop liking men, and when they realized that was impossible, the next step was making me hate how love felt. Hate the idea of love in the first place. I believe it had the opposite effect. Clinging to the idea of love during any of their homemade conversion therapy sessions was one of the *only* reasons I didn't just off myself at the time. Love was a lifeline that gave me the will to live. And hell, I wasn't even experiencing it yet.

One of their tactics to get me to hate the gay-love-lifestyle, was forcing me to watch gay couples fight, but more specifically, watch gay men abuse their husbands or boyfriends. Those videos made me cry more than the hitting did.

The abuse subsided the older — and the bigger — I got. Since I can fight back now, my parents use their voices more than their palms to persuade me to be strictly heterosexual. But despite them being the love-hating monsters they are, I still love them. So, hey, I guess they failed so much, they couldn't even stop me from loving *them*.

Shifting to my right, I tighten my grip on Connor, or at least what I have left of him.

The doll.

The moonlight sliding through my curtains barely helps, but I can slightly make out the doll's blue shirt and purple pants. It's colder and much, much smaller than him, but knowing that he can feel the warmth of me around him is enough to settle me down. Good night, Connor. And good night, cosmos.

CHAPTER 6

CONNOR

I hop out of my car, staring at the school I've known for years. God, I can't wait to get out of here. My body screams for the school day to never begin. On top of worrying about medical internships, I have Quinton to stress over too. But I can't help but miss him. My mind calls out for him at the slightest reminder that he's real. It calls out for his ability to distract me from my living conditions, his reassurance that my mother is lucky to be blessed with me, how funny he is, not his 'emerald-green eyes and bright smile,' but his comfort around me. Although, the charming smile and looming height are a plus.

My legs carry me through the school day in a breeze, but every other part of me stays locked on the thought of that boy.

Quinton.

The bell ending our last period rings, yet I stay sitting in my seat. An entire minute passes, and I can't stand. My teacher eyes me from across the room.

"Mr. Jones? Can I help you?"

I stay radio silent, wanting to talk, but worried about what might come out.

Mr. Mendrick sighs and returns back to his paper. "Leave before 5, I'm going then as well."

I nod, not giving any verbal response, and thankful he didn't require one. The clock ticks once more, and sweat forms on the back of my neck. It's time to meet up with Quinton.

Taking huge breaths, I get over myself and bolt to my locker. After collecting my shit, I hurry to the entrance of the school.

Readjusting my glasses, I scan the room for Quinton. After an unsuccessful sweep, I lazily jog forward to get a better view of my surroundings. Dread pokes my heart. Did he stand me up?

"Connor!"

My head flies up to see Quinton a few feet in front of me. I study his angular features, my mouth slightly open. I missed staring at him. His wide eyes and red face are a fair indication he's been searching for me as well.

I feel almost as though the world has dropped under my feet. Damnit, Quinton. *Damnit, Connor.*

The second thing I notice is he's dressed in a tuxedo? A full-blown tux, head to toe, radiating wealth. I scold myself for feeding on the pretentious smell of money.

"Quinton," I whisper, unmoving. He begins walking toward me and I step back in reflex. Once he reaches where I'm standing, he stares me down and slides his hand upward to cup my face. I feel my cheeks turning red as I lean into his palm. He sweeps my hair away from my eyes and opens his mouth.

"Come with me."

I am hesitant to take his hand and follow him. I still haven't gotten an explanation, but in that marvelous tux, it's hard to say no.

He drags me along and we enter his unnecessarily long, slim car. After a moment, I realize we've both entered the back seat. I give him a questioning look, but he raises a hand in dismissal. After no more than a few quick seconds, the car begins to move? Ah. He hired a driver.

Quinton makes no attempt to spark conversation, only casting a few sly grins my way and eyeballing me the entire car ride. He only scoots closer to me and takes my hand. I warm up to the atmosphere — this is far from the worst thing I'd imagined he had planned. He simply continues to smile, withholding an explanation still like the annoying tease he is.

The movement of the car eventually slows, causing me to perk up. I turn to look out the window and immediately, my jaw drops. "Quinton. What is this?" We pull up to a huge…mansion! With my head sticking out of the car, I catch sight of cypress trees lining the perimeter of the property. I have to laugh. "Quinton?!" I turn to him, demanding answers. *This* is not where he gets his beauty sleep every night — I've been to his house.

He chuckles, signaling the driver to stop the car with a quick wave. He pushes his door open and mine as well, still refusing to speak. He takes my hand and wraps our fingers together as we walk across the driveway. I look up at him and find a nervous look in his eyes, belying his confidence from a few moments ago.

Once he's stepped inside his mansion, Quinton gestures for me to follow. I walk into a wide, plain room with two sets of stairs running up and meeting each other in the middle. I scoff; if someone has *two* staircases in their entrance hallway, they've got too much money for their own good.

Quinton's face is, yet again, amused. He holds up a finger and just leaves me in the room, dangling clarification above my nose like it's a dog treat. "Wh — Quinton?" I call out to him but remain still. I shrug to myself, continuing to marvel at the shameless luxury. Does he own two expensive houses or some shit?

Quinton returns with a black tux, smaller than his own, and cups my hand over its hanger. "Go change." He nods in the direction of a door on the right. I comply, quietly celebrating that he finally spoke words. His voice tastes like nectar to my bee brain.

I gently close the door behind me and slip off my shoes, finding a mirror and a bench in a small four-by-four room. I barely know what's going on and frankly, I don't care. Sure, I've thought and said *things* about Quinton lately, but I was unfair. I amounted our time spent together to nothing, and I forgot how vulnerable I let myself be around him when we experimented with the doll. If anything, I've given him all the opportunity to harm me, or worse, and he never has. Except now, yes, but from the tux to the limousine, whatever his excuse is for ghosting me must be good. Or, at the very least, forgivable. Despite my attitude, I wasn't raised a complete pessimist, and if that results in more and more heartbreak for me, so be it.

I focus on the new outfit from Quinton. Putting it on is tedious, but I begin to admire the feel of post-dry-cleaned fabric hugging my skin. I feel around in the black pockets and pose in the mirror until a slip of paper in the right pocket catches my finger. I pull it out for further inspection.

It's a little envelope. It wraps a letter — I assume — neatly; it even has a golden rose emblem closing it, and the envelope's white is nearly blinding. I tear along the edges and grab the note inside.

It's written in literal fountain pen ink.

Unfolding it completely, I read.

Dear Connor,

I'm so sorry. I know I ignored you right after…<u>that</u> for three days and kissed someone else in that time period. I'm so, so sorry. I promise, I'm not unstable or anything, hear me out. Basically, my parents found out what we did. They swore they'd do, I don't know, something to you if I even thought about speaking to you. They can track my location, texts, entire phone screen, and they've asked other thick headed parents to ask their homophobic kids to keep an eye out for our interactions. I couldn't text you or risk being seen because of whatever they'd do to you. Extort your mother, actually physically harm you, sue your mother, get you in jail, anything. They're rich, they can get away with that, they've done it before. The girl I kissed, Nia, was nothing more than proof. I asked her to be my fake girlfriend so my parents would trust I liked girls, which I do, but I also like guys. I like you so much. I wanted a picture of her and me kissing so I could post it and my parents could see it and trust me again. It was to get privileges to talk to you back and I am so, so sorry I didn't try harder to speak to you. I'm sure I could've arranged something like this sooner, so I'm sorry, I was worried about the risk it would put you in more than anything. I'm meeting you at my second house because there are fewer security cameras for me to hack around here.

Anyway, you make me so happy, I genuinely think you're the best thing to ever happen to me. I still think of the night when we fell asleep on the rooftop, watching the sunset and karaokeing, with no speakers, all while getting fucked on candy & red bull. Messing with the doll, trying to solve that mystery…Sure, pretty horrifying, but it was still time spent with you. Lots and lots of time. 6 weeks has felt like 6 years and I want to get to know you so much better. I want to know everything about you because I've only met a small part of you and I'm already obsessed. So, with that said, leave the room and walk forward for a bit, you'll find the back door to a garden. Go there.

Love, Quinton :)

QUINTON

It takes everything in my power to slow down my breathing. *What is taking him so long?* The six p.m. sun's beauty is hard to appreciate while waiting for a gorgeous man that takes hours to change.

The simple pop of my backyard door opening and closing tears my attention from the sky. Immediately, I lower my head to meet eyes with Connor. The brown of his eyes is accentuated in the golden hour, and I quickly take back what I thought about the sun's beauty. The tuxedo hugs his body, allowing for a sleek, black fit. His hair, messy after a day of school, gently obeys the breeze. My heart flutters.

He's breathtaking.

But there's a troubled look in his sparkling eyes. His lean hand is clutching the letter, his cheeks are red, and there are tears in his eyes? He runs down the porch steps, trips, and manages to stumble toward me for an embrace.

"I'm sorry, Connor."

Connor breaks our hug and narrows his eyes in exasperation. "Do not be sorry. I can't believe you're apologizing. I'm sorry for not trusting you." Connor sniffs, blinking and finally looking around at something that isn't my face. "Wait, holy shit." His eyes dart all over the place, processing every perfect grass blade, every flower, and every decoration I've set up. His eyes land on the vintage jambox, quietly playing 'Careless Whisper' by George Michael. "Quinton, this is amazing. You didn't have to do this." And there it is. The breathless, captured voice I've been longing to hear since I first took him down to the school's garden.

"I know, but I wanted to make this unfortunate situation sweet. By the way, yes we do have security cameras — but don't worry! I dabble in CCTV and kinda found my way around un-suspiciously rerouting them. I've actually been coding HTML websites since, like, age twelve. My parents think it's a stupid hobby but *clearly*, it's served me well, so. Seriously, they talk all about how it's distracting me from my financing future — but I could seriously make a living without their cushioning." I look at Connor mid-rant.

He's smiling ear to ear. It's radiant. *Healing.*

"What? Why are you looking at me like that," I ask.

"You're just so beautiful, Quinton."

My brain goes numb. In a slow motion, I tug his face so it's resting right in front of mine. And I fucking finally kiss him. His lips are addictively soft, obnoxiously calm. I typically wouldn't pull back, and God knows I don't want to. But I'm a man of romance — and this scene could use different music. I step away from him, sliding an old disc into the radio player. It has a slow, rhythmic melody that sounds like moonlight and royalty.

I push my hair back and reach my other arm out to Connor. A plea to let me dance with the striking man.

Connor takes my arm and, apparently growing tired of the silence, says, "So why do your parents own two mansions in the same town? Seems a little excessive."

I chuckle and sway us side to side. "It's my grandparents' old house. They moved and offered it to my parents in exchange for some family business thing."

Connor's eyebrows knit. "A little transactional."

"Yep."

He grows quiet for a moment, then tilts his head down and smiles. "You know, it's always been on my bucket list to dance with a mysterious, rich hottie in a tux in the middle of a meadow to some ominous serial-killer-sounding song."

I snort, sweeping him around the field and straight back into my arms. "The song is 'Mellohi' by C418, dumbass. Know your shit."

Connor scoffs and swings me behind himself, keeping our hands locked. "I do know my shit, Mr. I Don't Know What SpongeBob, *SpongeBob* is. Until I told you at that gas station."

I spin Connor away from me and yank him back in so I'm towering over him. "Well, *mister*. I'm sorry I didn't stuff my brain with junk like SpongeBob when I was younger. Did you know that show has studies proving it can kill off your brain cells? Yeah I bet you didn — "

Connor interrupts by clamping his hand over my mouth. Swaying out and underneath my grip, he takes my hand and puts it on his waist. "For someone who parties every weekend, you can be a real nerd. Just shut up."

"Did you just tell me to shut up?" I whisper, stretching to my full height in order to curve over him again. I feel his grip on me weaken, just by gently moving him. Swiping a thumb along his jaw, I tilt his head until our foreheads touch. His brown eyes bloom and his breath quickens. But I never let our lips touch. I pull away, booping his nose for good measure.

His head falls onto my chest, and he presses deeper into me. "You're so annoying…."

I chuckle and continue to sway with him, enjoying the occasional tickle of grass on my ankle.

I've taken you and found myself.

"You love it. And you're way more annoying!" The rest of the world begins to fall away — I find it impossible not to stare at him.

Connor opens his mouth like he's about to disagree, but then nods. "I do love it. I love it a lot, I guess." He pauses. "And I'm *not* more annoying! Oh, 'hi I'm Quinton, today we're speed-running a hit and run — '"

" — Do you love it enough to be my boyfriend?" The proposal is cut, quick, honest. And Connor's face is worth millions. There's a chance we'll split as soon as college comes around, but I'd rather suffer the pain of losing Connor than never give myself the chance to experience him. Maybe even in some months' time, we'll be in love. I'll be in love. My heartbeat quickens at the thought.

Connor blinks. He seems to ponder — scaring me, almost. We did become friends just a month ago. Sure, we'd met back in freshman year, but what if it's too soon? Connor's medical pursuits don't mix well with my college ones, unless he would plan to move to Texas with me when my gap year is up.

But then he smiles. "Of course, idiot."

CONNOR

Sloppy and wanting, Quinton and I have trouble walking back inside the house without breaking our kiss.

"Connor." He breathes out my name with that deep, boyish voice, setting my heart on fire.

I pull my head away from him and challenge his cloudy gaze. "Yeah?"

He leans back, staring at me as though I'm the pot of gold at the end of the rainbow. "Nothing. I'm just so happy you're mine, doll." He chuckles and places one last kiss on my forehead. "Let's go get something to eat, I'm starving."

Though I'd love to kiss him more — just a few hundred times more — I nod and simply gaze at him as we walk to his car. *When and how did I get so lucky?* Eventually, I find myself too flustered to look at him. Quinton seems to notice how red my face is. He smiles, but continues walking.

He leads me through the door and locks it behind him in a quick motion, huffing softly afterward. God, his agility and effortless movements drive me crazy.

Once we're outside, I squint and look upward. The moon's all-too-soon invasion of the sky is disappointing. I send one last prayer Mum won't want me home for dinner tonight and hop into Quinton's car. My worries are shoved to the back of my mind once I've stepped fully inside. "God, your car is amazing," I mumble. "Didn't get to tell you earlier today 'cause I was pissed, though."

Quinton chuckles, his face round with endearment as he turns the key and revs the car's engine. "Thank you."

"Can we please go downtown? I'd *love* to see the city lights and stick my head out. I need fresh air after being next to your stinky body all day."

Quinton lets out a string of appalled sounds. "*My* stinky body? At least I don't wear pounds of cologne daily — "

"I don't wear cologne, you nimrod — "

He holds up a silencing finger. " — and of course we can go downtown. I'll take you wherever you'd like as long as we get home before — " he pauses and glances at the time in the car. Quarter to seven. "…before two a.m."

Two a.m.? "And your 'helicopter parents' wouldn't veto this decision?" I turn my head to look at him.

Quinton shrugs. "I'll tell them I was partying." He shoots me a *let me explain* look. "They were teenagers too — they know senior parties have a *plethora* of horny heterosexuals and encourage me to seize the opportunity. They want me to have sex with women at any cost. It's actually really gross, but may as well take advantage, right?"

"But lust is like a sin too, right?"

"They know. But it's sort of like, 'get him to be straight and *then* fix the sex part'. Their logic is never really clear."

"Oh." I scrunch my nose. "What weirdos. Well, thanks for the ride."

"My pleasure."

How long are we going to be out and about? My blood flows faster and faster, and I am less and less able to hide my smile. Quinton — *the* Quinton, and *my new boyfriend* — reaches a hand from the steering wheel to ruffle my hair as a way of saying 'you're welcome.'

Today has been too amazing.

Things are going too well.

I hum along to some Weeknd song until the city inches into view. The fluorescent lighting doesn't wait to slam itself into us, firing my dopamine in all different directions. No views excite me more than city lights. I spin away from Quinton and toward downtown Orlando as if to say, 'You see that shit?'

"Oh, my God, whoa!" I'd seen the city at night before — but never like this. Never marveled at such a view with someone like Quinton right next to me. I'd taken my one or two past boyfriends to downtown Orlando, and gone hundreds of times with Fritz and others.

But Quinton? He's special. I know these qualities shouldn't be my priorities in dating, but he *is* popular…and he's rich, and he is beautiful. And I can't help but let those facts excite me more.

"You act as though you've never seen the city before," Quinton comments, his tone warm and fond.

No, I'm acting as if I've never seen you before because you are one of the most gorgeous specimens I have ever met, and Lord knows I'm lucky that of all the people who could've had a doll of me in their closet it was this fine piece of —

"Here." Quinton reaches a red light and fiddles with a button to activate the sunroof. It slides open, and I get a bright idea. Unbuckling, I stand and start to poke my head out. It's definitely not the most dangerous thing I've ever done, but it's enough to cure my current desire for spontaneity.

"*Connor.* Be careful, come back down." I feel Quinton blindly reaching for my clothes to pull me back down.

But once my entire head is outside, his voice is nothing more than static to my ears. I take a breath, wishing I could taste what I was viewing. I turn from the windy side, cough twice, and turn right back around, leaning further out. Exposed and pumped with adrenaline, I watch the buildings fly past us. My eyes trace each separate skyscraper until my vision begins to strain. Once the wind is unbearable, I gently close my eyelids. And I let the moment burn in my memory.

The car stops, and my eyes reopen at another red light and the feeling of Quinton's hand sliding into mine. I smile and close my eyes once again. And God, as much as I never want this to end, my hair needs to look presentable for tonight. When I sit back down, this time in the back seat, the feeling of hunger returns to me.

Quinton twists back, mouth opened to speak, but he immediately gapes at the sight of my face. He swiftly turns back to face the road and explodes in laughter. "Connor, you're — you look ridiculous!" He's in hysterics for a second longer before sighing.

We hit another red light and I crawl back into shotgun, grumping at his words. "At least I'm not blond, idiot. Back off, I look like a little prince." I rest a hand on my chest, giving him my best, regal smile.

Quinton frowns, pretending to be hurt. "Wh — hey, don't come for me. And you didn't let me finish, I was going to go on about how you still look beautiful."

Damnit. He wins. I turn away from him to adjust my hair and blush. "Oh, shut up. 'I'm Quinton, and I only know how to flirt by lying and being a little shithead!'. But thank you, yes, I do look beautiful."

Quinton chuckles in agreement and glances at his directions. "And we'll be at a restaurant I made reservations for shortly, all right?" He flashes his phone toward my face.

I exhale and cover my face. "Jesus Christ, that's so bright." I rub my eyes, registering his words. "Wait, really? Where'd you make our reservation?"

Quinton cocks his head to the left. "You'll see."

I decide not to push.

When I feel Quinton begin to slow the car, I lift my head and glance out of the window.

Oh, my God. Cloak & Petal.

I've always had a slight resentment of this restaurant. As much as little me wanted to catch a meal here, I couldn't afford it. To set foot in the place, you needed a reservation and there was a *reservation fee*. "Quinton, this is so expensive. We couldn't possibly…."

Quinton pulls the car into a refined parking space for his refined, stupid car. "We could possibly. And you're gonna love the food here, sweetheart." He swings my door open and locks the car once I'm out. "But I can find somewhere else?"

I sigh with a smile. "No. This is good, thank you."

Kissing my hand, he leads me inside. The moment we step in, I'm hit with a cloud of blood-money cologne. The AC couldn't be above freezing — the low temperatures act as a status symbol. But I'd be a liar to say I dislike it completely.

A tall woman behind a marble stand gives us a quick wave.

Quinton stiffens, giving her nothing more than a curt nod.

His response to her prompts the woman to come closer to us. Wildly confused, I step closer to Quinton.

She props herself right in front of us before speaking. "Hello." Her eyes linger on me for a moment before speaking. "Do you have a reservation?" I bite my tongue, knowing I shouldn't be so nervous.

Quinton clears his throat. "Yes, ma'am. The name we put down was 'Hansley'."

She blinks, and her facial muscles relax. "Okay, great. I'll get someone to find your seats." Her heels click away, echoing on the pristine floor.

"Hello? Earth to Connor?" Quinton waves a hand in my face and slides backward to where I'm standing. He tilts his head to the side. "Are you gonna come?"

I blow out a stream of air and roll my eyes as high as they'll go.

He frowns. "C'mon, Connor." Quinton begins following a young, well-dressed waiter. I glance at the roof. I wonder how much it cost simply to paint it. I continue to space out and stare at Quinton until he speaks again.

"Come get the flower." Quinton chuckles, trailing a blue aster through the air.

I whack his arm. "I'm not some dog, Quinton. I was just distracted."

Our waiter pulls out a chair for each of us, and we kindly nod him goodbye.

Quinton sets his napkin on his lap. "You've been a little spacey all night." His tone lowers as he takes a sip of cold water. "Distracted by my irresistible beauty I presume?"

I snort. "Yeah."

His eyes widen. "Well, unsurprising."

I simply giggle, gesturing to the menu. "Shall we order our food?"

Quinton hums. "We shall."

Mum casts nothing more than a suspicious glance toward the boy hanging half-drunk over my shoulder. I lift my head toward my room and, although she looks conflicted, she nods with a sigh. I often feel guilty in moments like these. It feels like I'm taking advantage of her long work hours, and therefore her inability to question me when there's a boy hanging half-drunk over my shoulder.

However, I won't pass up the chance since it's midnight and Quinton is getting impatient. On the trek to my bed, Quinton finally stops leaning on me, wobbling to stand straight. "Connor, you look so," he hiccups, "cute."

I shush him, but still grin at the poor boozed-up boy. How did the server believe his fake ID?

Patting him on the back, I stroke his hair, whispering sweet nothings.

Quinton lolls his head back, staring up at me with glowing eyes. "What now?" He slurs his words.

I shrug and leave his side to properly remove my jacket. Quinton smiles in a suggestive manner, removing his as well.

I grunt in annoyance, averting my eyes from his sharp gaze. "Quinton, absolutely not, you're drunk. Let's sober you up a little, and then I'll drive you to your second house. You can tell your parents you decided to stay there." I scratch my chin and release a heavy sigh. "Even if they get upset at you for that, it's too risky for me to drop you at your first one. Ubering is suspicious, so."

Quinton continues to stir, completely ignoring my words. "Hey! Let's mess with the doll." My six-foot-three toddler of a boyfriend blindly reaches around in my bag.

"I'm…not sure. Mess with it?" I lower my voice to a small mumble. "The doll is basically me." I open my mouth to say more, but the raw touch of someone gripping my arm causes me to yell instead. Jumping to the side, Quinton crawls toward me, the doll in hand.

"Connor! You good? Oh, my God." He waits for an answer, lazily resting his palm on my forehead as if he's checking for a fever.

I move him off me, nodding. "I'm fine — I just got scared. I'm definitely getting more sensitive to that doll, or some shit." A thick anxiety grows in my throat while my heart rate picks up. That stupid doll. "God, you barely touched it. Am I really that sensitive?"

Quinton moves the doll to the side. "Okay, d'worry about it."

How could I not worry? We've already learned plenty about what this doll is capable of.

Perhaps pain.

Perhaps a sensory overload.

Perhaps worse.

I bite my nail and itch the back of my head furiously. "It's way too late for this." I take the doll from the bedside table and stick it in Quinton's tote bag.

Once the doll is out of sight, Quinton quickly becomes distracted. "Connor, this suit is uncomfortable, but I'm too tired to take it off." He drags his words and messes with the fabric.

I take the bait, groaning and crawling toward him. Better than thinking about the doll. Quinton's cheeks redden, clearly not expecting me to help him out of his button-up.

I position myself in front of him, loosening his tie and throwing it on the floor. Jacketless and tieless, Quinton whines again. "Connor, the shirt too please."

I roll my eyes before bringing my hands to his chest. But just as my fingertips reach the first button, he dips away with a smart grin. "Just kidding, not tonight, Connor." Placing a messy, quick kiss on my lips, he stands fully.

"Are you ready for me to take you home?" I sit up in bed.

Quinton swings his head left and right a little over ten times. "I'm gonna dial the, uh, limo person and have the driver take me home to — " a giggle breaks his next words — "prove my heterosexuality to my parents. Good ni — ght, darling." Quinton threads his long fingers through my hair and places a heavy kiss on my cheek.

I nod. "Goodnight, Quinton."

CHAPTER 7

QUINTON

My parents greet me, particularly my mom, with a grin that's a little too enthusiastic for a typical Tuesday morning. "You may be a little confused, but you know how we mothers at your school talk, and…Quinton, I can't believe you kept this from us. I'm so glad you found that sweet girl, Nia — Nia was it? Yes, Nia, she seems amazing, dear." My mom lifts to her tippy-toes, moving my hair to reveal my tired eyes. "I'm proud of you. We are still very angry about that act you participated in with Connor, but we're open to forgiveness."

I give them a tight grin, nodding in thanks.

After dishonestly hyping up Nia as the best girlfriend ever, I make my exit. The moment I'm inside my room, I slam the door shut. I pull out a notepad and scribble the following: Call Connor, Pick up Tux from the dry cleaner, English paper, Calc homework, Cheerleading prac. Seconds after I finish writing, my phone vibrates.

Connor: *Are we calling or hanging out/testing today?*

Me: *calling, i got lots of stuff to do today :/*

Connor: *Okayy message me when u can call :)*

I swing my seat back toward my desk and catch sight of a pen rolling off. Weirdly, my reflexes fail me, and it hits the ground with a click. "Goddamnit." I bend down and pat the floor, only to grab hold of the doll instead. "Fuck." I retract my hand.

Connor definitely felt that.

Taking a few short breaths, I compose myself. I can't think about doll anxieties while worrying about my parents while stressing about school *while* having a hangover. At least keeping Connor's doll does feel good in a way. The fact he trusted me with it to protect him warms my heart. It's a sick warmth, but I still enjoy it — I want to hold onto it forever.

And as long as Nia and I are "dating" everything will be okay.

CONNOR

"Ugh." I crawl along my bed, mindlessly flicking bits and pieces of food off my sheets. I debate if I should nag Mum on the phone more about my boredom or go out and flop down at my desk.

I move my hand across the stained surface, reaching for my phone. I fumble to unlock it, dial Quinton, and pray he answers. It rings.

And rings.

And rings.

And rings.

Until nothing.

Then a monotone "Your call has been forwarded to an automated voice message please speak your message at the tone."

"Fuck." I hurl my phone onto my sheets, standing and murmuring insults to the automated voice. I head to my closet, needing different air but wanting nothing more than to stay inside. I snatch shorts from the closet floor and throw on a different shirt. Does it go with my bottoms? No, but who cares, I'm so petrified by fear, it takes this much energy to convince myself to *change my clothes.*

All thanks to the doll.

The doll is a nightmare. I'd be pushing my luck to think the doll's connection to me won't result in a serious injury some day or another. Don't get me wrong, I trust Quinton's promise to protect it, but it's an eight-inch doll. No one on this planet has never sat on a doll by accident, stained one with marker or liquid, trapped one under a box. The worst part is, no one could even fathom my emotions because no one is experiencing this. There's no way to properly articulate the distraught feeling that comes with a doll who passes every physical sensation on to you, without sounding like a delusional person.

I kick a stray shoe to the side. My thoughts travel from my head to my voice. "No one could possibly understand. And it's not some day-to-day emo complaint about society or something, literally, no one on planet

Earth has a doll attached to their body that could hurt them at any second in any manner. At least I don't think so. It's hard to tell Quinton too.

He'd never say it to my face, but I know he might be offended. What if he starts thinking I don't trust him or…I mean, I'm afraid of someone sitting on a goddamn doll. I clench my jaw, heat pooling in my throat. "Who fucking cares, anyway?"

A loud beep tunes. "Voice message sent."

Oh, my God. I run over to my phone, and my eyes hollow.

Powering down my phone, I try to distract myself from steaming hot embarrassment. I drag my hands down my face, and I press on a pimple. The spot flares, burning with sharp pain. I press repeatedly, feeding on the hot jabs. What stops me is the feeling of warm tears I didn't realize were falling. Wiping my face, I continue to stress out.

Mid-cry, I hear the wonderful sound of a car pulling into the driveway. Mum's home. With a small hop, I weave through the hall.

But another face appears in the peephole. Quinton's. He wears a grave and serious expression, worriedly scrunching his eyebrows and his foot impatiently tapping the ground.

"Connor, I know you're in there. Open up, please, I want to help you."

I stand completely still, unsure of what to do. It takes a lot of willpower to see his calming, stunning face and say, "Quinton…I can't, I can't talk right now." I inhale, watching from the small glass peephole as his shoulders slouch. The movement causes me to notice his backpack. His rather *full* backpack. No way he brought the doll. "Quinton!" I swing the door open, spinning him around with full force to see if the doll is in his backpack.

He gasps, not expecting my roughness. But he overpowers me, quickly turning around and resting his hands on my shoulders. All his worry seems to vanish. He smiles, sweeping me into a hug and squeezing my waist. I melt into his arms.

"Connor…."A low, shaky voice manages to come from him. He buries his head deeper into my neck, leaving behind a dampness. Are those tears? I push him off me and look at his eyes. An unmistakable wetness shines there. "The second I heard your voicemail I drove over from cheer. Sorry if this is a little unannounced, and…I'm sorry I couldn't make you feel safe."

Guilt.

So, so much guilt. Here he is, wasting his tears on my fears.

God, I hate feeling like a burden. I tried my best not to complain too much when I was younger because it would make Mum's life harder if she was dealing with a whiny ten-year-old along with work. And I'd do the same for Quinton. For anyone for that matter. It's not a flaw; it's helped shape me as more independent. "Please, don't be sorry. You didn't have to come all this way. It was just a rant to myself — I'm okay now."

Quinton's fingers engulf my cheek as he kisses my forehead. "Don't lie to me about how you're feeling. It's okay and completely rational to be scared. I'm here for you, Connor, don't worry about my insecurity, or whatever, about protecting you. Your feelings are way more important." Retracting his hands from my torso, he slips his bag off his shoulder, casually revealing the doll.

Quinton never expressed a normal amount of freak-out over the doll's existence. I understand that given his homophobic parents, he's used to situations that call for quickly accepting strange circumstances. However, I still find it bizarre.

Quinton wraps his fingers around mini-me. The sensation is cold — invasive — but I accept it.

Quinton looks up at me through his lashes, head downward. "Through our tests, we've discovered that it responds to pain. We know if you cut it, you bleed. We know over time, you've gotten more sensitive to it." He flicks his eyes to the doll and back at me.

"We *don't* know if it could kill me...and there's no way to test that out," I add.

Quinton winks. "I can think of a way."

I shoot him a glare.

"Too soon?"

I chuckle. "Shut up. We don't know where it came from, or why, or if it's going to like...go away. Fuck. The internet was useless, but we can still have research sessions after school. I feel like we haven't thoroughly explored Reddit yet, and God knows what we can find there."

Quinton nods, still standing outside my house. "Yes, well, I guess we're on our own for this one. Let's agree to not tell our parents. Your mom might freak out that your boyfriend had a doll that looks like you from before we were friends. I wouldn't trust me if it was my kid." Quinton shrugs. "You told Fritz, but let's limit it to that, yeah?"

"Yeah. I already agreed I won't tell. Plus, I don't wanna further complicate Mum's life." I step backward. "Come inside." Sliding our hands together, I lead him through my halls and onto my bed. After releasing a breath held for far too long, I speak. "Let's just rest. I think we've learned the boundaries of the doll's connection to me, which is what I'm mostly worried about."

Quinton exhales through his nostrils. "Yeah, no. That sounds great. Looking forward to waking up next to you in the morning."

I smile. "Me too, weirdo." Pulling bed sheets over the both of us, I lie still. A fragment of peace.

"Thank you."

Quinton is quiet for a moment. "There's nothing to thank me for, Connor."

QUINTON

I rotate my shoulders and listen to the small cracks of my bones. I yawn wide while my eyes adjust to sunlight. Mornings are always fifty-fifty. Sometimes I wake up and Connor is next to me, other times, he isn't. The last time I woke up beside him was a week ago, the day I'd asked him to be my boyfriend, and since then I've been suffering alone in bed, awoken by my alien parents calling me for breakfast every morning.

I love them, I think. But every minute I spend with Connor, I seem to hate my parents more. Hate that they threatened him and his family. Hate the fact they can't see him like I do. Love the fact I'll never let them stop me from seeing him like I do.

I stretch my torso in bed, and my gaze falls to the doll's usual hiding spot below my desk. My eyes scan where it normally lies locked away in its glass case.

Wait.

I shoot up, eyes squinting hard at the empty chest beneath my desk. Anxiety crawls up my spine as I pull the covers off my body. The transparent case inside the chest looks empty, and the doll is nowhere to be seen. I hop out of bed, straining my vision and kicking stray clothes to the side. Heat burns my throat while I stumble toward my desk.

I'm just overreacting.

It's under here somewhere, right?

I search around for a few more minutes, trying not to panic. My dad calls me a second time for breakfast. Taking deep breaths, I wander down the stairs and focus on Connor's smile to distract myself.

My mom is standing by the dining table. "Good morning." As it's been since I was born, her voice is unreadable. Cold. But today, it sends more shivers down my spine than usual. Both of my parents have been sort-of strangers to me since the…incident of Connor and I having sex.

However, just the other day, they said they were beginning to forgive me.

Nia's my girlfriend; why is Mom acting like a robot again?

"Quinton!" Mom calls my name.

I clear my throat and lower my head. "Sorry, sorry, I'm half asleep. I'm very tired today." I coat my words with a small giggle at the end, wanting to avoid as much conflict as possible.

My mom seems satisfied enough with my response.

Dad is a different story. His eyes look me up and down several times. "You seem a bit more than 'tired,' Quinton. Are you okay? You look nervous." He sounds worried, but his malicious facial expression betrays his sympathetic tone.

"Don't question our boy, he just woke up!" Mom is seconds from sitting down, but Dad halts her.

"Honey, can I talk to you about something?" Dad's attempt at whispering is raspy and loud. I shift in my seat, unsure of their game plan. Unsure of what I did or forgot to cover up. Did they realize I've been hacking the tracking app on my phone? Did they find my notes app with future plans completely unaligned with what they have in store? Maybe they know I've been paying Connor one too many visits?

My efforts to eavesdrop are futile, but I can tell the conversation is over when Mom cocks her head and nods.

And then the plausible possibility hits me. What if they found the doll? Fuck. Did I not lock the chest? Who knows what would happen if they had it and recognized it as him? What if they destroyed it? *What if they hurt Connor?*

What if I just killed Connor with my irresponsibility. I feel nauseous, unable to look at my food. A sheet of sweat lays on my forehead, thoroughly polluting me with stress and heat.

"Quinton." Mom finally speaks.

And I know that tone. *Fuck*, I know that tone. With an unsteady breath, I lift my chin.

All my fears are proven correct. Connor's doll. Hanging by a thread — literally — in my mom's hands. Fuck.

No. No, no, no, no. "Mom, it's not what it looks like." Please.

Her calm outer shell cracks, revealing an uglier inside. "Not what it looks like?" She chuckles without a hint of humor. "Quinton. Why in the Lord's mighty name do you have a doll that looks exactly like that damned boy we told you to stay away from?" Her words increase in both volume and disappointment with every word.

I open and close my mouth, staring at the doll now squeezed in her hand. We'd bought it together *years* ago. She must've completely forgotten about it. If I remind her that we bought it together, she'd think I was lying, or go berserk at the fact it looks like Connor. Maybe she'd think it was a bad omen sent to lure me to him and destroy it.

So, I choose a safer option. Lying. "M-mom, please, please. It was a joke, he gave it to me as a joke." I hold my breath before adding, "I swear to God." She has no idea the power that scrap of fabric holds.

There's a second of silence. And Mom's face *shatters*.

Every bit of her skin turns to glass shards, bright and bloody. And she knows — I just broke a promise to *God.*

"You — " She lets out a laugh. " — you just lied. On a swear to the Lord." Her expression doesn't hold a lick of kindness.

My father clenches his fists, his upper lip twitching with disgust. Both of their faces radiate disdain, shame, and worst of all, they look destructive — like they want to break something. What better object to take your anger out on than the inanimate doll identical to your son's alleged reason for damnation.

My father finally contributes to the conversation. "What happened to our perfect son." He doesn't ask it as a question, he simply states it as a fact; his perfect son is gone. My father sounds sad, almost, like he's mourning a loss. How sick can you be to grieve the living?

I bring a hand to my temple, exhausted and scared by what they might do. My priority is calming them down before they get Connor injured. And judging by how hard my mom is squeezing the doll, I need to move fast. I shudder. "You guys aren't listening to me. I'm telling you it's not romantic or anything more than friendship." A sickness in my stomach begs me to not lie. Lying to them normally results in ugly outcomes, and it looks like even my body knows that.

My mom doesn't buy a word of it. "Oh, Quinton, we just — we don't believe you. We want to believe you, but cannot! When was the last time you told the truth?"

My ears barely function correctly. It becomes harder and harder to register a word she's saying as her grip tightens on the fragile object which is, unbeknownst to her, connected to Connor's body. *How long 'till she squeezes the last bit of life out of him?*

Fuck, I forgot to reply. I open my mouth to speak but Mom lifts a finger to silence me.

"Shut up. I do not want to hear whatever bullshit lie you just came up with in that secular mind of yours. We have been trying to save you from your temptations. We *moved* here from East Florida to get you away from your first little 'boy love,' which cost us money! This is how you repay us?" She inhales deeply, lowering her voice. "Why don't you get it, dear? We are trying to save you." She sounds hopeful for a moment, but my silence dissolves any last bit of her faith in me. "But you do not want to be saved." My mom's voice is grave, pitiful even. "You have chosen hell. We messed up in parenting you. We will discuss your consequences later."

Ouch.

I do my best to regain control of my breathing, uneven air falling in and out of my mouth. I swing my head toward my dad, who stares me down like I'm a rat that's been residing within their walls.

"Okay," I mumble.

Her eyes narrow into small slits, managing to soundlessly degrade me. "You are not my son." And with that, she turns to leave and sets the doll on the table.

Relief.

Relief blooms in my mind. I chase after the delicious feeling, so overwhelmed in relief, I audibly sigh.

My mom stops in her tracks and twists her neck toward the doll she left peacefully sitting. She connects the dots as to why I sighed with such pleasure and cracks a long frown. "This fucking boy."

There's no sound as she barrels toward the doll. But the thump of the doll slamming into the wall at full force is a louder noise than any other I have heard.

And black. My world loops into complete darkness as the kitchen crumbles away around me. Fear rips through me until I can no longer see my surroundings. I, in technical terms, faint. Mom yells something along the lines of 'call 911' before my body goes slack.

CONNOR

Earlier That Morning

A warm sigh leaves my lips. Quinton and I had an ice cream date yesterday. Cliché, but that in fact enhanced its fun. My mind remains on Quinton, as it usually does, while I find my way to the dining table. But I'm met with an urgent expression on Mum's face. "Morning, Mum?" I half-grin, slightly unsettled by the atmosphere.

She smiles and points at the chair. My chest tingles at her complete silence. Shit, did I fail my calc test?

"Connor, what's up with you lately?"

I blink, not expecting the question. I grow soft at her genuine and worried face, but I remember my promise to Quinton: don't tell another soul about the doll.

She reaches over, her skin rough as unweathered rock from constant hands-on labor. Her fingers gently brush mine, but soon fall on the table. "I can tell when you're stressed, but you normally get over it quickly — and it's been, what, two weeks since you've had this…sad vibe on you. Are you okay, sweetie? Are things with Quinton not going well? You can tell me anything."

I weigh different responses, shy of her questions. Half-truths are an okay option. Bluffing would normally be a good route, but Mum can easily force anything out of me. I settle for the safe excuse. "Mum, I'm fine. I've just been stressed about my, um, medical stuff." I sniff, knowing full well I finished my online self-taught medical course last week. "Thanks for your concern, but I'm an adult. You don't have to worry about me, promise." I stand up to leave, wanting out of the room.

But as most mothers do, she knows when I'm lying. "Connor, come on, sit down. I know you're an adult, but you're still young. I've been living with you for eighteen years — I can tell when something's up."

Despite what she says, I lower my head and begin to walk away. "Seriously, it's okay!" I can't turn to face her, she'd see the red that pollutes my cheeks every time I lie. Having such an obvious tell is never handy in these situations.

I walk off, managing to ignore her murmurs for me to come back until she slams her hand on the table. "Connor!"

I halt, but don't turn around.

"Come here, this is serious. You rarely ever lie to me." Her voice is stern.

Fuck.

I deserve a last place medal for my lying ability. I tense my shoulder muscles, but stay where I am as an odd amount of frustration piles in me. Sure, I'm lying, but I'm allowed to have secrets. I don't have to tell her my whole life story every single day. I am eighteen-years-old with my own life and interests. "Mum, I know you're concerned, but it's not my obligation to tell you everything. You raised me right. Trust I'm not doing anything stupid or risky."

Mum slowly shakes her head. "Connor, I know that, but I'm still your mother. I'm still in charge as long as you're under my roof. And, I can help you with whatever's going on, love."

My lip twitches. I try to avoid getting irrationally frustrated at Mum's innocent concerns. What could she possibly do to help anyway? Kill the doll? That'd kill me. Lock it away in a password protected glass case with air holes? We did just that, and I still don't feel exactly safe. I can't add more to her plate anyway.

God, normally I'm a fan of adrenaline and spontaneity, but this doll is killing that appetite.

With a tremor in my voice, I reply. "I said no."

Her voice is dry. Firm. "I said yes."

"I don't *care*." I spin back around, finally letting her get a good look at my face.

My mum can read a face like a book. She takes in the tears in my eyes and the red on my cheeks. However, rather than backing down like she typically does at the sight of me crying, she stands up even taller, and her gaze hardens. "What happened to you? Was I seriously so absent from your life and childhood working my ass off — so you could *live* — that I couldn't monitor your emotions well enough? Why can't I, as your mother, know what's wrong?"

I blink, taken aback at the conversation's sudden change of tone. "Mum…calm down. You're blowing things way out of proportion. My recent, um, sadness, or whatever, is a one-time thing. I get you're not always that present, but it's fine. It's made me stronger, and you try your hardest." I pause, noticing her dissatisfied face. What does she want me to say?

My voice raises with my annoyance. "But that has nothing to do with this conversation. I'll tell you what's up with me later. Relax, I just have no interest in speaking about my emotions right now. It's not personal."

She takes a step forward, scoffing. "I am calm! I just noticed my son was clearly upset, and now he's not telling me why? And now you think I'm not there enough for you. Do you know how concerning that is? You're always so composed." Her voice reeks of accusation.

So I have no choice but to be defensive. "*Always so composed?*" I snort. "Yeah, maybe you should be worried about how present you've been." I don't mean to snap, but what with high school, the doll, graduation, and my pending medical career, who can blame me? "I've had episodes like this in the past, but I'm not blaming you for that. Where is all of this coming from?"

Mum stutters out a few incoherent syllables before shaking her head. "All right, all right. I don't mean to bring it up out of nowhere; I've felt this way for a while…." Her voice lowers, expressing a cold sorrow. "I'm simply worried, and have been worried, you're going to go off the rails in an unexpected fashion because I didn't look hard enough for signs. A lurking fear I've had for a while now, I guess. And now you can't tell me what's up even after I've caught you lying about whether you're fine or not."

I step back further, losing control of my temper bit by bit. "I'm not falling for your little guilt trip. I don't need to tell you anything." I spit the words out, holding eye contact with the best of my ability, and continuing to move away from her.

"Guilt trip?!" She huffs a noise, one that sounds like a laugh tainted with a hint of rage. "What has happened to you? Why can't you tell me what the fuck's wrong?"

I slap my forehead and cringe. Mum cursing at me is rare.

I hate it when we fight. It's happened before, of course, we're mother and child. However, fights like these appear as blood moons do — rare, red, and impactful. "Nothing has happened to me, Mum. You're making this one small fight we're having into some huge thing that defines our relationship. Just, stop!" My vocal cords strain with my heart.

Mum finds her way around the circular dining table, creaking the floor with each step. "I'm not blowing anything out of proportion. Come to think of it, we've been needing to have this conversation. Or any conversation for that matter! When was the last time we spoke for over five minutes?"

"*You* never try to talk to *me* — where is this coming from!?" I swallow back any hint of regret sprouting in my stomach. "Just leave me alone." I try to slide past her so I can escape to my room, but she snakes around my blocking arm and pins me up against the wall. *Pushes me*, I suppose you could say.

It isn't a hard push, it really isn't.

It shouldn't feel like anything.

But, as if I had just plummeted onto hell's floor, my back punches in on itself. It's only a small push, but the action spirals into deep pain — whiplash, almost. I bite my tongue and gasp, overwhelmed by the unanticipated throb of agony. My bones feel as though they're utterly shattered for three hot seconds. The breath leaves my lungs, and I instinctively look at Mum.

Genuine concern flickers in her eyes. "Don't be so dramatic. And do not speak to me that way." Her voice is cold, but an ambiance of hesitance remains.

I take a few controlled breaths, and my body feels healed. I bring my hands to my chest and stare at them. Was that the doll? I mean, I feel fine. But that was pain like I've never experienced before, and now I'm fine and dandy?

My gaze floats back to Mum, and I remember the argument. I duck below her arm and head back toward my room. I ignore her dirty stare.

What the hell just happened to my body?

After a few seconds of exhausting myself by replaying our fight in my head, I resort to calling Quinton.

I walk over to my phone, but an intruding pain knocks me off my feet.

It pounds in my head, ripping my skull. I gasp, radioactive heat seeping into my head from every direction while shockwaves begin to catch up with the pain.

I grab my head and stumble backward to sit on my bed. My limbs scream in anguish at the simple impact of soft sheets. It's like how I felt just three or so minutes ago, but the extremity has increased *tenfold*. My vision strobes with all sorts of lights, and I cling to my abdomen, feeling its rigidness in my hands. The alarms in my head blare louder and louder until my brain blanks out in shock.

I move my hands to my comforter, squeezing the life out of it to distract myself from the throbbing afflictions until my knuckles begin to *sear*. With blurry vision, I lift my head to stare at myself in the mirror. My usual whitish-reddish skin has lost its color and tints blue. What the fuck is happening?

I hyperventilate in sharp, painful breaths at every arbitrary stab of pain. Air itself seems to be wrapping its hands around my neck and choking me to death. I try harder and harder to breathe until eventually, I fall back fully, and I'm unable to come to my feet. My body squirms on the bed, aimless, desperate, grabbing for some bit of survival to little avail. And, God, my *head* is so, so *hot*.

"Call 911!" My throat aches, barely allowing me to say any comprehendible word. It feels like someone has ripped my skin off and is beating my insides with a bat. I curl in a ball and let out a loud sob, relieving some bit of internal tension. After all, physical hurt is not the only pain wrecking me at the moment.

Fear runs equally rampant.

Adrenaline zooms through every inch of me, blocking any reality.

Regret and sorrow follow too, making me feel simply useless.

The blankets around me feel like they're pulling me into the earth, sucking me toward certain death. I'm in hardcore fucking survival mode. Writhing in my sheets, a question forged of pure fear passes my mind.

Is this how I die?

But my brain is screaming at me so loudly to do something, I eventually lose the thought, once again focusing on surviving and retaining a will to live. I obey the cries and attempt to stand up.

I can find Mum, she can help, she'll know what to do.

I trip over a few times, coughing as the invisible chokehold around my neck tightens. A hand ghosts over my mouth — an act of pure habit — to conceal the germs from my coughing. I pause, and spot a bright color staining the hand recently clamped over my mouth.

Blood. Red and luminescent. It takes everything in me not to faint at the sight.

The heavier my steps toward the door get, the lighter my body feels, as if it's already had enough. As if it's already chosen; death is better than this never-ending pain.

You're pathetic, Connor.

The scientific part of my head begins to take note of my symptoms — my medical instincts kick in fast. Primary pain, and then sudden heat? Pounding head? Jabbing strikes all over my body? Everything points to internal bleeding. I need a hospital. My brain seems to spurt, hot and heavy. By the time I reach my doorknob, my skull feels as though a meat cleaver has split it straight down the middle. Exerting every last drop of energy in me, I pound the door one single time with mighty force.

And I let myself collapse, more secure that I have a hope of being found. Mum's shrill scream is the last thing I hear.

CHAPTER 8

QUINTON

The loud, rhythmic beat of a heart monitor interrupts my comfortable sleep. I blink my eyes open, twisting my head left and right with a yawn. The desk beside me, the glowing monitor, the bed rails, the fucking needle in my arm — it doesn't take long for me to realize I'm in a hospital.

What?

I furrow my eyebrows, trying to recall what happened just before I fainted.

Or — did I faint?

Yeah, yes I did.

And then my memory slaps me in the face. My mom. The doll. She… threw it. *Connor.* He must've been severely injured. He most likely *is* severely injured. His worst nightmare might've come true.

I wipe a thin line of sweat from my forehead, and with little self-consideration, I slip the needle out of my skin. I exhale at the sting of pain, grab a stray band-aid from the bedside table, and slap it on.

After a few short breaths, I stand up quickly. My vision spins, blood pressure dropping at the sudden movement. My head reacts too, pounding and growing sore as I move around. I groan — I must've hit my head on the floor when I fainted. Is that how my parents convinced the hospital to admit me and give me an IV? I fainted one single time.

I take a deep breath, getting used to standing on my feet again. Multicolored lights outline the top of the door frame, and a miniature PVC Christmas tree rests on a porcelain desk. I chuckle at the odd amount of Christmas spirit in a hospital room and slowly stretch my tired muscles.

I step across the cold floor, barefoot. I quietly open the door and peek outside, trying to focus on finding Connor. Best case scenario, I simply imagined the doll hitting the wall. Worst, he's in critical condition, placing him here — or he's dead, and maybe in the hospital morgue. I shudder.

I speed-walk through the hallways, growing nervous. Employees are beginning to take notice of the six-foot-three, half-naked man running through their corridors, but I'm too quick to be stopped. I turn a final corner — sighing with relief — and find a receptionist.

Not waiting a second to catch my breath, I begin speaking. "Hi, sir, hello. One second." I pause, bending down to take a breather. "Do you — do you have a patient named Connor Jones here? Brown hair, brown eyes, short, you know?"

He doesn't respond for a moment, clearly surprised at my unprofessional, and apparently illegal, questions. "Well, actually, that's private information, I'm sorry. And two, your dress," he points a pen at my baby blue hospital gown, "indicates like you're not supposed to be here, young man. You're wearing the ICU gown, yet you don't have a nurse with you?"

Leave it to my parents to get me admitted to the vital section after I *faint*. I try to hide my anger, slouching and smiling with fake confidence. "Sir, I was given permission to visit my friend in this hospital. Is this going to be an issue? I really don't think you'd want to upset the Hansley's son, right?" I drop my shoulders to intimidate him more, hoping it's working as my worry for Connor increases.

It's cheap to threaten someone based on status, especially an underpaid employee…But this is regarding Connor. I will do whatever it takes to make sure he's safe.

He gives me a long look of disdain. He then murmurs something unsavory under his breath before begrudgingly providing an answer. "Connor Jones, room twenty-three, floor four."

Jackpot. I nod my head. "Thank you, thank you so much." I walk to the stairs, glad I found Connor.

Wait.

I found Connor. That means he *is* in the hospital. My previous high drops below Earth's core. He's in the fucking hospital. And because of my inability to keep one, tiny doll out of sight. Warm, thick tears pool on my waterline while anxiety boils in my stomach.

No. I wipe my sleeve across my eyes several times. Can't get distracted right now — at least he's not in the morgue, right?

The number **3** is painted in bold on the first wall of the next floor I reach. I sigh, relieved I don't have too far until Connor's floor — only one more to go. I turn and bolt up the stairs, ignoring the feeling of passerby's eyes on me.

I probably shouldn't be asking my weak and delirious body to endure physical toll like this, but I don't have a choice. Well…unless my body is strong and rested? I don't know how long I've been here, or when the last time I ate, drank water, or went to the bathroom was.

But I clearly don't care, because my legs continue to run. The stairs take a sharp turn, placing me directly in front of a massive **4** painted red. I let out a quiet holler at my success.

I take a moment to catch my breath before speeding down the hallway once again. As I run, I notice that this hospital wing is different from the rest. It takes on an abandoned asylum look, with chipped paint and walls stained with God knows what.

How injured *is* he? Why is he in this wing? Pretending not to hear the adult voices calling and questioning me, I continue my run, reading every number I whizz past. **1**, **2**, **3**, **4**…the numbers on the rooms I pass build until finally, a simple, black **23** greets me. Thank fucking God.

I brush my hair back and inhale deeply. Despite our situation, I can't help but want to look cleaned up for Connor.

I contemplate knocking on the door, but shrug and reach for the door-knob instead. It doesn't open. I fiddle with the knob faster as my knock slowly becomes a banging. Desperate, impatient, and exhausted after my run, the first tear leaves my eye. After this entire journey, the one thing keeping us apart is, what, two inches of wood?

"Sir? Sir!" A doctor coming my way picks up her speed. "Sir, I'm going to have to ask you to…" She pauses, recognizing my outfit. She squints her eyes at a pendant hanging off my hospital gown that I failed to notice before. The little badge has printed: 'Hello, my name is Quinton Hansley.' No chance my parents had them *tag* me.

She brings her hands together in a delighted clap. "Mr. Hansley! We've been looking for you; you're a patient. We need to get you back to your room. I hope you're all right?" Her voice is thick with urgency and relief.

I stare her down. Listening to her would make both of our lives easier, but I have to see Connor. I'm too unsure of Connor's state, plus, what will happen when I'm released from the hospital? What will happen when he's released? My parents will keep us hundreds of yards away from each other. What if this is my last chance to see him for a fucking *while*? I bite my lip. Connor is more important than her demands.

"Doctor, listen, I can't go until I see Connor."

She clicks her tongue, irritation eating at her smile. "Listen, Quinton, I don't know why you were pounding at that door, and I trust you know Connor, but there are visiting procedures that would take you only a quick moment to do. I can't let you in. It's against the rules. I'm sorry, kid. You have to come with me."

I scoff in horror, sputtering like a faulty circuit. "Sorry, Doc, but I can't do that! I need to see him. Seriously, I won't live not knowing if he's safe or not, he's my boyfriend." I press my tongue to the roof of my mouth. Hopefully mentioning our relationship wasn't a mistake. "At least tell me if he's alive or not and let me see him, even for one minute."

She stands her ground, not budging. "I cannot disclose any information. His mom asked for complete confidentiality; I'm afraid I don't know why. But I am not going to risk my job over some white boys who think they're in love. Let me take you back to your room so we can go on with our lives. I don't want your parents angry. I understand your worry for him, and I promise he's in good hands. Come with me. Please."

I stare at her and quietly wipe my tear away.

In a softer tone, she adds, "You'll see him soon, okay?"

I stare back at the door, glass fogged, wood thick, and let my tears wet my cheeks. I'm so close to him. Millimeters from Connor, and he's there because of me. I hurt him. I couldn't protect him. I grip tighter to the doctor's hand I didn't realize I took. She welcomes the touch, squeezing back, and begins to walk on her merry way because little does she know, she's feeding me to the wolves. My parents.

Or she's not feeding me to any wildlife at all? I gently swing my door open, the atmosphere quiet and cold, and best of all, empty. When I realize neither of my parents are in the room, my bones warm right back up. After pampering me briefly, the doctor leaves, promising to return.

Well, someone broke their promise. Rather than a five-foot-ten, older woman, a new young man slips through the door. I'm not sure if he's a qualified nurse or simply a medical scribe or assistant, because he can't be more than a year older than me. He greets me, holding a plain, gray tray. I'd say hello if my throat wasn't so numb.

He presents my food with a smile, slipping the tray into my hand. Jello, sandwich, and *more jello*. I study the jello, snorting bitterly. The bubbly substance ricochets within its space. Within its laughably massive space. Free, alive, and energized. You look at the jello and know it's better off than you, and…fuck.

I'm beefing with jello. I fight the urge to hurl the tray and its contents across the room — it's generally frowned upon to throw your food everywhere. The scribe — or whatever he is — must see my death stare, because he takes the tray from my hands with a chuckle.

"Trust me, laser eyes don't work." He grins at his own joke, and then frowns at my silence. "Hey, do you wanna have a chat?" He places the tray down with an irritating clank.

I wouldn't have to deal with my irrational hatred toward a plate of jello if I were in Connor's room right now. Still, I say, "Sure. 'bout what?" Small talk with a stranger is not wonderful when your boyfriend is in the hospital, but he seems friendly — and he's around my age.

Despite my doubts, as crazy as it sounds, the boy helps. His voice is tender, caring, easy to listen to. A year or so of training brought him to this moment, soothing me. And in a brilliant moment, I overshare. A few vague comments about my parents are all I dare to offer, but it still feels good to vent. Even if it's a heavily sugar-coated vent. He manages to flush my worries away for a few minutes and, fuck, it feels good, I even mention Connor by name, and how he's here.

My eyes flick to the clock, widening at the thirty-minute time difference since I last peeked.

The doctor's assistant follows my eyes, chuckling. "Someone's a talker. This was a nice chat, Quinton. But I gotta go report back to my boss. I'll see you around?"

I nod. "Thanks, man." I squint, wondering why I hadn't read his badge earlier. Karl Jones – *Doctor Ndiaye's Assistant*, it reads. "Thanks, *Karl*."

Time passes, and passes, and passes. I sleep for five or six hours and wake up at dawn, still exhausted. My raging guilt over the Connor situation does not go away. My mind finds no peace or quiet.

I eye the grayscale curtains, squinting at new light inching its way in. Lifting a few sheets off me, I grab my phone. It's wheezing for life, holding on dearly to the 5% battery left. I check if Connor had answered any of my panicky texts and sigh when I see no new notifications. Groaning, I peer at my reflection, and I can't help but smile. Having an ego can be so much fun.

An intruding noise from Karl disturbs my moment of joy. "Good morning, Quinton! I hope you slept fine." He fiddles with a pen. "You're going to have to leave the hospital at noon, so hooray. You're perfectly stable and in great condition — good news, I know. Your parents are here to pick you up since you came in their car." He hands me a warm tray of food. Fresh out of the microwave, yum.

I straighten up and attempt not to look revolted by the flaky pancakes. Karl stares at me expectantly. I respond with a thumb's-up so he'll look away. It does the trick; he exits in peace, and I trash the pancakes.

I yawn, hop off my mattress, and stretch my back with a few twists. Bored, I begin wondering what cheap excuse my parents gave for my hospital admission. I did hit my head, so they could've done some good old proportion-blowing.

I sigh — at least I have an excuse not to see them for now. Sun filters through the blinds, making the walls a little less plain. I smile at the sight, maybe I'll miss this place.

Wait a fucking second.

Connor. "Shit." The raw *franticness* in my voice catches even me off guard. The possibility I won't get to see him before leaving Holloway gives me the strength to throw shoes on and bolt through the halls.

Jeez, this is the second time in a twenty-four-hour period I've run full speed through Holloway in a hospital gown. I chuckle through my panting.

Worried and eager, I recite Connor's whereabouts to myself. Floor four room twenty-three, floor four room twenty-three, go, go, go. Halfway before realizing it, I'm at his door.

Connor. I pray, not to God, but to *luck* that it's not locked. My fingers wrap around the handle before it…opens. Perhaps his Mum just paid a visit? I laugh in victory, but my joy vanishes the second I see him.

I spot the heart monitor and random paramedic tools before I see his body. He's still and sleeping, hooked up to machines built to invade and fix his body and brain. I stare at his heart rate's level — low — but still pumping. I have to look away for a moment.

His tough skin is bruised purple and blueish. His eyebrows are slightly furrowed, and there are bandages covering his arms and legs. His steady breathing sounds thinner and thinner each time he inhales, turning my blood cold.

In all bluntness, he looks terrible.

I don't try to stop the tears. They're inevitable in this situation. Everything is inevitable when it comes to Connor. He's a force, an earthquake that rocks your world in the best way possible.

I finally step into the room, weary and hesitant. If I thought I could see how badly injured he is before, I was wrong. My hand hovers over my mouth.

My parents. My parents and I; we both did this to him. I lean down and pull him into a deep hug as a few sobs shake my body. I clutch Connor, smelling him, feeling him, adoring him until I have to cry again. I assume he's in a deep sleep, because no matter how long I hold him, he stays still. Maybe he could've hugged me back if I hadn't gotten lazy with protecting the doll. I should've hidden it in the *depths* beneath my bed — not out in the open under my desk. I thought it was an unordinary spot to hide it, meaning if my parents ever searched my room, they'd check the closet or under the bed. I guess I was wrong.

And that's the cruel pièce de résistance: He's here because of me.

I bring my lips to a small purple spot on his forehead, kissing it. He doesn't budge. Why hasn't he woken up? I scan the bedside table. A yellow folder rests on the wood.

Diagnosis (patient Connor Jones), written on the front. I pull the paper from the folder, growing more horrified as I continue to read.

Medically induced…coma. He's in a fucking coma.

My jaw slacks, changing the course of my falling tears. But I keep reading — as if to punish myself.

Broken bones in several parts of the body, cause unknown. Bruised rib cage, cause unknown. Internal bleeding, cause unknown. Could require surgery, cause unknown.

Cause unknown.

But *I* know. I continue to read until my vision is so blurred from tears, it's impossible. I turn my head away and set the clipboard down with a small thump. I want to be nowhere but his side.

But looming over a dormant Connor won't speed up the process of his awakening, or lack thereof. And on the chance he does live, I have to make it up to him.

I can only play the blame game for so long. From an objective perspective, I am at fault. I knew my situation. I was aware of my parent's antics. I'd known what they'd done to Marco, and I assumed the risk. I guess in the meantime, I could try to exterminate this *sickening* guilt.

My eyes flick to the clock, which reads twelve p.m. No matter how much I wish I could stay with him, I exit, stealing one last glance.

When I drag myself back into my room, Karl groans in exasperated relief, retrieves my hospital gown, and leads me outside. "Did you visit Connor **Jones**?"

I nod, a loose image of Connor's unconscious body still in my mind. "Yes," I mumble in a dark tone.

Karl sighs. "I think it may help to let you know that there is an incredibly high chance of survival — he's mostly stable, just very weak and injured. Unless something completely disastrous and unpredictable happens, Mr. **Jones** will be okay. Dr. Ndayie is his main doctor." He points to his badge while he walks, reminding me he is her assistant. "She has said there won't be lasting repercussions, but he'll need a lot of time to heal."

Life seems to return to my body. My heart blooms with relief, and I feel the urge to cry again.

I'm about to respond, but the moment I catch sight of my parents, I freeze. Hot fury burns my throat out of nowhere, almost like primitive hate. They also did this to Connor. They're also the reason he's in the hospital. Marco should've been my wake-up call but holy shit, they're broken in the head.

I fucking hate them.

I keep my eyes pinned to the ground while stepping inside the car. My parents wave Karl a goodbye, and they crane their necks to avoid looking at me. The car reeks of discomfort and anxiety.

And that's when I finally see my mom and my dad, fully. A quick look at them in the side-view mirror, and it's so clear. They aren't normal. My parents aren't normal. They're horrible people who need *psychological help*. Pastor and priest must've poisoned their childhoods too. After some religious trauma that closely mirrors mine, they grew up and tried to spread the same ideologies to me. I suppose the phrase 'abused becomes the abuser' accurately describes my parents. Either that or they needed zero traumatizing push to make them think it was okay to verbally and physically abuse their son.

No one says anything during the car ride back, not even when we step inside the house. I suppose having to speak to them less might be the one positive outcome of this situation.

I run upstairs to my room immediately and lock my door. Thankfully, neither of my parents bother to come check on me inside or, surprisingly, ask for my phone.

I soon fall into a nauseating brainstorming mode. Connor. How can I make this up to him? How can I make this guilt go away? I pace around my room, reorganizing my drawers to reorganize my thoughts for, I don't know, inspiration.

He got injured, or is currently in pain, because of how careless I was with his doll. I sit at my desk, groaning as I try to think of something to tame the guilt. Anything to get rid of the feeling.

He's hurt because of my irresponsibility with the doll…what if…I —

But no.

I couldn't. That's a crazy idea. But, then again, that's probably what Thomas Edison thought while sketching the first ever figure of the light bulb — what all the greatest historians and innovators thought.

I swing around in my chair, flip on my PC, and open Chrome. I type my question. Our research around the doll before this had come up short. We'd found some content, but none that'd help us deconstruct it. Maybe, though, we weren't optimizing the search engine.

How to make dolls that affect real life people

The first recommended video is like poison served on a silver platter: '*How to make magic dolls*'

I almost laugh. Connor and I researched the doll for hours and never found a video remotely like this. How were we stupid enough to never look up a tutorial on how to make them? Although I snort at the term "magic dolls," I remain so close to clicking it. But I can't.

That would be insane.

What if it worked, and Connor hated me for it?

I would be crazy.

Oh, but call me crazy. "How to make dolls…." Or irrational. This is, in all fairness, a great way to make up for what I did, and a great guilt escape…probably? Besides, it wouldn't hurt to make *one* tiny doll. It'll be of myself, too — I'm not dragging anyone else into this. Except for Connor, maybe.

I get back on task and look up at my screen. I'll watch one single video — and maybe it'll provide some answers on where Connor's doll came from. Win-win. Either way, I'm probably not smart enough to craft a magical doll. Right?

I laugh as I eye the creation below me. "Finally!" I look up at my clock: four-nineteen a.m. I slump in my chair.

I lazily reach for the doll and inspect it again, curious. Did I actually just…spend six hours creating a doll that could take my life at any second? That might not even work?

I swallow, trepidation creeping in at how well the doll mirrors my appearance. It looks just like me, even its features. With only thread and needle, I couldn't have made something this accurate. Maybe when I added my hair strand it…activated? What the fuck is — I giggle, a little terrified. But I quickly remind myself: this is for Connor.

Still, there's a high chance it won't even work. That this tutorial was made by an eight-year-old with a voice changer.

I tap my foot on the floor. What do I do next? There's no magical indication the doll is working, so I pick it up and curiously give it a hard poke on the head.

A sharp prod ripples through my skull. "God, fuck!" I look around, and then at the doll. I shakily place the doll back on my desk and try to come to terms with what I've done: the doll *works*.

"Oh, my God. Oh, my God, what?" I jump up from my chair, clap for myself, and rub my eyes maniacally.

I cannot believe I just did that. I bring the doll to my face, breathing hard. What's done is done.

The doll — my doll — has been made.

I unpause the video with a shaky finger. However, after I unpause, the video abruptly ends. I blink. I was expecting a tidbit at the end explaining how to disconnect the doll. Swallowing, I click on the channel's profile and look for more videos that explain how to deactivate it. Nothing shows up.

I power my laptop down. It'll be fine.

I can't see this as a mistake. It's simply too late to regret, which I don't. In hindsight, it is the perfect gift for Connor. A Quinton doll for him to keep. For him to use irresponsibly. For him to put me in the hospital with. Assuming he comes out all right — which he will, as Karl promised. A promise he better fucking keep.

I fall back on my bed with a smile, feeling my stomach ease a little. The guilt is still present, but calmer. A low tide.

I cuddle with my mini-me, lacing it with my scent for Connor, and sigh one last time before falling asleep.

CONNOR

I gently open my eyes, stolen from the safety of my own head, and am greeted with bright, noisy ringing and loud strips of light. My body glues me to my bed as panic leaks into my chest. Where and when the fuck am I?

All I can do is look around and huff. First thing I register: I'm in a hospital of some sort, far from what Mum and I can afford. My heart rate shoots up even higher as I recall inklings of what hospitalized me. The fight with Mum. Falling. Bleeding. Pounding. My head reels. What happened? My eyes flick all over the room, desperately hoping to see Mum sitting, cross-legged and relieved.

But I know she has work. All I find is a cheap, fake Christmas tree and fairy lights with the most displeasing color pattern — further disorienting me. I click my tongue and observe my surroundings. I crane my neck down, unsure of when my nails got so long.

I couldn't have possibly been here for over a week, right?

Within a few seconds, I can already feel life returning to my bones. It's delightful, thrilling, even, but only until waves of pain come with it.

I let out a hoarse grunt and feel my voice return as well. It's raspy and strained, like an unoiled machine. I twist my head, trying to get a view of the rest of me. I look as though a twitch would shatter every bone in my body. And it very well could, seeing as all my limbs are wrapped and propped up with extensive white Velcro.

My eyes shift to the armchair as I begin to freak out more. There's a pad, gray and small, to call for a nurse's help. It's right on my fingers, yet I'm hesitant to touch it. Operators pouring into the room and chatting about numbers and "my state" doesn't sound like music to my ears. I rest my wrist back at my side and allow myself a moment of quiet.

How long have I been here? What happened? Maybe…was it the doll? It can't have been Mum's push, she barely touched me, and I refuse to believe she'd ever exert that much strength on me no matter how angry she was. But maybe she thinks she *did.* Fuck, fuck, fuck, fuck that stupid doll; what else could it have been? Was I sat on? Did the Hansleys adopt a new, toothy pet? Dread weighs on my chest as my mind travels to money.

How the hell are we paying to stay in this hospital? Every second I spend in this room is another dollar added to the bill. My hands press the call button. I can't spend another day here; Mum's paychecks are probably howling at me to wake up. I fall back into my storm of emotions and pain, waiting for someone to arrive. God, if only I could summon Mum, Quinton, or Fritz at the click of a button instead. But my phone is nowhere to be seen, either lost in my covers, or at home in my room. I miss my room.

My longing for any type of family grows until a short, raven-haired doctor and her jittery assistant make an entrance. The assistant speaks into a walkie, then tucks it in a pocket and turns to me.

"Good afternoon, Connor. How are you? Are you feeling all right?" The assistant questions me with a pacifying tone, and my anticipation for news of how long I've been here grows.

But I only nod, cold and in pain. "Good. I'm doing good." I am not doing good.

The nurse's higher-up taps the desk next to me. She shuffles through papers and taps several buttons on my monitor before smiling. "You've been out for a week. Happy to see you awake."

My neck tenses as I try to eat my reddish jello. The doctor and assistant who first greeted me left a few minutes ago to call my mother. Within twenty minutes, I hear an urgent, feminine voice from outside the door. Mum. Mum!

My energy blooms. "Mum?!" I inch upward, but fall back downward wincing in pain. She comes into view, dressed in a white blouse and peach-colored pants, along with maroonish eyeshadow and her short, brown hair tied back in a low ponytail.

"Connor!" She finally swings the door open and rushes over, triple-masked. She'd kiss my forehead if she could, but it's not a great idea for someone immunocompromised to enter a hospital unmasked. Tears well up in her eyes as she stares at me. "Connor, baby, I'm so sorry. I'm so, so sorry, Connor."

I don't fight my tears; I let them fall. She wipes a finger below my eyes, pulling me in for a delicate hug. "Ah — careful. And don't be sorry, please." I manage to grab her hand. "What happened?" My chest wants to explode with bewilderment — I'm still confused as to how I got here.

"We…it doesn't matter what happened right now." She pauses, brushing my hair from my face. "You're the most important thing to me. Please never do that again." Giggles shave some of the sorrow from her voice.

I kiss her forehead, irritated she didn't answer my question, but too tired to care. I look at her face up close, and my previous bittersweet feelings morph into pure bitterness. Her skin is far paler than normal, and the circles around her eyes have deepened. "Mum…I'm sorry. I'm sure this cost a lot. Please tell me you didn't spend too much to keep me hospitalized here?" I prepare myself to say a million thank-yous in my head. This isn't my fault — it had to have been that fucking doll. But, still, I feel guilty.

Mum tenses, giving me a stern look. "Of course I did. You're my son." She looks away, crossing her arms. "Quinton helped a bunch with the cash, so don't get too worried, but I'm always going to spend loads of money on your life, even if it means every penny. You're the last thing I have to live for. I love you more than anything." She pats my head and *carefully* rests hers on my chest. She wipes her tears off my shirt before pulling away.

"Thank you so much," I mumble. "I'm sorry." Still very disoriented, I apologize again. I don't know what other way to react.

And, Quinton. He's probably riddled with guilt. If the doll was to blame in all this, I know he's beating himself up. I squeeze my eyes closed, quickly reopening them when I feel Mum leaving my side.

She stands at the doorway, solemn. "Fuck, I wish I could just stay, baby, but…rotary drill work today." Rotary drill jobs are among Mum's least favorite occupations to hop in and out of. She must've been desperate for a shift. I crumple more. "Look, you have nothing to be sorry about. I love you so much, okay? I gotta go to work; Quinton will be here soon." She blows me a kiss and I blow one back, cherishing her smile for a moment longer before she leaves.

I wait for Quinton and pop a few Advils the assistant left on the side table. Ten minutes later comes knocking so rapid, I nearly fly right out of my bed. But I'm soon exhilarated. "Quinton? Is that you?"

The door slides open, and a beautiful man bursts through. His face is frantic, hair askew, and eyes hazy, but it's *him*. I straighten my back, watching the boy laugh.

"Connor! You're awake. You're okay!" His voice has an eerie tinge of mania; however, that's soon forgotten when he walks over and hugs me with just enough strength to avoid triggering my wounds.

I chuckle, tears welling in my eyes. "Of course I'm okay. I'm literally invincible, remember?"

Quinton snorts, keeping his arms folded on top of me.

"I'm so glad you're here." I — try to — draw my hand down his back, feeling his tears wet my shirt's collar. Second person to cry on me today. "What's wrong, Quinton?"

His fingers dig into my hair, and I wince. "Connor, I'm so fucking sorry. It's all my fault. It's — I'm so sorry. I missed you so much. My…my parents. They got to the doll. I didn't hide it well enough — we fought. They, God, my mom threw it super hard against the wall. And I couldn't stop them." His guilt is practically tangible. He looks into my eyes as though he's eagerly awaiting punishment rather than forgiveness.

My chest twists, and I wonder how long he's been blaming himself. Then, the rage arrives. His fucking parents did this to me. "Quinton, Quinton, it's okay. Don't apologize. It wasn't your fault — it was your damn parents. And at least I've now suffered the worst of the doll, right? Like, it can't get worse than this."

Besides death.

But neither of us dare to point that out. Instead, Quinton frowns. "Quit comforting me. I should be the one babying you. How do you feel? What was being in a coma like?" He twirls my messy hair strands and kisses my lips for the first time in a week.

It sends me to heaven.

"It…just felt like a regular sleep. I dreamt sometimes, and I don't remember ever hearing or feeling things from the waking world. I was a little freaked out when I woke up and in a lot of pain," I chuckle, "but that's it.

Quinton kisses my forehead. "I'm glad it wasn't all terrible." He pulls back from my forehead with a new demeanor, though. It's trepidatious, silent. He turns away from me and retrieves an object from his bag.

"Quinton? What's that? A 'sorry for being the reason you're in the hospital' gift, perhaps?" I laugh to myself, but Quinton stays quiet.

Although I cannot see his face, I can hear the uneasy smile through his words. "You'll see, sweetheart. It is a three-in-one! An apology, commitment, and punishment, I guess."

I blink at his odd phrasing, slowly becoming more stressed. "Quinton, what is the gift?"

He hauls the bag over, places it on the bedside table, and pulls out the last thing I could've expected.

It can't fucking be.

A doll. Stitched to the last detail of Quinton's face — a small doll rests in his hand. A perfect replica of my boyfriend.

But no.

He wouldn't *make* a doll. He wouldn't take on every burden I have just to make me feel better. Plus, the internet holds nothing but conspiracists and useless information about the doll. How would he do that? Mine is a miracle — unduplicatable.

Right?

"Quinton. What is this?" My voice is like hard concrete. No fucking way he did what I think he did.

Quinton slaps a hand on his neck. "Well, Connor, I was thinking of the perfect gift for you." His low-pitched, bizarre tone throws me even further off. "I decided to make you a doll, but of me. Don't think I'm crazy, please. I…honestly didn't even know if it would work. But it did!" Quinton searches my face, desperate for a reaction. "Look, we're stuck with it, so — okay, my point is — just, okay." He clears his throat. "I know what it's like going through something no one else would understand. But now we both have to live with these burdens, you're not alone. We're even now! You get to keep mine and I can keep yours — if you still trust me. I know it's kind of strange, but it's a gift. It took hours." His excitement increases with every word, as if he's justifying what he did to both me and himself.

I chuckle, squinting to get a good look at his face. Perhaps it's a prank? "Quinton. You can't fucking — you can't just — "

Quinton only shakes his head and sighs. "But I did, Connor. Good idea or not, I made it. Accept it, please. You're the only person I could trust it with anyway." Quinton clicks his tongue, tossing the doll left and right between hands. "This is a punishment, and I'll forgive myself if I give it to you. I did this for you, but also for me, don't worry. I know, all right, I know it seems like a lot but…I'm a lot. And now you never have to feel alone. I'll always understand what you're going through." He wraps my hands around the doll. "I know it's kinda weird, but I need you to take this." His eyebrows knit, a want for acceptance twinkling in his eyes.

Is he *crazy*? Now he has to live with all my fears.

I glance at the doll, almost repulsed by its green button eyes. How much of a toll did my coma take on him? How guilty did he feel to conjure up such a danger to himself? I inhale, composing myself and carefully selecting my next words. Guilt really does things to people, huh. "I-I'll take it. I just don't really know how to feel. I see the thought process but… come on, you just willingly made a doll that could also put you in a coma." I exhale. "I'm accepting this because I care about you, but seriously, this wasn't a good idea. Do you even know how to, like, disconnect them?"

"…No." Quinton seems to understand my hesitance and shies away. "Yeah, no, you're right. It wasn't the best idea, but I'm glad you'll take it. It was just supposed to be a sweet gesture, you know?" But he still persists. "It's not so bad to be in such a bind with each other anyway, is it?" He keeps me from responding by sealing my mouth with a quick kiss.

Call this the *reddest* of flags — "I guess it is sweet…" — but I *am* colorblind.

I stare at the new *thing* in my hands. This doll exists. This doll is my responsibility. Oh, my God.

He did this for me, I suppose, so it's sweet.

Crazy sweet.

Quinton eyes me silently, then grins. "I'm just glad you're awake." He returns to his bag and pulls out a large, gray blanket.

I turn my head to the window. The moon is already high above the clouds. Is Quinton planning on sleeping here? My brain further dissolves into a confused mess. What about his parents?

Quinton, unfurling his blanket, twists his head to look at me. "I'm gonna sleep here, Connor. I wanna be with you for a long time after what

I…basically did to you. Or what my parents and I did to you. I'll watch over you…and over us."

"What do you mean over 'us'?"

Quinton pulls a pillow from his bag. "Well, you're my boyfriend. And despite everything, I want to protect that fact. If you want to as well, of course."

Quinton wears a weird energy tonight. "Oh, I see. Of course I do — I will be enjoying your company." Smiling, I add, "You're like my personal little guard."

Quinton lifts his head from his makeshift bed, smiling stupidly. "I guess I am, my prince."

I wrinkle my nose and wrap my arms with the limited movement I have around Quinton's doll. It's staying safe. Forever.

But just as I'm about to fall asleep, the door begins to rattle with furious knocking.

Before I can begin to lift my head, a five-foot-nine-inch frame appears at the door, dramatic and panting. "Connor! I was so worried about you, man. Also, a coma? That's kinda sick, dude. I put that on my bucket list when I was, like, ten or something." Fritz.

He trips over Quinton, not noticing his presence. His smile turns grim at my condition, and he then gives me an awkward hug. "The second your mom told me you were awake, I drove over. Or, well, I got gas and *then* I drove over — "

"*Fritz.*" I try to hug him tighter. "I missed you, and I'm okay. Sorry if you texted or anything. I think my phone is somewhere in the room, but I can't really walk or move." I make a small flailing movement to show how restricted my body is.

Fritz hums, amused by my playful struggle. "I love you, dude. I'm glad you're fine. And don't worry, I already texted the group chat you're alive. What the fuck even happened?"

Quinton and I exchange a glance. Neither of us answers.

Fritz finally pulls off me and stares at Quinton on the floor, raising an eyebrow, but not asking any questions. "I'll visit tomorrow. I really wanna stay and chat, but that history test you get to skip out on tomorrow…" He groans, tilting his head back. "It's killing me. I need to study for AP chem, too, but I promise I'll be back tomorrow right after school." He takes my hand, swipes a thumb over it, and then waves goodbye.

"Bye-bye, Fritz Cracker."

"Bye, love you!" And in a moment, Quinton and I are alone again, left behind for the night to swallow us whole.

Rather than blinking my eyes open to a gentle chirp of a bird, I'm awakened by Quinton's whiny ringtone screeching in my ear. "Fuck, Quinton, turn that off!" I groan louder and louder until Quinton finally answers his call.

But all my annoyance vanishes at the sound of his tone. I can tell who called — his parents.

Quinton stumbles over almost every single word. My heart sinks. "Y-yes. I'm, listen — no, you have to under — " He inhales. A feminine voice yells on the other line, nearly inaudible. "I'm sorry."

It's not very often I hear Quinton *scared*. The few times I have, it's normally after a conversation with his parents. Especially his mother.

"Please, you…you know what, fine. I'll be fine."

Very few times has he sounded so anxious.

"Where will you leave it?" He pauses. "Fuck you. You guys failed. I hope you know that. Not me, but yourselves. I can't believe how fucking terrible you both are. You are abusers. Guess what, I'm gayer than ever. If you try anything with Connor, I will call the cops. No — let me fucking talk."

His mother screams at him now, and I'm still unable to make out what she's saying.

Quinton grabs a fistful of his hair strands and tugs repeatedly. "You're — are you kidding me? You know what? Fine. That sounds great to me, actually! You won't hear from me for a long, long time. Fuck you, both of you. Go to hell." He slams his finger on the end call key and stands up, burrowing his head in his hands. His face is utterly *crumpled*.

"Quinton? Are you okay?"

His forehead crease softens at my voice and he sulks over to my bed to sit. I can physically feel the bands of stress coming off him in waves.

He offers a weak smile. "There goes the trust fund." He runs a hand through his hair, clicking his tongue. "I — they're kicking me out. Which is fine! Before you say anything. I've been wanting to move out, and they sent me…a little money, to be fair. Definitely not enough for college." He stills.

I fume, and my contempt for his parents solidifies even more. His dream has been crushed. They're *cruel.* "What? Oh, my God, I'm so sorry. Do you have anywhere to stay?"

Quinton clears his throat. "Not…quite yet. But I can figure it out. I don't have too much to worry about — I still got you." He pinches the skin on my cheek.

I bat his hand away, exhaling with a smile. After a beat, I slide my gaze up his figure. He has no place to go. "Okay, this might be super weird and way too early, but you could move in with me and Mum." I hold my breath, eyes widening. "But, you know, it's whatever. Like — only if you want. I'll ask my mum. We have enough space, I think," I look away, not believing I just asked that. I wouldn't have until months down the road of our relationship, but he has nowhere to stay.

Quinton looks at me with a hard gaze, as though he's trying to contain his excitement. "Well, I don't want to be too — we've only been dating for three and a half months, it isn't too soon for you or anything? I wouldn't want to, like, shake our relationship so much it breaks."

If I had the ability to slap my hand to my forehead, I would. "Quinton, this isn't a 'normal couples moving in together' situation. You got kicked out, and you're broke for the first time in your life." My throat thickens. "You have no place to stay and it would be a waste of money for you to buy a house or apartment when you can stay with us. Mum most likely won't really care." If he got a job, he could assist her in paying the bills and such. It'll work out. It has to.

Quinton chuckles. "You don't have to convince me, idiot. I'd love to move in with you — I'm just making sure you're completely game."

I roll my eyes in faux hatred. "Quit calling me an idiot — I'm a genius. You've never heard of Connor the science…guy?" Not many words rhyme with Connor.

Quinton smiles, teeth shining like the sun. "Not once. But, my answer is yes. I will happily move in with you."

I grin. "Let's fucking go."

When Quinton caresses my cheek, his gold-plated watch catches my eye. I take in his appearance, his attire, his *look.* Born into old wealth. Probably pampered daily.

He's unprepared, but I know he's adaptable, and he'll get used to my world. I know he can. "So, we're doing this? If my mum says yes?" I bite my lip.

"Yes, gladly."

CHAPTER 9

Day after day after day passes. Warm-cooked meal after visit after kiss. I'm simply experiencing, for a whole month and a half. Worst part is, I missed out on Christmas, a holiday that reminds me of chilly London mornings and ugly sweater parties hosted by Mum. I'm stuck with February, an objectively depressing month. But, thankfully, my body is now stable enough for me to leave. I'm allowed to join Quinton and Fritz during any one of their infamous escapades as new best friends. Turns out, when two people spend hours together in the same place, they bond. From constant homeworking to showing me their new hobbies, time has made Fritz and Quinton close.

Quinton leaves periodically to hang out with several groups of random friends he never bothers with talking about outside of school. He's still usually present enough to keep me company, along with Fritz.

Watching my two favorite people grow close is endearing beyond comparison.

It's been ages since I slept anywhere but this hospital — a month and a half to be exact. Believe it or not, the financial toll of booking a semi-perma hospital bed was more convenient and cheaper than the several casts, wheelchairs, and surgeries the doctors suggested as an alternative. As much as I don't like high school — never a ton of friends, took away time from helping Mum out with jobs and around the house — it's upsetting that some of my last months as a kid are being spent here. Healing has been painful and draining — and online school *sucks* — however, it's never lonely.

Not one second has been spent alone, in fact. Quinton doesn't have to pay a cent to sleep on the hospital floor, even though he does have cash left. On the nights the hospital decides he has overstayed his visiting hours and forces him to leave, he spends the night at mine and Mum's. Which would be awkward if Quinton wasn't such a natural at socializing and an excellent people person. Besides they rarely see each other, what with Quinton constantly researching new life paths that don't require a college degree and him only popping by late at night after school.

Apart from that, however, Fritz, Quinton, and I have become our own little distinct trio.

Quinton, in an attempt to be ironic, labeled us as the 'Holy Trinity.' It's not an awful name. Though, 'Connor & his little servants' is far more fitting in my opinion.

"Connor!" A large hand slides over my shoulder.

"Hi, Quinton."

"Connie-poo!" Fritz mocks Quinton's sappy tone. "Man, now you can come out into the real world with us. That's crazy, I've gotten so used to bedridden Connor." He yanks me up, forgetting my bones are still fragile.

Quinton pushes Fritz away, unamused. "What the hell is wrong with you?! Be careful, Fritz." He smiles at Fritz to ease the intensity of his tone and turns to me. "You okay?"

I grimace. "Oh, I'm so injured, Quinton. Please, save me, my knight in shining armor." I score a chuckle from Quinton and hop out of bed. I've gotten a little tired of the constant babying from him, though I guess I understand. He did blow almost every last dime his parents gave him on my hospital nights here. A little worrying, but I'm not going to scold a man for caring about me too much.

Fritz scrunches his nose, appalled. "You guys are so weird."

Quinton shrugs and stuffs his arms in his bag, shuffling inside until he finds of a change of clothes. I hum my thanks.

I bring the clothes to eye level, getting a whiff of my home's sweet smell. I sigh at how pleasant it feels and catch a familiar smell of honey and pine too. I blink. "Hey, where's my mum?"

A new voice chirps in. "She called. She'll be heading over soon!" Doctor Ndiaye's assistant, Karl Jones. Quinton has taken quite a liking for the charming eighteen-year-old. Quinton's fondness for Karl is understandable, of course. After all, he was the one to console Quinton when he woke up in Holloway hospital after fainting.

I click my tongue. "Ah, then — "

Fritz cuts me off, shouldering in from the bathroom. "Hey, doc! Still looking hella cute." He looks at Karl, biting his lip.

"Please, Fritz, call me Karl." He bows. Both boys smile in a way that'd make any fool think they've known each other for millennia.

And Fritz calls *us* "so weird."

"You guys are friends?" I ask.

"Yeah, *Connor*, not everything is about you. We've been talking for a while." Fritz sneers my name jokingly and glances at Karl beside him. Their dynamic feels familiar. I open my mouth to speak with Quinton but notice he's nowhere in the room.

I pull on Fritz's sleeve. "Where did Quinton go?"

Preoccupied with Karl, he responds distractedly. "Calm down, love-bird, he probably just went to a vending machine or something."

Karl butts in, moving away from Fritz and gathering my files. "Connor, *your mom* — " He chuckles. "…is here!"

My mind takes a sharp turn from Quinton as a smile spread across my face. "Fuck, okay. I'm actually getting out of here."

Karl grins. "We'll catch Quinton on the way there, most likely. But first, get packed and ready." He beckons me over and I follow. I slide into the bathroom and change into regular clothes. Turns out, it's not smiled upon to leave a hospital in their gowns. I run out of room twenty-three, not taking any time to say goodbye to Karl, and decide I'll visit him later. I step outside of the hospital. I breathe in the cold air and spot Mum.

As I trip toward the car, I notice something is off. My mum with her green mittens and brown beanie is standing by a car, yes, but the vehicle is untouched, new, and jet-black. I slow my run, squinting to make sure it's Mum I'm running toward.

It takes Quinton stepping out of the car door behind her to confirm that it is, indeed, apparently our car.

Once I reach the car, Mum pulls me into a heavy embrace. I chuckle, burying my head in her neck. "Hmm…I'm so glad I'm going home." The fight we had just before the doll put me in a coma has been forgotten for now. After the doctors confirmed it was external action that caused my coma and not her pushing me, Mum and I agreed to continue the conversation far in the future.

I feel Mum's smile against my shoulder. "Me too, love. At least while you were here I didn't have to wake up alone in that house every morning." She nods at Quinton. "It's like I've got two sons now!"

I snort, pushing off from her. "Don't say that, it makes it sound like we're brothers." I tilt my head toward the car and rest my hands on my hips. "Also — *hello*?! This car is sick! How did you get it?" I run a hand across the smooth metal, ignoring the stinging heat.

Mum quirks her shoulder at Quinton. "His grandad passed away in his sleep a week or so ago." My jaw falls, and just before I'm about to scold her for her bluntness, Quinton raises his arms.

"Don't worry, Connor! Seriously, I visited them once, what, twelve years ago? He was a homophobic, women-hating piece of shit, and he treated my grandma poorly back when she was alive." He shakes his head. "In retrospect, his death is a tragedy…but you didn't know him. I barely did. He never ever called or visited. And my calls went straight to voicemail, so he clearly didn't have a lot of interest in his grandkid. On the bright side, I am their only grandchild and inherited a bunch of cash!" He slaps the automobile. "A car, some jewels, and twenty-fucking-k. It would've been more, but the rest went to my parents." His voice lowers at the mention of his parents.

"Okay, weirdo. Sorry for your loss, but twenty-k? That's pretty awesome. Now start the car please, Mum, it's freezing." I kiss Mum's cheek, laughing as Quinton guides me inside the car.

We take a seat in the back, bickering about the sleeping situation at my place until my house comes into view.

And maybe things are okay after all. I'm not as afraid of the doll anymore, Quinton and I live together, and I don't have to see his parent's faces ever again. Both of our dolls are locked in separate glass cases in separate hidden spots in the house — far from Birdie and her teeth. We're okay. As incredibly strange as it is, we are okay.

QUINTON

"Hey, Karl!" Fritz sweeps the boy into a hug, eyes pouring out affection.

Karl yelps, turning his head until Fritz releases him.

I shake my head with a smile, but soon notice papers strewn across my desk. "C'mon, guys, we're at work. Let's try to focus." I look back down to face the blinding white papers in front of me. Hospitals are so white. The walls are white, the uniforms, aura, gowns, whatever you may think up…it's just *white.* Black is the supposed 'absence of color' but here, white seems to fill the description.

Connor's small palms close over my shoulders as he presses his body to mine from behind. "'Let's try to focus,' blah, blah, blah. Loosen up, idiot." He mocks me, taking a peek over my shoulder. "Whatcha doing?"

I rub my temple, attempting to shake him off me, and he moves in front of me instead. "Connor, can you please, just this once, take things seriously? Your sonography internship is almost up! And look at all of these files." I pause, gesturing toward the bright PC.

Connor only blinks up at me with wide, unconvinced eyes. "When did you get so bossy? You're literally not my dad." He snickers in harmony with Karl, continuing to mess around. "I have a boss — *she'll* tell me what to do."

Connor's work style, and overall ethic, are a true enigma. Two months ago when he was fresh out of the hospital, he made a sudden decision to return here at Holloway to work. He became familiar and friendly with the staff and higher-ups, who were later more inclined to get him an interview after his recovery. He'd now grown used to the white walls — and Karl, being a new friend, had given him off-the-record instruction and lessons about being a doctor's assistant. He's a networker at his core. His ambition is admirable, though still unpredictable. It just depends on the day. Fifty-fifty chance he'll either be a toddler or overwork himself.

Fritz slaps my back and turns to the other boys. "You two, get to work, come on, let's listen to Daddy Quinton."

I gawk. "Daddy Quinton? What the hell is wrong with you?" I shove Fritz before he can dodge.

Karl stands between us, his playful tone subsiding. "Okay, Quinton. Connor, he's right. We seriously need to get shit done."

Connor groans, but nods. "Whatever." It's difficult to tell if his annoyance stems from me being in the right, or his current disgust of paperwork.

I clasp my hands together in joy. "Okay, guys, start working. Fritz and I will stay for moral support. We deserve a break after practically babysitting this hospital's employees. And doing half your busy work, Connor." I shoot him a glare.

"Hell yeah, we will." Fritz grins.

Connor taps his chin as if he's calculating his next words. "Mmm… no."

I groan. "What do you mean 'no?' I already told you, I'm done doing the busy work you were assigned."

Connor yawns, still nonchalant. "No." He's taunting me.

I rub my temple. Connor needs to exercise some self-discipline. "Co-oo-nnor, do your work. They could, I dunno, fire you." I stretch his name out. It feels like we've had this same conversation a hundred times, and I consistently end up doing half his work for him. The boring work too — I don't know jack about medicine, so if he whines enough, I self-assign myself the busy work any idiot could do. He does the fun, specialized work.

"Hmm…no." Connor smiles.

This gets a chuckle out of Fritz, who shares a look with him.

Connor's tone remains matter-of-fact and indifferent. The thought of wanting to slap that lazy smile from his face leaves as quick as it appears. "Quinton?" Connor sounds concerned at my silence, and he places a hand on my arm.

I tsk, straightening my back. "Sorry, I'm just distracted by the fact you're such an idiot. Come on, where's all this inability to do work coming from?" I lower my voice. "Is everything okay?"

Connor laughs. "Pssht, are you worried about me, Quinton? I'm fine, just messing around."

I grin, spinning the boy around and shoving him forward. "Well, stop 'messing around' then, British fuck."

Connor gasps and stumbles forward. He catches himself gracefully, barely avoiding a collision with Karl and the metal desk. "Quinton — what the hell?" He pivots, whipping his head around. My chuckling amplifies at his deep frown and squinted eyes. "Quinton, you hurt me."

I step to his side and hoist him upward. "Oh, come on now, you're fine." I take his hand, still standing behind him, and kiss the back of his neck to apologize for sending him flying. Connor stiffens at our proximity, exhaling a low breath.

"I am fine." Connor grins. "It's nice being pushed and not, like, writhing in pain afterward. The doll really did a number."

I frown, and my chest swells. "Yeah. But, Connor, you and I both know that it is *locked in* a glass *safe* with *air holes* inside a *chest with air holes* cushioned with *four layers of cotton.* My parents and I cut each other off completely. You're safe now."

The beautiful boy laughs: the sweetest music to my ears. "I hope that's true."

I nod once. "But, seriously, get to work."

Connor remains still.

I sigh. "Come on. I'm going to help you, but get to your assigned room. With the laptop."

Connor drops his shoulders and faces me. With nowhere to back up, all he can do is accept our closeness. With a smile growing on his face, he finally responds. "Only 'cause it's hot when you tell me what to do."

I pull away from him with red cheeks. "Jesus Christ, Connor."

"Just being honest." And he leaves with Karl.

CONNOR

I roll out of bed and *nearly* avoid tripping over Quinton's and my clothes. Quinton breathes rhythmically, burrowed with covers and limbs sprawled across his half of the bed. I pick small bits from my eye to get a better look at my clock. Eight a.m. I glance back at my bed, unsure of what to busy myself with.

Why the fuck am I up so early? It's Saturday. Saturdays are always lovely for us. Which I can't say for Karl or Fritz or anyone not living in the boots of Quinton and me. Unlike them, we aren't going to college. No college applications to submit a day before the end of February deadline. Not a single college counselor to scold us for procrastinating the survival of our future. As blissful as it can be, though, this isn't by choice. We don't have the finances to support college, and a scholarship would be time-consuming and tricky — considering my lack of extracurriculars. Quinton could've, but that's no longer an egg in his basket. Now, although it's a curse, there's a blessing hidden in the inability to go to college: time. Time and decent mental health. With enough circling in my own thoughts, I can convince myself that the restriction of college is a good thing.

I never chose a dream school — never let myself entertain the thought. I suppose I always knew college would be out of my reach. That same pessimistic mindset is exactly what kept college out of my reach. Mum never encouraged it. Mum never discouraged it.

Sometimes, I wish she'd parented a little harder. But that's selfish. I mean, she mostly raised me all by herself, which no one is at blame for.

Dad died when I was a toddler. It was a work accident, and Mum was young as well. After it happened, my memory was a little hazy, especially since my two-year-old brain didn't hold information well. But overall, I was ready to mold into my world, to accept and heal from his death, which was particularly easy since I barely remembered his features. It makes me feel guilty at times — how can I struggle to remember my Dad's face until shown a photo of him? However, I don't miss his physical form. I just miss him. My thoughts of him linger on smell, sound, and presence. And I've spent countless days thinking about his death, why it happened, and what we did to deserve such a loss. Or I used to, at least. Reliving bits of his memory hurts like heaven.

Recalling him is more agonizing now than it was closer to when it happened. Time didn't heal, it prodded at the wound, infected it with knowledge. When I was younger, I didn't understand the scope of what happened — ignorance really is bliss. Death is truly the worst force out there, imposing on not only the victim's life, but also everyone else's around them. I hope, more than anything, death never touches my loved ones again.

I stand and stretch, realizing how much I've teared up. I quickly wipe my face and look at the floor. It's too early for me to be crying over Dad once again. After all, Saturdays are always lovely.

I turn back around and stare at Quinton's sleeping body, admiring his messiness. It's a lie to say he looks good — he looks like a drooling rodent (lovingly), but I can't help but kiss his nose because, God, he's still adorable.

I crawl back on the bed and ruffle his hair, deciding to not have a lonely morning. His eyes flutter for a second before he looks at me. He deeply inhales and gives me a small smile. It's the most beautiful thing I've ever seen.

I lean down and plant a kiss on his forehead.

"Morning, Quinton."

"Morning, idiot."

And I want every morning to begin like this.

Every day to begin and end with Quinton's face.

Not even two magical dolls can change that.

CHAPTER 10

My eye twitches in frustration. I run a hand over one stray hair strand for the thirtieth time and clench my teeth. Looking presentable is all I ask, just for these next few days. After all, Quinton's and my sixth-month anniversary is tomorrow — an early March day that still retains some of winter's chill. Of course, my typically compliant hair must be messy the one time…okay, one of the many times I want it to look nice.

I skid out of my room to find Mum waiting in the kitchen with lunch. Her eyes brighten when she sees me.

I kiss her cheek. "Hey, Mum! Where's Quinton?" I pull out a chair for myself. "And thanks for the food, 'm big enough to cook for myself, though."

Her face folds into a mix of playfulness and seriousness, and she drops her tone an octave lower than usual. "I'll baby you till the day I die." She turns away to collect an empty plate. "And I don't know, you find him. Isn't this the boy you're going to have been dating for six months as of tomorrow?" Her eyebrows quirk. "Oh, I hope you got him a present. I'd leave my partner if they didn't get me a present." She clicks her tongue.

I groan and lean back in my chair. "Mum, you don't have to micro-manage my romantic life. Of course, I have a gift. It's show-stopping, but who cares? I'll show my affection for him in a variety of ways tomorrow." I take a sip of water. "Presents are trivial if anything. But for the sake of Quinton, I'd say I outdid myself." I puff my chest and tip my glass of water to her.

Mum snorts. "Tch, okay, hotshot, don't act like presents are some superficial expression of love. What if Quinton's love language is gift-giving?"

I grab my phone from the seat next to me, mindlessly sifting through apps. "Which is exactly why I outdid myself. And quit saying phrases involving 'love.' We haven't said the three words yet."

Mum freezes. "You haven't said 'I love you' yet? Please, you guys are high schoolers, you don't have to do that weird waiting game adults play."

I rest my head in my palms. "First off, ouch. We're in a serious relationship, not some high school fling. And second, I just haven't found the right moment. He hasn't said it either, mind you." I face the ground. "We'll probably say it tomorrow."

"Well, do you love him?"

I smile to myself. "That's for him to hear."

Mum rests a hand on my shoulder. "Okay, sweetie." She rubs the muscle there. "But give him a quick text if you don't know where he is. I really changed the conversation topic, huh?"

I nod, switching to the messaging app.

Me: *Having fun without me?*

He responds with a picture of Fritz shirtless in the distance, the pixels blurry and undefined.

Quinton: *more than ever :)*

Me: *Boo what a mickey-mouse photo*

Quinton: *wtf does that mean*

Me: *Take a guess*

Quinton: *ur so weird*

Me: *You love it*

Quinton: *maybe a little*

Quinton: *anyway all we're doing is building sandcastles, going to war with each other, and yelling at each other*

Me: *Sounds delightful*

I shut off my phone and meet with Mum's brown, expectant eyes. I chuckle, scooting away from her. "Oh, my God, you're so nosy. He's at the beach with Fritz. They went to celebrate after Quinton completed his twenty-five-hour course. He did, like, an hour every week to really spread it out — but hey, now my boyfriend is officially a certified lifeguard. He originally wanted to be one for fun, but I guess it's out of necessity now."

She blinks. "He briefly mentioned that to me once…but that's a nice temporary job." She then smiles. "I'm so glad he gets along with Fritz."

I nod.

She sweeps her eyes over the table. "Hey, you haven't eaten anything."

I part my lips to reply, but an urgent knock stops me. It's unusual; a knock at our door is pretty uncommon. "I'll get it."

It's most likely a solicitor or canvasser. I twist my doorknob, foolishly not peeking through the peephole. I look around. My elevated house prevents me from seeing anyone till a voice from below gives itself away.

"Would you be interested in something?" A small-framed young man stares at me, grinning.

What a weird question. He couldn't be more than a year younger than me. In fact, I'd bet money we're the same age. One look into his eyes, and I can see stories of cheer, cleverness, struggle, and the epitome of being 'up to no good.'

I tear my gaze from him to look for Mum, but she's still in the kitchen.

A smile that could only be described as devilish takes over the boy's face. "I'll take that as a yes." Out of seemingly invisible pockets, he retrieves a boatload of mail, and hurls it directly at my face.

I yelp, doubling over instinctively. "Ow — what the hell?" When the mail falls to the floor, I tilt my head up, sharp. The boy, one hundred percent my age, bolts. I do not hesitate to run right after him.

It's unclear if he's aware that I'm behind him. To test, I call out, "Hey, stop!"

Boy, does he stop. His head whips around and movements falter, slowing him down just enough for me to grab his arm. Its thinness surprises me, and I have to tighten my grip quickly before he slips away. He has the nerve to smile as he lifts his free hand — for what I think is a punch — but instead, he adjusts his lopsided beanie.

The small, humanizing movement makes me believe him more when he apologizes. But he's still smiling. "Hey, man, fuck, sorry. I...sorry, I don't have an explanation prepared." He clears his throat. "I seriously meant no harm. It was a boring day and I thought a small prank wouldn't do much harm." A meager excuse, but I soften.

I stare at him, purely confused. "Who the hell are you, and what was that for? I literally have a paper cut on my face." I point with my eyeballs to the light red line on my cheek. When I glance down at him, he still has a damn smile on his face. "What's so funny?"

He shakes his head, chuckling. "I'm sorry, I — it's just hard to take your words seriously with that British accent you've got going." When he sees my face, he bites his tongue and looks away. "Sorry," he mumbles.

It takes guts to insult the one whose face you just papercut. I lower my voice. "Who are you?" For the first time in my life, I see someone frightened by my tone.

He nods, surrendering, yet still looking friendly as ever. "Okay, my name is Rafael."

I don't respond, only wait for him to continue.

He quits moving, defeated. "I didn't mean to hurt you. I just kinda don't live all that well and, I dunno, I wanted some excitement. But, hey, you're definitely my age. You get the adrenaline chase, right? Come on, it's fun living a little." By the tone of his voice, it almost sounds like he's trying to be relatable, to win me over. I snort. Maybe this is some obscure way of soliciting in America.

And if he is trying to win me over, it sort of works, because my feet don't move. "That's your excuse? Really?" I sigh. "Look, Rafael, it's not that deep. But this is an inconvenience. You can't just throw envelopes at people's faces."

He rolls his eyes. "Yeah, well, obviously. I was bored — and I'm sorry! Just, look, let me go. Please don't go to the cops, please. I'm not all that wealthy. I can't have that on my record. I'm — I got a scholarship for FAU and — " he pauses, turning pink — "…and forget I just told you the name of the university. They could revoke it." I stare at his pitiable face. He's just a kid, same as me, executing a poorly thought-out prank. At last, I loosen my grip just enough to lessen the hostile atmosphere.

"Oh, my God, I'm not gonna call the cops." I step back, giving him breathing room. "How old are you?"

Rafael relaxes at the more casual question. "I'm seventeen. But I'm in senior year. Actually — " He lowers his head as if to hide his pride. " — after Florida Atlantic Uni, I'm headed to law school, one hundred percent." He sees my disbelief. "Okay, don't let the baggy clothes and the trolling fool you, all right? I'm gonna be honest, I'm pretty fucking smart."

I narrow my eyes and bite back a laugh at his use of the term "trolling." It almost makes me trust him more. Almost. "Uh…huh. Look, we're both kids, I'm also a senior. I wasn't planning on doing anything. In all honesty, I'm surprised I chased you. It was sort of fight or flight. Your 'troll' was rude, though. Don't do it to us again." When I look up at him, he's grinning again. Seriously.

He notices my irritated expression. "Sorry, man, sorry! That accent is really hard for me to not mock." He kicks the dirt with his shoes. "I just, I wanted some bit of excitement. Being poor isn't easy and judging where you live, you probably understand. Even if that isn't an excuse, I really am sorry. You seem cool, though, if that's any consolation."

I squint. I guess I'll buy it for now. However, for someone so motivated and with so much at risk, how he chose to spend today's leisure time is odd…"You called us neighbors earlier. If you're from around here, how come I've never seen you before?" I try to shift our talk away from interrogation and toward more friendly conversation.

Rafael shrugs. "I don't go outside too often. Studying law to prepare for grad school after undergrad takes a hot minute." His eyes float to my hand, which still locks him in place.

I follow his gaze and release him. "Sorry, there you go. And already? You haven't even started at FAU." I pause. "Why FAU by the way?"

He scrunches his nose. "Someone's nosy. I guess British people are invasive after all."

I scoff with a smile — used to being made fun of for my accent. "What is your problem with British people?"

Rafael tuts, tapping his chin. "What *isn't* my problem with British people?"

I squish the bridge of my nose. "I was just being nice, starting conversation. I am interested in other people's lives, you know."

Rafael chuckles, drawing lines on the dirt beneath us. "Wow, so selfless."

I groan and lightly punch his arm. "Shut up."

He gasps, grabbing his arm as though I'd shot it. "How could you hurt me, stranger?" He waits for me to stop giggling. "For someone who's so curious, I don't even know your name?"

I fall silent, and think. Perhaps it's his wide smile, maybe his youth or spirit, but I trust him enough to tell him my name. "I'm not 'so curious.' And it's Connor."

Rafael hums. "Yeah, I think you are. You're like Curious George."

I shove him back. "Shut up, that makes absolutely no sense."

He giggles and pushes me backward. I stumble further than he probably intended.

Any bystander would assume we're friends of years — or attempting to kill one another.

I raise my hands after a particularly hard shove from Rafael. "Okay, okay. Truce!"

Rafael's composure is not holding up well, seeing as he's laughing harder than I have *ever* seen a boy laugh. It's refreshing, almost. Those who laugh at nearly everything make socializing a million times simpler. "You-you're so weak," he says through short breaths. "I, like, tapped you. You know, I can't believe you've just lived in the neighborhood being my age and shit, and we've never met." I nod in agreement, and he steps closer to me. "Still can't believe how far back I pushed you. Gonna fly away?" He flicks my jacket.

I'm just about to retort when a car stutters to a stop beside us. It's Quinton's car. The sharp, black paint of the automobile mirrors Quinton's dark expression. He peers from the window as his lips curl into a frown.

"Hey, get the fuck off him." Quinton slams the car door shut behind him while Fritz and Karl, pressed against the car's window, visibly snicker.

I exchange a glance with Rafael, both of us aware of the dirt stains on my clothing and our exhausted expressions.

Quinton looms over Rafael, careful to not touch him, but bold enough to stare him down.

I finally move, stepping in front of Rafael. "Quinton, calm down, it's fine. He's just — he's a friend."

Rafael turns to me at that, surprised, but smiles a note later. "Yeah, Connor and I are super good friends…" He throws his arm around my shoulder.

I cringe at the touch at first, but quickly warm up to it. "Quinton, seriously, it's fine. I just talked to him for a good ten minutes. He seems like a cool guy. We met a second ago when he tried pranking me by throwing mail in my face and he lives right down the road." I rest my hand on Quinton's shoulder and reach up to run a finger through his hair. "C'mon, have some trust in people every now and again."

Quinton backs off, his aura amending from hostility to geniality. "Oh, sick. Don't worry, I trust you, and I trust that you're smart to the moon and back. It just looked like you were upset so…but, whatever, nice to meet you…?"

Rafael lifts his head, deep in thought and not quite noticing our eyes on him. "Oh — Rafael," he says quickly.

Quinton shakes his hand. "Quinton."

I tune out their conversation, and call Karl and Fritz out of the car.

The five of us speak for what seems like an hour, laughing and chatting while getting to know Rafael. I look up through my eyelashes, and my gaze lands on Quinton.

As usual, he's breathtaking. Infatuating the other three with his rants and spiels as he always does with a strong, persuasive voice. I scan his body, pleasantly surprised to see Rafael's arm around him. I suppose an hour of talking to such an overtly friendly boy — Rafael — can form bonds after all.

Quinton catches me staring, and his eyes light up in a puppy-like manner.

He hops toward me, lowering his voice. "Can we keep Rafael? He's been here, what, forty-five minutes, and he's already the funniest of the group."

I frown. "I'm the funniest in the group."

Quinton chuckles and slides an easy hand through his hair. "Please, I am. I was just being nice to Rafael. But you don't deserve that same mercy, cocky bastard."

My jaw drops. "You better hope you're kidding. I'll kill you, you filthy American."

Quinton snorts. "At least I'm not British. You're all psychopaths."

I slide a hand down my face. How many times is someone going to bring up my heritage today? "Jesus. You're like a less vulgar version of Rafael. Speaking of, yes we can 'keep him'. I like having him around."

Quinton perks up, ruffling my hair. "Thanks, Connor."

"You don't need my permission, Quinton. In fact — " I raise my voice so all four boys surrounding us can hear — "since you three decided to leave me out of your vacation to the beach, let's all get dinner *together*. With Rafael, if he wants."

Rafael's smile blossoms wide before softening. There's an unreadable glint in his eye. "Really? Thanks, Connor. Mom and Dad are working late tonight, so I'd have been home alone." He pats me on the back

"No problem." I turn to Quinton and jab his side for his attention. "You ready to go? We can head to my house, it's, like, right there. Do some work, hang out, and head out to dinner?"

A look takes over Quinton's face and he pulls me aside. "Yeah, also, are you sure about letting Rafael into your house? I like him, but…what if he doesn't even live near. Or, I don't know, is lying."

I sigh into a smile. "I'm not just going to let a stranger into my house. I'm not that naive. I texted Mum a picture of him earlier. She recently became friends with his parents — they've been 'waiting for us to meet for the past few months,' or whatever." I eye Rafael. "Really weird that Rafael has never stumbled around here until now. I'm out all of the time doing yard work or walking Birdie and haven't seen him before."

Quinton's facial tension lifts, excitement setting in like a second skin. "Of course — I shouldn't have questioned you. That is kinda odd, though. Maybe he just doesn't go out much?"

"Who knows?" After ruffling Quinton's hair, I inch toward the car, sliding right into shotgun. "Everyone get in! Oh, and dibs on shotgun."

A few groans about me getting the best seat in the car float around, followed by the scuffling of three bodies in the backseats.

"We're in," Karl informs me, squished between Rafael and Fritz.

I eye the three up and down. "You guys seem snug," I flip on the radio.

Quinton raises an eyebrow with a grin. "Why'd you turn the radio on? You're so weird, we're basically at your house already." Quinton sighs dramatically.

I narrow my eyes, scoffing. "Do you have a problem with me listening to music? You gonna sue me or something?"

"I won't, but my parents might!" He references the threat we received, or he received, from his now unofficial parents way back in the beginning of our relationship. We share a traumatized laugh, and he taps the brakes, pulling us into my driveway.

The car halts abruptly. "All right, everyone out," Quinton orders us. We listen and hop onto the cement.

The moment all five of us are in the house, and then my room, a tiredness overtakes me. Perhaps it's the comfort of my home or the fact that I was socializing outside for the past hour. The other boys dance around together, settling on my bed. A cool quietness falls upon us, giving me strength to get off the bed and grab Karl's and my med-work.

Karl, clearly unhappy with the new silence, ruins the peaceful atmosphere by grabbing a pillow. "Quinton!" Karl hollers and slams a pillow on him. Quinton retaliates and hits him with a nearby pillow.

They proceed to accidentally hit Rafael and Fritz, who were practicing pick-up lines on each other. More of us are drawn into battle.

I exhale lightly, drowning out their screams and laughs to become something I rarely ever am: the only one in the room taking work seriously.

After an hour of my pencil scribbling and fingers typing on autopilot, I present a boatload of completed work to the gang. "Okay, guys, let's go. You three clearly seem to be distracting Karl, and he hasn't gotten anything done." I interrupt myself to scowl at their lowered heads. "But I have gotten stuff done for once, and I'm ready to leave."

Quinton slips off the bed, grinning. "You? Willingly doing work while the rest of us mess around? I'm shocked."

I scrunch my nose. "Wow, way to invalidate all my hard work, dick."

He snickers and pulls me to his side. "Not invalidating, simply voicing my astonishment. Now let's *go*." In a second, Quinton is packed and standing at the edge of my room's door. With no other option, I sigh, chuckling as I tie my shoelaces. I lean on him as we all walk out of the house, and the five of us skip into the car.

Fritz and Rafael slump in the front seats, Fritz driving, while Quinton, Karl, and I position ourselves in the back, electing Karl to sit in the middle seat. "Let'sa go!" Karl jumps in his seat while speaking, notching the energy up bit by bit. Rafael mimics him, and soon the phrase is bouncing around the car like a flock of birds chirping back and forth.

Fritz raises his free hand to silence us. "Okay, okay, guys, chill, we're going." He hits the gas, driving us into a bomb of midnight wonder — better known as "boys' night out."

The moon fully assists us, providing light for us throughout the drive. How could a simple rock be so bright? I smile. Not everything has to be a star to shine.

When we arrive at the restaurant, Quinton takes over from Fritz, drops us off, and parks. He meets us back after we've been seated, and we spend our time at the restaurant simply talking. Eating too, of course, but most is spent laughing and chit-chatting about the future, Cars 2, and our sex lives (well-rounded, I know). And it's *fun*.

I wouldn't have called myself a *loner* in high school, but my number of close friends never exceeded three or four. And I wasn't one to interest myself in making acquaintances or friends that I'd talk to in school, but never hang out with outside of it. This being, my close friends were also my *only* friends, shoutout to Fritz, Tina, and Theo.

This is different.

This is nice.

There were quiet, boring moments throughout the night, but what's light without darkness? Awkward silences can strengthen bonds...maybe, right? I'm not an expert in friendship, but I can tell we'll last. The, admittedly, funniest person in our group speaks up, kicking at the dust right outside the restaurant.

Rafael. "Hey guys, I just wanted to say thanks for inviting me. Especially you, Connor, seriously, man, I've been so busy with school, finding people to hang out with is harder. Pretty shocked you let me come, too. Like, not gonna lie, if this was the other way around, I probably wouldn't have let a random, scruffy boy in my car."

I squint, shifting my weight to my left foot. "Is that supposed to be a compliment?"

Rafael shakes his head in a flurry and laughs. "Sorry! Sorry, I wasn't finished. What I was going to say was, again, thank you. Tonight was super fun, and I wanna hang out again."

"Raf, you helped us go crazy tonight, no way in hell are you not officially added to the gang," Karl speaks for us, swinging an arm over his shoulder. "Besides, you have our numbers already. Make a group chat so we can hang out again sometime?"

The four of us nod in agreement, and I shift feet back toward the car.

"Let's all get out of here." Quinton kisses my head, and wraps his fingers around mine.

Fritz runs his hand up his arm. "Yeah, all feral nights must come to an end."

"I'm tired, we need to quit stalling. Let's go." I stand on my tippy toes and kiss Quinton's lips. I suddenly grow very self-conscious and recall that Rafael is ignorant of our relationship. I turn my head to see him looking; however, there's no surprise or reaction on his face. Yeesh, are Quinton and I that obvious?

Fritz speaks instead. "Guys. No more PDA. I swear, they were flirting the entirety of dinner. 'Ah, no, Quinton don't be so annoying, ugh, Quintie, help me open this ketchup packet, don't touch my food, ugh, I love you — '"

I kick Fritz in the shin, and he squeals. "I do not talk like that."

We arrive at the car, and I hop in with zero hesitation.

"Hey, Rafael, where do you live again?"

Rafael jumps after being spoken to for the first time in twenty minutes, and I drowsily lift my head off his shoulder.

"Oh, hope I didn't wake you two up, but we dropped off Fritz and you're the last person, so." Quinton rubs his neck, eyeing us through the rear-view mirror.

"Oh! Um, just drop me off where you picked me up, I can walk back home."

I look up at him. "Are you sure?"

Rafael nods.

"Okay."

QUINTON

"Quinton." A teasing voice comes from the boy wrapped around my back. When I turn to get a view of the culprit, Connor, I find him staring and smiling as moonlight highlights his hair. Though he still seems half-asleep, a smile remains on his face. He pecks my nose and exhales a soft breath on my cheek. I open my mouth to question him, but he shuts me up, resting his finger on my lips. "Let me look," he murmurs, "just let me look for a second longer."

I let him, sucking in a short breath. I inhale the comfort of his precious smell as he continues to grace me with his closeness.

Connor pulls back, no longer crowding my face with his swoon-worthy eyes. "Thank you." He inhales deeply. "You're perfect, you know? You give my life — " he lazily motions his arms in a circular motion. " — life. I dunno." His words are soft, real, and slurred in his sleepy state.

"I couldn't agree more." The rest of the world feels irrelevant when I'm with him.

Warmth trickles into my heart, spinning round and round. A slow process, delicate even, but definite. But this is stronger than my heart warming. It's heating. Burning, scorching, scathing, *loving*. My heart is loving Connor, and it's finally beating for the first time in its life.

I love Connor.

"You mean everything to me," I continue. "Please, Connor, promise you'll never go away, or, I mean, if I fuck up you have every right to, not to be toxic or controlling or anything it's a metapho — "

He silences me with a kiss, and his cold lips freeze my worries away. "I promise."

CONNOR

I jump out of bed, practically unable to contain my smile. I drag my gaze across the room in search of my newly six-month…boyfriend. He's not here. I don't dwell on his absence too long; my mind remains focused on the fact that high school is almost over and, of course, that today is our anniversary.

I splash my face with water and rush out from my door.

Mum sits on a small stool next to Quinton, and she greets me, blowing a kiss my way.

I reply with a grin, turning to Quinton. I slide into his arms and place a mighty kiss on his cheek.

Quinton chuckles with what could only be described as overwhelming affection. "Connor, good morning!" He runs a finger up my chin before effortlessly pulling me back in for a kiss on the lips. The loving action seems to hold residue of frustration, however. "You weren't supposed to wake up yet. I was gonna give you breakfast in bed." He gestures to the half-prepared plate before him, frowning.

I groan, pecking the down expression off his face. "The sentiment counts, don't worry."

Mum gives me a repulsed look while simultaneously trying to not grin. "Sheesh, get a room you two!"

If I had a penny for every time she used that exact phrase, we'd fall out of the margins of poverty. It's routine for Quinton and me to engage in some form of PDA, elicit a disgusted reaction from Mum, and yet later have her gush over how adorable we are.

I'd even dare to say we have a family dynamic. We live in harmony financially as well. With Quinton making money as a lifeguard, the weight on Mum's back has loosened enough for her to finally *relax*, if you could believe it. With her eye circles barely noticeable, and a new stream of income, it's safe to say we're happy. Stressed about the future constantly, but happy. As long as Quinton and I continue our daily checks on the dolls, I'm not thinking about potential death as often either.

I blow raspberries at Mum, facing back to Quinton and picking a hair off his hoodie. "Well, I am so sorry for ruining your little cliché gift. But thank you anyways. I truly appreciate it, I do."

Quinton knocks my arm from his shoulder and snickers. "It is so hard to tell when you're being sarcastic or not, you know. You have, like, an identical tone whether you're being genuine or satirical."

I stutter in defense. "Well…get better tone decipherers then! I was being serious."

Quinton snorts, amusement swimming up his smile. "Tone decipherers? Do you mean ears?"

I snatch the fork from the table and prod at my eggs. "Sure, yeah, whatever. Intellectualism hater."

Quinton sighs warmly before casting a longing stare at the food he's prepared. "I wish I could've delivered this to you in bed as you deserve."

I chuckle, patting his back. "It's okay, weirdo. You're still my lovely little cook, food delivered to me or not. Let's eat it here, anyway. I'd rather eat near you than you just serving me."

"Aww. You're fun when you're nice to me." He returns to his cooking and hums softly.

Mum stands to scrape her plate. "Well, that's my cue to leave. I'm gonna hang out with some friends. I'll catch you two later!"

I raise my eyebrows, clutching her arm before she can leave. "Friends? I mean, no offense, but since when?"

Mum spins to meet my eyes, and she rests her hands on her hips. "Well, first off, rude, you imp, and second, ever since your hunk of meat moved in and started paying some of the rent, I've had time to meet people. Only took six years after emigrating from Europe to make friends. So, thanks." She drops her gaze to her watch, sharply inhaling. "Okay, I gotta go, sweetie. Have a great day, you two!" She waves goodbye and gently closes the door.

Quinton eyes me from the side, arms still at work. "So, Connor, whatcha got planned for me today, hm?" His tone could only be described as sultry. Or playful. It's always a challenge to tell when he's trying to seduce me or just being himself.

"You'll see."

He flicks his wrist — it sends his pancake flying through the air. "I guess I'll have to take your word for it. And here." Quinton slides me a plate with a pancake on it, already covered in syrup, just how I like.

"Thank you." I bury my fork in the cake and take a large bite. My eyes widen, tongue welcoming the sweet bursts of flavor and fluffy texture. After swallowing, I smile ear to ear. "When the hell did you learn how to cook? Why are you this good at making pancakes?"

Quinton kicks back, resting his elbow against the counter beside him. "Thank you, thank you. Allow me to explain. I cooked a lot when I was little, but just as a hobby. Okay, God, I have such a privileged white male sob story, but my parents worked late almost every night. I was sick of ordering in alone from the thirty dollars they'd leave resting on the counters, so I'm self-taught." He puffs out his chest. "A self-taught, talented chef."

"That you are. Even if that is quite the rich white male sob story." I snicker.

Quinton shrugs carefreely, sticks his fork into his pancake, and takes a bite. "Delectable." His poorly constructed British accent throws me off guard. He looks up at me with big eyes and a wide smile. "Wouldn't you agree?"

And my senses short-circuit. Because here he is. Romance is a simple word compared to how I feel about Quinton. 'Romance' couldn't describe my instinct to be near him. It could never articulate my heart's erratic beating every time he smiles. My inability to grow bored with him, or how comfortable I am when I'm bored with him. My need to adore his body and his heart and his mind. There's a better word to describe how I feel about Quinton. A more powerful word to explain what we have.

Love.

I blink, staring at him through my lashes, getting a good look at his confused face.

I've completely fallen in love with this Quinton Hansley.

Quinton furrows his eyebrows, patience running out. "Hey, answer me. Too busy getting lost in my eyes?"

I slap his hand, intercepting its path to cup my cheek. "No!" Most definitely yes. I poke his nose and scoot back out of my chair. "Come on, I'm done eating. Let's make this the best day ever."

"Let's."

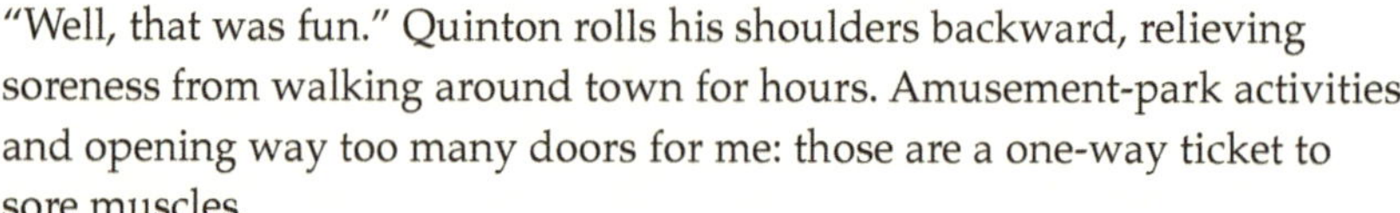

"Well, that was fun." Quinton rolls his shoulders backward, relieving soreness from walking around town for hours. Amusement-park activities and opening way too many doors for me: those are a one-way ticket to sore muscles.

I nod. "Mission accomplished, then."

Quinton hurls his bag to the side and yelps when it meets close to the edge of our home's flat roof.

"Jesus Christ, be careful." I rub my temple and sit him down on the dull, green folding chair.

He slumps in his new seat and stares up at me. "Connor, can I see the big gift you planned now? It's evening, and I already gave you, like, three." He slides his elbows to rest on the fragile chair arms as his eyes narrow at the blinding, orangey-yellow sun setting in front of us.

I try to contain my excitement. "Ugh, yes, yes, I suppose you may. I have a question though first, do you still *want to know everything about me because you've only met a small part of me and you're already obsessed.*"

Quinton squints. "Weird…oddly familiar phrasing of a question."

I haul my bag closer to my feet and pull out a card. *The* card. "It's probably familiar because you wrote a similar line six months ago." I display the card written in his handwriting.

Quinton's smile falters before widening once again. "No — no way, you kept my apology letter from the day I asked you out?" His hand juts out, and he snatches the letter from me.

"Well? Are you still obsessed?"

He nods, reading the letter over and over. "God, I am obsessed, Connor." He raises his head to look me in the eye. "Never doubt that."

I chuckle and turn to face the halfway-set sun.

Quinton shuffles in his seat. "Ahh, memories. Is that your gift, doll?" He opens his mouth to thank me, but I stop him by resting a finger on his lips.

"Obviously that's not the full gift, idiot. Here — " I reach into the handbag beside me, getting hold of a small slip of paper. "…you go," I mumble, growing nervous. Deciding on a good gift was difficult. There's not a lot I could give him that'd be super remarkable since he grew up getting diamond-plated Legos for Christmas. Pretty much everything expensive I picked felt like giving wine to Jesus, as if it was something special compared to what he's gotten from his family in the past. So I thought big. There's a chance he won't accept it, which is terrifying. But love is all about risks anyway.

I stretch back to my original position on the chair and present the gift in my hands.

Quinton gives me a questioning glance and takes the paper from me. "Is this another note I forgot I gave you?" He jokes.

I don't respond, watching him intently as his eyes drag across the page. His jaw opens further and further with every word he reads. "You — Oh, my God, no way! Connor, you actually — what? You — this is a contract! You got us a place? How did you, Oh, my God — this house is so cute! Wait, is this why you asked me about my dream house in full detail that one time? How long were you planning this?! Thank — thank you, holy shit." He meets my eyes with sparkling green ones.

While inspecting his face, I catch a hint of darkness behind the excitement. It's only for a trillionth of a second, but a pained, immensely distraught look takes over his expression before dissolving into joy once again.

I ignore it and kiss his lips for a few beats. "You're welcome, idiot. I'm so glad you like it. It's not fully paid, like whatsoever, and we're gonna have to pay it off in at least one year and a half. So try not to get fired, yeah?" I wink at him. "We're moving in the day after school ends! So, we have to start packing now…I don't know how feasible it is to get a moving truck, especially because we have to be very budget-strict now, but we can drive our shit with your car right? It's really close to Mum's place, actually, so very convenient if I do say — "

He cuts me off, sealing my lips shut with a kiss. It's emotional, rough. Firm and tender. Breathing slowly, Quinton pulls away from my face, and he presses his mouth into a thin line. "I…Connor, I love you. So much. I really, really love you. More — more than anyone and anything ever." He cuts himself off, though it seems like he wants to say more. But what more could he say?

He dives in for another kiss.

I accept it. I long to remain in the kiss, but I cannot go another second without replying, and I tug back. "I love you too, Quinton. More than anything and anyone." I nearly tip off the roof as I crawl in his lap and sink into his arms. "So, so much."

Quinton mutters something under his breath, burrowing his head into my shirt's blue hem. I crack my mouth to ask what he said, but he isn't done speaking.

"You're everything," he mumbles. "I'm sorry."

Sorry?

CHAPTER 11

You're such an idiot, Connor."

While my teeth grit and eyes twitch, I hit Quinton discreetly on the thigh. "Shut up and smile for the picture! Mum will kill us both if we don't get at least one cute graduation pic." I crank my faux enthusiasm up and pose with Quinton in the most platonic way possible. The camerawoman shifts on the stone beneath her, giving us a thumbs up and calming the storm in my stomach. The camera clicks and Quinton pulls me closer, ignoring our fellow students swarming around the area. "You're cute," he whispers.

I blush, chuckling. "Quinton! Get off me, the poor camerawoman is waiting for us." I roll my eyes at his antics, privately adoring them.

Or, at least that's how I expected this day to go.

He in fact did not pull me closer.

Or call me cute.

He didn't spare a single moment to look at me.

I sigh, wiping my sleeve beneath my nose. Just because he's not being a flirt 24/7 doesn't mean he has hidden feelings about me. Nit-picking Quinton's every movement and mannerism these past two months since our sixth-month are making me a little crazy. Calling him "closed-off" is too aggressive of a term, but calling him just 'off' doesn't fit either.

My inner monologue is disrupted by a rude yank on my arm. Yelping, I flick my eyes up and see the back of Quinton's head.

"We gotta go. They need us for more pics." His voice is low and distracted.

I yank myself from his grip. "Quinton, what the fuck. Give me a warning before you grab me like that."

His eyes wander to my hand and he grasps my arm delicately. He sucks in a pained breath before muttering an apology.

He doesn't owe me random compliments all the time. He's not obligated to shower me with affection, or tell me meaningful *I love yous* every single night.

However, his distance from me is becoming the norm of our relationship, and I can't help but worry. All I can do is hope his progressive detachment is just a fluctuation, soon to go away and bring us back to normal. But this is likely an anomaly, not the norm.

He loves me, after all.

That, I have no doubt. But there's more to a bond with someone than just love. A relationship of only love is superficial — the little things, the friendship, makes it a relationship.

He feels like my lover, but the "friend" in "boyfriend" seems to be lacking lately, and God knows why. Perhaps this is another relationship rocky road, a phase. I can buy that. His parents recently cut him off, we moved into a new house, and school is over for good. But I can't help but wonder what the *sole* push for the change was.

The behavior began after our six-month anniversary, but I read that day as wonderful, not a reason to become more distant. I suppose people change, and it's still Quinton. Just less goofy, more tired, and far less confident. A watered-down version of my lover.

QUINTON

I bang my head against the empty school bathroom mirror, overflowing with self-pity while Connor waits for me outside. Meeting my own eyes, I cringe.

What the hell is wrong with me?

Connor is the love of my life, and he's fallen for someone who lets their pride dictate their life. One who can't talk about their feelings without seeming like an absolute asshole.

I squint my blurry eyes, examining my own features. When did my hair get so brown? When did my eye creases get so…creased? When will

Connor have enough of me alienating myself from him? I have to play this *right*.

The desire to tell him my worries is a teasing nightmare. It seems as if it would be freeing to tell the man I'm in love with what's stressing me out, yet it's like a mental block. I can't help but think that telling him would do the worst thing possible — destabilize our relationship. I've forgotten how to speak when it comes to this. That could be because my problems are invalid. If someone's so scared to communicate a feeling, maybe it's because that feeling is unjustified. Or wrong.

But it's fine. It's okay.

"It's fine, it's okay." So long as we love each other. But if I keep acting like this, Connor might stop loving me.

"Quinton?" Speak of the devil. A pensive face appears from around the door's corner. Connor Jones. I watch him study my face with his lips pursed in a thin line.

Like a deer in headlights, I can't turn away from him, and I maintain eye contact for what feels like minutes. We cannot have this conversation now. Not here, at the very least.

"Quinton? What's wrong? You look…" But it's too late. His eyes darken. "You look so sad."

His voice softens and he brings a hand down to my cheek to wipe a tear. But, his chivalrous act only results in his nail striking my pupil.

I wince and clench my teeth. "Fuck, ow!" Writhing from the jab, I trip on myself, but Connor breaks my clumsy fall.

He runs a hand up my sleeve and warms my neck with breathy laughs. "I'm — sorry. Goodness, you are so dramatic, all I did was poke your eye." He brings a finger to my cheek and hauls me back to my feet.

I chuckle, almost forgetting my breakdown.

Almost.

It's jarring that a single man known as Connor could vaporize my distress with a wink, smile, and jab to the eye. Love truly does heal. "Jesus," Connor huffs, "who gave eyeballs the right to be so sensitive? I wonder, like, the adaptive reason for that." I tilt my head down to look at him.

He's smart. I'm sure he's noticed my behavior change — he won't settle for a lie, he knows me too well. "Hey, Connor. Listen, I'm fine. There's…a thing going on, and I will tell you about it, I will. I'm just not ready right now. But when I figure out how to communicate my feelings properly, you'll be the first to know. Promise."

Connor's face starts to crumple. "Okay, but what is so difficult about telling me specifically this? We've been together for, what, eight months? Known each other for a year? You always tell me things." He takes a shaky breath to stabilize his voice. "You've been so…different since our six-month anniversary, and that was two months ago. How much time does someone need?"

I smooth my hair down with a frigid hand. "Aw, Connor, you're so worried about me. Don't lose sleep over it, okay? I'll be — "

My hand travels toward his waist, but Connor snatches my wrist mid-air. "Don't deflect. I'm not an idiot." He looks at his feet. "Just tell me what's up?" Connor sighs. "I just…I feel like I have to *try* to receive love from you. Or affection. I mean it's not that big of a deal. But I cherish your compliments and, like, *affection* because now it seems incremental. Like I'm supposed to earn your love, or something." He loses his words for a moment before recomposing. "I'm definitely blowing things out of proportion, but…it feels like your satisfaction with me is something that could run out." His words fade off into a whisper, and he looks away with a lowered head.

And my head fucking *spins*.

He doesn't feel loved.

Connor doesn't feel loved. How could I work so *backward* from my goal?

I sweep him into a firm hug and begin tearing up once more. "Shit, Connor, I'm so sorry. Fuck. I'm sorry. Listen." I gently guide his jaw to keep our eyes locked. "I love you. Okay? I love you. To sell my love to you would be like selling time to a clock. Or — fucking, selling stars to space. I'm not gonna stop loving you; it's eternal. I promise. Our love means everything to me, I swear."

He snickers, sounds of joy seeping out with his tears. "Okay, fine, you little poet. But you have to tell me soon." He takes my hand. "Let me help you. I can. We'll do this together."

I grin, ignoring the boiling pot of guilt in my stomach. "Thank you, Connor."

He lets out a stretched breath. "You better be sorry. Don't continue this gimmick of being shitty when you're sad." He straightens his back into a regal position, enunciating his accent. "I simply won't have it."

I release a strangled chuckle. "I guess I must fix my ways then, hm? For you. Thank you for being awesome to me even when I suck."

Connor lifts his head from my hug, innocently cocking his head to the side. "But, you always suck?"

I snort and push him away. "C'mon, idiot, we have a ceremony to get to — grab your things. I promise I'll tell you soon."

Connor nods, looping his bag over his elbow and exiting.

I follow him. I exhale some sort of laugh through my nostrils. Now I have to tell him in time. Dread is the worst feeling.

"Woohoo, school's out, let's go! Also, Connor, y'all's house is awesome." Fritz smashes his can of beer against Rafael's and turns to rub the arm of our living room couch. He then throws an arm around Quinton.

Quinton responds with a nervous chuckle and looks at me.

I lift my hand — an attempt to be the voice of reason. "Guys, don't go too crazy. We have work tomorrow, and *Quinton*, we have our brunch thing tomorrow Mum really cares about."

"But it'd be so funny if we get the police called on us for noise complaints a second time." Karl's arm swiftly reaches for more rum that'd leave him blacked-out, and I give his wrist a brisk slap.

Quinton promptly nods. "I agree, Connor," is all he says. But, scant sentences that Grammarly would be *begging* to improve are typical of Quinton lately. Small, stale phrases are a luxury compared to complete silence, I suppose.

"Oh, come on, you two. Let's pop *off* tonight! We're men now." Rafael yanks Quinton and me closer to him and the others, sparking a new irritation in me. "At least drink one can. Come one, don't be a loser." He holds out two cans, fresh and icy, luring themselves to our lips.

I roll my eyes. "N — "

"Fine." Quinton gives a controlled nod and extends an arm toward the drink in Rafael's hand. Beer is disgusting, but Quinton seems to disagree tonight.

He dances his finger over the cap, prying it open with ease.

I brush off how attractive the skill behind his movement was and rest my hand on his arm. "Quinton? Are you sure you wanna drink? You're such a lightweight, and it's late."

This gets a *laugh* out of Quinton. "Okay, grandpa. When else am I supposed to drink? Midday?" He takes a long swig from the can, looks away from me, and asks, "What? Is everything okay?"

I narrow my eyes at his unpredictable changes in attitude. He's hard to read. He's impenetrable. *Mystifying.*

I shouldn't have the burden of dissecting my boyfriend's emotions like he's a fucking junior high English quiz. I'm trying to respect the wish he expressed just yesterday at graduation — to lay off and not question his behavior until he's ready. But I'm growing impatient.

"Yes."

Quinton grins. "Perfect. I can see it on your face, you know, I'm being boring and sad lately! This is my chance to show you it's still fun old me. Besides, I'll only have a little." He gives me one of his signature charming smiles.

An intoxicated Rafael snorts. "Come on, Quinton. Have a lot. Connor, you won't be too mad, right?"

I don't answer. Quinton's weird, unstable behavior is scary — instability always means change could happen. Something awful like a breakup — God forbid — or somehow something worse. People have left my life in the past, fast as a snap. In their defense, it wasn't always their choice. Dad, for example, didn't *want* to be crushed in the construction site that his boss warned him wasn't stable enough yet. Quinton taps my foot with his shoe, asking for approval.

I shake my head to clear my thoughts. "Okay, um, sure. Please don't get totally hammered, Quinton, okay? You have work tomorrow. And I'll have some beer too then, I guess, but only a little." And I do. I have a little. I keep my word and have a little.

But Quinton does not.

The butterfly effect is a wonder. It a spice of life — it allows the random to have meaning. The expected doesn't keep us sane, and the unexpected does, a brilliant balance that we can thank the butterfly effect for. It makes triviality a myth. And I believe it makes the little things important to life, granting worth to even the tiniest movements — how would the world differ if you placed your hand two inches to the right rather than three? Or if you decided to sneeze into your right arm rather than left?

The butterfly effect is bittersweet, of course. For example, the simple pestering from Fritz to get me off my feet and drive me to that one football game led me to Quinton. The man I love.

But, again, it has its drawbacks — like my coma, like Quinton's parents. And like last night. The awful decision to let Quinton take the beer can from Rafael. The awful decision to let Quinton and Rafael go out alone — resulting in Quinton's permanent suspension from his job.

"You. Got. Fired?" I squeeze my head, grinding my teeth with terrifying force. "Why are you telling me this while we're in the car driving?" I can sense Quinton's guilt, and his sense of self-worth deteriorating by the second.

I bite my lip, trying to sound more supportive. Quinton is probably far more stressed out than I am. When I meet his eyes, I'm greeted with his doe-eyes at full capacity, round and guilty, before he looks at the road again.

"I'm sorry I — Connor, you have to understand what happened. Rafael — look, I got dared to prank my, um, my, what's it called — boss, yes my boss. Or, not my boss, it could've been a coworker, but we chose my boss when we arrived. I was drunk, and I didn't mean to! Also, Rafael told me to, but it's not his fault. She fired me, but, hey, at least she cut us some slack and didn't report us to the police, but she basically swore up and down I'd never get a job as a lifeguard in Florida ever again. Which is barely mercy, what we did was perfectly legal, just annoying." He cuts his excuse short, morphing into an apologetic tone. "Anyway, I'm so sorry. It's all my fault and — Oh, my God, I deserve…I'm so sorry. You don't have to forgi — "

"Quinton, it's okay."

I rub his shoulder, not only to comfort him but to distract myself from the clawing rat of dread in my stomach. "You worked hard for that job and really enjoyed it, so are you sure *you're* okay? Forget about me for a second." Being a lifeguard was something Quinton heavily prided himself on. Not only did he love feeling like an overseer and protector, but he had a knack for swimming thanks to the athleticism gained from his cheerleading. He admired his tan in the mirror, and no matter the weather conditions, he remained an on-time, responsible employee. Even though the job was something fifteen-year-olds applied for, he didn't care. He simply seemed happy at work.

"I'm fine, in terms of my job. Thank you for asking. I'll just find work somewhere else, it'll be okay." Quinton lifts a hand off the wheel to touch my arm.

"That's good to hear." I bite my lip, debating whether to bring up our graduation conversation from yesterday. I decide to. "Quinton, I know I asked you this in the bathroom during graduation, but I was wondering if you were ready to tell me what's up yet?"

He looks down at me with his striking green eyes. He blinks just once before sighing defeatedly. "Look, ever since…well okay…Oh, my God,

I'm sorry, I don't know why I'm struggling so hard, I just don't want you to see me in a different light." The car slowly comes to a stop as Quinton pulls over next to the road right by our house. But he remains seated. The fact we're having a conversation tonight quickly solidifies.

"A different light? Quinton, I…I love you no matter what. What did you do?" Despite my gentle coaxing, I'm apprehensive about what he may admit to.

Rather than a confession, I'm hit with more stalling. "Not 'no matter what.'" Like a paper you couldn't even imagine folding any further, Quinton's face wrinkles in misery.

Twisting in my seat to look at him, I grow frustrated. "Damn, Quinton, just be honest with me, that's literally what boyfriends do for each other. Your ugly sides are welcome here — just tell me so you can stop distancing yourself from me as if you hate me."

He looks heavily conflicted for a moment, but then sighs. "Okay, okay. It's…" He holds his breath in such a theatrical way, he could be mistaken for a high school drama teacher. "It's guilt. It's guilt for not being able to take care of you like I wanted to. The — the day you bought us the house I was delighted to live with the most amazing person in my life. But — God this is so hard to word — I was upset that I couldn't be the one buying the place. And providing, like, shelter, or just in general. God, it sounds so stupid, but every time I was reminded I couldn't…. It sucked so hard. I couldn't stare at you as long without noticing your eye circles and really pale skin…you're having to work extra hours because lifeguarding pays so little and your mom couldn't help anymore. Rafael told me you'd probably want a little space now that we were graduating, moving, and having all these changes. I guess I gave you too much space." He speaks no more, staring at the wheel.

"So. It's a pride thing. Can't stand not being the number one provider?" My eyes bore into the side of his head. "Couldn't do something like get a new job? Instead you had to look away every time you saw my frail, porcelain skin?" Pride, a deadly sin, and the cause of two months of fucking…*torment!*

Quinton's lips tug downward, regret soon replaced with desperation. "Whoa, hey, no you gotta understand it's not, like, a toxic masculinity thing or pride thing. Well, I guess it's kinda a pride thing, but Rafael suggested a while ago — "

"I don't *care* what Rafael suggested. Why would you think I'd want space? I'm in love with you, you idiot. I want anything but space." I face the windshield in front of us. "You've been unresponsive because you feel emasculated by me making money — "

"No, no, no, I *just* said it doesn't have anything to do with masculinity. It's not you making money, it's me *not* making money…or, fuck." His voice trembles, begging for an inkling of understanding from me. "When I fell for you, I was excited to spoil you rotten — gift-giving is my love language! I feel like I'm failing you."

A cold breath swims from my throat. "…so, once again. I'm being told the cause of all my anxiety, was your self-pity? Was because *gift-giving is your love language?* Do you hear yourself!?" I cannot be calmed down with that classic explanation: the villain was tormented by guilt himself, the villain wanted to protect you, the villain didn't mean to, you felt that because *they* were hurting. I don't buy it.

Not that Quinton would ever be a villain in my book.

Quinton brings me back to the present, eyes wild. "This is exactly why I didn't tell you what was on my mind. I couldn't trust that you'd give me the benefit of the doubt and support me!" Quinton's voice sounds genuinely fearful.

"You truly expect me to help you after waiting a millennium for you to tell me? Now we're both hurt, and that has nothing to do with me. You should've trusted my 'benefit of the doubt,' but it's too late. Not my fault you don't trust me, or whatever."

Quinton's vision seems to shift, fear and worry flitting too fast across his eyes for me to keep up with. "No, I *trust* you, of course I do. But I'm still going to be cautious around my very…judgmental partner. I was worried you might like or love me less for it. This reaction is exactly why I didn't tell you. You're literally proving my point." Quinton takes a deep breath.

We go back and forth, spitting more comments neither of us means.

Quinton's hands cover his face. "Jesus, Connor. I still expected support. Especially after you basically forced this confession out of me when I wasn't ready — "

"You're a grown-ass man. Shouldn't take two months for you to speak to me. I'm *so* sorry for "forcing" something out of you that made you neglect me for two months! You're talking as if you didn't have time to figure out how to talk to me." I take a lengthy inhale. "You…you fucked me, Quinton. God, all that time spent worrying alone in our room, and for what? This completely handleable problem?" I shake my head, furious.

"Just because I don't tell you exactly how I'm feeling *one time* because I'm afraid you'll lash out, which might I add, you did lash out, doesn't mean I'm some monster."

My head slams into the seat behind me. I'm growing tired of this endless table tennis warfare. "Don't minimize it with a 'one time.' The 'one time' you weren't open lasted two months. Yeah, my reaction isn't ideal, but if you'd told me earlier, and if you were in touch with your emotions — "

Quinton's groan is guttural and demoralized. "You don't think I'm trying to get better at emotions? We can't afford therapy, so I'm learning the best I can, Connor. I'm growing out of the mindsets my parents drilled into my head. From day one I was taught to conceal everything real I felt, thanks to them. Point is, I wanna be in a relationship with you because I love you. I love our love. And I wanted to love you as best as I could, and when I felt like I couldn't, it sucked. So I didn't tell you why, because I was also worried telling you would jeopardize our love."

"What is it with you and "our love"? It's not its own thing, our love is composed of you and me, it's not a third party. Just, whatever. This fight is stupid and I'm tired. I'll try to be more friendly, I guess, but you still treated me poorly for two months straight."

"Okay, doll." Beatless, the words pass by with no inflection, no stutter. No care.

And he leaves.

And I leave.

I need a break, so I pass him on his way to the house and beat him to our room. I step inside, lock the door, and flip a small sign we have outside the door to read "Connor's >:(". We made it so whenever we seriously need alone time, the other doesn't knock or come in unless of emergency. It's only been used one other time by Quinton — after he and I had a huge argument about whether or not water was wet. I'm sick of the outdated debate but scientifically, it obviously is, by the way.

I flop onto our covers, kicking the door shut with an outstretched leg. I play with my fingers on the bed and scan our walls for distractions. But there are only framed photos I'm already too familiar with.

Jesus fucking Christ. I fall backward, hitting my bed with a quiet thump.

After angrily poking and prodding the pillows, I haul myself from my bed and fix the sheets. The wrinkles burnish out, leaving a polished look. I repeat this activity, until the room is spotless.

Pausing my stress-clean, I hang my head beneath our bed and look around for misfit objects. I suck in a sharp breath, finding two dusty dolls locked in their respective glass cases. The dolls. My stomach hollows more than before.

"You little…fuckers." The words leak with hate. I grunt, reaching for the safe. I punch the numbers in, the code simply being my birthday, and grab the doll that looks like me. As my fingers touch the fabric I feel that exact touch on the exact spot; the surreality never gets old. I gently set the safe aside and move my body back on top of my bed while inspecting my doll. A truth flits through my brain in a nanosecond, one brought from waves of anger toward Quinton. A logical dilemma I may very well need to decipher someday.

What will we do about the dolls if we ever need to break up?

I have to refrain from punching myself. What a stupid prospect to entertain. He's everything to me, even with all his flaws. But no amount of self-reassuring can stop the panic from flaring in my throat. It's a valid question.

My breathing deepens as I look back at the eerie lookalike doll in my hands. What the fuck even is this? It's a magical doll, from some random shop Quinton went to when he was small? My face contorts, every feature squeezing and stretching on my skin. Quinton has the ability to make dolls, seeing as he made one of himself, so what if he was lying? What if he was a stalker, or something, who made this of me? No, that's ridiculous. My thoughts run wild, each grotesque possibility stopping at nothing to reach the forefront of my mind. I bite my lip and allow my tears to flood my face. My shoulders wilt into a droop. Why am I so annoyed by this 'fight?' How will I handle myself when Quinton and I actually go through something difficult?

I deliberate my next move and settle on the idea of calling Fritz. My hands fly into the covers, finally touching my familiar cold, black screen. I dial his number and bring my phone to my face.

"Hello?" A tiny, sleepy voice springs from the speaker.

"Hey, Fritz." I pause, suddenly insecure about my reason for calling him. "Can I just…rant about Quinton for a sec?"

Fritz exhales; he's been hearing about Quinton's behavior for a while now. But he wouldn't say no to me. "Of course, man. What's up?"

Everything.

A half hour later, Fritz sniffs loudly into the mic. "Sounds like you guys are having regular relationship problems. But don't stress it too much! You're both mature…for the most part, and you know how to handle adult situations…I think. No way will you lovebirds be stopped by Quinton being wanting to spoil you with love and riches and shit. Even if it comes out annoying. Plus, his parents were literally physically and verbally abusive, of course he's not emotionally perfect."

I respond in a thankful, apologetic tone. "I suppose you're right. Thank you, Fritz. I do feel better. Quinton and I…we'll get through this." My bed sheets chain me down, drowning me further under the comforter.

"No. Say it like you mean it."

My head tilts. "Huh?"

Fritz shifts around on the other end, his voice growing louder. "Connor Jones, will you and Quinton get through this?"

"Uh, yes?"

"Louder."

"Yes." I snicker.

"Louder!"

"Yes!" A sweet syrup of hope washes down my spine. He's absolutely correct; Quinton and I are inseparable, or at the very least, have been remarkably close most of the time.

I grin to myself. "Thank you, Fritz. You're actually kinda tolerable sometimes."

Fritz's staticky voice chirps back. "Any time, man. Let me know how it goes. And don't worry," he adds, predicting my next sentence. "I won't say anything to Quinton, Rafael, or Karl. Bye-bye."

"Thanks, man. Bye."

The second I hang up, I'm met with a call from Rafael. I sigh, but on the last ring, I accept it in spite of my exhaustion.

An energetic voice muffled by food pipes up. "Hey man, I want to buy decor for my dorm at FAU — for when my gap year is up. Wanna join? We can head to your place after or something."

I smile, my depressive episode waning already. "You know what, Rafael? Sure."

I can hear the grin in his voice. "Sweet. Can you do, like, five?"

I think for a moment. "I have a shift at that time. My internship has upgraded to, like, an actual job as a medical scribe — more hours, less play. But I'll be done at six?"

Rafael sniffs. "Wait, really? Without a degree?"

I shrug, though he can't see me. "Scribe jobs don't require degrees."

"Sick. six works for me, then. See you!"

"See you, Raf."

I chuckle and drag my hands down my face. We've been dorm shopping for an hour, and I'm not in the right head space to deal with Rafael's shenanigans. "Rafael, you idiot. Just leave the stuff in the car. Why would you bring the chair we just bought with you?"

Rafael frowns, tapping his foot on the asphalt and resting a hand on his Chevrolet. "I wasn't talking about the chair. Jesus, you're so mean! I was obviously referring to the Polaroid camera." He lifts the blue camera higher for me to see, and I laugh through a sigh.

"Rafael — " I point at the bistro behind us "…why in the world would you need to bring your new camera to a restaurant we're gonna spend, like, an hour at?"

Lesson learned — never go dorm-room shopping with Rafael and get dinner with him afterward.

The boy looks at his car, and back at me, before placing the camera in the trunk. "Fine."

"Why not under a seat — you know what, never mind. Let's go now." I reach for Rafael's hand and haul him to the restaurant's entrance. The white double doors have golden handles for us to pull, complete with two equally plain pillars jutting out of the ground beside them. A small, silver stand props up a menu written in a font so cursive, it's practically unreadable.

I look at Rafael.

He looks at me, black hair falling above his eyes. "What? I'll pay, I promise!"

I roll my eyes and stride past him. "You better not be lying."

Rafael, who responsibly reserved our seats, leads me to our table and pulls my cushioned chair out for me. "So?" His eyebrows raise a little and gestures to his outfit.

I cock my head to the side, unfolding my napkin in my lap. "Um…can I help you?"

Rafael grins, fidgeting with his fork. "My outfit, Connor. Isn't it nice?"

I shrug. "Eh."

He rolls his eyes, smiling. "What'd I expect from you, a compliment?" He points to the unbuttoned black blazer hugging his arms and back. "This shit was expensive."

I raise my hands. "I'm kidding, you look very handsome. How are you affording all of this new shit? First dorm shopping, then this restaurant, and now fancy clothes?" I flick a speck off of my sleeve. "If you've found some way to make quick cash, please share your secrets."

Rafael straightens his back, eyes pinned to the floor. "Nah, still getting minimum wage at Sonic." He sighs airily. "Can't fucking wait for college."

I smile. "I'm excited for you. College seems great for you."

He nods vigorously and takes a long sip of water. "Thank you, thank you. How has work been? Karl told me you've been doing a *lot* lately."

I groan, head nearly dropping onto the tablecloth. "*God*, don't get me started. I miss when they went easy on me for being a high schooler."

Rafael's brows furrow. "Look, don't overwork yourself. I know you love your med stuff and shit, but mental health comes first."

I glance at the ceiling, a deep longing leaving me as a sigh. "It's just, my mental health will go down if suddenly Quinton and I have no cash in our account. So like, I have to work. Besides, working in this field has been my dream since I was little. I'll enjoy it at some point."

Rafael mocks my wording. "'At some point,'" he air quotes, "Have you ever tried working in a different field? Something…easier?"

I shake my head left and right sharply. "No. Again, I've always dreamt of doing medical work over any other type." I smile and chuck a sugar packet at him. "Dream crusher."

His eyes harden, face still worried. "I'm just saying, don't let your dream crush *you*. You look tired, Connor."

"Ouch."

He exhales deeply and folds his arms on the table. "Not like that, you look sexy as ever, don't worry."

I perk up.

"I just want to see you happier, you know? Can Quinton help you with work, or something?"

"No." I immediately shoot down the suggestion. Absolutely not. "Recently, I've strictly forbidden him from coming to help me at the hospital. I…it's complicated why, but he can't, and he knows this. And, thank you for your concerns, but still, I can't put myself first right now. Maybe further on in my career, but it's hard to move up anywhere without a college degree."

Rafael's expression changes. "He can't come into your work? Hm." He takes a second sip of water. "Well, I understand. I hope things get better with work soon."

I chuckle. "Thanks, idiot, me too. And congrats on making more money than me through Sonic somehow. But, yeah, no, he cannot visit me at work, like, whatsoever. Again, it is strictly forbidden. Can't wait to go see Quinton at home," I add sarcastically. We had talked about the fight.

Rafael's face loses some of its reddish color, and a gray hue clouds his expression. "Thanks, man. Oh, and don't be afraid to take a break if your guys' relationship becomes too much to handle."

QUINTON

Waiting is a fool's game, and I have no intention of playing it. Connor **Jones** deserves love beyond comparison. My complaints as of late have been petty and selfish. Love isn't only tangible — Connor wouldn't feel loved if I bought him a beach house. He'd feel loved through the time spent at the beach house, the memories made, the shared complaint of sand under our feet, the sentimental value of it all. I failed to see that. I misunderstood what would strengthen our love the most. I thought that Connor *wanted* me to be the main provider.

Now that I've fucked both Connor and myself over with my thoughtless antics, I have only one option: to apologize.

My eyes wander to the rearview mirror, making sure the rose bouquet hasn't tipped off the backseat or gotten crushed by a stray water bottle during the drive. I flick my turn signal on, growing anxious.

Connor *technically* told me not to visit him at work. But, Rafael reassured me, and I'm a man who loves grand gestures, i.e. I sewed him a doll of myself once. I need to apologize, to erase this quarrel from our history for good and get over myself.

Because I love him.

I pull into a dark parking lot, step out of our car, and grab the flowers from the back. Connor had Fritz drive him to work — Fritz had a film thing going on nearby — leaving the car to me. How lucky is that?

I'd tactically chosen to come at night, knowing there would be fewer patients to transmit their sicknesses to me and from me to Connor's mom. Hopefully, Connor will appreciate that thought at the very least.

I lock my car and quietly step inside the hospital. Holloway never fails to send a shiver down my spine. The eerie white walls and the floor seem brighter with the dark night outside. I turn away from the automatic doors and head to Connor's station. I clutch the blue roses tighter while I walk, quietly reciting what I have planned to say to him. *Time to serenade the halls of Holloway Hospital with my apology.* Mid-speedwalk, a hunched-over, coughing woman *barely* comes into view before I slam into her.

"Shit!" We both stumble backward. "I'm so sorry, ma'am, are you okay?" I rub my head.

The tan-skinned, blue-eyed woman chuckles through a cough. "I'm okay, thank you. I'm also sorry." She continues walking, leaving me slightly whiplashed.

I pick off a petal from a rose that was crushed during the smash-up and resume my Connor hunt, eventually finding his office area. I peer through the glass, spotting a slender, brown-haired boy hard at work in the far corner of the room. Connor. I flip around so my back is pressed against the wall, let out a deep exhale, and hold the flowers at my chest.

After I feel composed, I open the door only a few feet away from me. I step in, tip-toeing with such stealth that Connor doesn't notice me directly behind him.

I hover my chin above his right shoulder. "Boo!" I shout, smiling when he jumps.

"Jesus — what the hell? Quinton? What is wrong with you, what are you doing here?" Connor brushes his overgrown hair into place and frowns with all his might.

I, still laughing, bow. "Hello, Connor." I present the bouquet, meeting Connor's deeply confused eyes.

His gaze drops to the flowers, and he squints. "Quinton, I told you not to visit me at work. Especially not without a mask." He urgently shuffles around the room, sighing with relief when he finds a small box of surgical masks. "Here, put this on."

I oblige, stretching the elastic bands over my ears. "Okay, it's on. Here, take the flowers, I picked them myself." I nudge them toward him.

He looks at me like I'm crazy, but accepts them anyway. He maintains eye-contact as he sets them on the metal table behind him. "Thank you, these are beautiful. But, for the third time, what are you doing here?"

I clear my throat, lazily taking one of his hands. "I came here to apologize. Connor, I'm so fucking sorry for how I've been treating you. I...can't believe I ever made you feel unloved. That makes me feel so shitty — the fact I was making you feel shitty. So I'm so, so sorry. You deserve to be reminded every single day that you're the smartest, most beautiful man I've ever met. I owe that to you. If I ever make you feel anything remotely close to how I did ever again, tell me." I hold my breath and wait for a response.

Connor, blushing and with tears in his eyes, squeezes my hand once and let's go. "Thank you. I appreciate you telling me that a lot. I forgive you, all right? But, if your actions don't show for what you've just told me, forgiveness is redacted. Understand?"

I nod quickly. I'd have kissed him if we weren't both wearing masks.

He chuckles at my enthusiasm and watches me while his tears recede. "It's very sweet you did this, but I don't understand why it had to be here. Why couldn't you have given me these flowers where there's, like, not a chance of getting sick?"

I smile and scratch my head. "Well, two reasons, actually. One, I wanted to visit you during one of your a.m. shifts. I don't know about you, but if you showed up to my work when it was past midnight I'd be so fucking happy because that is just miserable." Connor snickers. "And two, I'm not quite done with my apology." I pull out a stool, sit down, and pull the bottom part of Connor's shirt toward me.

"Hi." Connor's wide, chocolate eyes stare at me from above, curious.

I swivel away from him, facing the dreaded paperwork. "I will do *all* of the rest of your work for tonight. That I'm capable of doing, obviously."

Connor's face lights up, but he calms down a moment later. "Are you sure? What if you — "

"Connor. Practically no one is going to come into contact with me, relax. I promise to stay in here and studiously assist you with your work."

His brows furrow, conflicted. "…Okay. I guess that's all right. But just this once — you are not allowed back."

I reply with a lilting, "Yeah, sure, whatever you say."

Connor crouches down to my eye level, face made of stone. "Quinton. This is my mum we are talking about. Promise me you won't come back here unless it's an emergency of some sort."

It's not a question, it's a demand. "I promise."

He chuckles. "Great. Let's get you to work then?"

I spin a pen in my hand and grin. "Your command is my wish."

CHAPTER 12

My retinas must be thoroughly burned at this point. No human being should be hunched over on their bed and staring into their full-bright laptop job searching for three hours straight. It honestly worries me how I can spend so much time looking for an adequate job and still come up short. I fall backward, our bed poorly supporting my large frame, and cough a few times. "Why is this so hard?" I rub my eyes, knowing the next time I look in the mirror, they'll be redder than blood. I flick my eyes to my screen and sigh.

Best plumbing jobs near you

No shame in plumbing, but that doesn't sound like it'd fulfill me. *Yet, here you find yourself, Quinton, researching qualifications to become a plumber for the past hour.*

God.

I close my laptop, shimmy off the bed, and slowly make my way out of the room. While scratching my chin and coughing several times in a row, I head for the kitchen. As I browse the pantry, a familiar figure materializes next to me.

"Hi, Quinton!"

I jump, chuckling and turning to see Connor's mom. "Ms. Frances, what are you doing here?"

She pulls me in for a hug. "I haven't seen you in so long, Quinton!"

I accept the embrace and grin. "I know, I've missed you. Connor is at work, if you're looking for him. But, be warned, I visited him at work, like, a day ago…and he wasn't too happy about it, so."

She smiles. "Oh, no, I'm not here for him. Connor was supposed to drop off my vitamin C pills that I left here when I spent the night. He forgot, so I figured I'd just come and grab them. Can't believe he'd forget about his own Mum." She rolls her eyes, her short, brown hair bouncing as she finds her way to the medicine cabinet above the microwave.

In a smooth motion, she pinpoints the bottle of pills, snags them, and turns around. "All right, done. Have a nice day, Quinton."

I'm about to thank her when *another* series of coughs take over. My body bends, trying to support the force of the coughing.

"Jesus Christ, Quinton. Are you okay?" Connor's mom begins to walk closer, but I lift a hand, stopping her with a serious expression.

"I-I'm fine." I stand upright and open my mouth with a smile before I cough once again.

Ms. Frances lets out a small gasp, and I open my eyes to see what elicited the sound. When I look at the ground I freeze. Red, gooey, and undeniably blood.

She steps back, grabs a towel, and throws it my way. "I do not think you're fine." Reaching in her purse, she pulls out a mask and straps it on her face. "Go to the hospital right now. Get tested — people don't just cough up blood." Worry laces her voice, but also strengthens it, leaving no room for me to disagree.

I nod and back away from her. If I am sick with something, she is at risk. While fishing for my keys, I remember an unfortunate fact with a long groan. "Connor has my keys. Um — okay, I think you should go back home."

Ms. Frances is already on it, the front door wide open. "You can call an Uber, sweetie. I hope you're all right."

I hope I'm all right, but mostly for her sake. I cough again, wave her goodbye, and whip out my phone. How did I get sick? Is it the flu? Tarchvirus? I massage my head with one hand and order a ride to grab me with the other.

And I wait. A cough leaves me breathless here and there, but I wait patiently.

A woman I have no intention to keep waiting pulls up at my front door. I hop into the car masked and offer her a hoarse thank-you. The least I can do is keep whatever I have from doing any more damage — by stopping the spread.

A few meaningless pleasantries are exchanged between us; however, I try to keep my talking at a minimum. Every time I speak, the vibration almost teases my throat, tickling the urge to cough and cough and cough.

But I manage. I tip the woman who has likely never had a passenger so eager to leave her car. I step toward Holloway's entrance, coughing up a storm, and only being able to tame my hacking once I reach the receptionist.

She grins. "Hello, how may I help you?"

With a burning throat, I reply, "I need to test. For Tarchvirus." Tarchvirus is one of the only vaccines I'm late getting this year. Judging by the symptoms, it's likely I'm dealing with that unforgiving virus.

She hums, clacking on her keyboard with polished, long nails. "All right, do you have an appointment?"

I shake my head no.

She tucks her hair behind her ear, requesting my insurance card and healthcare provider. I shuffle through my wallet, finding the card among hundreds of other useless gift cards and discount slips.

"Okay, sir, you're all set! I signed you up for the earliest walk-in, which happens to be in just a few minutes. You can wait there." She gestures to the small array of gray seats. I thank her and sneak a green apple lollipop from the complementary bowl.

I take a seat, picking at my treat with such focus, I almost don't notice Connor standing right in front of me with hands on his hips and angry eyes.

"Connor."

"*Quinton.*"

I clear my throat and scoot away from him. "What's…up?"

He stares daggers at me. "Quinton, just because I let you visit me once does not mean you're allowed to — "

"I think I have Tarchvirus," I state plainly, looking up at him with apologetic eyes.

Connor steps back, instinctively grabbing a mask from his pocket and wrapping it over his face. "Are you serious? I — are you okay? When did you get it?"

I don't answer him for a moment, pondering, because where *did* I get it? "Look, I don't even — " a cough, "…know if I have it. I coughed up blood, earlier, though."

"Are you here to test for it?" His voice is heavy with concern.

"Yes." I prod at my brain, desperately trying to recall incidents where I came into contact with someone sickly. I rarely leave the house, it couldn't have been — wait.

The brief moment returns to me; a memory that I had long forgotten. That woman. "Connor. When I…came by a few days ago, I did bump into a lady on the way to see you." I can't meet his eyes, and a deep guilt pools in my stomach. "She…coughed quite a bit when I was apologizing for slamming into her. She could've…" I trail off, zipping my lips when I see Connor's enraged expression.

A conflict of worry, blame, and anger pollutes his face. His slender fingers run through his soft hair three total times before he gives a final tug at the strands and looks me dead in the eye. "I fucking told you not to visit me at work."

The cold phrase freezes my heart. "Connor, I…I'm so sorry. This — I'm so sorry. I'm so sorry. Look, I might not even have it."

Connor remains silent.

My heart rate skyrockets.

However, not for long, because after a tantalizing thirty seconds, he speaks again. "I will stay with you while you test. If it's positive I…" He searches my face, defeated. "If it's positive, I'll figure out what to do. It's… both of our faults. I shouldn't have let you stay."

I rest my face in my palms. "It's my fault. I should've listened to you. I just — maybe it will be negative. Let's just hope for the best, yeah?"

Though Connor is still angry, it seems like the news has stolen his energy. He simply slumps down in a seat a skip down from mine. "Fuck."

Guilt eats at me as the silence grows more and more uncomfortable. I'm almost thankful when Dr. Putter calls me in. "Quinton?"

Connor and I slowly stand, walking toward her with no enthusiasm. Dr. Putter smiles — I think, she's wearing a mask — and leads us to a testing room, and she closes the curtain behind her.

Connor finds a seat, leaving me to sit in the patient's chair.

She works her magic, setting up every material needed for the test. With a long, *long* cotton swab in hand, she types something on her computer and hands the swab to me. "All right, so what you're going to do is push this up your nose until I tell you to stop. I might assist you at some point, is that okay?"

I nod and grind my teeth. I reach for Connor's hand, but find empty air, realizing he's staring at the wall ahead of him with tears in his eyes.

A green self-hatred paints my stomach as I begin to operate on myself. I shove the Q-tip as far as it can go. As Dr. Putter coaxes me along, I swear I can feel the cotton tickling my brain.

Once it's over, Connor and I wait the required fifteen minutes. It's silent and dreadful. Rapid testing doesn't feel so rapid when you've possibly sickened your boyfriend's immunocompromised mom.

The doctor returns with a grave look on her face and sits down. "Mr. Hansley, I'm afraid your results came back positive."

Connor lets out a breath.

Dr. Putter begins gently informing me of procedures and how to quarantine myself. However, I subconsciously tune her out, watching Connor's beautiful features *wrinkle* like a tossed sheet of scratch paper. So much for giving him a grand apology by visiting him with flowers and a helping hand.

Way to go, Quinton. Way to go.

CONNOR

I let out a shallow breath, eyes trained on the white task calendar, and I find today's date.

Tell Quinton 2 do taxes

I double-take, jaw unhinging. No way. Quinton's unwarranted two a.m. visit to my work happened four days ago. That morning, I had been recalling how I'd need to remind him he promised to do our taxes in 4 days. *That's today.* I drag my eyes to the clock. The taunting tick of its slender hand maddens me. Work is degrading my sense of time, especially since Quinton decided to venture into the hospital without a mask and get sick with Tarchvirus. Now his hunt for a new job has slowed even more. How much further south can things go?

I sigh at the reminder. I cannot believe he bumped into some lady carrying the virus. Just our luck.

"Connor! Hey." Karl waves, smiling.

My eyes follow Karl's, wandering to the evidence of hours of procrastination. Stacks of papers, unsorted files, and a cold coffee cup next to the laptop. I pry my mind from a sneaking thought of Quinton and hover over my unfinished work. I offer Karl a nervous chuckle. "Hey, Karl. Uh, I was just finishing up." Karl seems displeased with my response, so I continue. "You know, we could get food or something when I finish? I'm super hungry and really need a break."

The authority melts from his face, and he grins. "Ha, Connor, I'm not going to judge you for not being finished with your shit yet. You have a lot on your plate — just make sure it's not late or boss'll get mad. And yeah, that sounds fun! I'll drive you home after we eat if you'd like."

"Wow, my savior — please do. How'd you know I don't have a ride?"

Karl flicks a speck of dust from his shoulder, his smile still Gorilla-Glued to his face. "Your car wasn't in its spot. Guess I'm just super observant and a gold-star friend…"

Before I can make a quip, a way-too-familiar face blurs past my workroom.

Mum's face.

Whatever I was planning to say to Karl dies on my tongue. My brain focuses entirely on the fact that my *mother* just strode by in a *hospital*. A location she's needed to avoid since she was born with immunodeficiency.

Wishing no goodbye to Karl, I bolt out of the room and head in the direction she seemed to be going. "Mum?" The frantic tremor in my voice goes hand in hand with the speed I walk down the hall. What is she doing here? And in the injured subsection of this building? Mum shouldn't be near so many sick people unless it's an emergency. Ever.

Skidding around a final corner, I'm met with a half-closed door and a milky voice escaping from the crack. My mum's voice. I ram the window-less, oakwood door open. and my heart pounds with anxiety.

Dr. Ndiaye, one whom I am familiar with, lifts her head at my noisy intrusion. Dr. Ndiaye is a special one, with multiple degrees in disease and virus treatment. A medical doctor far above me in the hierarchy of skills here.

Mum's eyes round like she's an apprehended criminal. She straightens her back, and the paper on the bed beneath her crinkles. "Oh! Connor, hi." She gives me a weak smile. "How are you, darling? It's been a couple days since I've seen you and Quinton." She shies from my eye contact.

My hand floats to cover my mouth, fingers brushing my mask. "Mum? What are you doing here? Dr. Ndiaye, does she have a cold or something?" Her eyes shroud at my accusatory tone, as if she's hesitant to unveil the truth.

Mum purses her lips and trades a quick look with Dr. Ndiaye. "Connor, baby, yesterday I came by the doctor because I was feeling unwell. Like, really unwell. I…have symptoms presenting like Tarchvirus, so I thought I'd check it since Quinton has it. And — before you say any-thing, I was just about to get the shot, I promise, I just procrastinated and, well…"

Fuck.

Quinton.

If she is sick, he must've spread it to her — maybe before his symp-toms were visible. I shouldn't have let him stay when he visited me here.

I'm such an idiot.

Hot rage bakes with fear — if Quinton had just *listened* to me and not visited my work and worn a fucking mask…I mean, there's a chance she'll test negative, but it's unlikely. "Oh, Mum, why didn't you tell me?" My voice cracks, exposing a flood of fear. The Tarchvirus is a beatable opponent for most. But Mum? Over fifty? Barely eligible for working healthcare? And…*fuck* immunocompromised. Immunocompromised.

My horror must be obvious because Mum quickly speaks again. "I'm sorry, I should've told you. I just found out sweetie, but don't fret about me! I'm your good old Mum still, young as day and a-okay." She gives her chest a short pat to appear stronger. But the action ends up resulting in several coughs.

I visibly cringe, wanting to hug her but knowing the ramifications of doing so. "Mum, you're in a hospital, that typically means you aren't okay. I'm an adult, I can handle it if something's wrong." I give her a reassuring smile to hide my growing terror.

Mum has always had to walk through life carefully. Any wrong step could result in death. And with living below the poverty line, sickness tended to be an inevitability. Whenever her weak immune system fell victim to viruses, it was terrifying. But never had she caught something with the lethality level of Tarchvirus. Never.

Dr. Ndiaye's voice brings me back to the present. "Ma'am, we need to get you to your room now, if that's all right. And, Connor, don't forget to not get too close." The doctor assists Mum to her feet.

"You're right, sorry. Connor, I'll — " A cough ravages her body once again. "I'll be fine, don't you worry." She spreads her fingers, high-fiving the air. I high-five her back and watch as she exits with Dr. Ndiaye.

On any other occasion, I'd stop the doctor in her tracks, keeping Mum here. But I choose mercy, sparing the doctor my trouble and letting them pass with a defeated grunt.

An acid gurgles within my stomach, spreading to my head as dread joins the nauseating mixture. For a moment, I wonder why I didn't turn on my heels and chase after Mum.

My first thought is to dial Quinton. Seek his anticipation of my needs and his sympathy. But the thought is soon lost to anger. No. There's a high chance his dramatic gesture of waltzing into the hospital with flowers, and without a mask, has resulted in my mum's virus. My thoughts of Quinton are interrupted by a loud thud coming from the room Mum just walked into.

Panic. Immediate, mesmerizing panic.

Losing all care for the rules I run, turning the doorknob with such speed it bends. I stand, scanning the room and not finding her — that is until I look at the floor. Mum's lying, frozen and inert. Silent, like she's on the verge of death.

The doctor beside her, certified but definitely not Dr. Ndiaye, puts two fingers on her pulse, sighs with relief, and clicks her com. She mutters into the device inaudibly. I rush to Mum's left side, avoiding the doctor, hysterical tears erasing my vision. "Is she — is she okay? Doctor?" My eyes early vibrate in distress when I inspect the doctor crouched beside her.

I'm matched with a crisp, assured expression. "She's fine, don't fret. She simply fainted, nothing more, most likely from dehydration. Tarchvirus dehydrates people like hell. I promise, she's okay. But, please stay back. A sick son won't heal her any quicker." She gives me a secure and affirming smile.

Repressing my internal speech as to why I deserve to stay, I obey, standing and eyeing Mum's body with dismay. *Just dehydrating, just dehydration, just dehydration.*

I pace throughout the hallway. My careful pants gradually build into raw, horrified hyperventilation.

Karl.

I need to find Karl. I weave my way back to where I was initially working. "Hey, Ka — " He's not in the room.

I scan the area, convincing myself he could've gone to the bathroom. But, my hope is soon crushed — I find a note.

Hey Connor my mom decided to give me a surprise visit so i left bc she wanted me there immediately. cant say no to mother dearest ofc, <u>but</u> i did do your portion of work so youre welcome i know im the greatest most anti dogwater friend youve ever had okay bye - k <3

I see a damp circle on the paper, and a breath races up my throat. A teardrop. Mine to be exact. More tears drench the page, and I set it down, clenching my teeth. Will a day go by when I don't cry all over myself?

Catching a break seems to be a constantly unattainable outcome. The present bears no altruism.

I let out another sob. *Why do I never have any control?* I grab my phone from my pocket; my thumb floats over Quinton's contact, the call button jeering at me. I drop my shoulders in defeat and click the power button until the screen dims to black. I can't properly speak to him right now — at least not on the phone.

First, Quinton needs to know Mum's state. I cannot be alone in this, even if it is his fault.

Quinton?" For good measure, I knock on his half-ajar door. I flop beside him, and he lightly caresses my forehead to avoid my mask. Despite my anger, the act sends butterflies to every corner of my stomach.

He closes his laptop; his green eyes are now focused on me. "What's up, Connor? Oh, how was work?"

I look at him, and my chest grows heavy with blame for him at Mum's condition. The butterflies die. "Oh, it was…well, it was eventful. Karl wrote me a note because we were gonna hang out, but he ditched. But — " I cut myself off, a pitiful attempt to keep myself from crying again. Another second passes and my throat is still clogged.

Quinton inches forward. "Connor? What happened, is everything okay?" His voice grows more wary.

My eyes remain glued to the bed. "I'm sorry — um. Mum, she's sick. With Tarchvirus." The clock above us ticks once. "She — well, as you know — is immunocompromised. She's very vulnerable to disease…and it's a potential fatality." Tears rest on my eyes; they'll fall the moment I blink.

"Oh, Connor, I'm sorry," he starts, guilt taking over his entire face. "I must've…shit, I must've spread it to her."

I boil internally. "Yeah…you must've."

Quinton's eyes round as mine narrow.

"You absolute idiot." I spit the words out.

Holloway Hospital's ivory lobby is half the raucous fiesta it usually is during work hours. I'm grateful for the silence. I retrace my steps to Mum's room, twisting my key into the lock — an under-spoken-of privilege that comes with working in this hellhole.

This is the first day since Mum's diagnosis of Tarchvirus.

"Connor! Hi baby." A warm greeting delivered in a weak voice grabs my attention. Mum.

And once again, my throat constricts with grief. I set my sleeping bag down and inch toward her, but a frail hand lifts to stop me.

"No no, I don't want you getting sick. I'm okay, don't worry. Tarchvirus comes and goes." Her body trembles as she sits up.

The room is weighed down by a heavy aroma of heat, fever, and delirium. "That's good, Mum. Hey, what's your temp?" I don't make any remarks about her healing or being *okay*, since I know it's not true.

She shifts in her covers. "Oh, it's at 101 at the moment. It fluctuated for a while between 100 and 104…but I'm quite stable now. I'm not enjoying the bloody ice baths I've been having to take, though." She chuckles breathily. The noise barely makes it past her lips. "How've you been?"

"Me? I do not matter right now." I watch a *second* chuckle skate along her lips, my brows furrowing. "What's funny?" And she snickers once again. "Jesus Christ, Mum? How are you laughing right now? Don't you realize you could die?" To cover up my crudely blunt statement, I quickly continue. "Never mind — sorry, I'm sorry. I'm staying the night, too."

Mum's earthy eyes, far more grave now, flick up. "Stay here? Well, what about your husband?" Maybe she says it to lighten the mood, or even fluster me.

But I don't get flustered, rather, I get agitated. "Oh, he'll be fine. He's outside now. I'll take him home and catch you right back in an hour or so." One small taste of space from Quinton and it now seems I adore the distance between us. But I don't. Of course, I don't.

Her aggravatingly exceptional perceptive ability kicks off. "Is something the matter with you two?"

"No. Everything's fine." The lie dances off my lips. With glossy eyes, I wave her off, praying she didn't detect my expression. She's in no state to worry about Quinton's and my relationship.

That night, Holloway Hospital's marble floor fails to support my body — it's a bed of rock with sheets of cooled magma. My body contorts, trying to find an ample spot to rest. Alas, I continue to feel like a puzzle piece jammed into a spot it doesn't belong. I sit upward, souring as I recall my thoughts from earlier today; how while packing, I thought a floor could serve as a bed. I brought no extra padding to help with the inherent discomfort of sleeping on a hospital ground.

My makeshift bed is stationed several feet from Mum, close enough to hear her rhythmic breathing, but far enough to not contract the Tarchvirus. The faint tick of the clock above her head works against me, seeming to blare whenever the promise of sleep is near. I'm living an insomniac nightmare.

My thoughts wander to when the roles were reversed. When I was the one lying helpless in the hospital bed, others on the floor. Quinton on the floor.

Quinton used to lie on the floor, nightly when I was comatose, never leaving, never skipping, never moving from my side unless he was kicked out. He couldn't even speak to me for a month's time. He couldn't wake up greeted with my smile or laugh. He rested with me — and I wasn't even conscious. He did that for me, and I'm getting lazy with Mum on day one. Quinton stayed with me every single fucking night for two months, resting on this hard floor, only able to yearn for me to awaken.

How could a man do such a tedious thing? How?

I rise to my feet, and my eyes find Mum in the darkness. Her frail physique, unattended and quiet puts shame on the entire concept of serenity. My chest warms at her peace. I grow soft at the sight, feeling a need to revere her, admire her, and to never leave her side.

Oh. That's how.

I beam. That's how Quinton did it.

CHAPTER 13

I nearly doze off studying the hospital's cafeteria. Fritz and Rafael drone on and on with recycled advice. Rafael's hand roughly massages my shoulder as he speaks. "Look, all I'm saying is I think you and Quinton need a little space. Fritz's right! Sometimes, FAU and I get a little pissy, like I get all those annoying emails and reminders, so I take a break. Like I said earlier, never be afraid to take a break. Like, dude, he got your mom sick when he knew he wasn't supposed to go to the hospital." His casual voice doesn't fit the topic of discussion — Quinton's and my relationship.

Two pairs of eyes penetrate me as I, again, find myself angry with Quinton. "Everyone knows 'taking a break' is a segue into a breakup. Your fate's sealed when that happens. Rafael, you're right, we need a *little* space, but let's stop talking about it for now. I'm just so pissed at him and fucking terrified for my mum." I bat away Rafael's hand heading straight for my hair.

Fritz nods thoughtfully. "I'm so sorry, Connor, really. You know, I believe in both of you to get through this. I'm gonna take off, though. Lunch break's almost over."

I scrape my fork across a half-empty plate and nod at Rafael. "You should get going too. I'm gonna visit Mum."

He smiles. "You get to that! I gotta shit really bad, so I'm gonna hang around the hospital for a little bit to…yeah. I really hope she gets well soon, by the way." His eyes flick around nervously before he takes his plate and walks off.

I chuckle, disgusted by the detail. "All right, you weirdo."

QUINTON

The lousy beep of a heart monitor echoes across the hallway. It chirps from the room Ms. Frances lies in, where she waits patiently to recover. I sit on a cold metal bench near the door of her room and quietly observe the hospital corridors around me. I people-watch, studying facial expressions to gauge what brought them here. Some are children — maybe one stuck a bead up their nose or broke their finger during gaga-ball. Others are adults, praying for their aging parents to hold on a little longer. And a few are lovers, waiting for their partner to be okay. The lovers twist my heart the most.

Triple-masked, per Connor's request, I wait, until finally the man himself materializes to my right.

"Quinton," Connor states.

I scoot over, silently offering him to take a seat beside me. "Connor, hey. Don't worry, I've been staying eight feet away from everyone like you asked."

Connor makes some sort of approving noise. He looks at the newly opened spot on the bench with hesitance. "See? Not so hard is it?" Before I can respond, he continues, as if still wary of sitting down next to me. "What'd your Tarchvirus test come back as?"

I smile and lean against the pale wall behind me. "Negative."

Connor lets out a relieved gasp, finally sitting down beside me. "Oh, my God, why didn't you start with that? That's great news, I'm glad you're all better." Connor laughs, and as his giggling mellows out, we are left in silence. He soon breaks the quiet with a simple, "So, am I ever gonna know why you did it?"

Confused at the change of tone, I turn to look at him. "Did what?"

Connor sighs, pinning his eyes on the door leading to Ms. Frances. "Why did you visit me at work? You knew I didn't want you to. You knew about my mum's immunity issues."

I lower my head. It's rough being half the reason for all your boyfriend's contemporary anxieties. "I just…I really wanted a way to show you that I was sorry. Like, extremely sorry."

"But there are other ways for you to do that."

I exhale, readjusting my position on the metal slab below me. "I… understand that now. I was an idiot. I just wanted to make up as soon as possible, and that trumped my better judgment. I feel so shitty when we fight, and I get worried very easily that one of us could…like stop loving the other. I love *love*, it's beautiful to me. And when I thought ours was threatened, I made a stupid decision."

Connor chuckles, hair falling over his ears as he looks downward. "Yeah, you did. It's sweet that you have such a boner for love."

I snicker.

"But I do blame you for her sickness, and you're gonna have to really make up for it. Your heart was there, just…I wish you would've done a different, like, huge gesture."

I nod vigorously. "Yeah, no, I was going to, actually. I had a slightly different thing planned, but, I don't know, I really thought it'd serve you better to visit you and do a bunch of your work for you. Plus, Rafael agreed that it was a great idea. Probably wouldn't have done it if he'd told me not to." I pick at a scab on my arm.

Connor straightens his back at this and tilts his head. "Wait, what? Rafael told you to?"

I furrow my eyebrows. "Well, yeah, but it's not like he knew that I wasn't supposed to go — "

"Yes, he did." Connor looks confused. "He did. We had a conversation at Shallow Eddy's, like, a week ago. I told him several times how much I did not want him visiting me at work. Like, I verbatim said it was strictly forbidden."

This gets my attention, and soon, I'm searching Connor's eyes like my life depend on it. I stutter but manage to get my surprise across. "That's — Rafael — what? He invited me out to dinner the night before I got sick, and he told me you would love it. He told me you'd been so stressed with work lately, so it'd make up for it in the future. Raf even said you mentioned wanting me to help you out."

Connor shakes his head several times. "No, in fact, I specifically told him I didn't want you helping me with work. What the *fuck.*"

I try to collect my thoughts, remembering the night Rafael encouraged me to go through with my visit. He'd smiled, incredibly laid-back and self-assured. Telling me he was completely confident Connor would like it if I visited him at work. He lied to my face with zero remorse. And now, Connor's mom is hooked up to a monitor in a hospital bed.

What. The. Fuck.

Connor wrinkles his nose. "Why, though? What incentive would Rafael have to convince you to visit me? Like, did he want me to get mad at you?"

I shrug. "I don't know! I can't — literally not a bone in my body could've thought he wasn't being genuine while telling me to do it." I pause, still trying to find a moment that night where Rafael faltered and showed a sign he was being dishonest. "Maybe…maybe there's a reasonable explanation for this. Maybe he misunderstood what you were saying."

Connor looks uneasy, betrayed almost. "I don't know, I made it extremely clear…" He trails off, deep in thought.

I try to justify Rafael's actions in my head, leaving the two of us silent, confused messes.

"Maybe there is a reasonable explanation," Connor begins. "It's just not a good one."

I meet his eyes. "What are you suggesting?"

Connor fiddles with his white coat's strings. "I don't know…Look, Rafael has been off lately. Or not *off*, just never really encouraging of our relationship. In fact, just ten minutes ago, he went on a tangent on how taking breaks in relationships is okay and healthy. He also was insistent about us taking a break when I'd had that same dinner at Shallow Eddy's with him. Plus, wasn't he the one who offered you a bunch of drinks that ended up getting you fired?"

I try to recall, seeing as I was edging alcohol poisoning the night we graduated high school. "Yeah…yeah he did. He was also the one that suggested the prank." I rub my temple, feeling sick. "Maybe he's just a bit of a troublemaker but doesn't mean to be?"

"That's a lot of trouble for someone to accidentally make. And Rafael is a grown man," Connor points out. "I don't know if I can buy that when he's stirred up so much shit." He stands, reaching his hand out and staring down the hall like a man on a mission. "He and I just ate lunch together here. He's probably still around."

I raise an eyebrow. "Why would he still be here? That was, like, nine minutes ago."

Connor snickers, pulling me to my feet and beginning to walk. "He had to…shit, so for all we know, he has probably just finished up."

"W-what?" I double over in laughter as Connor drags me down the hallway. "It is ridiculously funny that you know about that. Couldn't he wait until he got home?"

Connor snaps his head back to me, continuing to speed-walk. "Let's stop discussing Rafael's poo-ing session, yeah?"

I ignore him and tap my chin. "What if we catch him mid-po — "

"Shut *up*," Connor exhales through a chuckle. "We'll make fun of him later, stay focused."

I giggle the entire run downstairs, until Connor leads me to the bathroom near the vending machines. "You know this place really well."

Connor shrugs. "Side effect of spending ninety percent of my time here." He pushes the men's restroom door open, peeking his head around the corner. "Rafael?"

"Yeah?" A voice responds, slightly muffled by the sound of the tap.

Connor gives me a victorious look, and we walk a little further, finding him by the sink. "Rafael."

Rafael twists the water off and rips a few paper towels out to dry his hands. "Be glad y'all didn't get here a second earlier." He tilts his eyes toward the stall while Connor groans in disgust.

"All right, Rafael, look." I step closer to Connor, taking a deep breath. "We kinda had a few questions."

Rafael furrows his brows, throwing the paper towels into the trash. "Sheesh, I plead the fifth?"

I snicker, trying to lighten the air before the blow. "No, no, it's not *that* serious — "

"Why did you tell Quinton to visit me at work when you knew I would hate it if he did?"

Connor's eyes eat Rafael whole as the latter boy shrinks in front of the mirrors and clears his throat. "I, um. I thought that maybe you would like it?"

Connor scrunches his nose as if Rafael's words are gallons of milk gone bad. "That literally doesn't make sense, Rafael. I told you I'd be mad at Quinton…I think. Just be honest."

I speak up, leaning against the white wall. "Yeah, you told me to do the one thing Connor didn't want me to do. Come on, man." I lift my eyes to find Rafael absolutely *pale*.

The three of us stand in silence. Connor and I watch as Rafael fidgets and gathers his thoughts.

Connor soon grows bored, checking his watch and groaning. "Rafael, I don't have a lot of time. Just give us a fucking explanation before we assume the worst, like, that you're trying to sabotage us, or something."

Rafael's eyes, if possible, widen further. But after a few beats, he sniffs, untenses, and lets out a long sigh. In a swift movement, he pulls out his phone, clicks around, and stuffs it back in his pocket. "Okay. I'm going to explain something to you, but you have to promise to keep your cool and just let me talk. All right?"

Connor and I exchange a look. "All right," he says for both of us.

Rafael looks down and balls his hands into fists. "I kinda was trying to sabotage you guys," he blurts in one breath.

"*What?*" Connor steps forward, lightning zapping across his face. "You were fucking trying to what?"

Rafael sighs as he continues to eye the floor, unable to meet our betrayed faces.

My rage begins to pick up, having every red, hateful suspicion confirmed. "Rafael, why? Literally, what did we do to you that would make you want to break us up? Are you, like, in love with Connor or something? How long have you been…doing whatever the hell you've been doing?"

My mind runs in circles, recalling the number of times Rafael's advice had seemed off and counterproductive. When he'd suggested Connor didn't like being the breadwinner, or when he encouraged me to get blackout drunk so Connor would find me exciting again, promising me these were all concerns Connor himself had confided to him. What a *liar*.

Rafael lets out a nervous laugh, and Connor tenses up. "Guys, it's — it's not like that, just give me a moment to collect my thoughts."

And after mustering all the kindness left in me, I let him speak rather than punching him back into the bathroom stall he came from.

"Yes, I was trying to kinda monitor your relationship when we first became friends. But then…they started asking me to go to further lengths, like sabotaging for example. I didn't want to but, Quinton, your parents *suck*." He turns to Connor. "I was poor, you know that. I needed quick cash and Quinton's parents found me. With a lot of desperation at the time, I was posting my email on almost every social media platform saying that I needed a way to make quick cash. They DM'd me on Insta. We started talking and met up, and they seemed pretty legit. Once they had me stuffed on their grapes and bread and butter, the task to essentially be friends with you two for a boatload of cash was impossible to say no to." He looks up at the wall. "Besides, no offense, but I didn't care about you guys at the time. I didn't know you, but I did — do — have a family, and they were suffering. So I did what they asked. Including…sabotaging your relationship."

My head reels. My parents are still intervening in my life, after all this time. They've still been right next to me, guiding me, influencing my decisions, and all without my knowledge. They have had control over me, contrary to the disownment documents they signed. Ever since Rafael walked into our lives. I don't think God would be happy to hear they've been busy playing Him.

Connor draws a few shaky breaths and, at the sight of my shocked expression, takes my hand. "So…Quinton's parents hired you? To watch him and sabotage him? They disowned him, why would they still want ties with him? Plus, why didn't you stop once you started caring about us?" Connor hits Rafael with the most disappointed elevator eyes I have ever seen. "Unless you don't care about us?"

Rafael blinks several times. "What — no, of course, I care about you!" He takes a breath. "I just don't know if I should…" He pulls out his phone, as if he's double-checking something. "Quinton. I wanted to stop a few months ago. But your parents, fuck, they threatened me."

Connor's anger morphs into worry. "What?"

Rafael fiddles with his shirt. "They told me some shit like they'd get me in prison for smoking weed, or something. It was one time — and I was peer pressured, all right — "

"We don't care if you've smoked, but Oh, my God, what the fuck?" Connor seeks help from me, staring into my eyes with deep confusion.

"They threatened that?" The same threat they had used against Marco. They're back at it again. "Connor, he's telling the truth," I state.

Connor tilts his head to look at me uneasily. "Look, I want to believe Rafael but come on. He's already lied to us once, what if he's lying to us now?" Connor makes no attempt to whisper or keep Rafael from hearing us.

"I'm really sorry, by the way," Rafael pipes up.

"Don't be," I butt in, knowing how horrifying my parents can get when you make the mistake of disobeying them. "It's not your fault."

Connor swings his head toward me, adding force to the movement for dramatic effect. "Quinton. We still don't know if he's lying or not."

"I know. But this would be such an elaborate lie. Plus…" I meet Connor's confused eyes. "A similar thing…There was once a guy who — okay, basically, Rafael, you're not the first victim to my parents' threats. Including this very specific one."

Connor remains quiet, watching me with questioning eyes. Rafael remains rendered silent by stress, but his face reveals subtle hope and curiosity.

I close my eyes for a moment. "The first guy I ever liked, or at least where it was mutual — his name was Marco. *Is* Marco. Um, when my parents found out they basically threatened us similarly. Except, I handled it very poorly, and they actually went through with it. Like, he got sent to prison for marijuana as well." I suck in a breath, not keen on breaking down in a hospital bathroom. "And — and I wouldn't be shocked if they did the same thing again." I study Connor as his expression grows more sympathetic. It's expected, Connor's contrarian bone is still significantly smaller than his kind heart. "Listen, this was why I didn't try and find a way to speak to you when my parents threatened you. I saw what they were capable of. So, Rafael, I forgive you. As long as you promise to quit it."

Connor scrunches his eyebrows in thought while Rafael nods vigorously. "Obviously, I want to quit it! But they make me record us speaking for, like, evidence I've been doing my job. I was turning off the recorder earlier." He shakes his phone in the air for a moment. "I want to stop, one hundred percent. But if I could, I would've a while ago."

"Shit," Connor mumbles. "It's okay, Rafael. We gotta help you out of this for all of our sakes, though." Connor takes an uneasy breath and looks me in the eyes before turning back to Rafael. He mutters a simple, "I forgive you, Raf. But, I don't really trust you too much. And thanks a lot for inadvertently getting my mum sick."

I nod. "All right. Well, that was a lot of emotional exhaustion. I need a nap." I take Connor's arm.

Rafael steps forward. "Wait, what about your parents? Don't you have more questions, or wanna fix...this now?"

I sigh. "We will fix this tomorrow. I can already kinda answer my own questions based on simply knowing you were trying to sabotage us. And, fuck, I am so sorry you got wrapped up in our bullshit. My parents will pay."

Reluctantly, Rafael smiles. "...All right. It's your call. Both of your calls." He gestures to Connor. "I'm sorry again. I'm glad we are still friends, even after what I did."

I nod courteously. "Of course."

Connor scoffs before following me out of the bathroom and into the hospital lobby. "Plot twist," he murmurs.

I chuckle dryly, trying not to lose my mind over the fact my parents found a way to monitor me *still*. I shove the tall glass doors open. "Fuck, Connor. I hate them so much. Those people are not my parents."

Connor sighs, resting a hand on my shoulder while we take a seat on the benches outside.

CONNOR

Quinton kicks up dust and squints at the bright sun. "It's just so weird. And the fact they ordered him to try and separate us."

"Terrifying," I agree, twisting my body to get comfortable on the bench.

Quinton groans. "They never liked the idea of me and love put together. Mostly because of my attraction to men." He clears his throat.

"They tried a lot to get me to stop liking men, or just reject the idea of love entirely. This is a new tactic, though. Interesting, but awful of course." The wind blows Quinton's hair from his face, giving me a crystal-clear view of his distressed expression.

"I'm so sorry, Quinton. That must've been super hard — growing up with all of that." I pause, trying to find the right words through my Rafael-induced haze. "You don't talk a lot about your childhood."

He shrugs, and I relax a little. "Why dwell in the past when I can relish the present." He reaches for my cheek and squishes it.

I laugh, pushing his hand away. "I guess," I start, smile slowly dropping. "But, do you…like, have a bad association with love now?"

Quinton's head snaps over to me, and he takes my wrist in his palm. "No, of course not." He squeezes it softly. "Quite the opposite, actually. I love you so much, my parents couldn't break that if they tried." He sniffs and wipes his other sleeve over his nose. "Plus, I had my ways of keeping my mind safe from all of their anti-love rhetoric."

I listen intently — it's rare to hear even a snippet of how Quinton was raised.

"One of the ways I avoided insanity was remembering that, like, every emotion we have is a result of evolution. That includes love. It's almost romantic — that it helped us survive, like, during the cavemen times and shit."

I ponder for a moment. The sentiment warms my heart. "Yeah, that is pretty sweet, actually."

But something in Quinton's tone changes when he twists to look at me. "Isn't that crazy, Connor?" His grasp tightens around my wrist, and his nails begin to dig into my skin. "How love is survival? Love is a result of evolution? We *needed* love for survival of the fittest at one point or another?" He could draw blood.

The atmosphere grows uncomfortable, and my wrist begins stinging.

"Quinton — "

"I find it romantic." Quinton continues. "What is survival without love?"

I decide to humor him and think for a moment. "Survival?"

"No, love, it's death."

Um.

I chuckle nervously, finally able to rip my arm from Quinton's grip. "You're so funny, Quinton. Yeah, it's cool, but you don't need to be so grave."

I regret my words when his face falls. But it soon picks up again, returning to normal and bringing me relief. "Ha, yeah, it's kinda stupid, and I know it doesn't really work like that. But I still like it as an idea."

I stare at the markings drilled into my wrist from Quinton's nails. *Fuck,* that *hurts.* "Me too."

Quinton clears his throat once more and stares absentmindedly at the parking lot. "Well, anyway, back to Rafael." He turns to me slowly. "I'm not going to let something like that get in between us again. I'm so sorry for everything, truly. I love you. And my parents definitely won't get in the way, if anything."

I frown and lean forward to kiss his cheek. "I love you too, and I'll put in my all as well. I hope your parents choose to leave us alone someday."

Quinton's bright eyes bore into mine. Promise smolders behind them. "They will."

QUINTON

I parallel park a few inky streets down from my destination. Not out of self-preservation, but out of my car's preservation. I could outrun my parents easily, however, they *are* capable of wrecking my car with bats signed by superstars and silver clubs usually meant for their small private golf course. This is why I parallel park a few inky streets down from my destination; my childhood home.

I lock my car, stuff the keys into my jacket pocket, and look out at the rolling asphalt.

My neighborhood has always been beautiful, with its long green columnar trees, and its sidewalks re-paved too often for their own good. I wish I could feel similarly about the home I grew up in. My mother and father stripped its beauty away with their words and their palms, forcing me to associate my house — my supposed safe space — with violence and abuse. Which is perfectly fine. But to meddle with my life — to mess with Connor's and my relationship after *they* kick *me* out?

Fucking ridiculous.

The ugliest spot in the neighborhood comes into view. I let out a short breath, mentally preparing to face my parents for the first time in many months. When they threatened Connor and Marco, I was too scared to truly stand up for myself or for them. Sure, I dated Marco secretly anyway, and Connor, but I never marched over to my parents and demanded they stop. I whined about their rules, but I never threatened enough for them to create change. I just got disowned without complaining. But I'm older now. And I won't stand that kind of control.

I cross the driveway and head up the three simple steps leading to my former front door. Nearly kicking over a glass-beaded flower pot, I bang several times on the wood. When my hand meets the door, I shudder. I can't believe I willingly brought myself here. For Connor, though. *For Connor.*

Footsteps approach the door. There's a flat, heavy clack, of my father's prized fucking Louboutin shoes, indicating it's he who will answer.

Without bothering to look through the peephole, he swings the door open, and his creased eyes immediately widen.

The breath leaves my lungs, and my fight or flight response nearly kicks when he makes eye contact. The grayish mustache peeking out of his skin sickens me, along with his polished suit and equally shiny bald head.

We stare at one another, waiting for the other to speak.

I soon remember what I planned to do. In a swift movement, I slightly bend my knees, twist my body, and slingshot my open hand directly into his face, sending him backward with a surprised grunt. Watching him stumble and nearly fall in unbridled shock sends a warm vibration up my spine. *Invigorating.*

"Quinton, what the fuck?" My mother's voice is shrill and commanding when she appears at my father's side. She rests a worried hand on his arm.

I silently wait for them to recover from both the pain and the shock of my slap and clear my throat with a small smile. "Thank you so much, Not-Dad, sincerely, for teaching me how a slap like that feels so I'd know to use it on you."

My mom's eyes search me wildly, a mix of fear, anger, and regret taking over her face. "What are you doing here, sweetie?"

I let out a high-pitched laugh and push my hair back with a sigh. "Did you just fucking call me sweetie after disowning me?"

My father finally returns to his regular strength and steps closer, but not yet out of the house, as though he's about to sucker punch me in the chin. However, my mother tugs him back slightly, clearly not wanting to make the situation more violent.

I keep myself at a distance, smiling at him. "I bet that didn't feel too pretty, huh?"

"Why the hell did you come here? I thought we made it clear we didn't want some gay son." My father, unable to use his fists, uses his words instead, almost hitting the right places.

I maintain my composure, fighting the urge to weaken beneath my stone-cold appearance. "I showed up unannounced for good reason." I grow silent, increasing the suspense.

"What reason, Quinton?" My mother's straight, short bob cut bounces as she shares a nervous glance with my father. I cherish the fear I find myself capable of making them feel. Maybe they're finally realizing they raised a ticking time bomb.

"Stay the fuck away from Rafael."

My father sniffs. "Ah, so he told you. I knew we couldn't trust that *fucking* — "

"Stay the fuck away from Rafael," I repeat myself before he can make any rotten comment.

My mother sighs and turns to my father. "We will have to keep him quiet. Does he have any in-text evidence of us threatening him?"

"*Guys*," I bite, raising my voice. "There will be no keeping him quiet, understand?"

My father takes this as an opportunity to reassert his dominance. He stomps closer until I can smell his sewage-like breath. "Oh, yeah? What the fuck are you gonna do about it, cry to your little boyfriend?"

Probably. I take in a shaky breath. I refuse to crack under the pressure of the mere sound of their voices. "Gonna ignore that comment and continue. I will involve the law if these threats continue. Rafael has evidence of you threatening him and isn't afraid to use it." Okay, I didn't stutter or quiet down, good.

My mother begins to smile. I'd bet she's going to bring up how *untouchable* they are compared to him, so I quickly continue. "And, I know how much you care about reputation. Me, Connor, Rafael, and our other friends will not stop pushing until this story makes the headlines, even if you avoid jail. I know you care about reputation. I know you care about becoming a public spectacle 'cause it's bad for business. Cut all ties with Rafael except for one final call promising you will leave him alone, and we won't have to go through all of that or get the police involved. Your choice — don't punish him and exit quietly, or possibly face all of upper-class Orlando despising you, have your business damaged, and be forced to deal with the law." My eyes dig into theirs and I slightly lean forward, making sure they understand just how serious I am. In the world of persuasion, confidence is more powerful than truth. "One more thing: If God is real, he or she, or whatever the fuck, hates you severely. You will go straight to Satan simply for being such horrific parents, whether that's a sin or not. Goodbye, you shit-stains, and burn in hell." I lunge forward, and my father flinches. But I only wrap my fingers around their doorknob and slam the door shut so hard I swear the wood chips.

Depending on their response to this, Connor and I just may be able to stay safe from their reign forever. I may be able to love freely for the first time in my life.

I pull into Connor's and my driveway, spotting Connor hurrying toward the car. I step out and lift an eyebrow.

"Hey, Connor. Where are you in a rush to at night? Emergency shift you need to cover for someone?" I rub my palm, the skin starting to hurt from how hard I'd slapped my father.

His legs stutter to a stop, and his previous determination transforms into nervousness. "I was just gonna go to the grocery store. We are out of rice, and like, eighty percent of our meals depend on rice."

Before I can offer to search the pantry to double-check, Connor has snatched the keys from my fingers and slammed the driver's seat door shut.

I stand in the driveway, disoriented. "Oh, um — okay! Bye!" I call out to him, smiling as he quickly waves to me through the windshield. Left alone in the expanse of night, I sit on the steps near our front door. I stare at the sky, annoyed with the summer crickets for polluting the northern hemisphere with their never-ending drone. It's August, why are they still here?

My annoyance is quickly enhanced by my loud ringtone. I lift my phone, squinting to read that Rafael is calling me. I accept the call, wondering what he could want at this hour.

"Quinton!" Rafael shouts from the other line.

I groan. "What is it?"

"Oh, my God. Quinton, I don't know what you and Connor said to your parents, but I just hung up with them and they promised to leave me alone. They deleted my number and said our business was over. They did say they'd follow through with their threat if I told anyone about this, but still! It's a win to me. Just, fuck, thank you so much. I don't know how I can ever repay you for this — just, thank you."

Oh, my God. What I did actually worked. In everyone's favor. "Wow, Rafael, that's amazing."

A small, emotional giggle comes from his end. "Yes, thank you so much. I don't know what you did, and I won't ask, but, fuck, thank you."

I sigh with deep relief, and I feel my body physically repair itself at the news. "Of course, man. I'm sorry again. I know it wasn't technically my fault, but I'm sorry my parents are monsters."

There's another fuzzy laugh from the other line. "You don't have to apologize. Thank you so fucking much. I'm going to go to bed now not stressed for the first time in a few months."

I smile and rise off the concrete steps. "Of course; enjoy it, Rafael. And just know, I forgive you, but obviously, I'm going to be a little more skeptical of you for a little while."

"Yeah, no, I get that, one hundred percent. Thank you for being so forgiving, man. I appreciate it."

I nod, even though he can't see me. "Mm-hmm, go get some rest now. Bye, Rafael."

"Bye Quinton!" And the call ends.

I smell the familiar neighborhood scent, taking in the grasses and floral Orlando fragrances. They've promised to leave us alone. Sure, we basically have guns pointed at each other, but mutually assured destruction is easier when I'm also at least armed this time. It gives me some semblance of peace.

I tilt my head up to the sky and observe the few glimmering stars I can see. "Thank you, God."

CONNOR

"Fuck you, God." I lower my eyes from the sky to Dad's marked grave in front of me. "First you take my dad away, and now Mum's sick. Not cool."

I used to come by here more often, pulling into the parking lot of the Umlauf Cemetery, chock full of stories to share with Dad's rather unresponsive grave. It hurt, never receiving any message back, but when he was alive, according to Mum, Dad was always a listener anyway. He's sort of like a pen pal that never writes back.

Today, his lack of responses is equally in character. "Dad," I murmur. I place a pretty rock I'd collected by the tombstone. "Here." I place another rock with its own charm. "What have you been up to lately?"

Silence.

I clear my throat. "Sorry for coming by so late, you're probably tired." I would chuckle at myself for sounding like a weirdo if I hadn't been paying him one-on-one visits like this for years now. My trips used to be once a week, but during freshman year and after, they shortened to more of an every-two-months, type thing. At this point, it has been four entire months since I visited. "I would've come earlier today, but work is taking up quite a lot of time. Mum's sick, too. So there's that."

More silence.

"Do you think she'll get better, Dad? I mean, I think she will. I don't know if I'd be able to handle it if she doesn't…" I let out a dry laugh and turn away from his grave. "We miss you a lot. But," I add with a smile, "I really hope neither Mum nor I see you soon. No offense." I brush my hands across the rough stone, gradually applying more pressure until my fingertips are red and blistered, and my nails are filed. I slow my scrape to a stop and rest my hands on the rock. "Please don't let her die. If you died and like, got reincarnated as one of heaven's cabinet members, don't take her life. You probably miss her and want to see her, but I need a little longer with her myself. I know that is dramatic, and we are still in the early stages of her sickness, but tell me there is zero possibility of her…dying."

Another simple silence.

I sigh and drop my shoulders. "I love you, Dad. I hope the rumors are true and you really are in a better place." I cough, raising my voice to its regular, less solemn volume. "But thanks for the talk. I, um, needed this." Although my words indicate I'm planning to leave, my feet remain glued to the tough soil. I stand, eventually sit, and daydream.

Seconds, minutes, and a few hours pass until I decide my father-son activity quota is filled. I trudge toward my car and curse God at the 2 AM sky one last time before slipping inside the vehicle.

Day two. Day two confined in a hospital with Quinton for Mum's sake and day three of her illness. At this rate, by the time I die, I'll have spent eighty percent of my life inside these walls. Thankfully, Mum's condition has improved dramatically in the morning's time. But I'm unwilling to set myself up for disappointment again.

Dad's breath lasted longer than the doctors expected, but he still died.

It's still good news. I spit my toothpaste into the sink and abandon a disorganized space for someone else to fix.

"Morning, baby." Mum beckons me over.

I keep a reasonable distance and blow her a kiss. "Good morning, Mum."

Her smile falters, and in an instant, I know she's planning on bringing up some sort of concern. My mother is anything but discreet, always wearing her intentions on her sleeve.

"Hey, sweetie, so what's up with you and Quinton?" There it is.

I smile. There's no reason to lie. "Honestly, we were a little strained, but I think there's progress. We're doing better than before." I bite my lip, deciding to give her the gist of what's happened. "Basically, we just — he was distant for a bit because of personal problems that he was scared to tell me about. I reacted poorly when he told me about it and yelled at him, and when he tried to make it up to me, he got Tarchvirus and…got you sick. We both kept doing the wrong things and then we discovered…" I pause, laughing. "Okay, don't call me crazy, I swear I'm not lying, but Quinton's parents…they sort of hired Rafael to be my friend and, like, break us up."

"*What?!* I swear to *God* I am going to kill those evil people — "

"Mum! It's fine. Rafael decided to stop. We kinda caught him, and he told us he wanted to be actual friends with us. But, the Hansleys threatened to get him imprisoned for some drug-related thing they discovered. Psychopaths, I know. Anyway, apparently last night, the Hansleys told Rafael their business was over — Rafael texted me about it — and, yeah, it's over. I don't know why, but I think Quinton and I will be fine. Of course, I'm still pissed he got you sick, but.…"

Mum's jaw drops. "Jesus — I mean, what the fuck, I'm in a hospital bed for two seconds and all of that happens? That is some insane…how does that even — what is wrong with Quinton's parents? I don't want to imagine how he grew up with them, poor boy."

I nod. "I know. But, in terms of Quinton, whatever happens, he's always very…grand about it, I don't know. He believes in our love a *lot*. Like, sometimes I think he's in love with how much he's in love with me."

Mum chuckles, followed by a gentle cough. "That's so sweet. It makes me happy seeing you happier. I'm glad you're not being too hard on Quinton. He has been through a lot."

A shy grin finds its way to my face. "Thank you." I am still upset with him, but it's hard to stay angry at his charming, lovely face. How could I not be quick to forgive? Besides, I was angry with him mostly for ignoring me and shutting me off — now he's showering me with attention. He's being better. I ignore his fingernail marks on my wrist.

"Hey, guys." Quinton sends a quick wave our way, emerging from the bathroom.

I wave back. "Thanks, Mum. Don't know what I'd do if I didn't have you." My eye catches her white dress and hospital bed, and my throat dries. Though my last sentence was lighthearted, I could very well need to seek advice from someone else if her condition becomes extreme again. My insides harden to rock as I work to form some verbal Band-Aid for the careless statement I made.

She smiles back with strong, loving eyes. "Awesome, now run off and get me breakfast like you promised. Enjoy your work-free day." She motions for me to go to Quinton.

I stand awkwardly beside Quinton and look up at him. "Uh, ready to go?" Good. Great, even, considering I didn't fuck up my words. Our recent Rafael discovery of betrayal apparently makes me nervous, and we've had one too many vulnerable conversations for just two months.

He seems unaware. It helps calm me down. "Yep! Grab your things."

"Okay." I sling my bag around my shoulder. Time for a nice, normal day. Funny how rare those are lately.

CHAPTER 14

Outside the hospital, Florida's August punishes me and Quinton with intolerably humid airs. A proclamation of summer's death and fall's takeover.

We suffer, but we eventually make it inside Waffles Galore, Quinton's favorite. We had discussed the Rafael debacle during our drive. It wasn't completely pleasant, but we both happily acknowledged there was far less between us than we thought. Given that, I jokingly declared I would consider forgiving him for the grim months I endured after our six-month anniversary. Okay, half-jokingly declared. "Waffles Galore?" I mutter. "What a stupid name." Though the comment is meant for me, Quinton responds.

"Oh come on, it's better than the name 'Connor'." He scooches forward in line.

I frown, gasping as if I'm offended. "What? Your name is literally Quinton, that's so British."

"What — so are you!" His eyes flit to his nails, and he picks at the cuticles half-heartedly. "What were my parents thinking when they named me?" Quinton musters a hearty cough, shifting his body to face the menu hung above the cashier. "What do you want to eat?"

I tear my gaze from Quinton for the first time since we stepped into Waffles Galore and search for the menu.

Quinton's eyes lower to mine. "Why didn't you answer me? What are you ordering?"

I squint at the menu above the cash register. The lime green text blends far too well with its yellow background. What were the...menu manufacturers, or whatever, thinking? "Fuck, are there any paper menus here?" Protan color blindness beats me once again.

Quinton chuckles fondly. "Ha, colorblind idiot. Need help?" He mocks in a childlike tone and snickers.

I can't stop the smile already surging across my face. "Shut up, you are so mean. And yeah, actually, I do need help. Go find me a menu, *idiot.*" I say the last word in the same tone he did, and shoo him away with one arm.

Quinton pretends to ponder on what to do. "Hmmm, how about instead I read you the menu options because you're a blind little baby?" Quinton points to the large menu above us.

Through a clenched jaw, I agree. "I — fine." Shyly asking the cashier all the way up front for a menu is less ideal than dealing with Quinton's patronizing.

"As you wish." In a swift movement, Quinton shifts me closer to him and crouches so he's bent down to my height. A teasing smile pirouettes on his *very near* face. Quinton slides a finger beneath my chin, tilting my head up to see the menu. And after the smallest touch, I've let Quinton manhandle my gaze to meet the menu in one smooth motion.

My cheeks burn. In my defense, with all our bickering lately and his sickness, he hasn't touched me much in a while. "This — this is so — you're so annoying." The insult is a weak attempt to hide my fluster.

Quinton — inches away — raises an arm toward the menu. "Oh, poor thing." He smiles before moving his pointer finger along the menu from afar, softly reading out every option. His hand still rests beneath my chin. He occasionally steals a glance at my face and grows slightly pinker every time he does. "So?" He finishes reading and patiently lets me think.

Breathily, I pull myself together. "Hm, waffles and eggs sound good, with a side of fruit too, and — oh God, it's our turn." I gingerly shove him forward to the front of the line. He sends a hurt look my way before taking it upon himself to order for the both of us.

The cashier hands me my fruit bowl starter, and after thanking her, we pitter-patter away. Quinton speaks up. "Hey, I need an apology for you pushing me earlier." He settles at a round table, his fingers dragging across the wood; he has forgotten we were planning to get the food to go.

But I don't mind, and I join him with a contented smile. "Hmmm, I don't think you deserve one…" I splay my arms, colonizing the table's space and making myself at home.

Quinton's eyes stay pinned on my thin arms as they gradually take up his table space. "Fine." Through gritted teeth, he smiles. "I'm eating your fruit bowl then."

In an unforgiving millisecond, the small plastic bowl is no longer in front of me. It's instead held in Quinton's palm, and his sturdy fingers are plucking one of the grapes out.

I have to keep from shouting while Quinton's eyes sizzle *sadistically*, almost. He dangles a grape just above his grinning, gaping mouth. He knows that grapes are the only berries I enjoy from restaurant fruit bowls. Well, pineapples are appetizing as well, but Waffles Galore's fruit bowls do not include the tasty fruit, so I'm left staring at Quinton in horror as he continues to tease me.

"Quinton!" I laugh. "Quinton, give it back. Now." I lean over the table and nearly fall straight out of my seat.

Quinton only hums, completely unaffected. "You know, maybe if you tried asking nicely…but oh, what do I know?" The entitlement dripping from his words makes me seethe in the best way possible.

What a choice he's presenting me with: Get what I want at a cost, or get what I want at a cost. "No…no, just give me my grapes." With another futile attempt to snatch the grapes, I'm met with Satan's smile and a maroon berry dangling above it.

"Okay, your choice." To my surprise, he pops the grape in his mouth. He crunches it with such a *slow speed*, ensuring I see every delicious flavor swim to his mouth. Yet he never fully crushes the grape.

My smile is soon replaced with an unhinged jaw while I chuckle in disbelief. "What the hell! Okay, fine, oh, my God. You win."

With a darkly triumphant gaze, Quinton tilts his head expectantly, reminding me of what I just agreed on. Once again, my grin is stolen from me. "Uh — please? Could I please have my grapes back, Quinton?" I begrudgingly follow through on my end of the deal.

But Quinton remains silent. I sigh. I use the most sultry and seductive tone I can possibly muster and look him dead in the eye. "May you please hand me my grapes back? Pretty please?" I can't help but burst into laughter the second I finish my sentence.

Quinton, on the other hand, goes beet red. His lips silently part, creating just enough space for the second grape to roll from between his pearly whites to directly before me. "I — uh," he stutters out.

During his short-circuit, I grab the fruit bowl from his right hand and slide a grape into my mouth.

Quinton finds his voice and whines. "Connor! What the hell was that, so unfair." The rose color fades from his cheek, and I already miss his blush. "You're evil," he accuses.

My hands lift in defense, swallowing the all-too-worth-it fruit. "You asked for it, not my fault." I look around, wondering when the rest of our food will get here.

Quinton lets out a deep breath. "Hey, Connor, after we eat, can we drop off your mom's waffles but go somewhere else after?" He scrolls on his phone.

I look at his screen and notice directions plugged in on his map app. "Sure. Seems like you have a specific place in mind?"

Quinton nods. "Yes, I've been wanting to go there for a while. Why not take the love of my life with me?"

I snicker.

"It's a botanical garden — Unnatural Gardener. They have, like, bizarre freaky plants." He powers the phone off and rests his chin on his hand. "What do you say?"

I meet his dark, hopeful gaze. "That sounds fun. Drive me there, figure out the directions by yourself, and I'll go anywhere."

His lips curl into a great smile, as if there was any chance I'd declined. "Can't wait."

➶

"We're — " Quinton takes my hand and locks the car "…here!"

I chuckle. "No shit." Upon registering my surroundings, I lightly gasp. Although the majority of the garden is hidden by the hill's slope, it is still, simply put, *beautiful*. "Wow…this is really pretty." The reply somehow floats from my lips, despite the flowers having captured every breath I thought I had.

Quinton jabs me with his elbow and tips his head to a reddish subsection of flowerbeds I hadn't noticed. "I know, right? I went here, like, once when I was really little. Can't believe I forgot how beautiful it is." His voice is nearly inaudible as I stare in awe.

In a zip, Quinton is halfway up the middle of a garden's section. I rush to meet him and rest a hand on his shoulder. He grins, turning his head back to the meadow we came from. I follow his gaze, and an appreciation warms my heart. The flowerbeds are so *bizarre*; there is no order or consistency. Blue chrysanthemums grow alongside red azaleas, clashing colors and species. Similar mismatches make the whole ensemble look like an illustration of the word *anomaly*. What drunkard decided to plant pink tulips behind the buds of a hydrangea plant? It's peculiar, and entrancing, even, when every flower is so methodically planned yet so randomly arranged. This garden was either planted by a poetic genius or a disappointed idiot.

There's no rhyme, but there is reason.

Quinton notices my fascination and prods my side. "It's gorgeous," is all he says.

Our shoes faintly thump on the pavement of smooth stone, occasionally tripping on vines neatly curled over either side of the path.

I tilt my head up, lean closer to Quinton, and point out trees we consider "most amazing" throughout the walk.

A bright hydrangea further ahead catches my attention. There's not much in the bed, at least from where I can see. I abandon Quinton and speed up.

He catches my arm and *yanks* me back. Before I can react to how harshly he pulls, he grins and begins speaking. "Calm down, you buffoon. We'll reach there in a second." His eyes are pinned on a second flowerbed, just beside the hydrangeas. A flourishing semi-section of red roses.

I rub my arm, and decide he didn't intend to exert that much force on me. I turn away from the sun and walk backward, directly in front of him. "What can I say? I like flowers, jeez."

"Okay, flower boy." Quinton places a kiss on my cheek. We both pause. "I picked this a second ago," he continues. "I think it's illegal, but, whatever, I thought it was really pretty." In a rushed motion, he slips a faded flower behind my ear. "Um, you can have it."

I bring my finger to my ear and graze the petals. My body feels warm. "Thank you, Quinton."

"I'm glad you let me take you here." Quinton brushes his finger on my back, and his eyes grow hooded. "I like having you alone, where I can appreciate your beauty privately, with no distractions for either of us." Any crumble of nervousness from the earlier morning seems to shed completely from his cadence.

I tilt my head up. "Thanks, creep."

He chuckles. "You have no idea how much you mean to me, or how terrifying losing you feels."

I bite the inner skin of my lower lip. "Let's hope you never face your fears, then." Not saying anymore, I take his hand. And he steals mine.

I yawn from the hospital floor, groggy and tired from the garden walk the previous day. But I have to get over it quickly, because Mum is leaving Holloway today. Her symptoms no longer hold a threat of fatality. She's not in sufficiently critical condition for our awful insurance to cover the payment. No doctor will drag her from the doors, of course, but she's insistent on not spending a dime more.

Her better condition could be a blessing or a curse. Tarchvirus can be extremely unpredictable, tricking people into thinking they're all better before going in for the kill. But the hospital decided to discharge her, and they know best.

I spot Mum beginning to wake up from her bed.

We have a lot to pack today.

At the very least, Quinton and I are doing better. He apologizes daily — I have little to be mad at anymore. He helps with the stress of Mum's illness, is constantly job searching for someplace that will accept his record, and supports me all that he can. Any concern about him not paying attention to me has shattered as well; if anything, he's sometimes too possessive nowadays.

My friends struggle to provide as much presence as he does. With Rafael wrapped up in college, Karl's equally busy shifts, and their combined romantic ordeals with Fritz — which, great for those three — there's hardly anyone around to talk to but Quinton. Which is fine by me.

Quinton is complicated, but I don't crave simplicity by any means.

"Morning, Connor." Quinton's voice tugs me from my own head as he hovers over our suitcase with my clothes in hand. "Wanna pack?" His eyes glitter through the bathroom door's crack, and I push it open.

"Yeah. Let's get to it. Hey, Mum." I tilt my head toward her pleased face.

After lazily hurling scraps of clothes and toiletries into my suitcase, I turn toward Quinton. "So, how's job searching going?"

"Good," he mumbles, gravelly and bitter. Since this morning's news of Mum officially being kicked from the hospital, Quinton has made his agitation clear. Justifiably so, I suppose. He's always been a rebel with a cause, and therefore a firm believer that Mum should stay hospitalized free of charge.

I zip up my toiletry bag, aware that Mum too is in the room. "Wanna elaborate?" Maybe Mum's discharge has ruffled his feathers more than I thought.

Quinton clicks his tongue. "I mean, I don't have much of a resume. Would've loved to go to college, but even community is above our budget. There's not a lot of, like, worthwhile jobs who are okay with the fact that I was drunk-fired." His packing grows less neat, more hurried. "I screwed us over."

I nod dryly. "Yeah. That sucks, Quinton. You know, I spent a whole lot of high school accomplishing all that I could. Internships, jobs, paying half my rent, but even the half-ride scholarships I got…It's too much of a risk. Too much debt." My eyes narrow, and I glance toward Mum. "Too much to lose."

Quinton zips his suitcase roughly. "It's so fucking unfair. You, Connor, you're so smart. You don't deserve to be held back from your dreams because you weren't born rich. Or because you didn't kill yourself working every second of every day."

With my hushed, "It's messed up," the conversation dies out.

In record time, two suitcases are neatly perched by the door, ready to roll out. I slump, happy it's done with. Quinton's soft sigh indicates his satisfaction as well.

Mum smiles. "Thanks for packing, boys. I'm so glad I'm getting out of here and feeling a little better. *Finally*, when I leave the hospital for a stroll they won't yell at me for 'vitals,' or whatever." She chuckles and yawns deeply.

Quinton's fingers enfold my wrist, snug as a sweater. I part my lips to question the touch, but before I can, he has pulled me into the bathroom. He cranes his neck toward Mum. "Just a second, Ms. **Jones**!" His eyes flit back to mine, and he lowers his voice. "Sorry. I just — I don't know about her going home. What if the symptoms return?"

I whisper with him. "Wh — Quinton, we just packed our suitcases. And she's recovering! It's…fine."

Quinton lowers his head. I can't blame him for his adamance — especially because he's responsible for her sickness. If anything happened, the guilt that would come would be unbearable.

I kiss his head. "Trust me." Squeezing his hand, I raise my voice from a whisper to its regular volume. "You watch Mum, okay? I'll be back in no time." I lift my head toward Mum, who has fallen back asleep.

Quinton stops me in my tracks. "What? Go? Where are you going, Connor, stay with me."

I chuckle and sweep a hand through my hair. "Karl needs me for something. I'll be back, you know." His frown only deepens. I sigh, pulling him in for a kiss on the lips. "I'll be right back."

"Ok, Connor."

It doesn't take long to find Karl in the hospital's corridors.

He senses me before I can greet him, his hair falling to the side as he turns his head to look at me. "Connor, hey! How are you, what's up?"

I open my mouth to speak but soon fall victim to uncertainty. Karl instantly reads my body language and sets his papers down. That's one of his many talents — an expert at the universal language of movement. "It's, um, they're discharging Mum today, as you know. Just stressed, is all."

He pats my shoulder with worried eyes. "I'm so sorry, man. I'm glad you feel like you can come to me. Do you wanna tell me what happened? Why you found me?"

My response comes quickly. "No."

Karl hums, understanding without a second thought. His hazel eyes stare at the ground for a moment, a small grin cracking. "We will not discuss your mom then — but, you know…after you bring her home safe and sound, you wanna come hang with me and Rafael? Fritz couldn't make it. His grandma has some high blood pressure thing going on so he's out of town. Rafael and I were planning on going out tonight." He lazily leans his body on the side of the desk. "It could be a nice break from, you know, Quinton. Give yourself some fun?"

A break? I bite my inner cheek at the mention of Rafael. I guess neither Rafael nor Quinton told the others about his initial intentions. "Um…I mean, I don't know. Quinton and I are getting better — "

"Really?" Karl interrupts. "You were complaining about him for like, two months straight a second ago." A breathy chuckle spills from his smile. I guess Rafael didn't tell him about his initial intentions in being friends with us. "Are you rejecting me? Just come! We haven't seen you in a while. I can find a way to excuse our absence so you don't have to do — " his hand presents the scattered white papers " — all of this."

I bite my lip. If I agree to this, I'll have to take the a.m. shifts. But I miss my friends. "Okay, okay. Fine, but I need to drive Mum home first."

Karl pats me on the back. "Let's go! I'm so excited, we haven't hung out enough."

I smile. "Me too, freak. I'm gonna go bring Mum home now, all right? Catch you…"

"Rafael'll pick you up at five p.m."

"…at five p.m." I offer him one last smile and slip back down the hall to Mum's room.

After I explain my plans for tonight to Mum and Quinton, a nurse walks in with a wheelchair and a few papers to sign. Mum is officially discharged from the hospital.

"I still cannot believe this," I mutter grimly as we roll through the lobby.

Once outside, we help her from her wheelchair and trudge through the parking lot. Mum coughs a single time and unlocks the car hurriedly. "It's not worth the battle with them. Besides, there are patients with more need for urgent care. You two sit in the front. By the way, I'm still a little contagious." She squeezes into the backseat.

I remain quiet as Quinton hits the pedal and murmurs, "Sayonara, Holloway."

All right, Connor, we're here. So glad you could come." He enunciates the last word of his sentence and snorts.

I wrinkle my nose. "Karl, you're so weird. And, yeah, sorry I took a while to say goodbye after we got home. Hope I didn't leave you waiting in my driveway for too long."

Karl loops his arm around mine, leading me to the restaurant's entrance. "Pff, don't apologize." His fingers tap the car lock.

With an itching need to, I add, "No thoughts tonight, okay? Don't ask me about Mum or Quinton, I just want to have a normal fun night with the Sex Do'ers Plus Fritz. Or minus Fritz today, I guess."

Karl giggles. "Our group name is so long. We should shorten it." He hops up the miniature staircase at the restaurant's front and pushes its door open.

I'm greeted by homey designs and a warm atmosphere. "This place is so cute." I smile at Karl.

"Not as cute as you, Connie." A deep voice tremors behind my neck, blowing on my skin.

Rafael.

I spin around, not expecting him to be inches from my face. "Rafael! Hey, we were about to look for you." I grin at him. Though I'm still slightly unsettled by the whole betrayal ordeal, it's easy to remember that he's still Rafael. I'll have to keep reminding myself that throughout the night, and pray I can return us to our regular flow.

He smiles till his gums show. "Connor, I'm glad you could make it. How's your mom?"

Karl and I exchange a glance. "She's good," Karl answers for me. "Connor wants to only have a fun night tonight, though, right?" He glances at me for confirmation.

I nod my head, following Rafael who has begun to weave toward our table. Once I've slid my the seat, I'm met with, unfortunately, non-alcoholic drinks. "Tonight'll be great."

Rafael quirks an eyebrow. "Connor being the word of optimism? This is so rare. But you're not wrong, we're gonna go crazy." He shimmies closer to Karl.

"Go crazy? With what, club soda?" I scoff, eyes sloping to the fizzy drink before me. However, I end up smiling, because poking fun at Rafael makes it on the top ten things-to-do list.

Rafael rolls his eyes until the dark russet is barely visible. "Silence, lightweight."

And he and I are back to normal.

CHAPTER 15

Rain is lovely. It's nostalgic; it produces a certain scent that cannot be replicated. Every droplet came from somewhere, every droplet tells a story — a little girl splashing in a puddle, a deep blue sea, a polluted river. Like liquid poetry draining from the sky.

I stretch in bed, lower my head from the window, and decide that any more time spent staring at the rain is less time helping Quinton prepare dinner. I catch the time on my phone. *August 10, 6:19 PM.* My heart sours at the date, an acrid memory of the sixth returning. August 6th barely happened — the night before Mum's initial incident. I spent it cooking parched chicken in a somber hush and sitting across from my equally tired lover.

Speaking of Quinton, he's most likely waiting for me at our dining table. I exhale from my nostrils and leap from bed.

The kitchen comes into view in a matter of seconds. I barrel toward a blond head bent over a steaming dish. However, I catch a glimpse of brown hair as well. Mum?

"Connor!" Mum's eyes brighten, but they also appear slightly exhausted. Downturned, almost.

"Mum! What are you doing here? Everything all right?" I move to kiss her on the forehead but halt and pull a mask on from the counter instead.

Mum's mouth twitches. "Yeah, everything's fine. Why?"

I narrow my eyes. "Nothing, just — oh right — you are infected with a virus!" I carefully add, "You also look a little tired."

Her gaze snaps back down. "I'm still sick is all." And, perhaps the excuse would have worked if she wasn't my mum. Whom I've lived with my entire life.

I choose my next phrasing delicately. "Mum, are you working again?"

Her expression fractures. "No."

A pause.

"Yes — " She lifts a hand to my already incredulous face " — but it's none of your concern. I just took care of a few shifts this morning. I'm getting better, and I'm a grown adult — since Quinton isn't working, you can't have only one provider."

Quinton hears his name and looks up from his plate. But he quickly wilts. "Sorry about that, Conn — "

" — Quinton, don't start." I turn back to Mum. "And you — you don't have to work. I've got it covered all by myself."

Mum rubs her temple. "You're barely nineteen. I can't have my baby providing for three. It's just too much."

My lips pucker to a tense fold. "This isn't a normal-case scenario."

Mum drops her shoulders, signifying some sign of defeat. "Okay, Connor. Still a grown woman, and you cannot control my work, I'm sorry, hon."

I grunt with dissatisfaction and sweep some chicken casserole into my plate. "Okay. Just, don't overwork yourself. I love you." I take a seat.

"Love you too."

⸺

"Hey, Quinton." I lean on our kitchen door frame, eyes stapled to Quinton's body sprawled across the living room couch.

"Hi, Connor." He lifts his head from his position with a smile.

"So, I don't get a greeting?" Mum's voice peeps from Quinton's and my couch. "Jeez, Connor."

I grin and smooth an easy hand through my locks. "I was talking to you a second ago — we literally just finished dinner."

I claim a spot next to Quinton, shifting around on the couch. After a few moments of silence, Quinton speaks up.

"Hey...Ms. Frances?"

I blink.

She twists her neck and smiles. "Yes?"

He clicks his tongue, giving her a moment to finish coughing. "Nothing, just the thing you said earlier...about only Connor providing." Suddenly, his eyes are locked on mine rather than Mum's. "I'm sorry for putting him through that. Really. I'm trying to get a job, and I will for him, and — "

"*Quinton.* You do not have to apologize." She offers a halfhearted smile.

He relents. "But I do. You should still be in that hospital — Connor shouldn't be so worried about you still."

I scrape a hand down my face. "Quinton!"

Mum coughs.

I continue. "She told you to stop — no one wants to hear your symphony of mope. Remember what you promised you'd do better on?"

Quinton lowers his head. "I'm sorry, you're right. Thanks for your forgiveness either way."

I nod, though I find it strange his thank you is said while staring directly at me.

Mum coughs twice.

I stretch my hand to Mum's calf, wanting to provide comfort. However, seconds before I can reach her, she explodes in movement. A sort of spasmodic heave seems to wreck her throat with a series of coughs. Any quarrel between Quinton and me quickly becomes old news.

"Mum?!" My voice breaks first. Quinton and I are soon hovered over her as my frantic hands cup her head.

She attempts to raise a hand in dismissal, though her plans are ruined by another violent number of coughs. As if desperate to breathe, she gasps out several more times. Her whole body suddenly seems inflamed. My medically trained hand immediately finds her chest, and I feel over the red skin. Fuck, how did I not notice this discoloration earlier?

"Mum, please answer me. Are you okay?" The Tarchvirus does not follow a linear process. The virus is efficient, and worst of all, fast.

Tarchvirus doesn't kill everyone — it wouldn't exist if it did. However, Tarchvirus's murder technique is engineered to jump-scare you before swiftly killing you. It makes you believe you're healthy for a few minutes before hurling you back in front of death's door. The idea that Mum could be a victim drops my heart down to my stomach.

The fatal stage of Tarchvirus begins with rapid coughing and inflammation.

"Connor, is she okay? Why is she so red?" Quinton's arms freeze above Mum's face.

My ears pop until I can barely hear, horrified as I watch her writhe. "Quinton...I don't know! Mum, why aren't you answering? And, fuck, call 911 right now." Please, please, please, God, *no.*

Near the end of the Tarchivurs' life-taking process, it calms down, no longer causing coughing fits — like a promise of life. However, this promise often breaks.

Mum's gasping body emits one last cough, for the time being. Her breath is irregular, but it is much more improved.

"Ms. Frances!" Quinton squirms closer to her with a phone in his left hand. He looks at me with deep sympathy.

I watch her intently. "Say something. Can you hear us?"

Mum draws a guttural sound from her throat. "Yes — yes, Oh, my God, Connor." Her breathing evens out, bringing relief to all of us. All of us except Mum. "Boys, you both know how this — " a cough " — virus works."

And what more could be said? Both she and I know there's more to come.

My mind pounds with fear. Mum's coughing and spasming begin once again.

"Fuck, I thought she'd calmed down?!" The unaware Quinton checks his phone, as if the EMS has a tracker instilled.

Please let them arrive in time.

I feel paralyzed. I link eyes with Mum, and my heart shatters.

My eyes blaze in denial.

Hers shroud in acceptance.

"Mum…no. Don't look at me like — that. Please, please don't look at me like you're…Please." I bury my head into her chest. A period of serenity passes through me. Mum has little time left to speak before the virus goes back into offense mode, and she wastes none of it on silence.

"Shh…please don't cry, you two." She looks as though she yearns to wipe the hot tears from our faces.

Quinton inhales shakily, and he pulls me in closer. "It's okay. You're okay, you're gonna be fine."

"I'm not." Her tone lacks color. "And that's okay." The truth leaves her lips in a small whisper.

I wish she'd tell us she'll be fine. I wish she'd call me an idiot — that I'm wrong, and this is in fact not how the Tarchvirus kills. But who am I kidding?

"Connor, what — She's going to be fine!" Quinton demands that Mum be okay — the impossible. Demanding time to freeze, demanding a fish to breathe.

"The…the virus. She's showing every sign of how i-it kills you. But she could very well be fine, the hospital just needs to — they just have got to come quicker. *Please* come quicker."

I look at Mum to reassure me, but she's already been rendered inaudible, violated by coughs and spasms once more.

Just because she can't speak doesn't mean I can't.

I lightly drag my fingers across her face, trying to smile through tears. "It's going to be okay, all right Mum? I love you. I love you so much, you're gonna be okay as long as Quinton and I are here."

Quinton's trembling arm rubs my back.

"You're going to be okay. I love you," I whisper.

Mum's coughing calms down once again. "I love you a lot. Someday, you're going to live far more happily than I could provide, Connor." She rubs my hand.

"Yeah, and you'll be there to witness it," I warn, voice cracking with a quiet sob. I cannot sit here and watch my mother die.

She begins coughing. If the virus has gone fatal, her time is running out. "I'll miss," a cough "… you a lot. But that's okay."

I collapse onto her, pepper her with kisses, and immerse myself in her soft hair and rough skin. "Don't say that." Maybe, I can play pretend a little longer.

"I love you, Connor. I love you, Quinton. Just — don't be annoying to each other."

Quinton chews his lip till it bleeds. "I love you too."

Nausea convulses and ferments in my stomach. It's worse than any sickness I've ever experienced, an indescribable pre-game for grief, almost. "God, Mum, I love you so much. You can't leave me here all by myself. Please don't leave me."

Mum herself now looks scared. "I'm sorry, Connor. Hopefully," she coughs, "your father hasn't found some other chick up in heaven." Her eyes flick upward.

"Gross…" I latch onto her torso with a grief-stricken chuckle, screwing my eyes shut till there's nothing in the world I can feel, hear, or smell but her.

"You're strong," she encourages in a hushed voice. "You don't need your dad or me to do great things. I love you, kid. " She coughs several more times and slowly thrashes once more.

Reality infects me like a disease, and I come to terms with one thought.

Dad's death.

I might be an orphan.

Any remaining tears left in my eyes unleash. "Mum, I can't do this without you. I can't lose another parent, seriously. Please, please, please…" The topic of debate for many philosophers, " — I love you, please, this isn't happening." Which is more traumatizing: Losing a parent you have a full memory of or losing one who you wish you could remember?

I suppose I'll be one out of an unfortunate many to find out. I caress her face, tracing my thumb over every feature as she breathes rapidly. "Mum, Just hang on a little longer, the EMS has gotta be — they've gotta be here soon."

I lay my head on her chest, whispering airy mumbles of affection. Tears drip from my eyes onto her skin, and I pat them off, knowing Mum doesn't like the sting. "Don't go away, Mum."

I rest my head on her chest, and soon come to a daunting realization.

Her breathing is not quickening frantically anymore, or evening out — it's *weakening*.

Panicking, I tug the hem of her shirt, silently urging her to fight it. To fight against death.

Slowly, her breath begins thinning. Her body quits its thrashing. Quinton's voice has drowned out to total silence at this point. I watch her as my heart *breaks*, drenched in a moment that is becoming *all too fucking real*. "Please…" I know the plea is useless. I know what's happening.

Mum is going to die right in my arms.

The longer I look at her, the more memories flood back. My mind replays moments that I had long forgotten — the day she gave me fifteen dollars and told me I could buy any toy car I wanted. It was the first time I ever actively spent money. I think she was trying to teach me how valuable every single dime is, but I'm not sure six-year-old me got that. She told me not to leave it on the living room floor, and return it to my blue bin every time I was finished playing with it. I once ignored her rule and ended up stubbing my toe on the toy car. I sobbed my eyes out, but then, she used her thumb to wipe my tears and taught me a second lesson: whether or not I was to blame for my tears, she would undoubtably wipe them away.

I wipe a tear gently traveling down Mum's face, then swipe my thumb beneath her other eye. "I love you, Mum."

And her chest stills.

I choke out a gasp. "She's not breathing. She's not breathing, fuck. What am I — what the actual *fuck*." I press my ear against her chest to hear her heartbeat. Silence. Through a sob, I place my hands on her chest and recall my training. I begin pumping her chest, and after what feels like hours of pushing, her heart remains unresponsive.

No.

Quinton's eyes glaze, unreadable.

I squeeze Mum, and I cry as loud as I possibly can.

With the world unaware, Frances Jones dies.

Time no longer seems to pass. It jogs, skips, floats all over the place. Reality feels logical, but fantasy feels safe.

My phone is what reminds me it's been two days since Mum's death on our couch, though it still feels like moments ago. Quinton has been gracious enough to deal with the legal BS, such as getting an official pronouncement of death and negotiating an autopsy with the EMS that arrived a few minutes too late.

An autopsy would be necessary. Suspicion is natural, but, of course, she was sick, and Quinton and I don't come off as murderers. I hope.

So she currently lies in a morgue, soon to be plucked and transferred to a goddamn grave. The thought makes me sick.

At this point, everything makes me sick. Everything antagonizes me. Brushing my teeth is a chore, every stranger is an enemy, and every morsel of food feels like poison at its core. My own stomach has betrayed me, forcing vomit out of me if I think too long about August 10th. The day she died. My stages of grief must have had their order scrambled considering all I can feel is rage, the supposed *third* step. Torrid rage.

I hate everything.

A curt, poorly penned sentiment — I hate everything.

Living life in either a constant state of tears or rage is tiring. Not to mention, funeral debt plus very little income is a dangerous duet I'll have to dance for the next…however many fucking months. I curl tighter in my bed sheets, teeth grinding like a wood chipper left running too long.

Quinton is a suboptimal support system at best.

Every time he apologizes for getting Mum sick, I blame him a little more. He's decided to shower me with love and affection, despite my reminding him countless times that is not what I want. Or need. I need *empathy* — someone to sit in grieving silences with. Not someone who seems to have forgotten about Mum completely while making it their life goal to help me forget too.

Let's just say, his offers to take me to an amusement park or the movies aren't ideal. His constant cheap gifts and handmade presents aren't as heartwarming when your mother has just died.

When I finally find it in myself to lift off the bed, I trip over an object and feel an immediate sharp pain in my upper arm. Yelping, my hand flies to the painful spot, and I catch sight of the perpetrator.

My doll.

I sigh. Quinton and I have gotten lazy with looking after the dolls. I pluck the uncanny figure from the floor and grimace. I fiddle with the fabric, prod sewn skin, and search for a tag I know does not exist. The doll that brought Quinton and me together. That led Quinton to my office when he contracted Tarchvirus.

Because of one football game.

That *begs* a question — was meeting Quinton even worth it?

If I hadn't, there would've been no one to recklessly get Mum sick with Tarchvirus.

I clutch the doll, squeezing its torso until the pressure on my stomach is too much to bear.

I set the doll down. "Quinton?" I call for him immediately, as if I've been trained. After all, who else do I have to shout for when I'm on the brink of tears?

When there are no pattering feet or rapid knocking, I flop onto my bedsheets. In a way, I'm grateful. I have the pleasure of crying solitaire, I tell myself. What could be better than that — sobbing with no one to judge you?

So I sob.

CHAPTER 16

O h, my God, just — do you have the flowers ready or not?" My hand abuses the wooden table, leaving an already sweating Rafael quivering.

"I…uh well, you see…Karl was being a little clumsy, and tripped me, and I dropped them." He pauses. "And then fell on them." He tries to justify losing my mother's funeral flowers, and guilt floods his features.

Karl sends an evil glare his way.

Rafael clears his throat. " — but! It wasn't completely Karl's fault. I'm really sorry, Connor, we'll grab more. Seriously, I'm so sorry." Rafael turns to leave and wraps Karl's arm around his.

I stop them. "No! How did you even manage…and why did you come back before buying more?" My hand chops their arms' link, and I snake my fingers around Karl's wrist. "Only you go, Rafael."

I pivot to the boy trapped in my grip. "Karl. Make sure everything else is prepared. We're running on a schedule, there are other funerals being held at this parlor today. *Serene Spirit* has others to attend to." What an ironic name. Way to provide serenity to anyone's spirits with little customer care and zero time to hold a ceremony.

Rafael nods, set on fulfilling his task correctly this time. But Karl stays put. He looks at me. "Karl, I said — "

"Are you okay?"

I blink, frown faltering. "What?"

Karl clears his throat. "I mean, it's only been five days, Connor. Five days since she…passed. You spent a lot of money for this funeral to even happen, and I can only imagine how stressful it is."

I sigh into the hand resting on my shoulder and smile. "Thank you, but I don't have time to think about that. She's already resting in the coffin, the least I can do is throw her a good funeral."

"Well," Karl removes his hand, grinning, "I think she would've appreciated the lengths and efforts you're going to over the actual funeral. You're an awesome son, Connor. I'd tell you to take some stress off planning because you need time to grieve, but I know you're not going to change your mind." He begins his trek off, shouting back, "I love you, Connor!"

"Love you too." I wave the man off and set out to prepare the final arrangements before the service. I head outside toward the sand-covered podium near her open coffin. To avoid combusting with tears, I look any-where but at her preserved body.

Instead, I stare at the small audience who bustle with conversation, as if they're not ten feet from a decaying corpse. There are around fifteen people actively walking around the beach, most of whom I've seen once or twice and quickly deemed unremarkable. They're likely the numerous friends and coworkers Mum gained from frequent job hopping.

I scope the crowd, quietly surveying their micro-movements till my eyes rest on Quinton. He chats with a rando, vexingly *useless*. I wiggle my arm to calm down. "Quinton," I call out. His gaze snaps to mine, taken by surprise at my tone.

He nods his chit-chat buddy a rushed goodbye and straightens his back as I come near. "Connor, how are you? You doing okay? Randal, the guy I was just talking to, invited us over to dinner. Won't that be fun? Socializing might help you take your mind off…everything."

My eye twitches. "No."

He clears his throat.

"Anyway, can you gather everyone at the front? And find Ms. Singh. We can't start without the funeral director."

He nods several times, shifting his weight from one foot to the other. "Of course."

I nod, pat his back, and spin back toward the podium.

Please let this go well.

QUINTON

A distant relative pays her last respects to Ms. Frances, bringing the funeral to its final leg.

It's time to seal the coffin.

I stand at Connor's side, watching him witness dirt cover the woman who raised him. I want to shield his eyes, turn back time, keep him far away from such an awful, surreal sight.

Thankfully, the process ends soon. A few people hang around while Connor beside me cries softly under my arm.

Eventually, the last guest leaves, and the ground is burdened solely with Connor and me. Connor leaves my side, wordlessly taking a seat in one of the chairs. The boy who makes moonlight look like a shadow squeezes himself tight. I step closer and hear him mumble a low, "I'm sorry for failing you." He stares at his mom's grave as he speaks, a small lapping of distant ocean waves filling the silence.

I move behind him and shake my head. "You didn't fail anyone."

"Oh!" Connor jumps. His eyes tearing away from her marked stone several yards away. "I, um, I was just — "

I place a hand on his shoulder and take a seat beside him. "You don't have to explain yourself." I reach for his hand, tracing it and peppering the skin below his ear with kisses.

He turns his head to look at me, and his brows furrow, as if he's planning to say something. But instead, he looks at his feet with a frown. "I miss her."

I let out a deep sigh. "I know." Connor received piles of love from his mother. Love is a healing agent. When it's stripped away, many people find themselves defenseless.

I lean into him, wanting to scoop him up and make him feel *better*. Against the gentle sound of the tide crashing, I whisper, "Connor, why do you think you failed her?"

He looks at me like I'm stupid. "Pfft, I just buried her body. Of course I failed her."

How ridiculous. A highly uncomfortable buzz grows in my stomach. I'd do anything to prevent him from feeling this way. "You couldn't control that."

Connor finally leans back into me as jagged breaths leave his mouth.

His mom was a wonderful person. I can't blame him for his constant crying. I join him in his cries, and hold him closer. As we remain linked, liquid spills from our eyes, forming a sort of sea of our own.

His tears burn my skin until my only wish is for his pain to evaporate with them.

CONNOR

Considering Quinton's nonexistent self-awareness, I wouldn't be surprised if I woke up to a 'Happy two months of your mother's death anniversary!' banner strung across the ceiling written in black ink.

Luckily, I'm met with none. A grumble, followed by a stretch, is the only movement I make before leaving my room. I'll admit, it's lonely forcing the one you live with into "no speaking" terms, for even just a few days. Sometimes, people need breaks from the ones they love. True, genuine breaks, hence the whole "no speaking" thing.

My chest twists.

I travel down the hall and turn into our kitchen. I swing the pantry open, and I'm met with stray bags of chips, cans, and heat-up soups, all topped off with ready-to-go DIYs in the form of dry macaroni, stale Goldfish, and soggy oatmeal packs. Delicious. Not to mention the void of space on half the shelves.

In an awkward fashion, I reach toward the Goldfish, stretching further than my body can manage. I lose balance and jolt forward, but I'm quickly caught in one of Quinton's arms.

He hauls me to my feet and brushes a small red fuzz from my shirt. His eyes wander to mine. "Are you okay — "

"Yes." I cut him off. He sinks at my tone. "Just hungry." I try to keep from feeling guilty as I brusquely slide past him and head back to my room. That is, until he wraps his fingers around my wrist.

He looks at me with desperate eyes. "Wait — Connor." He moves closer and rubs my shoulder.

When I flinch away, he looks dejected. He removes his hand from my back with a wounded frown, but gently increases the pressure of his grip on my wrist. "Why isn't my love enough?"

I tug at his hold a single time. "Quinton, what? I just don't want to be touched right now." I break my own no-speaking rule, and I tug against him a second time. "Enough for *what?*"

His shoulders droop as if I'm missing some huge point, but his grip tightens. It starts to hurt. "For you to be, like, happy."

I squint. "Be happy? Mum just *died*, like, what?" I use the force of my body weight and finally break from his grasp. I use my new freedom to cross and hide my arms.

Quinton slightly stumbles and nods wearily. "I know! And you have the right to be sad, it's just…again, why isn't my love enough? I keep… trying so hard. Giving you words of affirmation constantly, picking you flowers, taking you to nice places, yet you still act like you want to be left alone 24/7."

I scoff, tearing the Goldfish packet open. "Dude, thank you, but no offense, your love doesn't just cure my grief, or whatever. I appreciate those things, but I can't just get over her death because you love me."

"But why *not*," Quinton persists and has the audacity to look hurt. "Okay, that sounded ba — "

"Grief — " I shove one of the orange crackers into my mouth, appalled at his lack of empathy " — isn't linear." I make a square motion with one of my fingers. "It doesn't have a solution except for time, why won't you get that? The phrase "love conquers all" is bullshit when it comes to grief."

He tilts his head, confused. "But love got me through my…" He looks at the floor, and his tone lowers. "…tough times, I don't know, sometimes."

I begin to laugh. "Are you kidding me? We are not the same person. I don't care if you're offended that I'm not feeling happy. I won't apologize for sulking all the time. Get over it — need I remind you my mother just died." My heart sizzles the longer I look into his wholeheartedly confused eyes. Why doesn't he get it?

"Connor, I've given you time. I'm the only one putting effort into us. It's been two whole months! Of course I'm going to worry that I'm not enough when after all that time, you still — "

My fingers curl into a fist. "*After all that time*? Are you crazy? Two months is nothing, she is my mother, for fuck's sake!"

"Wh — " Quinton looks defeated and meets my eyes " — What about us?"

"What *about* us?" I lift a finger accusingly. "Mum is the only thing on my mind. You need to get the fuck over that and read an article about how everyone grieves differently, or some shit, so you can get it through your thick head. I love you, Quinton, but Jesus Christ. How could you act like I'm the bad guy because gestures don't get me over Mum? I want to remember her, I want to grieve for her, and I want to heal with *time.*"

With blank eyes, he mutters, "I just love you, Connor." He slowly leaves the kitchen, most likely headed to our room.

I remain frozen. I flinch when I hear our room's door slam shut. My brain tries to justify what Quinton said, partly convincing myself that I imagined the words. *It's been a whole two months*, he'd said, purely confused.

In a moment of insecurity, I pull my phone out of my pocket and open Google. In the search bar, I type "how long should it take to get over family death." Several websites suggest the peak of your grief is at six months, and that for some, it takes years to feel better. Admittedly reassured by the internet, my mind floats back to Quinton's words. He didn't grow up with a loving mother, or a loving father. No siblings, and no cousins to my knowledge. When his grandparents died, I didn't see a single sign of grief.

To cope with the fact that my boyfriend basically just told me to get over my mum's death because he feels bad, I choose to believe that he has no family that he loves or has ever loved. Grief like this for immediate or extended family is just something he can't fathom.

I hope that is the reason for his behavior because if it's not, I've dedicated my heart to a sociopathic soul who refuses to help me in my darkest time.

So he sucks now?"

"Karl! He's still our friend."

Karl twirls his straw, examining his juice. "A friend who, the last time we spoke to, promised to be designated driver and then got drunk because Connor sent him a slightly passive-aggressive text that *could* be interpreted as a little rude. Need I remind?"

"Guys!" My head drops to my arms. I want nothing more than to end the drawn-out debate of Quinton's and my relationship. "Please."

"Sorry, sorry," Fritz says. "We'll lay off the deliberation for now. But, yeah, I haven't spoken to Quinton in ages, it's kinda sad. He hasn't shown a lot of interest in speaking to anyone but you lately, but…" Fritz trades a careful look with Karl. "…want us to have a talk with him or something?"

My head springs up from my sleeves. "No, no, no, definitely not. He'll know I was complaining to you guys, and then probably whine more about how I don't think he's enough."

Rafael chimes in before Fritz can disagree, saving me from the argument. "It's really shitty for him to suggest it has been enough time for you to finish grieving. Maybe he literally just can't comprehend how you're feeling because he has never felt it. You're in a tough situation. And ignore Fritz. His toxic trait is having a boner for conflict."

This elicits a simultaneous chuckle and offended gasp from Fritz.

"I…guess. I dunno, I just miss Mum. I never want to forget about her." My head twists to the side, avoiding their intent expressions.

Karl clears his throat. "I'm really sorry, Connor. She was an amazing person. Keep us posted. We'll always be here if you need us." He shoots finger guns at me and grins.

I smile warmly. "Thanks, guys. I'll think about it. Sorry if it's annoying for me to talk about my tragedies 24/7."

The three glance at each other before politely smiling at me. Rafael signs the check and hugs me goodbye. Karl trots after him with a wave.

I start to stand, but Fritz touches my arm. "Connor, wait."

I face him. "What's up?"

His eyes fall to his phone and rise back to mine repeatedly, a classic sign of nervousness in Fritz. "I know you don't want us to, but I'm going to try talking to Quinton. He's still our friend, and it seems weird he'd be so insensitive. Maybe fully understanding where he's coming from might help. Again, he's my friend too." He's not asking for permission.

I let out a long breath, eyes pleading. "Fritz. No. Do not involve yourself, it won't help. It won't help me, or anyone, or him. Plus, I don't trust that you'll be…nice exactly."

He rolls his eyes. "You care about me being nice after what he has said to you? Connor, come on."

"*Fritz.* Don't, okay? Do not call him."

Fritz contemplates and then *nods*. "Okay. Fine." His agreement is oddly quick. Upsettingly easy. The Fritz I know always puts up a fight if I tell him no.

I grunt. "You better not be lying."

QUINTON

"You're fucking stupid," Fritz spits at me. "I get you want Connor to go back to normal, but Christ, Quinton, his mom just died."

I sigh and fall flat on my bed. "I just hate seeing him so sad. I'm lost and have no idea what to do. Every single day there's work to be done, and I barely get enough time to be with Connor or help him. I just — I can't stop feeling like shit. Ever."

"What work, you're unemployed? You're not the one with a dead mom."

I may as well also be. "I know. I feel horrible for Connor. And he's complained about me so much to you, and I worry so often about his and my relationship, and — " my voice breaks " — I have no fucking clue what to do."

Fritz's hard voice rebukes me one final time. "Then ask your friends for help! I hate seeing you two act crazy and irrational, and I'm tired of hearing Connor talk about how annoying you're being every fucking time we hang. I wish you'd hang out with us, too. Just understand Connor doesn't want to move on from her yet." And then three monotone beeps.

I let out a gentle breath. Tears roll off my face like little boulders. Alone, I cry, releasing a few whimpers and shaky breaths until a small voice knocks me out of my wallowing.

"Quinton?"

I jump, snapping my head to see Connor in the doorframe. Surprised under the weight of his presence, I quickly wipe the tears off my face. "Oh — hey, Connor! I'm just, um, what's up?"

Connor kicks the ground. "Hey…" We both cringe. "I heard you talking to Fritz." He bites his lip as though he's conflicted. "Are…you okay?"

I look at him. "Do you care?" The question reeks of emotion.

His head tilts upward. "I do care. I don't like seeing you unhappy."

"So you're talking to me now?" The phrase comes out challenging, but I mean it to sound hopeful. He didn't seem happy after what I'd said during our fight from a few days ago, and he's barely spoken a word to me since.

He shrugs.

I drop my head. ""Thanks — thank you, by the way, I'm all right. I don't like seeing you unhappy either."

Connor scoffs dryly. "Trust me, you've made that *very* clear."

I've yet to understand why that's a bad thing. I clear my throat, eyes trained on the bed sheets.

"So. Um." Connor's fidgets with his fingers timidly. "What'd Fritz say?"

"Uhh…he told me what you said. Um, when you were out with Karl and Raf." I try not to sound too accusatory. Don't want to start another fight.

Connor fiddles with his pockets. "I'd told him not to call you. I knew you would react poorly — or how you act now but, like, worse."

I offer a sad smile. "I wish you'd have talked to me instead of talked to them. Fritz gave me a lot of…necessary criticism, I guess. But he was definitely not happy with me."

Connor chuckles. "Neither am I, so." The brown of his eyes burns. "Look, I know I've been, rightfully, mad at you recently. But I didn't want Fritz butting in like that. I didn't like listening to him dig into you. I'll have a chat with him." Connor inches closer, and my breathing quickens. "Can't have you whining about how 'your love isn't enough' even more."

I ignore the last remark, and focus on what's important. Connor is *concerned* about me. It provides a little reassurance, warms my heart, even. "Why did Fritz do that? Like, talk to me even though you said not to."

Connor blinks. "I dunno. Fritz has always liked arguing, but it'd be weird for him to apply that to my situation. When we're…grieving, and suffering financially. He seems pretty anti-us lately, but it's not like him to not listen to me." It's difficult to tell if Connor dislikes Fritz being "anti-us" or not.

"Maybe he's jealous." The words flow from my mouth against my will.

Connor looks up at me with big, confused eyes. "What? He just doesn't like how you've been treating me is all."

I sour. Fritz is an obstacle. "Connor, think about it." An obstacle to love. "You guys had been best friends for years. Spent all of your time together." An obstacle to survival.

"*Have* been best friends," Connor corrects me, "*spend* all of our time together."

"That's the thing, Connor. It's not 'have.' It's not 'spend.' Fritz knows that." I sigh. "You've been wrapped up with work lately, and spending a lot of your time here, with me. I take you out places a lot — "

"That I rarely want to go to," Connor interrupts.

"Doesn't matter. You don't hang with him as much as you did in high school. He probably thinks I'm stealing you from him or something." I take a deep breath. "While we were calling, he told me to stop making you 'fall for it,' or whatever. He literally suggested several times I was manipulating you because of this thing you said when y'all hung out."

Connor's eyebrows twitch inward. "All I said to Fritz was I didn't trust him to be nice to you if he called…"

I look him dead in the eye. "He thinks you don't have a mind of your own — that I have the capability to control you." I barely feel my face as I speak. "Instead of literally just asking you to grab a burger, he's shit-talking me. As someone who experienced the fuck out of high school, I know all shit-talk comes from jealousy."

"You're accusing him of a lot right now — "

"And he hasn't accused me of a lot? Just — " My stomach twists when I see annoyance at my interruption plain on Connor's face. "Just think about that for a second. I love Fritz." Care about him, at least. "But he obviously has a major problem with me right now. With us. I don't know about you, honestly, but I value our relationship so fucking much. I am loyal to you always. Is Fritz?" The words coming out of my mouth barely feel like mine. But I love Connor, and I can say what it takes to make sure he always feels the same way, right?

Connor shakes his head. "What he did was stupid. But, he's still my best friend." That's all Connor says in defense of Fritz.

I consider it a win.

"I love you, Connor."

The boy sighs, beginning to stand up. "I know, Quinton."

My heart sinks as he leaves, and I wonder if that was a victory or a loss.

CONNOR

"Hey man, why'd you call us to this little coffee shop? White Rock Coffee or whatever the fuck?" Fritz pulls a chair out for Karl and himself, voice buttery.

I swallow and straighten my back. "Fritz. I know…okay, let's just get right in, I know you called Quinton. I know you yelled at him after I told you not to."

Fritz's eyes widen, and he throws "did you tell him?" glances at Karl and Rafael.

I follow Fritz's gaze. "Did they know too?" I don't require verbal confirmation. "Also, of course, I figured that out, you nimrod. We live in the same house."

"Look," Fritz starts, bewildered. "I just wanted to, like, help. You know that, you know me." His justification falls short. Fritz's motivation and ability to argue always plummets when he knows he's lying or in the wrong. Right now, nothing about his face looks like he wants to continue talking.

I scoff. "No, you wanted to argue because you get sick pleasure from yelling at people."

He sits in the booth beside me. "No, Connor, I really just wanted to help. I'm sick of seeing him be so shitty. Sick of you being upset all the time with him, and talking about him, and watching him take you places — "

"What, is my grief getting old for you?"

"No!" Fritz's eyes open too wide, and he exchanges too-long a look with Karl. "No, of course not. I didn't mean it like that."

"Then what the fuck did you mean it as?" I recall Quinton's words from last night, before pondering Fritz's points. *Talking about him, watching him take you places.*

"I mean he's being shitty and you're letting him."

I laugh and lean against my booth's back. "I'm not 'letting him' do shit. And you calling him has made the entire situation worse." Quinton had mentioned Fritz telling him to stop manipulating me, or some condescending bullshit.

His eyes narrow into tiny, fiery slits. "Oh really? You're not letting him? Connor, Quinton is the root of half your problems and you still spend all of your time with him. Someone had to tell him."

"It's not your place." I cast a desperate look at Karl, searching for an ally in this battle.

Karl disappoints. "I dunno, Connor. He's kinda right. Sometimes the solution you need isn't the one you want, and he has been a bad boyfriend lately."

I stare at him, feeling slightly betrayed. "He's — calling Quinton wasn't the solution. He feels even more determined to make me feel loved after you did that because he now knows I was shit-talking."

Rafael remains silent and obviously conflicted, however, from their body language, it's still clear that the three have a subtle preference toward each other.

I quickly exhale from my nose to relieve the stress. I hate getting ganged up on. "All three of you are objectively wrong. I cannot fucking believe you two are defending Fritz, did you not hear me? Quinton got worse."

Karl places a hand on Fritz's shoulder. "He was trying to help, at least"

"Well, *did* he help?" I snap. "Show me where he helped. I'd love to see it."

Fritz shakes his head. "Connor, it's unhealthy for you to be spending this much time with someone you're, rationally, angry with frequently. Seriously, I'd — "

"God, Quinton was right." *You probably are jealous, or something.* I can't bear to say it out loud, but Fritz doesn't pry about what "Quinton was right" about.

Instead, his eyes darken. "Connor, please don't be an idiot. I just think it's unhealthy."

I glance to the side. "Do you? Or are you just upset that I'm spending loads of time with someone other than you?"

Fritz rolls his eyes to the top of his head. "Is that the bullshit idea he fed you? Connor, don't be stupid."

"Shut *up*." I boil in annoyance. "I am not being stupid or being an idiot. You told me you wouldn't call him. You're barely helping me more than Quinton at this point."

Fritz tilts his head up, as if he's experienced some divine realization. "Look, Connor, I'm one of your best friends. I will be there for you, but like, our friendship can't be measured in how much I 'help' you. I know you're going through a very rough time, but the three of us have lives outside of you. You never ask about our problems, and we never complain about that."

I blink. "No offense, but what do you have going on that's more important than your mum dying? Who says that? I don't care what you 'went through.' I'm going through a crisis." My anger beats any empathy out of me, and for a moment, I regret my words.

Fritz lets out a quick exhale. "If you're not going to take my problems seriously, then I won't take yours seriously." His eyes dart down.

"Fine," I mutter. My heart aches.

"Fine," Fritz states coldly. "And by the way, I'm not jealous of Quinton for taking you away. Maybe I'm a little grateful that I don't have to deal with your self-centered ass all of the time." He looks at the ground, as if he's a little ashamed of his words, before rising from the booth and leaving.

—

I twist my key in a haze. The moon is high in the sky by the time my door pushes open. I lose the motivation to put my briefcase in its proper spot and allow it to slip from my sore fingers.

Slightly tipsy, I cough, finding a sleeping Quinton splayed on the couch. It's a lazy spread, his limbs splayed out unnaturally, evidence that he fell asleep by accident. Surrounding him is…half-eaten Chinese take-out. I don't miss the untouched box containing my order.

I raise my eyebrows and recall his text messages, which timidly requested I come home earlier. I'd said I would, but I quickly forgot the promise.

Fuck, he must've planned this.

I inch closer and slip the blanket further up his chest. Though I'm tempted to kiss his forehead, I can't. Not until his behavior changes. Not until his tantrums about my grief cease.

I throw my boots toward the front door exit, weave toward my room, and find a photo pinned pretty to the wall.

Quinton is a sucker for documenting memories by pinning up doodles we've made or old Polaroids from back when he could afford a Polaroid camera. He calls them "reminders," often providing no further context. He enjoys relishing the positive past, and I can't blame him. This photo, for example, is from before our six-month. A simple picture of Mum attempting to steal my glasses while I fail to duck away from her attack. My eyes flick to another one before I can cry. Quinton and I at an arcade, taken by Fritz, I believe. It's hard to remember. I smile, but soon stop. I wonder if these are reminders of what was, or of what can never be again.

I speed up my pace to my room.

But I'm not quick enough to avoid the baby picture of me swaddled in Mum's arms that she insisted I hang up. I'm not keen on shedding tears over her for the third time this night, so I swiftly step into my room.

I shut my door. When did my breath grow so shaky? Fourth stage of grief, commonly known as *depression,* hits me like a truck. I had thought anger was the most trying stage to tolerate, I was constantly bothered by everything. But now I yearn for the anger. I *miss* feeling that hot, enraged energy because at least it was energy. Hell, I can't find it in me to be mad at Fritz.

I hop into bed, having spent another day as a ghost. My eyes close, and I let sleep swallow me whole.

I hurl my covers off me a second after I check the time. "Shit, shit, shit, shit, shit." I harass any tiredness from my eyes and force my pupils to adjust to the sun.

Quinton is still in his clothes from last night when I rush to the kitchen. "Oh, hey," he says, "I was just going to tell you you're late."

My lid twitches, and I summon what strength I can to shove him out of my way.

"Ow — Connor!" He grabs my arm and pulls me to face him.

I look him up and down, staring with a penetrating glare. "What is it, Quinton? Please, I'm late."

Quinton's hand stays locked. "I just — how long are we going to be like this? I want to…I wanna get better already. Between us, of course. I feel like I've been trying really hard to make that happen, like last night I ordered us Chinese, and — "

"That is why we aren't better." I sniff. "You're still on about the same shit. I'm sorry I couldn't make it to dinner last night. But when you change and prove you actually understand why someone would be sad for a long time after their mother died, we'll chat." With a sour chuckle, I add, "I enjoy our occasional hang, like how things used to be. But, Quinton, I have seen zero change. Maybe you were a little right about Fritz, but that doesn't change what you said, or the fact that he could be a little right about you. And you still haven't taken it back."

Quinton releases a drawn-out sigh.

"What's with the sigh?" My eyes flick to my watch. When will he let go of me?

"Nothin'. It's just, as much as I'm not showing change, you're not either. You still don't show any signs of wanting us to improve. Do you want us to keep living with each other while you basically hate me?" Quinton releases my arm, knowing I'll stay. Knowing me.

"I don't hate you. I hate how you have been acting. I hate the fact Mum is dead. I hate the fact my friends aren't standing with me. I hate how much my job demands. I don't hate you."

Quinton clenches his jaw, and the volume of his voice slowly increases. "Then prove it, Connor, please. I've been waking up every morning without you by my side — you've always gone to work before we can properly talk. It just leaves me to think and think and think until I've convinced myself you don't want me anymore."

My shoes pity him and keep me in place. "Quinton. Sorry for not being the world's best boyfriend, I'm grieving."

"It's been *three months*, Connor. I know you're griev — "

My stomach drops, and I let out a breathless laugh. "I cannot fucking believe that is the second time those words are coming out of your mouth. You are saying all of the wrong things, like, what the fuck, Quinton? Are you really that incapable of feeling empathy? Do you seriously not understand that I can't just choose to get over what happened to her? I don't think I have ever heard such un-self-aware, shitty words from someone, and I'd least expect them from someone I supposedly love. I'm going to work."

Quinton wrinkles his nose. "Fine. Perfect, actually. You can go to work while I bend over backward figuring out how to meet your impossible standards of love!" His arm flies left to exaggerate his point, and it slams into a cabinet. A bowl is knocked clean off its shelf, and it shatters into pieces right beside Quinton.

I jump backward and bend down to grab the larger shards, "Fuck, relax!"

However, Quinton's eyes do not leave my face. He acknowledges the plate with a quick glance before continuing. "I have tried so hard to please you these last three months, Connor, Jesus fucking Christ. Of course, I feel empathy. I'm so sorry about your mother, and I miss her every day. But moving on is important, she wouldn't want you to be so sad all the time."

The bulb above us flickers. "Dude, you just broke a fucking plate, calm down." Quinton remains standing, and I slice my finger on a piece of glass, sharply inhaling. "Do *not* fucking speak for her — "

"It's true," he mumbles dryly, and he finally takes a step away from the hazard by his feet.

I stand up, deciding he can clean his own mess. "Also, there are no impossible standards. All I wanted was for you to be there for me, was to listen to me if I asked you to do or not do something. I wanted comfort, and I wanted someone who could accept the fact I was going to be different for a little while because I was, and still am, going through something. You are literally so *dense*. You made everything about *you* and *you* not being enough, *you* not feeling loved, *your* obsession with the concept of love. It's fucking weird, man." I bite my tongue to refrain from hurling every insult I can think of at his pretty face.

Quinton's expression darkens. "It's not an obsession. And, what? Do my concerns not matter?"

"If it was your mom who died I would put every single one of your needs before mine." My voice cracks mid-sentence. "Fuck, why did I ever say yes all those months ago?"

Quinton's pupils seem to shrink into tiny specks. "Why did I believe you when you told me you loved me?" He exhales, deep in thought, before a look of acceptance takes over his face.

Confused and horrified beyond comparison, I watch Quinton leave the kitchen and head somewhere I don't care to find out. Leaving me to sob the entire drive to work.

CHAPTER 17

My eyes stay trained on the ground as I walk to my station. I can't risk meeting eyes with a stranger and finding disgust, or even worse, pity.

I head to my assigned room, and a fluff of brown hair appears in a room near me.

I assume it's Karl and head toward him.

With a small tap, the door opens wide, and a familiar face greets me. He's a sick reminder of my recent fight with Fritz, but I'm still mostly happy to see him.

"Oh, hey, Connor!" His head draws to the sound of the door. His pupils round at my appearance. "Um, you look…are you okay?" He slips to my frozen side, resting a palm on my shoulder.

I flinch from his unwarranted touch. "I'm perfectly fine." *Still a little pissed at you for siding with Fritz, though.*

Karl pretends not to notice my rejection and pats my head. "Well, I wish I had good news for you, but…Dr. Thompson is giving you more shifts. Said if you wanted to stay you need to accept them, that is. It's not personal, she said, it's that they're having a huge layoff and you barely make the cut. But Dr. Thompson adores your diligence and knows about your mother. They're trying their hardest to give you a chance. But…no extra pay." He catches my face before it can fully fall, cracking a joke with an awkward laugh. "The shrinking middle class, amiright?"

I stare at him. "Are you…kidding me? No more pay? Is that even legal?"

His fists ball. "I'm really sorry, Connor. I've got a few new shifts too, but hey, she said she can't control it. The cutoff is the cutoff, something she didn't set. The *big* big dogs did. The ones who don't really give a shit about us."

"Hm." I grit my teeth. "Seems she 'can't control' a lot of things."

Karl's head turns side to side, cautious. "I'm so sorry. But, she did say it's your choice!"

"Not much of a choice."

Karl nods. "Yeah. I was just about to say…but, yes. I'm sorry, Connor. There's not much wiggle room since you don't have any college degree in medicine, or any at all, from what she told me. Your options are limited."

"Ha…so she's just telling you my life story?" A small noise escapes my mouth before a hurricane of laughter ambushes my body.

Karl, maybe unsure of his next move, stays quiet.

I turn away once my laughing fit is over. "I'm sorry," I mumble.

"Hey, it's all right," Karl offers a sad smile. "I'll leave you alone so you can get started, yeah?"

I nod, watching him exit with stones in my stomach.

My life is a fucking mess.

⁓

There has gotta be a word for unintentional lack of eating. I suppose there are two reasons — forgetfulness, and a borderline empty pantry. My hands crawl over thin skin. My protruding rib cage says enough. I promise to take care of myself — but a delayed promise is a stretched one, not a broken one. I will, but only when I have time.

I remove my hand from my waist and wonder if it will ever feel plump. I open my camera app, and my mood rots over how I'm presenting myself in *public*. Rots despite knowing no one is still roaming the halls of Holloway Hospital. Even Karl left hours ago. Left alone in my borderline useless department, I've lost a fair share of my passion for assisting victims of America's (terrible) healthcare system. For studying med. Fun in theory, hell in practice. I take another look in my selfie view and wipe my nose. Hopefully, if I earn enough, I can safely switch to a different path that may appreciate my medical experience. Hey, at least I'll have the appeal of allowing employers to exploit me and subject me to hours of nearly unpaid work.

⁓

My belongings clatter to the floor as a loop plays in my head. My brain never quits singing: from mantras cursing Quinton, to hating work, to grieving Mum, a thought is always on my mind. I can't believe I haven't visited her grave since her burial three months ago.

I kick a stray shirt to the side and ignore Quinton's presence. I head to my room and go limp until my head hits the mattress. And again, as I've done a multitude of times, find sanctuary in sleep.

I wake up to a pokey intrusion near my upper arm. A groan leaves my lips, but I soon grow quiet when I realize it's an envelope. Remembering with a brief joy that it's Saturday, I tear it open, assuming Quinton left it.

"*:(we should talk abt this. get plenty of sleep tho,*" reads the first page, painting my chest with anxiety.

I pull the next piece of paper out and skim the text.

With a churning stomach, I throw it to the side.

We are on the brink of going into debt, and we've already met this month's budget limit. Fuck.

There's only around two weeks of November left, so we don't have to wait too long. Carpooling with Rafael is going to be necessary, maybe cutting lunch too.

I bang my head against the headboard and mutter curses for what feels like minutes. This will result in a long conversation of *finance*, easily the second most lethal germ sickening our relationship.

Though we're still together, we remain that way for mostly convenience. If one of us moved out, they'd be homeless. We…love each other, I like to believe. And still have hope, *I like to believe*. But what he says about Mum can be unforgiveable.

I rise, slow and weak, like a dying plant reaching for the sun. After a few seconds, I crumple back to the haven of my sheets. When slumber arrives, worry leaves.

Quinton's clamorous return home wakes me right back up.

I chuckle at his obvious attempts to be quiet: the door is closed so carefully, it betrays him and creaks with a shrill yelp. I roll out of bed. May as well get the budget conversation over with.

Quinton sees me and blinks stupidly. "Oh, hey, good morning." He sets the car keys on the kitchen counter. "I assume you read the letter."

"Yes, and where were you?" I tilt my head with neutral eyes.

Quinton's lip twitches, hiding a smile. "Well, I got a shitty-ish job! I'm now a library technician-slash-associate. It's…well, it'll take up a lot of time — they're really understaffed — but still. More pay."

"That's great, Quinton." I grant a small, congratulatory smile and feel a crumb of relief. He expects curiosity, but I focus on the task at hand. "We still can't spend any more this month. But I'm glad I'm not the only one paying it off now though. Nice job."

Quinton swallows. "Thanks. We'll work hard."

He reaches to touch my arm.

I flinch away.

It's once again Saturday, also known as Laundry Day. Last week was Quinton's turn, though he groaned about his new job as a librarian's associate the entire time. He did top it off by expressing gratitude that he could now take us to carnivals, and "cute shops," and buy me ice cream again. As if I've ever mentioned wanting any of that.

More importantly, Quinton's and my one-year anniversary is in two days.

Quinton's and my one-year anniversary is in two days, and we won't be celebrating.

It's bittersweet.

I activate the washer.

I plan on surviving my current situation. It is not an accomplishment to complete a day's workload, it's a given, and it's not rewarding to work overtime, it's an expectation. Weekends aren't breaks, they're simply ends of a week.

Mum didn't emigrate and then die for me to not pursue whatever she hoped I could someday. I owe it to her. But the American dream is letting me down at the moment.

Not to mention, Quinton is still constantly attempting to make me feel better, which sounds sweet in theory, but actually contains guilt-tripping me for *feeling down,* as he puts it. Despite all this, I won't quit, whether my future includes a medical career and Quinton or not.

The minute I give up, the minute Mum truly dies.

Waking up to a paper note on my chest is strange enough. But twice in the span of two weeks is just pushing it. I yawn and squint as I try to read in the dim cheap lamp-light.

Morning Connor. We need to talk, this is unhealthy for either of us. Meet me in my room.

I can't stop a giggle at his last sentence. His "room" is a makeshift pile of cushions and couches, formerly a general office and living space. I'd kicked him out of the bedroom a few October nights ago in pursuit of mental space. I'm unsure when he'll come back. Or if he wants to.

After a few minutes, I persuade myself to stand and stretch.

Time to go see Quinton, my *beloved*.

I clean myself up quickly — arriving presentable despite being asleep minutes ago is second nature at this point. I can thank my horribly unreliable phone alarm for that skill. I drag myself to his room, greeted by Quinton sitting on his…"bed."

"Connor, good morning."

I flop beside him, far from elegant. "Hey. What is it?"

Quinton taps a finger on his thigh. "This isn't healthy."

'Healthy.' "What, our relationship? No shit."

Quinton frowns, and the clock ticks louder. "Hey, don't be hostile. I just — well this isn't good for either of us. We can't keep sitting around waiting for things to go back to normal, you know?"

I surprise myself when my heart hammers. "So what? I mean, clearly, but we can't really do anything about it."

Quinton drags out a sigh and steps closer. "Connor, can you please just cooperate? I'm not asking you to be happy right now, just take your mind off…her, and have this conversation with me."

My mouth fouls. "Pfft, seriously? Now you're just trying to piss me off."

His patience must be at an all-time low this morning. "Yeah, but I'm not. In fact, I've been spending quite a bit of my time trying to get you to be the opposite of pissed off, Connor."

I scoff, tilting my head up while he tilts his down. "You're still trying to force me to move on."

Quinton crosses his arms. "I'm not doing that. I'm just trying to address the fact we've had thirty fucking fights in the past four months. "

"And whose fault is that?" I raise my hand toward him, incredulous.

But before I can return it to my side, Quinton grasps my hand and lowers it slowly. His eyes tangle with mine for a moment. "Both of ours." He breathes out heavily. "This conversation was supposed to be pleasant, but you can't hold your tongue, can you?"

My frustration skyrockets. "You're one to talk. You brought Mum up first."

Quinton sighs and rubs his temple. He locks our fingers, squeezes once so tight it hurts, and forces my hand back to my side. "God, Connor. What happened to us? How long are we gonna be like this?"

I don't reply, biting my inner cheek. "Maybe when you stop being destructive." I rub my hand. "And hurting me."

Quinton continues, watching me with hooded, accusatory eyes. "You're torturing me, Connor."

"Oh, how am I *torturing you* — "

He huffs and takes a step closer. "I am in love with you. And you don't love me. Why are you still here? With me?"

My eyes tear from his equally inflamed ones. "I…you know why, don't be an idiot."

"Why don't you just leave me?" The tease that drips from each syllable is far from gentle banter. He should be growing, but a smile tugs at the corners of his lips. "You seem to hate me so fucking much." He takes another step toward me. "So fucking much, yet so hesitant to lose me." He leans in even closer, taunting me with a dark expression. "Hence, you are torturing me."

My head spins. I try with all my might not to be the first to look away from his eyes. I babble the first gently thought-out sentence I can formulate with Quinton inches from my face. Before I can stop it, the words slip out. "Shut the fuck up."

And there are a number of things he could've done with that sentence.

Slithering a hand beneath my chin and pressing his thumb into the cleft was not exactly a possibility I had in mind. Tilting my head up to face him with a *slow* force wasn't either. Or him snaking an easy hand around the curve of my waist.

"No, you shut the fuck up," he whispers in a breathless, heavy tone — a faintly familiar one.

The least expected of all, though, is a barely-there kiss on the lips.

"Fuck." I pull away, breathing warily. *What is he doing?* "Fuck, Quinton." My gaze blisters red, matching his rage-colored cheeks as he tugs me forward.

I hate him so much.

He hates me too.

So I kiss him again.

And again.

And again.

QUINTON

"Wow, that sex was magnificent." I stifle a giggle at my own words, eyeing Connor as he effortlessly slips his T-shirt back on.

Connor scoffs. "Oh, my God, what is wrong with you? Who says that?"

I press a small kiss to his cheek, extremely nervous about how he'll respond despite the fact we just… "Me, apparently."

Connor's eyes look everywhere but into mine. "Right, well, I'm going to…go back to my room I guess. Get some work done."

And he…begins to *leave*, but he quickly stops when I grab his wrist. "Wait, what? No, let's talk about what just happened." I scan his face for agreement. Why is he so eager to leave? "That was kinda progress, right…?" I try to chuckle my nerves away, hoping I'm wrong about everything, and sex was a sign he does still love me after all.

Connor quirks a brow, and my hope shatters. "Progress to what? We had a huge fight, and then fucked. Not much of a fairy tale." But he does stay still, allowing me to speak.

I frown. "Well, but, that was fun, wasn't it?" I lean against the bed frame and look down at him.

"Sex is always fun," Connor murmurs.

"So, did that mean anything to you…? Like, actually something?" I wait, concerned for the state of my sanity if Connor answers my question negatively.

Connor tries to be polite, clearing his throat with a smile. "It was nice. Either way, it's over now, Quinton. Nothing has changed."

Oh. "One more question." I tighten my grip on his wrist. So, what if I come off as desperate. "Do you love me?"

"Quinton — "

Not a yes. "All right." My heart splits. "Got it." It comes out in a whisper. Connor's silence continues to thoroughly break my heart until it's no longer bearable. "I have an idea."

Connor looks up at me with big, brown, apologetic eyes. "I'm sorry — "

"*I have an idea,*" I repeat.

Connor's sympathy morphs into his regular annoyance with me. "Okay, Jesus, what is it?"

I offer a wimpy smile. "What if we…I don't know, spent, like, the day together?" May as well try one last time to revive our love. "After that, maybe we'll progress, and I can understand what you're saying a little more." Connor practically twitches in disapproval of the idea but stays quiet. "That's not crazy, is it? Spending a day together like it's senior year again? I'll take you to more casual places than I normally do. It'll be nice… even if you're faking your smiles and shit."

I catch him muttering a few snide remarks to himself before he begins speaking. "Hm, I mean." He turns his head to the window. "I guess we haven't tried it. But only today, and, I swear to God, if you make one comment about Mum I will take the car and leave you wherever we are. Do not expect anything out of this tomorrow," he adds sharply.

I nod, shocked he had agreed. "I'm going to get into more proper clothes, and so should you." Connor remains still, so I smile, deciding to respond with risk. "Unless you want to stay and watch?"

To my surprise, he blushes. "Shut up, no," he says, exiting with a low chuckle.

Heart still recovering from his comments earlier, I sit down on my bed. We have to be salvageable.

Okay, you little weirdo, hurry up and pick something!" Quinton nearly vibrates in line, antsy to take me to a new store. I snag a small, clearance Harley Quinn figurine from Aisle 2, but still don't return to the line. A market stocked with nothing priced above three-ninety-nine, a toddler's heaven, and Quinton's first stop on our date.

"Give me a moment, lord." I fail to subdue Quinton's pestering. I didn't know what to expect when I agreed to this extravagant date. I'm trying to keep an open mind, maybe something will change. But every time I'm not laughing at one of his jokes, I'm reminded of what Quinton said about my mother's death. It's hard to put it past myself, and it's conflicting since I love Mum and *hope* I love Quinton.

"So angry. You're, like, the definition of a rebel without a cause." Quinton looks at me fondly, clearly enjoying this new, not sad version of me. It's true that Mum hasn't been on my mind as much today, but I credit time and less work-related stress for why I'm happier. Not Quinton. With his library assistant gig, it's easier to calm down if I sleep in a day or spend a Saturday out. Plus, the initial overwhelming grief is waning. Mum died over three months ago, and although thinking about her still twists my heart, it doesn't snap it. My bursts of sobbing usually have to be *caused* by something, not simply random. It does feel nicer, but everything still stings.

I cut the line to Quinton's side, earning irritated grunts from strangers behind, and I set my toy in his hand. "Rebel without a cause implies I don't have a reason to be annoying to you. Which I definitely do."

Quinton grins, lifting his toy-filled hands. "Okay, okay, I take it back." His eyes flick down to the inscription *Ages 8+* on my trinket of choice. "Quinn. Really?"

I sputter and squeeze my box closer. "Fuck off, she's amazing. At least I don't still play with marbles, you literal two-year-old." I gesture to the pouch of fifty cent marbles in his other hand and flick them.

To an outsider, we'd come across as new lovers. Fishes of the sea who'd finally swum into each other, vibrant, innocent, *youthful*. We certainly wouldn't look like we'd have the label "orphan" had we been seventeen.

"Two-year-old?!" Quinton's near screech tugs me back to the present. "I'm — look, marbles are interesting to everyone! I just thought they'd be cool to look at, or play with, or whatever…" He trails off at the sight of my taunting expression. "You're such an idiot."

"Sure, I'm the idiot. Okay, Quinton."

We leave the store in a fit of quiet chuckles and walk parallel. It's a miracle we haven't fought tooth and nail once since we arrived together an hour ago.

"Where to next, oh, great and mighty Quinton?" I'd be lying if I said Quinton's and my default dynamic isn't fucking cocaine. I know I'll regret allowing him to hear my laughs and see my smiles again after the shit he's said. I know I'll regret letting him be around me, as if he deserves that at this point. However, it's hard to get enough of him, and it's so easy to forgive a man like Quinton. There should be rehab for human beings. Well, I guess that's therapy…whatever. For the sake of us I'll grant him pieces of me *just today*. Yeah. This is simply a new method of improving our relationship. I'll obey my heart for today, not my head, as much as I don't want to.

But I'm growing infatuated once more.

Quinton's eyebrows lift and, get this, he *blushes*. I'd almost forgotten what a nice sight that is. "Don't call me great and mighty, what the hell!"

I grasp his arm to halt him, inspecting his face as a grin grows on my own. "No way you're *actually* blushing at me calling you great and mighty. Ha, you are ridiculous!"

Quinton pries my wrist from his arm, throat clearing. "Shut up, you just caught me off guard." He tears his eyes from the sidewalk ahead of us and back to the infrastructure. "How about we go to that thrift shop, huh?"

"Yeah, elude your weird kinks with a thrift shop, why don't you." I dodge his lazy push, and before I can think of retaliating, he skids to the shop's entrance.

He beckons me over with an urgent flail of his arm. "That's not what I'm doing! We just need to make the most of our time today. The absolute most." Quinton walks inside the shop and immediately calls out, "Holy shit, it's freezing in here!" He's hugging himself by the time I've entered the store.

My nose wrinkles. "You poor American thing. This is *hot* by European standards."

Quinton scoffs. "Oh please, at least we have better accents than you."

Before I can open my mouth to object, Quinton's finger rests on my lips, and he smiles in mockery. "Let me guess what you're gonna say: I'm so fancy and British! I love tea! I have bad teeth!"

Despite his anguish-inducing accent, I grant him a chuckle. "I hate you so much."

"Maybe you do," Quinton says, and although he's smiling, his tone sounds all too *real*.

However, the conversation becomes irrelevant in moments. Quinton, in record time, has left my side and returned back with several articles of clothing hanging from his fingers. My jaw drops at his speed.

His eyes roll, and he ruffles my hair. "Oh come on, it's not that much. Besides, you slip in and out of clothes fast." His second sentence tumbles from his lips with nonchalance. He almost sounds oblivious to the implications.

I sniff, refusing to fluster. "God, okay. But we aren't buying any of this unless it's under three dollars. We'll just try them on for fun, got it?" I snatch the *laundry load* from his grasp as he nods, and I head toward the dressing rooms.

"Fuck. There's only one available room." Quinton sinks. "Connor, you go first. Put on a fashion show for me." He points at the door, dismissing any employees that look too eager to assist with polite no's.

I grimace at his wording, but I can't stop my cheeks from heating up. "Okay, Quinton." With Quinton in the waiting area, I press the door shut, triple-check that it's locked, and strip completely. Without looking, I mindlessly reach for the first thing Quinton picked out. It's a sweater, perfect for the late fall season. The saturated brown is an appealing look, and despite the simplicity, it sings a modest chorus of color.

It's safe to say I like it. *But* it feels like a size too big.

I twist the doorknob, anxious for Quinton's reaction.

He blinks once. "It's so adorable."

I grin. "Really? I thought so too."

He beckons me over, and his smile widens with every step I take closer. Quietly, he runs his hands over the fuzz, careful to trace every bit of fluff with his fingertips. Like he's handling an injured animal, his hands travel up and down my torso softly. It knocks my brain out of function.

For a moment, it's like nothing ever even went wrong.

At the dangerous feeling of forgiveness, I retreat from his touch. "I don't think I'm gonna get it, it's a little big. You try on your clothes next, freak." With a quick subject change and insult, the moment ends.

Quinton replies airily, as if he's still reliving the moment. "Okay — right, thanks." He grabs a dress at random from the pile. "Just try not to faint when you see how beautiful I look." His hand lingers on mine a nanosecond before he darts into the dressing room.

When Quinton finishes, he struts out like a model, and he tips an imaginary hat with a wink. "Well? Dashing, aren't I?"

I burst before my heart can, and I nearly fall backward in laughter. "You — you look like a fool!" The dress sticks to his shoulders like a second skin — enticing — but it disappoints when it meets his stomach, where it heaps a *load* of unnecessary fabric. "Why the fuck did you pick that out? It looks like a maternity dress, Quinton, and I'm pretty sure you're not pregnant."

"Hey!" He feigns offense, covering his stomach with a frown. He twists the dress around and looks at the tag. "Wait, I think it is. Why was it in the wrong section?!"

I continue to laugh, and with no warning, he wraps his hands around my waist and switches our position per his will. "Your turn."

As my laughing mellows out, Quinton meets my eyes, holding them there until I look away. I slide into the dressing room. Before the door fully shuts, Quinton sticks his arm through the crack, a new garment in hand. I take it without asking any questions.

The second the raven dress properly hugs my body. I look in the mirror. And, God, I wish this was an exaggeration, but my jaw falls lax. It's almost halter, however, there's a sort of window in the middle of my chest, complete with black sleeves that almost act as gloves, stopping midway up my upper arm.

Before I can drool over its sleek fit, black palette, and neat folds, I hurry to present the medium-length dress to Quinton.

And just as expected, his mouth too hangs open, and the "O" slowly forms into a grin.

"Hey, Quinton." I give a feeble wave, growing shier as I try to forget my less positive emotions about him.

He rises to his feet in an instant. "Damn, Connor! You really pull this shit off." He lifts his hands with a sneaky curiosity before dropping them. His mind gets the better of him.

Good. "Well, should I get it?"

Quinton blushes a thousand shades of red. "Get it? And like…have it at the house? And…wear it?"

I release a warm laugh. "Quinton, you really short-circuited there." I pat his head once before quickly retracting my palm.

With an absentminded voice, he airily defends himself. "Sorry… you're just really pretty. I don't know, sorry."

I stutter, taken aback by the compliment. "Pretty?" He tends to butter me up with compliments — you know, to make me feel better about Mum — but this one feels more honest. Natural, and *real*.

"Yeah?" His pupils round. "You just look cute, what can I say?" He's shy.

I'm shy too. "Heh, thanks — um, Quinton. Your turn now, and try on something that actually looks good."

Quinton cocks an eyebrow. "Wanna see me in something pretty, Connor?"

I nod. "Whatever helps you sleep at night."

Quinton and I leave the thrift store with my new dress, and my eyes flick down to my phone. "Two-fucking-p.m.?"

Quinton nods, flicking a stray hair from his tank top. "It wasn't just a thrift store, idiot. It's an entire chain with a number of stores, and we went to quite a few." With a cocky smile, he adds, "You were just having too much fun to notice." He collides our heads, bumping mine probably harder than intended.

I jump. "Ow! I was *about* to say I'm getting tired, but I guess not so much anymore." My feet ache in complaint. Maybe I'm a little tired.

Quinton intercepts my path. With a frown, he searches for a solution — very typical of him. "You could just be hungry? Tell you what, how about we eat, sneak into some badly guarded theater because tickets are so overpriced, and then afterward take a quick car nap?" And in moments, his quick mind has conjured a plan that checks every box.

"Sneak into the theater?" A distant, long-decayed memory of sneaking into a theater at seventeen with Fritz crawls back. The thought tugs at my lips until a bittersweet grin has formed. "I did that once, and bro, it was so fun."

Quinton scrunches his nose at the nickname. "Yeah, let's do it!" He cups my face, a playfully serious look in his eyes. "Will that satiate your utter boredom and complete famine?" He runs one honey finger down my cheek and looks pleasantly surprised by my lack of protest.

I pull back from his touch. He frowns. "Yes, Quinton."

The wind slaps our hair left and right as we hurry back. Quinton's heaving breath is periodically interrupted by laughter.

We run with no purpose.

Having just eaten, the sickly combination of food, exercise, and strained giggles makes me nauseous. But it doesn't stop me. We skid corners and curves until we realize we've slowed to a lazy walk, drained of energy. I pull Quinton to a stop. We latch onto each other and breathily sink onto a near bench.

"Why — why the fuck did we *do* that?"

Quinton squawks out what I hope is a laugh before tugging me to my feet. "I don't know. But, Connor, I'm running out of time with you. We gotta get to the movie theater." His eyes lift like a hawk as he surveys the perimeter. Until his face goes pale.

"…What's up, Quinton?"

"We ran in the opposite direction of the car."

I blink, refusing to let the mood be ruined because of an inconvenience. "Then explain to me the movie theater plan while we walk back?"

Quinton perks up, grinning. "I'll explain when we get there."

After a slow walk back, we fumble back to the car until Quinton is successfully in the driver's seat. He drives us to the movie theater and parks.

"Okay, just tell me, you nimrod."

Quinton fiddles with a string hanging on to his shirt's hem as he leads me inside. "Well…all we gotta do is, um, borrow two tickets from people. Once we're in the movie wing, there's no way they can tell if we're watching what we 'paid' for." He smiles like he's some mastermind.

"You guys are going to do what?" But he's soon knocked off his high. A lovely dark-skinned woman behind us cocks her eyebrow directly at me. My eyes immediately find her certification tag. Shit, she works here.

She notices my stare. "What? Going to explain? Or…" Quinton turns around to look at her, and her face suddenly lights up like a Christmas tree. "Wait — Quinton!?"

Quinton's head flies up, and his eyes widen to ovals. "Nia! Oh, my God, how have you been?"

She chuckles. "Good, just making quick cash for college housing expenses next year. Call me over-prepared, but it's necessary. However, I'm probably better than you two have been. I mean, come on, who steals movie tickets? That's just weird." Her eyes glint with questions, Quinton laughs.

"Let's just say…the world isn't treating us great lately. We wanted to be spontaneous," Quinton explains.

Nia, Nia, Nia. The name is so familiar.

"Find spontaneity in a way that won't lower my pay," she jabs back, turning to me now. "And…" She squints. "Connor! I see you two are still together, very adorable. Maybe you're not so bad at getting some, after all, Quinton." She elbows him, bringing a small chuckle from his lips. Her eyes narrow at me till they're pouty slits. "Come on, you don't remember me? Ouch."

I scramble around my thoughts until an understanding hits me. "Wait. You're the girl who pretended to be Quinton's girlfriend, right? So his parents wouldn't, like, throw him out? Nia, good to see you, oh, my God."

She chuckles nervously, rubbing the back of her head. "You too. And sorry about that again, I didn't like him, promise. But are y'all on a date or something?"

Quinton and I exchange a heavy glance.

I press my lips together, and Quinton's face falls. Demoralized, he lets out a quick, "Yes." We both wince.

Nia grins. "Aw, cute. So cute, I might just let you two see a movie without y'all needing to illegally sneak it?"

Still pondering Quinton's 'yes,' I barely register Nia's kind favor. "Wait, really?"

She nods, nudging her head toward the theater hall to encourage our movement.

We follow, watching her chat up the ticket-taker with a sly smile. With a quick thank you, she returns to her post and nods at us.

Quinton and I return to our plan.

"So this is a date?" I test the waters.

Quinton blinks. "Um — well, whatever you want it to be, you know? Is it a date to you?"

My turn to blink stupidly. So stupidly, I forget to respond.

Quinton's eyebrows contort, and he looks to the side. "Okay." It comes out dry. But I don't dwell on Quinton's tone for long, as I'm quickly distracted by the theater he pulls me into.

When my eyes crack open, I'm instantly bewildered by my surroundings. The first words to leave my lips come with a wide yawn. "What the… fuck." That was certainly not the twenty-minute power nap we promised ourselves to have after the movie — that was a whole REM cycle. "Quinton." My sense of touch returns to me, leaving me in a comfortable panic with my body's closeness to Quinton's. Our limbs are pressed together, our noses are brushing too nearly, and our eyes are millimeters from each other's. "Quinton," I whisper-yell with more volume this time and try to lean away.

His temple twitches several times before his eyes open. Equal confusion spreads across his face. "What…" He stretches, inadvertently sliding further against me. "I don't think your alarm went off."

I look down and blush bright at our proximity. "My alarm? I thought you set one." I manage to sit up.

He chuckles and rises with me. "We are such idiots."

We remain quiet till Quinton pipes up.

"It's okay, look, it's only five minutes past six! That's not so bad. Whatcha wanna do?" He cranes his neck, stretching it out.

I tap my chin. "The sun's setting soon. We could drink a little later. Not crazy drunk," I add; don't want a Rafael-Quinton firing repeat, "but, just some light drinking. In the meantime, let's play…hm. Oh, let's play that one game where someone says a color and we race to whatever object has that color. Until we're totally lost, of course."

Quinton perks up. "I heard about that game, yeah! Great way to spend the final hours of the day." He looks down before smiling. "And when we drink later, we can play spin the bottle." He winks one of his green eyes at me.

I cock my head. "There are only two of us, Quinton."

"Exactly."

I swing my car door open, careful not to hit the curb. Quinton sucks at parallel parking. "You're a weirdo. Let's play." Once Quinton has the car locked and secured, I reach him and drag him toward the shopping center's sidewalk.

Quinton's eyes flick away as he thinks. "How about we spice up the game with this idea? We could make it competitive. Like if we chose blue, whoever spots and reaches the next blue thing first can make the other person do whatever. Within reason, of course."

I shrug, suspicious of Quinton's idea of "within reason." Still, I say, "Okay," and in an attempt to throw him off, I mumble the word 'blue,' nearly inaudibly. But apparently, Quinton is Superman, because he hears my sly insert and immediately flies toward a blue billboard with terrifying velocity.

I catch up to him, panting. "How did — how did you register me saying blue — I practically whispered!"

Quinton graces me with a casual glance. "Doesn't matter. Now, what should I make you do?" He thinks for a moment, raking his eyes over me and stopping at my hand. He grins. "My request is for you to hold my hand while we run to the next spot." He takes my hand and grips it as if it's the last time our fingers will ever touch. From the way he's holding it, part of me mildly believes it is too.

"What do you mean 'next spo — '"

Before I can finish speaking, Quinton's arm is extended and his legs are running as he drags me along with him. "There!"

I follow his finger and spot the blue object he's pulling me toward. "Quinton — that is a bird. A bluebird in motion and moving."

Quinton continues pounding the ground. "Nature waits for no one, Connor. Once it stops, I'll make my demand."

And after fifteen seconds of unbridled gasps and pants, the bird blesses us with a pit stop. I swear I see pity in its black, beady eyes. "You are…the worst." I point an accusing finger at Quinton.

"I know. Now do fifteen jumping jacks." He tilts his head. "Oh also, let's have a grace period when we arrive somewhere so we don't spot something before the other is looking. We'll both look at the ground for thirty seconds, and then see who spots the next blue object first, yeah?"

"Fifteen…are you fucking *kidding* me?" I pause. "Also, yeah, I like that rule."

"I never kid. Now get to it, sweetheart."

I stare daggers at him the entire time and perform his request, lazily, of course. He counts out loud with every hop and chuckles at my exhaustion. "Okay!" I cry, sinking to the ground. "Done. I'm done."

Quinton lowers himself to my side and traces a hand up my back. "You all right? Ready to go again?" He grants me a break and stares at the sky the entire time.

Rounds pass by, elapsing faster than seconds. Quinton wins for the fifth time, concluding the game.

"Yes! Okay, it's around ten till seven, let that be our last round?" I nod and he continues. "For my prize this time…I want a kiss. Just on my cheek?" He nudges a finger to his freckled cheek. He quietly adds, "I-I mean only if you, like, want to, it's…yeah."

I chuckle softly. "Yeah I'll kiss your cheek, it's not the end of the world." I rise to my tippy-toes, press my lips onto his soft skin, and pull away with a speed that leaves Quinton looking hurt. "You're welcome," I awkwardly squeeze out.

Quinton doesn't speak for a moment. He lightly touches the spot with a sort of *boredom* in his eye before clearing his throat. "Car?"

I nod, trailing behind him.

Quinton, a natural navigator, has us back to the corner where his car is parked in five minutes flat. "Since this car technically has some blue on the license plate, and I technically spotted it, could I give another request?"

My eyes flit over and link with his. "Sure."

Quinton abstains from a single fidget. "Well, you kissed my cheek earlier…I was wondering if — well, a kiss on the lips?" He chuckles at his own poor sentence structure. "One, that's all I ask?" He looks on edge, nervous.

Until "I guess you could," leaves my lips.

Quinton wastes no time sweeping me into a kiss.

He is swift, but not messy.

He's always messy.

I welcome it, allowing him to position our bodies against the car. I grow pliant and look up. Warmth invades my heart as he looks down, emotion wrecking his eyes. The kiss is sweet, but deep. Though both of us are afraid of overstepping boundaries, Quinton keeps the kiss passionate.

He incorporates every touch he can, as if he is to be shipped to the front lines of war at dawn. As if he's kissing his lover goodbye.

Despite this, it lasts no longer than nine or ten seconds, and when he pulls away, my stomach burns for *more*.

"Uh, thanks," Quinton mutters, exhaling deeply.

With a fuzzy mind, I blush. My state is pure. A pure frazzle over the simple but loving act of a kiss. Considering we had sex this morning, my reaction is nothing short of amusing.

"Relax, Quinton." I ruffle his hair, hypocrisy seeping through my words. He seems far more relaxed. At peace, even.

Quinton chuckles and smooths out his hair. "You first."

After the swathes of butterflies finally migrate from my stomach, I find my words. "That wasn't…forgiveness, for the record." I can't tell if I'm telling him that, or myself. "Let's get in the car, yeah?"

Quinton nods.

We pile inside, with Quinton (hopefully) sharing my grin. He informs me he already made a reservation for dinner ahead of time. After lollygagging for a few more minutes, Quinton hits the gas pedal, and we set off for the restaurant.

Excitement begins to muffle the annoyance I usually have associated with Quinton. I can't help but wonder where the rest of the night will leave us. Since it's fall, the sun has already sunk. However, when the true sun sets, a new, equally bright one rises.

City lights.

They blaze and pop, coating downtown Orlando in a bright blanket. Sure, light pollution sucks, but this is sheer *beauty*. It's today's cherry on top. It's hard to believe, really: I enjoyed an escapade with Quinton for the first time in *months*.

I enjoyed being Quinton's friend again. Not just boyfriend. Quinton is one of my best friends. As much as I resent him, I believe we have hope. Admittedly more so than I did yesterday. I couldn't say if I love him or not, and I honestly don't care. I believe I *can* love him again. God, I better never be labeled as someone who holds grudges — I'm on the brink of forgiving someone who wasn't there for me when my mum died.

If he makes up for all this shit. If he apologizes and grows. That's enough for him to stay with me, right? After all, he worships being loved. And I'm taking that very thing away from him.

I tear my eyes from the delicious city view, casting a risky glance toward Quinton. His head nods faintly with quiet music squeezing from the car's speakers. It's turned to nearly the lowest setting — he knows I'm not a fan of his musical taste.

As I observe him, my heart puts Newton's first law to shame. Honestly, where did all these thermal energies come from?

I tilt my head toward the window once again. Today was a reminder. A reminder that Quinton is still Quinton. My Quinton. The one I shot dangerous glances at in the hallways from sophomore to senior year while knowing his unattainability. The one I pursued not believing I could score Quinton Hansley. And the one I sit in a shared silence with now.

I believe we can get back to normal one day. The thought was a fairy tale last night, and today has proved me wrong. Sue me. Sometimes, you have to work to keep your soulmate. Love isn't its own force with a mind of its own. It's encouraged, built, created, given, and taken. And only if Quinton is willing to fight for us, I am too — unless he insults Mum ever again. Even if it causes "thirty fucking fights."

The venue of Quinton's choice is Thai Palace. The tiles are either all yellow, all lime green, or a mix of both. The similar hues mess with my Protan disorder. Before I can decipher the color, Quinton gently tugs me toward him.

He links his left arm with mine and opens the other arm to the tall wooden door. "Shall we?"

When I nod, he walks us through the entrance and straight to our seating. "I also ordered our spot ahead of time." He smiles proudly.

I quirk an eyebrow. "This place is nice. Look at you, taking initiative and making a reservation."

He rolls his eyes. "So snarky," he mutters, but he grins as he looks down at me.

I chuckle. "So. Why did you choose such an expensive restaurant anyway?" I take in the detailed beige glass panes and blue ceramics dotting nearly every ledge.

Quinton shrugs. "I don't feel guilty stealing from big corp restaurants."

My head flicks up. I open my mouth to ask for elaboration, but a waiter strides in beside us. After a simple order of Pad Thai from me and a second, lengthy order involving oyster sauce and champagne from Quinton, he leaves us.

For the next hour, conversation trickles from a steady stream of chit-chat to waves of banter.

I had forgotten Quinton's mention of stealing until the idea resurfaces again. "So…Connor. How much energy do you have left to run?"

My eyebrows twitch inward, and I gulp my water before speaking. "What? What are you talking about?"

He opens his wallet and displays it to me. My stomach drops. The pouch contains a single ten-dollar bill.

Our meal is at *least* two hundred. My first reaction is to scold myself for not questioning how Quinton planned to pay for this sooner. My second reaction is to scold him. "Quinton, you idiot! Did you…do we have to — my, God." I grow alert, glancing around to ensure no one had seen the empty wallet.

"Connor, it's fine! This place is so, so far from where we live, we'll be alright. Actually kinda annoyed about that because now we have to pay for gas — "

"*Quinton.*" There's a playful glint in his eyes, sending adrenaline to my stomach. His mischief is contagious.

I desire a bullet in my skull. "A heads up would've been nice."

Quinton is clever. I trust he'll get us out of this; however, I still boil in my seat. "Come on, don't act like you don't like the spontaneity of this." Quinton stands and gestures for me to do the same.

"Now?!" I whisper yell, scanning him up and down.

He nods steadily, takes my arm, and drops a small brown rectangle on the table. It's certainly not his actual wallet — the real one has a green stain — but it's meant to deceive. I think? "Just follow my lead." He pulls me forward.

So many objections. I have so many objections. But, all I can do is vibrate in silence, torn among rage, adrenaline, and *excitement*. Quinton knows me well enough to tamper with my boundaries for fun, analyze them, and grace me with experiences of his choosing. He knows that any slightly illegal activity triggers my inability to take any situation seriously. And my love for stupid fun.

We're *stealing*. We ordered hundreds of dollars of food and drinks. My heart beats faster.

Quinton meanders along, softly bringing me toward the door without a hint of worry or suspicion in his step. "See? This is easy." He flicks a piece of dust from his shirt, yawning.

"Shut the fuck up. This is unforgivable," I spit through a gritted smile.

We approach the front waiter, and a different usher waves. "How may I help you?"

Oh, god.

Quinton puts a hand on my back to calm me down. "Our friends are a little lost and were planning on grabbing a table near us. We thought we'd go outside and wave them over." Quinton's eyes never tremble, and his arms never flail — he speaks with an unwavering voice.

The man clicks a pen and nods slightly. "Right…" He leans past us and zooms in on our table. He catches the counterfeit wallet and relaxes. "Would you like to claim a table for them? Grab the seat beforehand," he offers. How lucky of us to catch such a cooperative, gullible worker at their shift.

Quinton smiles and pretends to think. "No, that won't be necessary. They're basically already here anyway! And — " Quinton points to our table " — we left my wallet there, for collateral."

I try not to shake, clutching Quinton's hand as he grins easily. Quinton charms the man with a few pleasantries before the usher finally smiles.

"Sounds good, sir. I'll watch your table — and wallet — for you while you're off." His voice tenses. "Be quick, and thanks for choosing to eat with us tonight!"

God, Quinton's masterful. "Pleasure's all mine."

We walk outside at an ordinary pace, chuckling like law-abiding lovers.

Quinton's grip on my hand suddenly tightens, indicating — I think — that we're out of view of the front desk.

And we run.

We run fast around the corner. There are no shouts or calls imploring us to return, so we find no reason to twist our necks back in any cold sweat.

After skidding down the streets for at least two minutes, we halt, panting and laughing. "Holy shit, Quinton, I must've burned a million calories by now."

"For — " a gasp " — real. That was so nerve-wracking, oh, my God." I lean against Quinton for support. "We did it! Hah! We just committed a crime together." Quinton finds my eyes.

I want to laugh at his romanticizing of the ordeal. As if it's some couples bonding experience to rob uptown restaurants of hundreds of dollars. "It was fairly exhilarating."

He doesn't reply. A few beats pass, and I grow worried. Silence breeds conflict when it comes to us.

Dreading the quiet, I continue. "I'm so full. Can we wait before we drink?"

Quinton clears his throat. "Yeah. Let's get back to the car for now. Also — " here the conflict comes " — I'm so sorry, Connor." Oh. "I'll try to understand you. It's true that it hurts a lot that you don't love me — " he sighs when I don't object " — And, I know I haven't been the best to you. And I'll try to get over myself until…yeah. For you. Even if it's not what I'm truly feeling, I want our time together to be loving and fun." He looks deeply sad as he speaks, in contrast to his hopeful words. "I can't promise to not get offended or to not desire your attention and love. But, Connor, I love you so much. And I can't have you being angry with me until the day I die. That'd just suck."

My heart spills over. "Jeez, chill. I won't be mad at you for that long, good lord. I'd have to be upset with you for, like, seventy years."

Quinton's polite smile spreads over his tan skin. "Let's avoid that then." He nudges my slouching body off his. "Also, no getting tired yet. Our final waltz is not over yet."

I lift a brow at his wording; it's said in a teasing tone. Maybe it's a reference I didn't get. I stretch my back and vigorously blink any sleepiness out of my eyes. He's right, I can't let the day end. "I'm not tired!" And it won't end. Quinton's confirmation that we *can* fix this brings me joy incomparable with any other activity we've done all day. "I'm not letting this fun stop yet," I declare.

Quinton's smile falters for a second. "Yeah…come on. Let's go." Quinton takes my hand. And I steal his.

Coiled up in Quinton's car, I squint at him and notice his concerned expression. His eyes remain trained on the road ahead of him; however, he soon catches my stare. "Look who decided to open their eyes. We're just about here, Connor. Hope you enjoyed your twenty-minute car nap." Immediate excitement.

"Oh, nice." Then reality hits. "Wait. You've got fake IDs, right?!"

Quinton tuts and rolls his eyes. "Of course. Fritz made them for the five of us as a graduation gift, nimrod. How could you forget? How do you think I got the alcohol that resulted in me getting fired?" He parks and exits the car.

My chest twists at the mention of "the five of us." Fritz, Karl, Rafael, Quinton, and me. I miss the group's bond. I haven't had the focus or time to speak with them for the past two or so months. Or to make up with Fritz. But maybe that's good. Maybe when I set up a date, we'll meet up, and time will have made us sweeter and more forgiving — we can laugh about our fight, even. If I don't have that mindset, I'll break down at every reminder of Fritz.

I quickly crush the thought. Tonight is a night of blissful forgetfulness, not grieving over dead mothers and stressing about friends.

Quinton knocks on my car-side windows with a vigor that bangs me from my head. "Hey idiot, you good?"

"Oh yeah, I fucking am. Wait up." I scramble out of the car.

"Sorry, just excited." He hands me the fake ID.

After at least forty re-reads of the ID's information, I shoot my head up to the club.

"Dude, you've gotta chill." Quinton ruffles my hair, only pushing me further on edge.

Still, I nod and take a breath. Fuck nerves. After I memorize the ID — the only way to steady myself — we walk inside with a recklessly youthful awe. We conceal our excitement by slowing our pace and keeping our eyes trained on the wall.

The bar's activity is nothing short of explosive. Skin on skin, alcohol turning the floor into a river, and pulsing lights that adorn the air in shimmer and shine.

If not for my colorblindness, I'd probably have a sensory overload. Quinton seems quite at home, however, he's been to tenfold the number of parties I have.

He combines our cash — a ten and a twenty — and orders for the both of us. He exploits his more-defined jaw and deeper voice to act like a twenty-one-year-old. I observe him as the light paints his skin. I suddenly wish I could decipher the light's color and suffer the sensory overload after all.

When the bartender is finished preparing our drinks, I snag the booze and take a hefty swig. I scrunch my nose. Way too hefty. "Is this vodka?" Perhaps zoning out during Quinton's order wasn't the best decision.

Quinton nods. "And some gin's in there too. Along with a bunch of non-alcoholic flavoring. Good, right?" He drinks, eyes widening and lips hooting. "Fuck, that's strong, like, 80 proof or some shit."

At his display of weakness, I suddenly feel compelled to finish the large glass resting in my fingers. "What's wrong, can't take it?"

He looks at me, the green in his eye shifting from emerald to neon. "I can, probably. Better than you, actually." Competition conquers his beautiful smile. "In fact," he twirls his straw, "I bet I could finish before you."

I blink and feel a slow grin stretching on my face. Could that be a poor decision? Maybe. But that's not what's on my mind.

What is on my mind, is the enticing blond perched beside me while offering me the best night of my life. "I bet you couldn't. I accept your challenge, Quinton. Why don't you count us off?"

"All right then." He slides his chair, increasing our proximity scoot by scoot. "Three…two…one."

I snatch the glass up to my lips, open my throat, and *swallow*. The liquid channels downward in large surges, and tears prick at the acidity. But, it doesn't stop me, and I chug the vodka. It tastes of bitter rage as it punishes my liver. This definitely isn't the safest way to consume alcohol, but then again, there's no such thing as safe underage drinking anyway. Yeah, that makes sense.

Relief pervades me when the final drop of liquid touches my tongue, and I slam the glass on my table. "Done!"

Quinton's eyebrows furrow at his loss but soon soften. "Wow, Connor, didn't know you could take alcohol so well!" There's a sharp, tipsy enthusiasm in his tone.

I let out an absentminded giggle and attempt to unblur my vision by blinking repeatedly. God, we are both such lightweights. "Daaaamn right I did!" I aim for a loving punch at Quinton's arm but miss, KO-ing the air beside him.

Quinton chuckles. "Let's drink more later. I think it's high time for some dancing while the effects really hit us." He clumsily links our arms and drags me toward the glowing ground of the bar's center.

The lights burn brighter and the music somehow screams louder.

"May I — " a charming burp from Quinton " — interest you in a dance, fair prince?" His smile *smolders,* wonky and lopsided.

Strobing light comes from every corner of the room. It rejects the laws of physics to swim around the two of us. "Only if you promise to protect me, knight in shining armor," I yell over the noise.

Quinton stares at me in deep thought for a moment, before producing the most goofy grin I've ever seen on him. Which is saying a lot. "Why, of *course*, Connor."

The man lazily swerves me across the floor, and his eyes shine as we try to dance in sync. We waltz in a graceful mess and rummage over each other with shameless glances. We eventually break apart, spinning and laughing and spinning and laughing and spinning and laughing until I eventually fall back onto his chest. I bury my head in his shirt, and Quinton runs a finger through my hair.

"Someone likes my shirt, huh?" Quinton peers from above, a grin teasing his lips.

I barely hear him over the blasting stereos but manage to mumble, "Mmm, shut up." I tilt my chin up to search for his eyes, but I only find his head outlined in light.

"Did you just tell me to shut up?" he whispers, dipping me drunkenly. He attempts to grab my chin, misses, and then laughs before trying again. Successful this time, he presses our foreheads together, rum-smelling breath mixing between us.

I tear off him and trip back toward the bar. "You're so annoying…"

Quinton shouts back, "You love it!"

I roll my eyes. "I don't." When I arrive on the bar stool, a bit of sensible Connor returns to me, and I remember the entire concept of rationality. "A-are you sure we should drink more?" Quinton sits on the cold, metal stool next to me. "Can't we get, like, alcohol poisoning if we drink too much?" The walls seem to chuckle at the thought.

Quinton shrugs dramatically. "I won't pressure you, but, you know, I'mma drink. You do you, bud — "

"Nevermind, pass the booze." And sensible Connor is left for dead.

I take another swig because alcohol poisoning can suck my dick. For once, I'll detach from responsibility. Let go a little.

Quinton lays a hand on my palm and pulls me forward. "Let's dance some more."

"Yes, sir."

The physical sickness of vodka still gurgles in my stomach when I wake up. "Ugh…" My surroundings materialize; a cab's interior. As I shift around, and a large object topples off my shoulder. It groans when it collides with my lap. Quinton's head.

"Jesus…Connor, a little heads up before you move." His head snuggles back up, still mid-slumber.

I stare at the sight, feeling for my phone and clicking it on. I find no history of a cab being ordered and try to piece together what happened. Quinton must've sobered up just enough to catch a cab for us. I look at my screen and notice it's half past eleven. I flip the device off, relax my upper body, and sigh into Quinton.

When we step into the house, Quinton suddenly appears sober. With that, he also appears…ominous. I note it but say nothing. We walk into my room, and Quinton flops onto the covers. Sober Connor would've skewered me for allowing Quinton to rest on the same sheets as me, but today, Quinton gets a pass. He deserves this, I guess.

After delirious pillow repositioning and repetitive kicking of sheets, I settle in the bed with Quinton at my side. Quinton presses a lazy kiss to my forehead before whispering, "Night, Connor."

And I fall asleep.

Or Quinton *thinks* I do.

I keep my eyes pinned on him through my lashes, watching as he observes *me* instead of sleeping. He stares, peering at and inspecting and surveying my features. Not with fondness, not with malice. Maybe with love?

But one thing I'm sure of is the glint of liquid in his eyes. Exhaustion and rum steal me before I can ask what's wrong. And I dream. And I forget.

CHAPTER 18

I fucking hate hangovers.

My head constantly makes some sort of sound, never ceasing, never giving me a break. Nausea hits next, enhancing my headache and pulling a groan out of me. But, strangest of all, Quinton has left.

There's no boyfriend to kiss my head good morning. I don't need to sit up and check to know he's left either. I've grown used to misfortune, of course, so it can't ruin my day — especially considering my poor decision-making has led me to a hangover on *Monday* morning. Work.

The sun naturally woke me up before my alarm clock did, so I opt for simply lying in bed and thinking hard.

I enjoyed yesterday — without hesitation, it was worth it. It was a good idea. Quinton made more progress than he ever has. Yesterday was a good sign, and it proved we can be how we were. Just, with time. Time is everything.

I let out an audible yawn, and my head clears to an extent. After the mental battle fought every day, I'm convinced to rise from bed. Even a little earlier than I usually do.

My fingers drape over a rough edge somewhere in my sheets. I feel around more and realize it's a slip of paper. I scoff; leaving a note for me a third time is just pushing it. Curling it open easily, I read.

Connor. Meet me in that room. The empty wine cellar I think it is??? Anyways. Go there.

The wine cellar? I chuckle at his misspelling of cellar before suspicion steals the laugh from my throat. The wine cellar is a peculiar meet spot. Before questioning why he hadn't suggested the living room instead, I fold the letter and head down toward the cellar.

—

QUINTON

A petal pluck, a petal fall, a petal pluck, a petal fall, a petal pluck, *a petal fall.*

Don't kill myself, kill myself, don't kill myself, kill myself, don't kill myself, *kill myself.*

The rose falls.

I don't know why I bother — I've cried all the tears, contemplated all the reasons, considered every outcome. How would stripping a red rose bare of its petals help me in a decision that has already been made? Maybe it's symbolic. Maybe I want to depart with style, so they can write a story that reads something like — *young blond male takes social media dare too seriously — kills himself because a rose told him to.*

They'd be wrong. I'd never take my own life over something so trivial. And love isn't trivial.

Connor and I are doomed, frankly. I love him to the moon and back, but he doesn't feel the same. I failed to win at *life*. He is beautiful. He is the sky, the sun, the ground, the sea, the planets. Connor is the world because he is love. But I am not that to him. Yesterday, he made that clear several times by saying nothing. Never reassuring me when I suggested he didn't love me anymore. Yesterday, I spent a day with a different Connor, and he spent a day with a different Quinton. The old Quinton. We took on the persona of who we used to be, but high school is over. Yesterday was closure. It was *everything*; and everything comes to an end.

It showed me what I should've come to terms with a while ago, which is, again, that I have lost the right to Connor's love. If no one else loves you, how are you supposed to love yourself?

So what do I deserve? Why continue to live?

I have no one to call my friend, my job barely pays, I have a magical doll attached to my body, I fall beneath the poverty line, I hate myself, my parents disowned me, and yet, all became irrelevant when Connor walked into the room. My issues became minor inconveniences that could be dealt with once I decided I was done kissing him.

However, that's no longer our reality. There's no bright side anymore — there's nothing to combat my iron-clad *misery* without love on my side. And he left my side long ago. If Connor proves there is nothing between us anymore, I will humbly seek refuge in death.

I went to therapy one time when I was in the sixth grade. Hated it. So, when my parents abused me every time I showed a hint of interest in men, I didn't bother with therapy. Plus, it was forbidden — probably out of fear I'd snitch on their abuse. My parents had tried to make me believe love was an idiotic thing altogether, that it was evil, even. Unfortunately for them, they got the opposite reaction. I formed a concept of love that I believe is correct — that it is what we live for. No thesaurus could ever offer a synonym to rival the term love. And what if my therapist tried to tell me it was crazy? That it was wild to dedicate your life to pleasing your heart alone. I would've lashed out — therapy wouldn't have been a good or healthy option for me whatsoever.

I had what I wanted. Connor's smile was more healing than any therapist I'd ever encountered, so why go? I placed all my bets on him, while he ended up investing a single dime.

Point is, life fucking sucks.

Which is why my next steps are crucial.

My eyes wilt down to my phone, and I suck in a sharp breath. Connor should be up by now. Five minutes pass, and I decide to set out to find him. I feel like a ghost as I walk.

Not two seconds pass before I've collided with an alarmed Connor.

"Ow! Fuck." He rubs his head and bats his eyes a few times. "Quinton? Why are you so dressed up?" Yesterday was definitely an act for him as well. Roleplay. Because, fuck, his voice has gone through a massive change — from sunny skies to a blizzard, from warm to below-freezing. I take his icy tone as more evidence in support of my decision; there is no hope. But I'm still going to test…

"S-sorry. Sorry. Come on, let's go."

Connor starts to whine about how I didn't answer his question and grouses over being late to work. However, it's an hour before he'll need to leave. It can wait.

I hush him with an annoyed look and turn to the cellar. "Come in." I open the door for him, growing nervous.

I study as Connor's expression mutates, gradually, slowly. It contorts from dry lack of amusement to…*fear* even.

He hasn't taken a single breath since he walked in. I suppose it's difficult to properly breathe in such a tight space — especially with a table taking up room.

Especially when two pairs of scissors lie flat on the table's wooden surface.

And especially with the two dolls lying beside them.

"Quinton…" Connor moves deliberately, *carefully*. "What is this?" His bewildered hand attempts to reach for the doorknob without me seeing. But I notice, slide past him, and shove it closed.

Perhaps I slammed the door with an ounce too much strength. He looks *scared*. "Don't worry Connor, my goddess. I'm not going to kill you, Jesus fucking Christ." I scoff at the thought. I'm not technically lying.

Wide-eyed Connor snorts, humorless. "Oh — yeah, really? Then why are our dolls here next to pairs of fucking *scissors?*" He stands in place, apprehensive.

But Connor's nerves seem to relax at the sight of my face. "Hey, what?" He reaches a still *so* careful hand to my cheek. "Why are you cry-ing? What is this, Quinton?"

I wipe my face clear, not having noticed my own tears. I don't reply yet, plucking the dolls from where they're stationed.

Along with the scissors: one pair handed to him, one for me.

I stare him down, looking for love in those deep, brown irises. Nausea bleeds into my stomach. *What if he disagrees?*

"Answer me!" Connor's voice cracks. "Why — why did you give me these? What the fuck are you doing?" His questions stack up. He links his eyes with mine before they travel down to my doll and scissors.

"We aren't happy."

I only have to whisper a few words. Just a few for Connor's smart mind to connect the dots.

"Are you…oh, my God." Connor buckles his shoulder muscles with a brutal tightness. "Oh, my God. Are you really suggesting *suicide* to me right now? What the fuck is *wrong* with you?"

What the fuck *is* wrong with me?

A hand floats to his mouth. "Q-Quinton, don't — why? We were… aren't you, don't you want to fix things? Please don't. You can't just leave me." Connor begins crying. The tears flow down his cheeks, drip down his chin, and hit the floor.

"We?" It's a small word that Connor whispers. "*We* aren't happy?" But I know what he wants me to confirm. That I'm asking him to join me.

I nod. "We. Both of us." I can hear the craze in my voice, but I have to be sure…"Please, don't cry. You don't…love me anymore. As you said several times yesterday. I cherish love. And I don't have it anymore from you, so what's the point? Let's just leave this awful life behind." I inter-twine our fingers, staring into his soul. Please say yes. "Die with me. I have nothing. You have nothing. Perhaps we can love each other up there, doll." *Please agree.*

Connor rips his hands from my grasp. After several frustrating pauses, he murmurs. "Oh, God. What happened to you?" His face mangles in distress. He looks down at his doll and scissors in his own hand with a shaky exhale.

I frown, trying to keep my voice stable while my stomach loops. "Come on, Connor, please just think about it. We have no one but each other. Your mother and father died. My parents disowned me because I'm gay. We have no friends, no siblings, and not a damn soul in the world cares about either of us but each other. You depend on me for nearly everything down here. Wouldn't everything be better with us up there?" My words thicken. "And you fucking *hate* me."

"I don't," Connor cries. "I don't hate you. Please don't do this. Please." His body shakes with sob after sob, hurting my heart, but not enough to keep me from pressing on. "How could you ever think I'd agree to kill myself, Quinton? Do you think I have the willpower to do something like that?"

I stay quiet.

"Also — " he continues " — what the fuck?! How could you ask that of me? Are you crazy? I don't depend on you for everything." He accuses me in a shrill tone, squeezing his doll.

I scoff. "You basically have zero friends besides me, which, no judgment, neither do I besides you. You have no family except me, and you have no house without me. *Think* about it, Connor."

He takes a step back, and his voice shrinks. "What the fuck is wrong with you. I'm not your fucking marionette that'll slip and shatter the second I'm without you. When did you ever start thinking you had all this fucking control over me?"

Every sentence is a blow to the jaw, but I refuse to give up just yet. "I–I didn't mean it like that." What I said still stands, but telling someone who's headstrong that they need you to survive isn't exactly convincing. "Please, Connor, please. There's no way you think we'll make it out of this hellhole. We're in debt. We go hungry at least twice a week. Once again, we have no family. We're the only people we have on this entire planet, and you don't love me."

Connor steps back a second time. "Who the hell tries to convince someone they, quote-un-quote, *love* to kill themselves?" He whispers this time, eyes wide, and for no longer than a nanosecond, those eyes appear to consider.

"I'm going to do it whether you join me or not," I lie. This is it.

Connor scrunches his eyebrows even more. "You're going to leave me?"

Shame begins to leak into my senses. "You don't even like me, Connor."

I lean toward him, plant a warm kiss on his cheek, and seize his small hands.

He simply grows paler.

I decide we've been silent for too long and continue with persuasion. "Connor. You're late to work. When you go, they'll yell at you. Give you more shifts — "

He breaks our hands apart. "I-I do," Connor stutters out, staring at me with broken eyes.

"You do what?"

Connor can only hold our gaze for so long before hanging his head and sobbing softly, this time with slightly less volume. "I love you," he whimpers.

My heart blooms before I can stop it. "Then…don't — Be honest."

"I do, really! C'mon, let's just leave the cellar and go out, on me. Celebrate our one-year!" He grasps my hands and tries to pull me away from the scissors.

I rip my hand from his. "Then join me, Connor. If you love me, you won't be able to live without me. Come with me. *Love* me."

"Love is survival," Connor begins. "You told me that a few months ago. How did I not pick up on your *fucked up* ideas of love? You made me a magical doll out of *guilt*, you made it a habit to dig your fingernails into my wrists anytime I exercised independence, you thought love could trump grief, you idolize the damn thing. Love is nothing if we are dead, right? Didn't you say it yourself — love is survival?" Connor desperately tries to convince me, but he is grasping at straws. My mind has already been made up. My ideology doesn't say death stops love, it says lack of love stops life.

"Join me."

"No." Connor wields his scissors in the air and before I can process what he's doing, he jabs them into the wooden table. "No. No, Quinton. I'm not going to commit suicide. I had hope in us. I love you, I do. But I am not giving up so easily. Please, Quinton — " he swipes for my scissors, but I quickly move my hand out of reach and forcefully shove him back " — don't do this."

My head slowly lifts from the floor, any light left in me leaving. "You're not joining me?"

Connor shakes his head and raises a hand toward my cheek, but I flinch away. "Just put the scissors down," he begs. "I can't do it. You don't have to either, please, I–I love you so much. Do you fucking hear me, I love you, Quinton! Just hand me your doll, please, I love you more than anyone."

"Understood." And before Connor — or I for that matter — can react, I hold the scissors above the doll and stab the blade right into its heart.

My vision goes *red* in agony. I twist the knife with a deep grunt, ensuring this will actually kill me. I huff and sink to the floor as my chest sears, feeling every inch of the rip into my organ. Adrenaline is too weak to conceal the pain of a popped heart. Fuzzily, I look toward Connor.

I see a pair of frozen shoes, and I tilt my head up as much as I can.

And there he stands, sobbing. He weeps, disbelieving, hurting, crying.

He shakily squats for a moment, as if unsure how to move his limbs, how to *walk*. His hands brush my cheek, and he kisses my forehead with burning force. "Why. Why, why, why, why, how could you do this to me?"

I release a shaky breath. "Because, Connor, you failed. You d-don't love me. You…have made — you have made that so clear." I gasp through my words. Finally, I cry, and realize that I am dying.

Pain increases as my heart loses the motivation to continue pumping. "Connor," I croak softly. Maybe I wouldn't be here if I wasn't drugged with love, drunk on misery. It's a killer combo, literally.

"I'm so sorry, Quinton. I'm sorry." His eyes are glued to my body, his surrounding skin pale with horror. "I thought maybe you wouldn't have done it if I said no, I — " His words cut into fractions with hiccups and cries, and he eventually turns away.

"Oh Connor," I mutter, losing myself in death, not considering the weight of my words. "I — it's quite the opposite." But perhaps a part of me wants to punish him too, for not loving me as I loved him.

"What?"

I cough up blood. "I — I wasn't going to do this just based off — " I gasp in pain " — yesterday. This was a test. I — was gonna see if you really loved me, and if you had agreed to die with me, I would've known you did. B-but you didn't. Why didn't you say yes, Connor? Why — why didn't you prove your love to me and *agree*?"

I'd still be breathing if he loved me.

I'd still be breathing if he agreed to die with me.

I'd still be breathing, but I don't blame him.

Connor whips around, eyes wide. "No. No, no, no, this is my fault? No! You cannot just say that, you…sociopath. You can't blame me for this. Please, Quinton, tell me this is a prank. Holy fuck, I should've forced you to go to therapy. Stand up, please, I love you." Connor's screams for help and desperate declarations of love quiet down as my pain eases. Memories of my parents, Marco, my long-dead college aspirations, and *Connor* float around my head aimlessly. My vision blurs while the shapes and colors around me begin to make a little less sense. Connor's voice quiets to nothing, and my ears relish the silence. I see Connor above me, screaming and clutching his head. Blue with guilt and grief. I think he leans down and kisses me. Until that image disappears.

Until his screams disappear too.

Until my love for him disappears.

Until there's nothing.

CHAPTER 19

CONNOR

"Happy birthday, Connor."

"Yeah, twenty-three is old, you're literally a senior citizen." Karl prods at my side, and I yelp.

"Does this make you a boomer now? Twenty-three is basically forty." I scowl at Rafael and shove him away from me.

"Hey, Rafael, remember when you literally betrayed me."

Rafael goes pale. "Hey, man, look, that was a while ago, and I'm sorry — "

I punch his arm, rolling my eyes with a smile. "I know, I know, I was joking. But fuck off, you two. And *thank you*, Fritz, for being the only one to give me a regular happy birthday." I trace my fingers over granite countertops, bathing in the glory of my new house. It's living space number three by now — just the thought makes me feel like a spoiled brat. Little me'd had pissed himself if he saw current me owning a kitchen this size.

Rafael wanders to the couch and twists his head toward Fritz. "Hey, can you grab my phone? I left it upstairs — in the bathroom, I think? I don't know, this place is new."

Fritz sneers, but he waddles up the staircase anyway. I chuckle, joining Rafael on the sofa as he extends his arm ungracefully to grab at the remote.

I snicker. "It's right there, idiot. I keep the remote in its own special tray."

Rafael frowns and snags the device with an unamused face. "The upper-middle class life has made you so posh, freak. I miss having to dig up your couch's cushions to find the remote like a normal human being."

I click my tongue. "Times change, Mr. Law School Sheep."

"They sure do, Mr. Med School Bootlicker."

Karl flops onto the sofa with a grunt. "Let's watch something while we wait for the donuts to arrive. They should be here fairly soon."

Fritz, panting and just returned from his adventure upstairs, nods in agreement.

Karl flips through the channels and settles with the news.

I squint at the reporter and scrunch my nose. "Karl, put something fun on! Can't believe I'm the quote-unquote *senior citizen* here and you want to watch the news on my birthday."

Karl lifts his arms in defense. "Hang on. Jeez, I just wanna watch for a second. My mom and I love discussing the news every single Friday night. It's like our thing — and it's Friday!"

I sigh. "Okay fine, only for a minute."

After a moment an all too familiar structure appears on the screen, and all my previous snarkiness vanishes.

No.

It can't be.

And the reporter opens her mouth.

"Hello, Hema Raja here, and we report findings of a body in a semi-rural area, a modest neighborhood in south Orlando. Discovered by a couple moving into the abandoned, seemingly quaint, house in Seminole County — a house they were planning to renovate before coming across the body. Police report that the victim was likely male and fully decomposed."

I let out a small gasp as her voice drones out.

Fritz's eyes narrow and his mouth opens. "Oh, my God, Connor! Isn't that your old house?"

I remain silent.

Rafael pipes in, laughing. "Oh — hey! What if it's Quinton," he jokes, swatting my back. "Crazy how the joker's still MIA. Where did he move? Like the Philippines, right?"

I sweat. "Yeah...the Philippines."

Quinton's death. *Fuck.*

I click the TV off in a flurry. Any more details could expose my lie about Quinton packing up and moving to Southeast Asia with no warning. "Let's not right now. This is weird. I need to go to the bathroom." In the least suspicious fashion possible, I scramble to the restroom and close the door behind me. In an eerie moment of quiet, I sit on the floor, breathing heavily as I try not to relive the traumatic experience. *It wasn't your fault, it wasn't your fault, it wasn't your fault, it wasn't your fault.*

Quinton.

Quinton was such a man.

The police won't question his death further than suicide, given his note — one sentence saying, "I killed myself," classic Quinton. I flop to the marble floor. Besides, it's not like they'll find anything pointing to me. Vivid memories of the day fester inside me, all hot misery and dark melancholy. I felt like a sociopath. Closing the phone app once I decided his and my story was too unbelievable. Putting on gloves, scrubbing droplets of blood that didn't quite line up with the trajectory — because it sprayed onto me — burning it off my own skin, disposing of any evidence that suggested I was present, shredding the Quinton-doll, but placing the scissors in his hand with a glove, and leaving Quinton there in a muddle of his own organic matter. To top it off, hiding Quinton's suicide from all my friends. At least I had one less mouth to feed. Fritz and I quickly made up, and with overwhelming sympathy from my friends, I had financial assistance from three separate people. Their small donations were enough for me to live in a modest apartment. And *finally*, I found myself at a shitty but acceptable school a few years too late. With the help of a generous scholarship, of course. Apparently, watching your mum die before your eyes is great essay material. I work hard to make it all worth it. So that Mum didn't die for nothing, and so Quinton didn't die to ruin my future.

I prefer to think of him as a true crime story I once read — never a real-life event I experienced. It gets me thinking too much, especially about Quinton. What I missed, the signs that were there, the red flags I ignored, and what I could've done differently. Who was he? What did his parents do to him that fucked him up so extraordinarily bad? He never got into detail — perhaps physical or mental abuse. Probably both. That poor, poor little boy.

They are all questions that can never be answered. And they leave my head reeling.

I can pinpoint moments of Quinton being bizarre. When he sewed a doll of himself to beg for forgiveness; when he tried to poison me against Fritz, his lack of empathy toward my mum's death, and when he gripped my wrist a little too hard or broke dishes during fights — all were pointers to his troubled mind. I barely remember the warmth he made me feel, and when I do, it's wildly addictive. Dwelling on Quinton is dangerous. And it's hard keeping a secret like him.

I slide out of the bathroom and tiptoe up the carpeted staircase. Once I'm sure none of my friends have spotted me, I head to my room and slip inside. Flipping the light switch on, I sift through my closet for a special item. Quinton's apology letter. The same one he wrote me the day we became official. *Love, your Quinton,* he wrote. I accepted him, unaware of how much he truly considered himself to be mine.

I stare at the slightly crumpled paper resting next to my doll, and my jaw tightens. What did either of us do to deserve such a gruesome outcome? Who did this to us? I guess, if someone did, the answer would be God. But if God is real, they are not someone I want to worship, or pray to, or respect. If anyone would willingly create a world where people suffer as Quinton did, they are sick in the head. Even you, God. You're not exempt from being a good person because you live in the sky, dickhead.

With little thought, I rip the frail letter in half, disposing of five-year-old paragraphs written with love that is long dead. I tear the letter several more times, and I watch the scraps slip out of my hand. Quinton was completely wrong. Love isn't life, or anything good, for that matter. Love is a wellspring of despair.

I look at the paper scraps left in my hands. And I let them trickle into my trashcan. By Sunday morning, ten a.m. sharp, the remains of my attachment to Quinton will be shipped to a landfill.

New beginnings, right? Hurray.

Unless you count that damned doll.

THE END

ACKNOWLEDGMENTS

I will start by thanking my parents, Ranjeev and Arati Singh. You both always gave me the space to write — letting me skip dinner or family hikes, or looking the other way when I did not wash the dishes. Dod, I love you so much. You're an inspiration, and without you, I wouldn't have the determination to write this book. I hope I'm as smart, determined, and self-reliant as you when I'm older. You have given me an incredible childhood, and the time and guidance to publish my first book! Mimi, I love you. You're a role model for me, and I hope when I grow up I share your strength and contagious joy. You both have given me so much; I could never fit all my gratitude into these acknowledgments.

I, of course, have to thank the person this book is dedicated to — my older sister, Avni ("Ali"). There is no one I love more in the world than you. You're a huge reason behind my passion for learning, reading, and writing. You introduced me to books and taught me half of what I know. You're supportive, selfless, and loving. I didn't have to think twice when I was asked who I wanted to dedicate my book to.

I'd also like to say thank you to my mom's side grandparents, Nana and Nani, or Jayant and Jyotsna Pandya. I am eternally grateful for your presence in my life. I never would've had the opportunity to write a book without your sacrificing so much for our family. I find myself projecting my appreciation for you in my book — namely that Connor's wish is to make his mom's immigration to America worth it, since she worked day and night to give him a better life. Similarly, a lot of my motivation to try to succeed revolves around the dharma of living up to my ancestors' hopes for me. I feel a sort of duty to repay everything you two did for me, and the world you two gave me. I would not have the time or means to publish a book if you both didn't come to America and build a life from the ground up. Thank you for spoiling me and loving me endlessly, and *Iloveyoumorethanyouloveme*!

I have just as much adoration for my grandparents on my dad's side, Dadaji and Dadiji, or Dr. Vijay Singh and Dr. Tripta Singh. Even though you aren't here on Earth, I still feel your presence sometimes when I stand near your photos or if a beautiful bird visits the backyard. I didn't know either of you as well as I wish I did, but I love you both and wish you could see this book. Thank you for raising the best son ever and working tirelessly for your family and yourselves. As the only doctors for miles around in rural Himachal Pradesh, India — doing everything from delivering babies to helping accident victims to treating tuberculosis patients — you set an example for all of us. We will always honor you for that. Without everything you both did for your future generations, I wouldn't have the ability or ambition to write this book.

I want to also acknowledge my aunts and uncles who always encourage me, and my cousins Cabir, Jeevun, Sana, Sara, and Anshu, who make me laugh like no one else can.

Next, I want to thank two friends who are very dear to me. I'll start with Ellie Thompson. Ellie, thank you for being my best friend for the majority of this process. You're always there for me in all my social/academic hardships. Thank you for all the laughs, good times, and sleepovers. Now onto Zoe Moreno. Zoe, you are someone who is unimaginably dear to me, and this book would not be the same without the influence you had on my recent years. I love both you and Ellie so much.

I have to thank my eighth-grade English teacher, Mr. Kevin Mullen from Clint Small Middle School. Mr. Mullen liked to start classes with a "writing workout." This workout consisted of four image prompts, and we were given ten minutes to simply write about one image. You could write absolutely anything about the image you choose, as long as it was coherent. On January 6th, 2021, Mr. Mullen assigned a writing workout, and one of the image prompts was of a football game. I thought it'd be hilarious if I wrote fanfiction about *two characters I refuse to name*, flirting at a football game. This ended up being the first page of my novel, *Marionette*. I didn't intend for it to become a book, I just…kept writing the weekend after it was assigned, and eventually it got to 250 pages. The original characters did not make it in the final cut, and their names were changed to Connor and Quinton in the second-to-final draft. So, thank you, Mr. Mullen, for being the entire reason this book exists. Keep up with those writing workouts; they were fun!

I'd also like to thank the Austin Badgerdog writing camp I attended many summers ago. My teacher chose me to read my poem at the camp graduation, which meant everything to little me. This was one of the first times I felt validated as a writer.

I had some amazing editors and helpers with this book! Rachel Carter and Katherine Catmull from Yellow Bird Editors, thank you for helping me improve this book. You helped turn a wandering manuscript written by an ambitious fourteen-year-old into a real novel I'm proud to call mine. Rachel, you told me what I needed to hear, and reassured me that my book was worth publishing. Katherine, thank you for your funny comments throughout my manuscript; this kept me going through arduous revision sessions. I want to thank my book designer Jen Payne from Words by Jen who served as a *critical* guide, and friend! Usually emailing adults stresses me out, but I am always comfortable communicating any question or concern to you, and I can expect a super helpful answer every time.

This book was a COVID project. Being stuck at home for eighteen months during an international pandemic can certainly help a person develop a hobby! I am aware of the privilege I have for being able to spend my lockdown time writing, while many of my classmates were helping their younger siblings with online school, or earning money to help pay the family's bills, or caring for elderly relatives. Your contributions are so much greater than this one little book.

Finally, a special shout out to the characters Connor and Quinton were based on.

I know I'm supposed to be an author here, but I *wish I had the words* to describe how thankful I am for everyone who helped me reach this achievement. You're all why I never gave up on this project. I'm grateful for my family, my friends, and my team.

ABOUT THE AUTHOR

Annika Singh is a sixteen-year-old self-published author of the novel *Marionette* from Austin, Texas. She's a picture-perfect-romance fanatic and watches the world through an idyllic lens. Annika has won first place in both the PBS kids writing competition and at her Badgerdog writing camp. And when she's not busy writing or reading love stories, she's practicing *Howl's Moving Castle* on the piano, coding a game with Python, or preparing for a Bharatnatyam—Indian classical style—dance performance. (Unsurprisingly, her favorite dance is a reenactment of two deities falling in love). Annika also has a knack for politics and debate and has won first and second place at tournaments. She's president of her Government program club and has won first place in three separate years during the club's state-wide conferences. In 2023, she was selected to participate in "Off the Shelf: Book Challenges, Bans and Promoting Inclusive Literature," a panel discussion hosted by the Anti-Defamation League and American Association of School Librarians. She combines social advocacy and romance into her first-ever novel, *Marionette*, reflecting two out of three of her most favorite things! (The third would be her precious malti-poo puppy, Shairoo.)

www.ingramcontent.com/pod-product-compliance
Lightning Source LLC
Chambersburg PA
CBHW020105310726
48970CB00002B/489

9 798218 260576